NOLLE PROSEQUI

A Novel By

Christy R. Diachenko

Nolle Prosequi (nol-le pro-se-qui)

A Latin legal phrase meaning, “be unwilling to pursue”, a phrase amounting to “do not prosecute”. Used in many common law criminal prosecution contexts to describe a prosecutor’s decision to voluntarily discontinue criminal charges. (Wikipedia.org) To abandon prosecution.

Forgive (for-give-ness)

To stop feeling anger toward (someone who has done something wrong); to stop blaming (someone). To stop feeling anger about (something); to forgive someone for (something wrong). Merriam-Webster.com

Publishers Note:
This is a work of fiction. All names, characters, places, and events are the work of the author's imagination. Any resemblance to real persons, places, or events is coincidental

ISBN 13: 978-0692696644
ISBN 10: 0692696644

I would like to express my heartfelt thanks to the people who shared their experiences and thoughts with me while I created this story and the book trailer. I couldn't have done it without you! I would also like to thank my editors and dear friends, Marie McGaha and Debbie Roppolo, for their willingness to teach me the craft of writing and editing.

John Abdalla
Allan Barton
Brianna Barton
Gerry Diachenko
Steve & Jennie Diachenko
Mike Ellis
Ryan Holloway
Leanda King
Joelle Lanfear
Lucas Marchant
Greta McIntyre
Judge Edward Miller
Judy Munson
Bryna Seay
Janine Sharney
Mary Troup

Sermon "Are You Sleeping With Hagar?" used with permission from Peter Hubbard

Sentencing charge used with permission from the Honorable Judge Edward Miller

~ One ~

I hate red trucks. Lizzy Godfrey glanced nervously at the vehicle to her right, and the smell of diesel fuel infiltrated her nostrils. *Red truck. Carl. Danger. Death.* Beads of sweat formed on her upper lip and she gripped the wheel tightly. Lizzy's heart pounded while memories of that horrible day filled her mind. The physical and emotional pain. The humiliation and helplessness. The horror that this was actually happening to her. She could still feel the sting of gravel hitting her face and arms. She remembered the questions swirling along with the terror in her mind. What drove Carl to such cruelty? What had she done to deserve this? Had she failed to be the right kind of Christian wife yet again? Was he going to kill her? Was he going to leave her there all night?

Glancing to the side, Lizzy sighed with relief when the huge truck slowed and turned right. She shook her head, chagrined. How could she be transported back to that moment so swiftly? How could the memories still be this vivid? She was no longer a victim. She was a survivor—strong and confident. God had healed her pain and restored her heart. Although, at this moment, Lizzy felt as weak and vulnerable as she had when she fled that day ten years ago.

Lizzy took a deep breath and looked ahead, eager for the comforting view of the distant mountains she usually enjoyed on her way home. Today the beautiful vista was shrouded in a layer of fog, the opening act for the storm to come. Disappointed, Lizzy began to pray. She knew that even though the peaceful majestic mountain peaks were hidden from view, her Lord was always available. *Father, I don't know what just happened here, but I need You. Please help me to conquer these fears for good. Give me wisdom and strength to look to You at all times. Help me not to allow my past to haunt me. I don't believe you want that for me. Help me, Father God.* Lizzy continued to commune with her Heavenly Father while she drove down the highway, and slowly, her pulse returned to normal.

~ * ~

Sweat ran in rivulets down Carl Greene's face while he gasped, trying to breathe. His heart pounded so hard he felt as if it would come out of his chest. The woods around the shed were still as though respectful of the life he just snuffed out. The air was cool and the eerie unnatural quiet creeped him out. Carl shivered.

He looked at his wife's face. Her body lay crumpled where it had fallen. He grabbed her feet and straightened her out, then ripped the duct tape off her mouth. *Crazy chick had wretched taste in clothing*. He eyed her bulky extra-large sweater and men's jeans, both filthy from the struggle. *Where are her shoes and socks?* He looked around but didn't see them. He retraced his steps to the house and found her socks balled up along the way. One small loafer lay halfway to the shed and the other by the back deck. *Must have come off from dragging her.* He tossed the footwear into a rusty metal barrel behind the shed.

Carl wiped his forehead, surprised to see a splotch on his hand. *I can't believe she scratched me hard enough to draw blood. She was usually such a wimpy little thing*. He wiped his hand on his jeans and walked to the shed where canvas tarp was stored. *I never expected her to put up such a fight. Good thing I bought those zip ties.*

With much effort, he rolled Marcie's body onto the canvas, then tied it with baling twine so it wouldn't shift during transit. Carl shook his head with a sigh. *I was willing to teach her how to be a Godly woman but she just would not learn*. His face was set with determination. *I had no choice. 'If thine eye offend thee, gouge it out. If thine hand offend thee, cut it off.'* He remembered the scriptures well and made up his own twisted addition. *If thine spouse offend thee, cut her down so that the evil be destroyed from the earth.*

He went to the shed once more and brought back a two-wheeled garden cart. The effort of getting the canvas-wrapped body into the cart caused anger to rise within him again. Carl cursed in frustration. *I thought she was such a tiny piece of crap. She must have been packing more weight than I realized.* He took a deep pull from his water bottle, then set it beside a tree, grabbed the handle of the cart, and started down the trail through the woods. He cursed again when the left wheel lodged in one of the many ruts. The handle wrenched from his hands, and the load nearly overturned into the brush. He angrily grabbed the handle with both hands, rocking and yanking, until he finally freed the cart. Carl stood for a moment, breathing hard, and wiped the sweat from his brow. *I'm burning up.* He removed his jacket, tossed the garment on top of the bundle, and continued down the hill.

The path ended at a metal gate. He rolled his burden through and began the trek across the field. Thankfully, his neighbor's horses were in another pasture today so the beasts wouldn't bother him. Carl grunted while alternately pushing and pulling the cart through waist-high grasses topped with seed heads. *I wish this was Beth.* Fury welled within him anew as memories of his ex-wife filled his mind. *I don't know how she managed to get away. She was supposed to honor and obey me. I can't believe she had the gall to leave me after she vowed to stay with me until death.* He stopped for a break. *I could have arranged that if she had stayed.* A laugh burst from his lips, hovered for a moment in the air, then dissipated into the landscape.

The sun disappeared behind a cumulous cloud, while a soft breeze caressed his face and arms. Carl pulled up his t-shirt and wiped his sweaty forehead, absorbed in the day-dream of killing Beth. He looked at the bundle. There she was. He did kill her. She did not get the better of him. He asserted his dominance and there her body lay to prove it. Triumph made him feel powerful. *Yes! I took care of them both.* He picked up the cart handle and started forward with new vigor, then stopped and looked at the bundle again in confusion. *Wait. Is it Elizabeth? No, her name was Lizzy, wasn't it?* Then he remembered. *No, no - I made her stop using that trashy name. I made her use the name Beth. That's right.* He frowned and thought hard. Demons of confusion and madness wreaked havoc on his troubled brain. *No, this isn't her. This is Marcie. The other one. The second little hellion-wife.* Somewhat disappointed, he trudged forward. *I guess in the grand scheme of things, ridding the world of one evil is better than none.*

Carl reached the other side of the pasture and pulled the cart through the gate. Hoof prints marked the ground in a wide area around the entrance. *They've been riding again. Good thing I planned this for a weekday when they're at work.* He followed the riding trail for about ten yards, then turned, angling sharply off into the woods on an old abandoned hiking trail. About a mile up this long-forgotten path was a small meadow surrounded by trees, the perfect spot to bury Marcie. He began watching for the trail markers he constructed several weeks ago to ensure he wouldn't forget the way. In a few moments, he spotted the first small pile of rocks. *Good, I'm on the right track.*

~ * ~

While Lizzy made her way closer to the polling place, her thoughts began to drift to the day's defendants in court. Her job as Deputy Clerk at the county courthouse made for some interesting days. *I don't know why they seriously think the judge is going to believe some of those stories.* Defendants blamed all manner of things for their actions but few took direct responsibility. *I know some are genuine, but still...* Despite her occasional cynicism, Lizzy prayed silently for each defendant who came through court. She knew the love of Jesus Christ could heal them and change their lives if they would accept Him as their Savior.

Lizzy's attention returned abruptly to the present when she nearly missed her turn into the Riponville East Elementary School parking lot. Election Day was here and Lizzy took her right to vote seriously. Pulling her coat more tightly around her, she quickly made her way to the door of the gymnasium and groaned inwardly when she saw the line. *I should have come before work. Too late now. At least it's warmer in here.* Lizzy waited about half an hour before presenting her voter-registration card and ID. After a few minutes in the booth, her votes were cast, and she returned to her car, satisfied her voice would be heard. *Lord, please help the right people win these elections, especially for president*, she prayed while she drove home. *This country needs someone who will be a good and godly leader.*

~ * ~

The shovel carved through the rich forest loam with ease, then stuck fast on an unseen root or stone. With a frustrated oath, Carl moved the tool slightly and tried again with the same result. Clenching his jaw, he felt a spark of fury rise within him. *Even in death you still won't submit, stupid little witch.* His face contorted with rage. In spite of the cool temperature, more sweat rolled down his temple. He looked at the canvas-wrapped bundle on the ground and ranted. "I have to take care of everything, don't I? Absolutely everything!" He lifted the shovel high and brought the tool crashing down across the middle of the bundle. His words faded away like steam into the trees and brush. Nothing stirred but a few red and yellow leaves that danced a waltz along the forest floor.

Limbs trembling, he took a deep breath and leaned against the shovel. *I've got to calm down and get this finished, so she can never sass me again. She got what she deserved.* He began to dig, this time in a different spot. A pile of rich black earth soon mounded up to one side. The woods around him was silent, its occupants frightened away by this strange, angry visitor.

Finally, Carl tossed the shovel aside and surveyed his work. *That'll hold her.* He grasped one end of the bundle and began to pull, moving it a few inches before he had to rest. *All that digging must be wearing on me but I can't let that witch beat me, not now.* Cursing, Carl pushed until the bundle rolled into the hole.

A rush of power gave him a high akin to the most potent drug. ""No six feet under for you, tramp." "You will rot here forever like an animal. And nobody will ever know." He covered the body with dirt and packed down the earth firmly. When the heady feeling of invincibility began to fade, he carefully arranged leaves and fallen branches over the grave. Satisfied the spot looked no different than the forest floor around him, Carl gathered his jacket and tools, and began the trek back to the house, stopping to carefully kick apart each trail marker he came to. *Nobody's ever going to find her, but there's no sense in being careless.*

Gray storm clouds had filled the sky by the time he opened the gate on the forest side of the field, reminding him of past conversations with Marcie. A twisted grin curved his lips as a plan formed. *Ireland. I'll tell anyone who asks that she went on a trip to Ireland. She always wanted to go there. I'll be the grieving, heartbroken husband when she never comes home. The poor abandoned spouse who misses his beloved terribly.* Amused by his own wit, he laughed. *They'll buy it. Her stupid parents are as moronic as she was.*

A half hour later Carl arrived back at his garage. Leaning the cart against the wall, he narrowed his eyes at the sight of blood speckles on the floor. Grunting, he grabbed a bottle of bleach, a cleaning brush, and prepared to destroy the evidence. *This is so ridiculous. She is not worth all this trouble.* He wanted to be done with it. Marcie did not deserve all this attention and labor.

A string of profanity burst from Carl's lips when the bleach trickled over a cut on his right hand. *Stupid thing came open again. I thought it was healed.* He clenched his teeth, told himself to man-up, and thoroughly scrubbed down the cart and shovel. Tossing the empty bleach container into the trash can, he hurried to the deep sink to wash. He dried his hands, then returned the cart and shovel to the shed and retrieved a box of matches and a piece of newspaper. The baling twine sat where he'd left it after tying up the bundle. *I'd better burn the twine, too. Can't be too careful.*

He watched mesmerized. as the paper seemed to come alive in the flames. The newsprint, twisting and gyrating while being eaten by fire reminded him of Marcie's struggles. Evidence slowly transformed into white ash and cinders. Suddenly, he snapped to attention while he watched Marcie's shoes melt into a plastic blob. *My pants,* he thought in panic. *I wiped my bloody hand on them*. Agitated, he yanked off his jeans and tossed them into the barrel as if they were poisonous to the touch. He grimaced. *That was close. Can't get careless now. Not after all this work*. Carl's body relaxed as he watched the hungry flames devour the denim. *Man, I gotta settle down.* He wiped the beads of sweat off his lip and chuckled. *What am I so worried about? Nobody's ever going to find her anyway. Besides, it was just my blood on the jeans anyway.*

He slowly took one final look around. *I think everything is done*. A loud tapping on the window made him jump. Carl looked outside and sighed relief. *Perfect*. How beautifully everything was coming together. *The rain will wash away anything I might have missed.* Standing in the open garage, he paused, enjoying the sound of the downpour.

Eventually, Carl made his way to the kitchen and stopped by the refrigerator. *Crap. This is Election Day. I forgot to vote*. He checked the clock on the stove. *Still an hour or so before the polls close*. Filled with indecision, he looked out at the flowers bordering the front walk. Was his vote worth the effort? Finally, he shook his head. *Nah, I don't feel like going out again. I'm hungry. Besides, this has been a long day and I deserve a rest*. Satisfied with his decision, Carl made supper, grabbed his laptop and plopped down in the recliner, ready for an invigorating Tuesday evening with the ladies on-line.

~ * ~

Cold raindrops flew off the windshield of Lizzy's sporty two-door Honda Accord as she left the polling place. A small smile of satisfaction touched her lips. The Rain-X she'd applied was working. Lizzy braked carefully when a large utility truck pulled in front of her. Warm air flowed from the heater and soothing instrumental music by Josh Kramer poured from the speakers. The time spent waiting to vote and anticipation of a cozy evening at home had caused the earlier fright of the red truck to dissipate from her thoughts. The snail's pace set by the utility truck irritated her, and that was messing with her sense of calm. Since her turn was fast approaching, she decided to swallow the aggravation and resist the urge to pass the offending monstrosity. Finally, she turned off the main highway and left the truck to crawl his way up the road, irritating other motorists.

Lizzy pulled into her driveway and slumped against the seat, eyeing the house gratefully while the garage door began to rise. The light from within echoed the love and comfort she was sure to find contained within those walls. She pulled inside and turned off the engine. Her eyes closed while she enjoyed the feeling of finally coming to a stop after a busy day.

After a moment, a gentle tap on her window startled her and she opened the car door. "Coming in, or planning to camp out here all night?" her mother, Rose, teased. Lizzy grinned, grabbed her purse, and exited the car. As soon as the women entered the house, they were bombarded by two leaping dogs eager for their mom's attention. Lizzy was just as eager for theirs. "Down kids," Lizzy ordered firmly. The Pomeranian and the Sheltie sat obediently, tails wagging in anticipation of what would come next. Lizzy smiled widely and dropped her things on the floor. She knelt down and hugged them close. "I love you, Nugget, and you, too, Downton." In moments, her elderly tuxedo cat, Jack, rubbed against her in greeting. She gathered him into the group hug, and a loud purr erupted from his chest. *It was good to be home.*

~ Two ~

Tucker Bates ran a hand through his dark hair and sighed deeply. Should he make the one-hour trip home to Riponville tonight or stay in his condo here in Clifton? He loosened his tie and stared unseeingly out the window of his Senate office. The meeting in his hometown wasn't scheduled until ten in the morning, so he would have plenty of time if he waited until tomorrow to return. His last couple of days were what a friend termed "rich and full." After winning re-election to his office as state Senator on Tuesday, Tucker had been constantly on the go. Any other time he would have rescheduled his meeting and spent the whole weekend in Clifton. However, his client truly needed help with a complicated legal issue, and Friday was the only day the man was available. Even winning the Senate seat didn't mean his law practice came to a halt.

Tucker leaned back in his leather chair and put his hands behind his head. Ten years ago, he would never have dreamed he would end up here. His father's constant teaching about conservative personal finance held him in good stead as a young adult. He worked hard and lived within his means during his pre-law and law school years. He graduated with honors and served as a law clerk with a county judge for a year, after which he was debt free. He still remembered the pride he felt when he hung his *Juris Doctor* certificate above the desk in his own practice. Assisting clients with wills, real estate transactions, and other legal issues brought fulfillment and provided a decent living. While he hoped someday the Lord would bring a woman into his life who would be his best friend, confidante, and soul mate, he was content to wait on God's timing. Life was good, and he was happy. Change was not something he craved.

After five years in business, however, he received the shock of his life. The governor appointed him to a state Senate seat vacated when the previous office holder lost her fight with cancer. He'd never had aspirations for life as an elected official, and though he held more than a few personal doubts about how well he would handle politics, he accepted the challenge as an opportunity from the Lord. He forged ahead with a positive attitude, determined to represent his people to the best of his ability.

A smile touched his lips. He'd been so unsure of himself that first day in the legislature. He assumed he would serve his appointed term, and then some seasoned politician would take his place. But the people re-elected him by a landslide. He leaned forward once more and looked at the stack of mail on his desk. Cora, his administrative assistant, insisted he needed to read each letter personally. He shook his head. *More groupies.* Cora assured him they were nice notes of congratulations on his re-election, but his brief time in the public eye had already made him a bit cynical. So many women were after him for his money, his position, and perceived power. *I wish I could find somebody who cares just about me. All they care about is what I can do for them and my money.*

He felt his partially-digested lunch rise into his throat as he read the first card, "I'm so glad you won. You're so cute," the note read. "You're my favorite Senator. If you ever want to get together, just call me, baby." *More of the usual.* Disgusted, he tossed the note into the trash.

Sometimes I think being single and successful is a curse rather than a blessing. He picked up the next missive. Another sappy note, only this one included a photo. *Good grief! She must be only sixteen. I'm forty-four years old. I wonder if her parents know about this.* The card, envelope, and photo landed in torn pieces in the circular file. *I don't think I can handle this tonight.*

Tucker leaned back in his chair gazing at the richly carved bookcase which housed a large collection of law books. *It's been such a hectic day.* He groaned at the stack of mail still sitting on his desk, mocking him *They'll still be sitting here when I get back. Might as well finish.* He made his way through the rest of the pile. Several more letters were of the same ilk. But one from a World War Two veteran struck his heart. The man expressed his heartfelt thanks for the work Tucker did to help veterans with their increasing health-care needs. Another was addressed in feathery handwriting from a Mrs. Ida Johnson, who thanked him for helping her son get his business established.

The last card, decorated with a photo depicting a field of American flags fully unfurled as though invisible hands were holding them taut, intrigued him. The sky was a beautiful stormy blue-gray, and bright green grass made a carpet underneath. Below the picture the sentiment 'May the Lord Bless You and Keep You' was printed. Tucker stared at the shot for several seconds. *I would love that as a large framed piece for my office*.

Finally, he opened the card. "Mr. Bates," he read. "I want to offer you the warmest congratulations on your win. I knew you would do it. I have always felt there are two types of candidates in the race for office: the politicians and the public servants. The things I've heard and read about you have led me to believe you are truly a public servant for the people of our state. I'm especially impressed by your volunteer work with seniors and veterans. My dad passed away at age eighty-five, and my mom is seventy-six. Your ministry to this dear group of people means so much to me. Thank you for your hard work and for not being a typical 'politician'. Take care and may the Lord richly bless your life as you follow Him and allow Him to guide and direct you. You will continue to be in my prayers."

The note was signed "Elizabeth Godfrey" and below her name, she wrote, "Psalm 1". Tucker re-read the note and a surrealistic feeling washed over him. *A nice one*. He actually received a note from a woman who did not sound like she was on the prowl. He could not recall if he'd met her. *I meet so many people along the campaign trail. I wish I remembered her*. He grabbed his iPad, pulled up the YouVerse app, and tapped to Psalm 1. After reading the passage through, Tucker closed the app and picked up the card again. The corresponding envelope was nowhere to be found.

Cora must have thrown it away by accident. The stamped information on the back of the card listed a web site, and indicated it was produced by a local photographer. On impulse, he grabbed his iPad again and tapped in the web address. Stunning photography greeted him on the home page. The site advertised framed prints and note cards. An *About the Photographer* page revealed the artist lived and worked in the southern part of the state.

He turned back to the card on his desk. *She must have bought it from the artist or at a shop somewhere.* Disappointment swept over him. *I'd like to have sent her a response. I'll keep this. Maybe the photographer knows her.* Tucker yawned widely and shook his head. The clock read 8:30 p.m., and he knew he needed to get supper and a good night's rest before starting out in the morning. He laid the card on the corner of his desk, then grabbed his suit coat and keys. After giving a friendly greeting to the cleaning crew on his way out of the building, he drove to his condo on the outskirts of town with the words of Psalm 1 echoing through his mind.

~ * ~

At 8:45 p.m., a janitor made his way into Tucker's office. He dutifully dusted whatever bare surfaces he could find, then dragged the vacuum cleaner in from the hallway. Engrossed in his work, the janitor bumped into the unwieldy piece of furniture. He grimaced, rubbing his hip bone ruefully, but continued his task. When finished, he rolled the vacuum back onto his cleaning cart and returned to collect the trash. He dumped the contents of Tucker's waste can dutifully into the bag. *Too bad the Senator is throwin' away such a beautiful card,* he thought. His own father fought in Vietnam, and the picture of the flags stopped him in his tracks. After a pause, he reached into the bag. He retrieved the card, carefully tore it in half at the fold, and put the picture portion in his shirt pocket. *After all, he was throwin' the thing out,* he thought. *I didn't keep the personal part. Daddy can put this up in his room at the nursin' home.* He proceeded with his chores and did not give the incident another thought.

~ * ~

Lizzy grabbed a tissue from the cup holder beside her and dabbed her eyes. She was in the middle of her Friday morning drive prayer time when, *Write Your Story*, one of her favorite songs by Francesca Battistelli, came on the radio. This particular song had been such a comfort when her father passed away six months earlier. The book of his life contained God-ordained chapters, including children's ministry, service to his country, and the love, care, and provision for his family. Only eternity would testify to the number of children who were ushered into God's kingdom as a result of Justin Matthew Godfrey's spreading the Word so faithfully. Lizzy played the song almost continually during the time her father was dying and in the weeks afterward.

She sighed and swallowed one last sob. She tucked a lock of dark hair behind her ear and continued her prayers.

Father, please watch over our President-elect today. Please give him wisdom to lead our country and keep him close to you. Thank you for allowing a man of integrity to be elected this time. I pray he will lead our country to safety. Use him to help in healing the wounds inflicted on this land during the past few years.

The light turned green and Lizzy slowly accelerated. *I also pray for Senator Bates today. Please watch over him and keep him safe. Keep him from evil, Lord, and draw him closer to you each day.*

Smiling, she gathered her things and locked the car She pulled her coat more closely around her. The temperatures had been cool all week, and Lizzy wished she had remembered her gloves. She hurried across the parking lot to the welcoming warmth of the courthouse. Her recent promotion required her to work in court often, a task she enjoyed immensely. She settled at her desk to process a few bits of paperwork. When 8:30 approached, she gathered her supplies and headed to the courtroom with a smile. She loved her job but was glad a relaxing weekend waited in the wings.

~Three ~

Tucker chuckled. "Yes, Mom, I'll be careful. I promise." He sat in the driveway of his Clifton condo, ready to start back to Riponville.

The cool air coming from the heater gradually turned warm, taking the chill off the car's interior. His cell phone rang just as he was about to pull out, so he stopped to take the call.

She reminded him about coming over for dinner that evening, and he assured her he wouldn't forget. She reminded him to be careful on his trip back, and he reminded her he'd never been in a wreck and had only received one speeding ticket in his life.

"I know, dear," she replied. "I just worry about you. There are so many crazy drivers out there."

"I understand and I love you, Mom. I'll see you tonight." He tapped the phone off and tossed it in his briefcase. After inserting a CD of worship music produced by a group who recently visited his church, he pulled out and headed north. The fall colors made the drive beautiful, and Tucker smiled. He loved fall and hoped he would have time for a trip to the mountains before the leaves were gone. *I need to find a weekend soon when I can get up to the cabin.* He visualized the retreat his grandfather left him on Whitby Mountain. *I would really enjoy the cool air and hiking with Porter.* He smiled at the thought of his energetic Jack Russell terrier, who was always up for a trip to the cabin.

Tucker had just crossed the outskirts of Riponville County when he remembered his gas gauge. *Don't know why I didn't think to check it before I left. Guess I'll pull over when I get into town.*

Tucker tapped the steering wheel and sang along with the music, oblivious to everything else around him. Unaware of the tractor-trailer coming up behind him, Tucker continued on down the highway singing with the music. A few minutes later, he glanced into his rear-view mirror and saw the enormous vehicle tailgating him.

A surge of irritation ripped through Tucker's body as he gripped the steering wheel. *Just pass me, buddy. There's nobody else anywhere close.*

As if on cue, the huge truck lumbered into the passing lane. Tucker relaxed back into the bucket seat of the Accord. *I don't know what's wrong with these guys. Why do they feel the need to be so pushy abou...*

Tucker's thoughts where ended when he felt the large truck slam into the side of his sedan. Terror gripped his heart as the small car flipped end-over-end before coming to rest on its roof at the base of a large oak tree.
The truck careened onto the shoulder and smashed into a cement bridge piling. An eerie silence was broken by a loud *boom* as the cab erupted into flames.

~ * ~

Mike Branson carefully steered his Chevy from the highway, followed a gravel road through the trees, and finally pulled into a wide turnout. The early morning sun cast rays through the trees which mingled with low lying fog. Light caught the frost on the brightly-colored leaves, causing them to sparkle as if encrusted with diamonds. Mike's son Frank immediately jumped out of the truck and pulled his Nikon D300™ from his camera case. The mystical appearance of the forest caught his eye, and hiking was forgotten for the moment as he took multiple shots of the grandeur from different angles. Mike watched his son with pride.

The older man had taken Friday off and pulled his son from school because he felt the need to reconnect with the teenager. Frank was involved with some friends Mike and his wife Ginny found questionable and after much prayer, they felt a father-son weekend together might be of benefit. So far, everything was shaping up to be all he hoped.

Today was to be spent hiking in the Thirskton State Forest. Tomorrow they would spend fishing on Thirskton Lake, and Sunday after church they planned to go golfing. During the two-hour trip to the forest, Frank opened up to his father about his fears, the pressures he faced at school, and trying to take a stand for Christ in a world where the lines between right and wrong were becoming increasingly blurred. Mike was pleased with their meaningful in-depth conversation.

Frank pulled out his camera and zoomed the lens onto the distant mountains. *Perfect*. A breeze kicked up, bringing with it the stench of decay. The boy covered his nose. "Phew, man what's that odor?"

Mike, who was slightly behind, caught up to his son. "What odor? What's it smell like?"

"Nothing like I've ever gotten a whiff of. It's beyond nasty." The boy coughed as another wind gust the breeze blew across their faces. "There it is again. Don't say you didn't get a nostril full of that."

"It's something alright," his father mumbled, looking through the weeds for the source of the smell. "Ah, here we are—looks like the coyotes have been at something." Mike grabbed a dead branch and eased the brush back. "But..." His ran cold as he stared at the mass on the ground. He shook his head trying to comprehend what he was seeing. *No way...*

Frank frowned and tried to push past Mike. "Hey, let me have a look. What did you find?"

The older man stuck his hand out to stop the boy from getting any closer. "Don't touch anything, Son. This may be a crime scene." He removed his cell phone from his pocket and breathed a sigh of relief. His hands shook while he quickly dialed. *I'm sure that is a dead body. Someone died here. What on earth...*

"9-1-1 what is your emergency?"

"We just discovered a dead body down here. Get someone down here now!"

"Sir, I need you to calm down."

"You don't get it," Mike yelled. "There's a body..."

"I can't help you if you don't stop yelling, sir. I can't understand what you're saying," the dispatcher explained. "There's a body... where?"

Mike's voice came in short gasps despite his efforts to calm himself. "My son and I are hiking in the Thirskton State Forest. Get someone here now."

~ * ~

The judge left the bench early in the afternoon to take a conference call, and Lizzy used the time to prepare more paperwork for the day's pleas. "At this rate, we'll be here till ten tonight," she remarked to Phoebe, the court reporter. "They just keep handing in more."

"We never get to them all, thank goodness." Phoebe took the paperwork from Lizzy. "Besides, I am so ready for the weekend." The women laughed and shared their weekend plans while they worked.

The room buzzed with activity. Defense attorneys and assistant district attorneys talked together about plea bargains. Spectators in the gallery conversed loudly among themselves. The courtroom coordinator prepared stacks of files and handed sentencing sheets to Lizzy to be paired with indictments.

Lizzy was usually able to tune out the hubbub that was plea court but while she worked, she suddenly picked up on the conversation going on between Stephanie, the probation agent, and one of the defense attorneys.

"Yeah, the accident happened this morning," the lawyer said. "I got a news bulletin on my phone."

"Wow," Stephanie said. "Senator Bates, huh? Did they say what happened?"

"Rumor has it he was talking on his phone. You know, mister-busy-all-important senator."

Stephanie pulled up the local television channel's web site on her laptop. "Oh, that's not what happened, Jim," she said exasperated. "Channel 5 says right here he got hit by a tractor-trailer that lost control. The truck driver was thrown from the cab and only sustained minor injuries." She *tsked* and shook her head. "Can you believe that?"

Lizzy frowned. *No way.* "Is Senator Bates all right?"

"Let's see." Stephanie perused the article. "This says he was hurt pretty badly. Lots of scrapes and bruises, some broken ribs, his hand was crushed, plus he's got a bad concussion. He was unconscious when they found him, and he hasn't come to. Oh, and for your information, Jim, his phone was still in his briefcase."

Jim shrugged and strolled away. Stephanie shook her head, sighed, and continued to prepare the paperwork for defendants.

The news began to sink in, Lizzy blinked away tears. "Oh my. That's so horrible." Silently she prayed earnestly that the Senator would recover from the tragic accident.

I'm going to buy a get-well card from Joy. She thought about her photographer friend. *Senator Bates is going to need a lot of cheer when he wakes up.* She hoped everyone in her office would write an encouraging note to the Senator.

Judge Blake returned to the bench, and court resumed. Lizzy pulled indictments, published pleas, administered the oath, and entered case dispositions on her laptop for the rest of the afternoon. She prayed often for the Senator's healing and checked for new updates whenever time allowed.

~ Four ~

Flags whipped and snapped in the breeze. The stormy sky swirled with masses of clouds in every hue of black and gray. The plaintive sound of a lone bagpipe playing Amazing Grace wafted through the air, but the musician could not be seen. Tucker stood watching, mesmerized by the scene. He pulled his suede jacket closer around him to ward off the chill. Tears streamed down his face. The beauty of the song and thoughts of those who gave their lives for their country overwhelmed him. He noticed a lone figure emerge from the flags, the slim form of a woman. Her dark shoulder-length hair danced around in the wind. She wore jeans, a turtle-neck sweater, and a leather blazer.

"Tucker." She called to him, her voice full of laughter. "Come and stroll with me. It's amazing to walk among the flags." Her blue eyes sparkled with enjoyment and wonder.

He felt an unseen force urging him to follow her. "I'm coming," he called out, trying to be heard over the wind's steady roar. "Wait." She turned back into the mass of flags and beckoned. He wanted more than anything to go with her, but found he could not move. His body felt trapped, and pain began to throb from his left hand and from the left side of his head. He had the sensation of plummeting, and was helpless to stop the descent. He cried out in pain and fear as the earth opened up, and he fell into darkness. With a jolt, his eyes opened.

He heard a slow beeping sound and gradually his parents' anxious eyes came into focus. "Oh honey." His mother Emilie sobbed. "You've come back to us." She gently grasped his hand and held it against her tear-soaked cheek.

"We thought we were going to lose you, son." Gilbert Bates impatiently brushed away his own tears, "How do you feel?"

Tucker's entire body ached, and the pain in his hand was nearly unbearable. "My hand." He did not recognize his dry scratchy voice. "It's killing me—my head, too." He looked at the machines and unfamiliar décor in confusion and felt completely disoriented and afraid. He was thankful his parents were there. "Where am I? What happened?"

"You're in the hospital." Gilbert's voice caught in his throat as tears trickled unchecked down his face. "You were in an accident, Son. Semi rammed into you."

Pain and concern shone in Tucker's eyes as he asked, "Is the semi driver okay?"

Emilie caressed her son's cheek. "Yes, honey. He came through just fine. Don't you worry."

"When they first got you here, they thought you had a severe concussion, a crushed hand and broken ribs. But they did an MRI and found no major head trauma and no broken bones. The ligaments in your hand were damaged, and you've got a lot of swelling but nothing broken." Gilbert cleared his throat. "God protected you, Son. It's a miracle you're alive. Your car flipped several times." Gilbert brushed away a tear and smiled at Tucker. "You'll be good as new in no time."

Tucker tried to smile back. He swallowed and nearly choked. "I need some water, Mom. My mouth feels like cotton."

Emilie immediately pressed the call button to summon a nurse. She filled a cup with ice water and guided a straw to her son's mouth. Tucker sipped eagerly, the liquid gliding down his parched throat, offering momentary comfort. The nurse arrived and injected a dose of morphine into Tucker's IV. Within minutes he fell back into a deep sleep.

~ * ~

Mike and Frank waited downwind of the sordid scene until the first responders arrived. A sheriff's deputy, struggling to regain his composure after the hike up the trail, approached the duo. "Mr. Branson? I'm Deputy Paul Wilson."

Mike stepped forward and shook the proffered hand. "Yes, sir. I'm Mike and this is my son, Frank."

"Where is the body?"

Mike pointed. "Just over there under that oak tree. Whoever did it buried the body but I suspect animals have been around." He lowered his voice and turned so his son would not hear. "There's some torn canvas that must have unearthed. I saw what appeared to be feet but looks like..." Mike paused and grimaced. "It looks like the toes are missing."

Deputy Wilson nodded grimly. He walked slowly through the tall grass, making his way to the tree where the body lay still partially buried. He then walked the perimeter of the small meadow, watchful and alert.

Soon, two EMS workers came around the bend in the trail. Deputy Wilson greeted the men and introduced them to the Bransons. A burly man who wore a shirt with an EMS logo on one side shook Mike's hand. "Hi, Mike. I'm Chief Freeman." He looked at Deputy Wilson. "The coroner is just behind me with forensics."

At that moment, Riponville County Coroner Ellis Michaels, the forensics team and a German shepherd came around the bend. Deputy Wilson conferred briefly with them. "Not much to report. The hikers over there discovered the body. The scene is secure."

"Great. Thanks, Paul." Ellis shook the deputy's hand. "I'll take it from here."

Mike and Frank sat on a fallen log, watching with a mixture of interest and horror. Deputy Wilson began to make his way toward them.

After twenty years on the force, he'd become a bit hardened to some of the crimes he saw daily. Still, a violent act of this magnitude got to him. And judging from the look on Frank's face, there would be a lot of sleepless nights for him as well. *Poor kid. He's too young to have to see something like this.*

He stood before the shell-shocked hikers. "Gentlemen," he said kindly, "I'll need you to come with me. I'd like to get a statement from you when we get back to the vehicles."

"Of course." Mike rose to his feet. "Frank may have some pictures you can use. That's how we noticed something was wrong. He spotted the pink yarn in his viewfinder."

"Great work Frank." Deputy Wilson clapped the teenager on the shoulder. "Let's get back and I'll check out your shots."

The county coroner EMS finished their assessment and officially handed off the scene to Ellis and Sam, the forensics team captain. "Okay, lady and gentleman." Sam looked at his co-workers. "We only have one chance to get it right. Let's get to work."

They secured the extreme outer edges of the scene with crime tape, then began to take photographs. Ellis walked along and left markers anywhere visual evidence appeared. Additional photos were then taken with the markers in place. They moved to the area where the body lay and began carefully collecting anything that could be considered evidence. Only the feet and part of the legs were exposed and contaminated by animal activity. The team carefully scraped away then dirt and removed the canvas to discover the body, face up. Forensic technician, Sally Patmore, moved in with the camera again. She photographed the victim from every angle, paying close attention to the marks on her neck.

"Thank goodness for these cold days and nights," she mumbled. "Not too much decomp yet." Then she moved to the other side to continue shooting, *Interesting*. "Guys, can someone bring me a fingerprint strip and some solution? Looks like there's a bloody fingerprint on her neck."

Sally took the bag, removed the strip, and cut a piece to fit the size of the print. She sprayed activating solution on the pre-treated side and pressed the strip firmly against the victim's neck to lift the print. When she was sure the impression had adhered properly, she carefully placed the strip in a small manila envelope, sealed the flap, and labeled and initialed the front. She then took a container, unscrewed the lid, and deposited a small scraping of the dried blood for DNA analysis. Once the team was satisfied nothing had been overlooked, Roki, the cadaver dog was allowed to check the scene. He did not alert on any other remains, so the team wrapped up and waited for the transport unit to take the body to the morgue for autopsy and attempt at identification.

~ * ~

"Bill, do you have a minute?"

"Sure, honey." He put his newspaper on the end table and looked over at his wife in the recliner. "What is it?"

Martha twisted her hands in her lap and tried to think how best to word the thoughts swirling around in her mind. She stared unseeingly at the news blaring from the television. "I'm worried about Marcie. Bill, this is Friday and we haven't heard from her since Tuesday morning. I've tried calling her cell, but keep getting voice mail."

"Hmmm... You know what Carl said about the trip to Ireland when I called the house last night."

"But don't you find that odd?"

"In fact, Martha, I'm glad you brought this up. I've felt uneasy ever since I talked to Carl. I can't see my little girl running off to another country without telling us." Bill shook his head. "I just can't see it."

Martha nodded in agreement. "Me either. She's dreamed of visiting Ireland for as far back as I can remember. I'm sure if she finally had the opportunity to take the trip, she would have told us all about it. She would have been so excited."

Bill narrowed his eyes." Something doesn't feel right, Martha."

"I agree. And after those times when Marcie told us she was scared of him, I'm just afraid..." Her voice trailed off into painful silence.

For several minutes, they sat quietly, each contemplating thoughts they hardly dared give credence. Bill sighed deeply. "Honey, come over here and let's ask the Lord for guidance." His wife joined him on the couch, and they took each other's hands. "Dear Lord Jesus," Bill prayed. "Give us wisdom. I believe Martha and I are thinking the same thing and ...." His voice broke and for a moment, he could not continue.

"Help us, Lord, to find our little girl," Martha whispered while tears ran down her cheeks. "Something is wrong, Lord. We feel it. Help us to know what to do."

The couple sat for several minutes, weeping and holding each other. "Let's go over to the sheriff's department tomorrow and file a missing person's report." Bill wiped his eyes and took a deep breath. "That seems the best place to start."

"Yes, I think that's a good plan." Martha rose. "I just hope she's okay," she whispered, her voice laced with pain and concern.

~ * ~

Tucker was scheduled for rehab when he was released from the hospital. His original diagnosis of a severe crush injury to the left hand was officially downgraded to a minor crush injury and sprained wrist. Though stiff and swollen, his hand would heal, and he would regain full mobility with physical therapy.

While his mother and he approached the Riponville Rehab and Physical Therapy Center, he inwardly groaned. *Help me, Lord. I know this will be painful and difficult.* The stories he'd heard about rehab were none too encouraging. *But I want the use of my hand again, and I'm willing to do the work. But Lord, I don't have the strength on my own. I still hurt all over. Please help me to get through this, and teach me what You would have me learn.*

"Thanks, Mom." He gave her a gentle grin. "I appreciate the ride. Hopefully, I'll have a new set of wheels soon."

"I'm happy to help, son. You know that." She touched his cheek softly. "No matter how old you get or what position you hold, you'll always be my baby boy."

Tucker chuckled as he opened the car door. "Love you, Mom."

"I love you, too, Tucker. Your dad will pick you up in a couple of hours. I'm praying for you, honey."

Tucker looked at her with a twinkle in his eyes "I need it. I feel like I got hit by a truck or something."

"Oh, you." Emilie laughed. "Even when you're in pain you're still joking around." She was smiling while she waved and drove away.

Tucker slowly made his way inside the building. After checking in, he waited only a few moments.

"Tucker Bates?"

"Yes, that's me." Tucker rose, wincing at the soreness in his muscles.

"Hi, Tucker. I'm Steve Phillips. I'm going to help you with your hand."

"I appreciate it, man. I never realized just how much I use both until now. Thank the Lord I'm right-handed." Tucker shook his head. "But even so, it's been really hard."

"Don't worry. I've seen worse than yours and haven't lost a hand yet. You're lucky no bones were broken." Steve grinned broadly and led the way back to the therapy area.

"God was looking out for me, that's for sure." While they walked along, Tucker noticed people of all ages performing various exercises, stretches, and moves, some using equipment, some on the floor. *Looks like a gym.* People exhibited various facial expressions, from boredom, to intense concentration, to the tense strained look of working through extreme pain.

Steve put a tennis ball in Tucker's left hand. "This doesn't look like much, but trust me, it'll help. "I want you to squeeze this as hard as you can."

"Seriously? That's it?"

"Yep." Steve grinned and gave Tucker a knowing look. "That's it. Give me fifty reps. Keep count, and I'll be back in a bit to check your progress."

Skeptical, Tucker got down to the job at hand. Gingerly he attempted to grab the ball. Pain shot through his hand and radiated down his arm as he grasped the orb. *Wow. Not so easy after all.* He grimaced as he tried another rep. Stiff muscles and ligaments with no desire to move screamed in protest. Tucker clenched his teeth and beads of sweat formed on his upper lip. *Help me, Lord. I need to be able to do this.* He resolved not to think of how many total reps must be done. *I can do this with Your help, Lord. Just one rep at a time. I know I can do this.* He pressed onward trying to force his stiff fingers to squeeze the ball as much as possible. When he finally finished, he felt completely drained.

Steve returned and handed him a towel. "You're doing great, Tucker. The first couple of days are always the hardest. But you'll get there, I promise."

Tucker wiped his sweaty face. "I surely do hope so." He surrendered the tennis ball and rose. "That was some workout. I feel like I've run a marathon."

"You'll work with me three times a week and in the meantime, continue the reps at home *if* you want to recover." Steve walked Tucker back to the check-out area where they set up his appointment schedule for the next week.

Tucker slowly walked out of the building. The rehab center was accented by breath-taking landscaping. Tucker followed the sidewalk, bordered by a rock wall, and discovered a bench beside a large evergreen tree. On one side, a small fountain sent gurgling liquid along its bed of river stones. Tucker drank in the peaceful serenity while easing himself onto the bench to await his father. The cool fall air caressed his sweaty face, and he took a deep breath, thankful the pain in his bruised ribs was finally beginning to lessen.

Lord, I feel so weak. He looked at the sky. *I can't do all this in my own strength. Help me to trust You and trust these folks who are experts at this kind of thing. Help me not to give up. I want to use my hand again. Help me not to forget my goal.* He continued to commune with his Lord in silent prayer until his father arrived to drive him home.

~ Five ~

A week after Marcie's parents filed the report, two grim-faced men arrived at their home. "Mr. Carson, I'm Deputy Coroner Ellis Michaels, and this is Detective Lucas Howard from the Riponville County Sheriff's Department. You filed a missing person's report last week on a Marcie Carson Greene, correct?"

Bill Carson's heart filled with dread. His stomach clenched and for a moment, he thought he might vomit. Up until now, he'd had hope. Hope that their Marcie was just incommunicado for some innocent, understandable reason. But now the police were here. Right at his door. He motioned Martha over with a violently shaking hand. *I've got to be strong for my wife. I've got to be strong. But how can I be? Lord, help me.*

"Yes, sir, that's correct." His voice shook. "Do you have information? Do you know where she is?"

"Mr. Carson, an unidentified female body has been located." Ellis' eyes conveyed his heartfelt feelings. "We truly hope she is not your daughter. Would you feel comfortable looking at some photos to see if you can help us identify the victim?"

"Of course. We'll help." Bill heard, but couldn't comprehend what the man was saying. The only things he was truly aware of was the vice-grip his wife had on his arm, holding on as if her own life depended on it, and the thudding of his heart in his ears. *Dear God no...not my baby girl.*

Detective Howard opened a folder and handed them an 8"x10" close-up of the woman's head and neck. Martha shrieked. Sobs welled up deep within her and spilled out in an anguished wail while tears began to flow down her cheeks. "No. No. Not my baby girl. Bill. That's our baby girl." She turned away, unable to control her gut-wrenching sobs. "Oh, Marcie, Marcie no!" She wandered back into the living room and collapsed on the couch.

"Yes, officers, this is our Marcie." Bill's hand continued to shake violently while he handed the photo back to Ellis. He looked lost for a moment, then cleared his throat. He could not wrap his mind around what he'd just seen. Tears began to flow in a steady stream down his cheeks and through sobs, he choked out, "What happened? Where was she found?"

"Mr. Carson, your daughter's death is still under investigation by law enforcement and the coroner's office." Detective Howard was as gentle as possible. "But we can tell you her death has been ruled a homicide. Right now, there's not a lot more we can share due to the circumstances but when new details can be released, you will be contacted immediately."

Bill nodded, the logical part of his brain vaguely able to understand their obligations, but he was still confused. A homicide? His sweet, caring, kind daughter, who never had an enemy in her life? Who in their right mind would want to kill her? A familiar face flitted through his mind, but he dismissed the thought immediately, feeling ashamed. Sobs continued to shake his body while he shook the officer's hands. "Thank you for your kindness." Then, as an afterthought, "Have you contacted her husband Carl? He thought she was on a trip to Ireland."

"No, sir." Detective Howard shook his head. "Since you filed the missing person's report, we contacted you first."

Martha wandered back to stand by her husband in the doorway. Her eyes were bloodshot and puffy, and her hand clutched a handful of sodden tissues. "Where is she? Can we see her? I feel like I need to see her face. Is that possible? And I know Carl will want to. He's going to be heartbroken."

The officials nodded their assent and Ellis spoke. "Yes, ma'am. Her body is at the morgue."

"Thank you," Martha whispered brokenly. "We'll call Carl so he can come at the same time."

~ * ~

They found her. I can't believe they found her. Of all the rotten luck. A string of expletives burst through Carl's mind while he drove toward the Riponville County Morgue. He slammed his fist on the steering wheel of his pristine BMW sedan. After fuming for several minutes, he realized he needed to calm himself. *Chill, man. Just chill. You're cool. Remember, you're the grieving husband. Your wife ran off after an argument but she was alive when she left you. You have no idea what happened.* He passed a billboard advertising reduced airfares on Delta Airlines. *No, wait. I told her parents she went on a trip.* For a moment, indecision gripped him. *Which story is more plausible?* He drove another mile before he decided. *I'll stick with the trip story. I think that's the safer route.* A sense of well-being spread over him. *People are so stupid. I can fool anybody. I didn't expect to have to deal with this, but that's okay. I'll have them all eating out of my hand.*

~ * ~

Martha nervously smoothed her skirt after she got out of the car. Bill shut the passenger side door and watched while she fiddled with the hem of her sweater. Gently he took her shaking hands and wrapped them with his own. "Are you sure you want to do this, sweetheart?"

She squeezed his hands tightly. "Yes, I'm sure." Tears which had hovered at the edges of her eyes during the short drive, now spilled over. "I know she's gone, Bill, but I keep hoping somehow that this won't really be her."

Bill pulled her close and hugged her gently. "I know, honey. I know. I feel the same way." They stood for a moment, attempting to regain their composure.

Martha pulled back and looked around. "What time is it? Carl was supposed to meet us here at one."

Bill checked his watch. "It's ten after. I'm sure he'll be here soon." They sat on a nearby bench to wait. When Carl finally pulled in nearly thirty minutes later, they all headed inside.

Bill and Martha Carson wept when they viewed their precious daughter's face. Her bluish-white and lifeless features confirmed what they saw in the photograph. Their little girl was gone. Carl glanced at Marcie's body, then turned quickly away and put a hand to his mouth. Tears squeezed from his eyes.

"Yes, that's our Marcie." Bill could still hardly believe it. "That's our little girl."

Carl clutched his chest and sank to his knees. "My wife, that's my wife. Oh, no...no..." he wailed.

Ellis Michaels mercifully pulled the sheet back over Marcie's face and returned the body to the compartment. He escorted them to a small conference room. Martha was thankful to leave the inner area where the bodies were stored. She was beginning to feel nauseated by the faint smell of death and chemicals that lingered in the room. Now that she knew without a doubt her daughter was dead, she wanted all this to be over.

Ellis looked at Carl. "Since, as her husband, you are next of kin, we are free to release the body to you, Mr. Greene. The autopsy is finished. Do you want us to call a funeral home for you?"

Carl looked up, struggling to control the anger that was consuming him. He *still* had to keep dealing with issues about Marcie. When would this end? Quickly he squelched his fury and put on a look of pain and anguish. "Mom, Dad, could you take care of this? I just can't do it." He turned from them, his shoulders shaking with sobs.

"Is that okay, doctor?" asked Bill. "We can take care of the arrangements."

"Of course. We'll just need you to sign here." Ellis opened a file folder and indicated the line.

After settling on the funeral home details, the group was free to go. As they left the morgue, Bill noticed the overcast, gloomy sky threatening cold rain to come. *Fitting. Fitting that the sky weeps with us on this horrible day.*

Carl, shoulders slumped and his face a mask of confusion and pain, turned to Bill and Martha while they walked toward the parking lot. "Mom and Dad, what on earth could have happened? She said she was going to Ireland. How could this happen? I took her to the airport. I saw her get on the plane. She was so excited and..." his voice broke and he began to sob. "Oh, Marcie, Marcie. Oh baby, what happened?" He shook his head helplessly. "Why did God take my wife?" His voice became angry and he shook his fist at the sky. "Why, God? She was the sweetest woman on this earth. Why did you take her? Why did you allow this to happen? You could have protected her." He bent over double, sobs overtaking him.

Bill and Martha put their arms around Carl, their own tears flowing freely. "Son, we may never know for sure," Bill said. "But our girl is gone. She was such a light in all our lives. But you can't blame God, Carl. You cannot. His will is perfect and His ways are ..." Bill's words trailed off when he pictured his daughter's smiling face. The day she was born. Her kindergarten graduation. Her brilliant smile on her wedding day. Her precious faith in Jesus and her dedication to serving Him. "I don't know why this happened, Lord Jesus, but I will trust in You. I will trust You, God," he whispered, teeth clenched against the pain.

Martha grasped his hand as sobs erupted once more. "Yes, dear Father God," she affirmed. "I will trust You. Thank You that our baby girl accepted you as Savior when she was a tiny girl. Thank You that she is now safe in Your arms." Anguished parents stood with their grief-stricken son-in-law, holding each other and offering what comfort they could.

Finally, Bill and Martha stepped back. "What do you want to do for the memorial service?" Martha dabbed her eyes with a tissue.

"I just don't think I can handle that." Carl's lower lip trembled, and the tears began again. "Is there any way you all could plan it? You know the things she liked. She might have even put something about her desires on our computer." Carl studied his wingtip shoes for a moment, then looked at Bill. "Seems like I remember her mentioning that once. You'll want to come down to pick out something to bury her in. Of course, you can have any of her things you want. Come to the house anytime." He reached into his pocket. "Here's a key. Whatever you plan will be fine. Just let me know when." He took a deep breath, wiped his eyes, and strode toward his car.

Bill and Martha watched him depart. "Poor guy." Martha's tone was tender. "I think we were wrong about him, Bill. I feel guilty for even thinking badly of him. He wouldn't be so upset if he didn't love our Marcie, would he?"

Bill looked at her, unconvinced. "I'm just not so sure, honey." His eyes were thoughtful. "Something doesn't ring true but I can't put my finger on what. Let's just say I'm very glad they did an autopsy. I want to know how she died." They walked to their car and headed for home, knowing the coming days would be difficult while they came to terms with the death of their only daughter.

~ * ~

"I'll call before I go home," Tucker's assistant, Cora, said while he climbed from her vehicle. "Just in case you don't find what you want today and need a ride home."

"Thanks, Cora. You're a doll." Tucker smiled warmly and closed the passenger door. He waved while she drove away, wincing when pain shot through his hand. *Even waving bye is a chore.* Despite the discomfort, he flexed his fingers while he entered the Honda dealership. He was determined to do as much rehab as possible on his own in order to more quickly regain the full use of his hand. The general soreness of his body was beginning to abate, and he felt ready to take charge of his life again.

A salesman immediately approached. "Senator Bates, welcome to Riponville Honda. I'm Matthew." He extended his hand with a smile. "How can I help you today?"

"Hi, Matthew. Nice to meet you." Tucker shook his hand firmly, and grimaced. "Unfortunately, my Accord was totaled last month."

Matt's thousand-watt smile faded. "I heard about your wreck on the news. How are you feeling?"

"Not too bad, considering," Tucker said. "God was with me. My hand is still not too cooperative, but I'm in physical therapy for that. Most of the bumps and bruises are healing well. Really, it's a miracle I wasn't killed. God is good, all the time."

"And all the time, God is good." Matthew laughed. "So you've seen *God's Not Dead*, too?"

Tucker nodded. "Great movie."

After a bit more chit-chat, the men got down to business. "May I show you one of our new Accords?" Matthew asked. "They're fully loaded and get fantastic mileage."

"I'm sure they're incredible, but something a couple of years old is more my speed." The overly-practical Tucker then grinned. "Although, I'm kind of hoping you'll have a pre-owned one with a little flash and wow value."

Matthew thought for a moment. "You know, we had one come in yesterday that might just be the ticket. Let me see if we still have the car on the lot." He made a quick phone call to the pre-owned division, then grinned. "We're in luck! C'mon."

Tucker followed the man outdoors to where a beautiful burgundy two-door Honda Accord was parked. "She's only two years-old and has just fifteen thousand miles." Matthew caressed the hood. "She had the dream owner, too. Drove carefully and no accidents. She needed to trade for a four door, but said she loved this car."

Tucker looked over the shiny vehicle appreciatively. "*Very* nice. Shall we take her for a spin?"

"Absolutely."

Tucker climbed into the driver's seat and felt the comfort of the bucket seat envelop him. They drove around town, and Tucker was pleased. The car was everything he had hoped to find. Back at the dealership, Tucker and Matthew haggled a bit, but finally settled on a price both felt was fair. Within an hour the car was paid for, and Tucker drove off the lot. He was halfway home when he remembered Cora. He pulled into a parking lot and dialed her number. *Can't forget to call her. She'd be beside herself if she didn't hear from me.*

"I've got a nice new ride, Cora. Not too fancy, but enough extras to make driving fun."

Cora giggled. "Another Accord, I presume?"

"Yes, ma'am. I'll show her to you tomorrow. Might even give you a ride if you're really nice to me."

"Ha!" Cora exploded. "You'll give me a ride whether I'm nice to you or not, young man."

They both laughed and wished each other a pleasant evening. Tucker tapped the radio on and returned to the highway, grinning with contentment and thanking the Lord for providing a new car that suited him so well.

~ * ~

"Carl, we'd like to come down and look through Marcie's things tomorrow, would that be okay?" Bill asked. "We want to find just the right things for her service."

"Sure, no problem." Carl tempered his voice to sound sad. He fingered the blonde curls of the woman he'd met earlier.

"I'll be away this weekend, so come anytime starting tomorrow."

"Thanks, son, we appreciate that."

Carl tapped the phone off and looked at his date appreciatively. "We'll be having a wonderful weekend in Vegas, won't we, baby?"

~ * ~

Bill and Martha drove down the long drive to Carl and Marcie's home, four manicured acres near the Thirskton State Forest. The couple joined hands, prayed for strength, then proceeded to the house. Marcie's touches were everywhere. On the porch, pots of carefully tended plants still bloomed, though some were drooping from frost damage. *No one to take them indoors*, Martha mused. *Carl would never think of that*. Inside, they slowly took in her collection of antique books, the paintings she loved, and her tasteful décor.

Everything spoke of a woman who had made the house a home. *She could have been an interior designer*, Martha thought sadly. *She was so gifted.*

"I'll go look through her clothes." Martha sighed, wiping tears from her eyes. "Why don't you check the computer?"

Bill nodded and headed for the office. He booted up the desktop computer and waited until the home screen fully loaded. *Where to start?* He thought for a moment. *Guess 'My Documents' is as good a place as any.* To his surprise, while he scrolled through the various documents, he found one named "My Funeral". His heart beat faster. *Wow. I didn't really expect to find something so obvious.* He opened the document and sure enough, there was a listing of the songs Marcie wanted and the scriptures to be read. The listing was in rather a haphazard fashion, given Marcie's usually neat and orderly style, but there it was. Puzzled by something he could not define, he printed the document. When Bill closed the file, he noted it had been created on November 2nd. A cold chill spread over his body. The deputy coroner estimated the time of Marcie's death to be on or around November 2nd. Bill took a screen shot of the file showing the date, then copied both to a flash drive. He looked again at the printout of Marcie's funeral service requests. At the bottom of the sheet, he noticed the words "The Cloud of My Thoughts" listed as a song.

What? He took the sheet in to the bedroom where Martha had several of Marcie's dresses laid out on the bed. "Martha, look at this? Do you know this song?"

"'The Cloud of My Thoughts'. Hmmm. No, I don't recall ever hearing that one. Honey, which dress do you like?"

Bill folded the paper and put it in his pocket to review later. Right now he and Martha must decide on the right clothing and mementos for their daughter's service.

~Six~

The aroma of roasting turkey trickled out when Lizzy and Rose opened the door to welcome Deborah and her family. Deborah's husband Marshall Jackson gave Rose a wink. "That drive gets longer and longer especially when you know there's an amazing meal waiting at the other end."

Six-year-old Millie's face was wreathed in smiles. "Mama, it smells so good in here." As soon as she spotted Lizzy, the young girl and her twin, Kate, made a beeline for their aunt.

"Oh, girls, I've missed you." Lizzy enveloped them both in a massive bear hug. Then she beckoned to Rose, Deborah, and Marshall. "C'mon, guys. Group hug." The family embraced with lots of laughter. Lizzy dabbed at her eyes. "I know we only live a few hours apart, but we still don't see each other often enough. I'm so glad you're all here."

She sniffed, put her hands on her hips, and looked at her nieces with a serious expression. "Now girls...I need your help." Millie and Kate followed her to the kitchen, eager to take part in the preparations. "Before we start, we need to take care of those sleeves." Lizzy carefully folded back the arms of the turtleneck the girl wore. "There," she said with satisfaction. She stood back, looked them over, and smiled with delight. Her nieces looked so adorable in their bulky fall colored sweaters, jeans, and tiny loafers. Deborah had pulled each girl's hair back on one side with a barrette that looked like a leaf. "You are lovely, ladies. We'll have to ask your Mom to get a picture of us together later. We're all dressed like fall." Millie and Kate nodded eagerly in agreement.

"You look pretty, too, Aunt Lizzy," said Kate shyly. "I like your hair." Lizzy had styled the ends in a flip and was happy the girls approved. She knelt down on one knee to give them a hug. "Thank you, Kate." The girls returned her hug exuberantly.

The youngsters chattered away, sharing the events of their lives while they finished preparations for the meal. Lizzy smiled to herself, thoroughly enjoying the time with her nieces.

Rose and Deborah went into the large dining room and covered the table with a tablecloth. In the center, Rose placed a wicker cornucopia and filled it with fruit. She asked her granddaughters to scatter silk fall colored leaves on the table, and they also helped arrange a set of praying pilgrim figurines on each end of the centerpiece. As the final touch, Deborah lit two candles, which filled the air with a spicy aroma.

Thirty minutes later when everyone gathered around the table, their mouths were watering with anticipation. "Marshall, would you lead us in prayer?" Rose asked with a smile.

"Absolutely." Marshall nodded. "Let's join hands."

While her brother-in-law thanked the Lord for the food, Lizzy felt her heart clench. Her nieces each held one of her hands. The feel of those tiny soft fingers in her palms made her heart momentarily yearn for the child she would never have. She squeezed their hands gently and forced her mind back to the present.

"Father we also thank you for the incredible blessings you've brought to us. We thank you that our Lizzy is safe and has such a wonderful job. Thank You for Mom and her love for us and the wonderful, Godly example she is. And Lord, I personally thank you for my wonderful wife and girls. Help me to lead them well and to be the husband and father You want me to be. Amen." His voice broke for a moment, then he cleared his throat and said, "Okay, ladies, let's dig into this feast!"

~ * ~

Tucker returned to his Riponville office, eager to get back into the swing of things. His left hand was still painful, but flexibility was already starting to improve. He hoped in time, complete mobility would return, and he would have the full use of his hand again. With a sigh, he slowly sat at his mahogany desk. He was glad to be out and about, even though the doctor insisted he take it easy for the first couple weeks. He was thrilled to be back at work for the people he represented, both his clients and his district. He began to look through the neat stack of papers Cora left for him and then turned to the stack she brought from his Senate office.

All at once, he stopped. *The card. Where is the card with the flags?* He looked the desk over thoroughly and found nothing. He methodically went through each piece of paper on the desk, intent on locating the missive. Finding nothing, he proceeded to look through each drawer as well. Frustrated he gave up. *It's gone,* he thought sadly. *I know I set it aside to keep, but now it's gone.* Then he remembered. *Oh wait - that card came to the Clifton office, not here. I must have left it down there.* The words on the card had filled his memory while he lay in the hospital recovering from the crash. He wanted to contact Elizabeth Godfrey and thank her, but there was no return address available. He thought he might contact the card's producer in hopes of finding Elizabeth, but now he had forgotten the name of the artist. He leaned back in his chair and sighed. He certainly had means at his disposal to find her, but what was the use? *It's more than just her kindness that caught my attention,* he thought. *Her note was different, and I actually wanted to meet her.*

Lost in thought, Tucker stared blankly at the dark computer monitor. Suddenly he started. Of course. The computer. He booted up the machine and googled Elizabeth's name. *Maybe she's on Facebook*. Elizabeth "Lizzy" Godfrey's name immediately popped up, and the first listing was her Facebook page, but the privacy settings indicated only friends could view her profile. *I could send her a friend request*, he mused. *But she'd probably just think somebody was playing a joke on her.*

Not to be discouraged by one dead end, Tucker kept looking. Finally, he found a site that listed an article written by Elizabeth Godfrey. He clicked on the link, and a page for victims of domestic violence popped up. Disgusted, Tucker grunted and leaned back in his chair. *Not this again,* he thought with a trace of sarcasm. He knew full well there were genuine cases of abuse, but he was completely flummoxed by the fact that the women involved so often either stayed in the situation, or would leave for a while and then go back. Dread trickled through his heart while he clicked on Lizzy's article and began to read.

"For many, domestic violence is a never ending cycle. You feel powerless to stop it. You feel trapped and that you're losing your mind. My own experience with abuse was the darkest time in my life."

No thanks. He closed the web browser. *Forget it. I don't want to be involved with anyone with who has that kind of background and baggage.* He purposefully began sorting through the mound of work on his desk, determined to put all thoughts of Elizabeth Godfrey and the card out of his mind. But a sense of profound disappointment spread throughout his being, and he found himself fighting a feeling of letdown.

~ * ~

Lizzy surreptitiously glanced around. Everyone in the office appeared to have their attention focused on their computer monitors. A small grin tugged at the corner of her mouth. She eased her chair back and looked with delight at the bulging Christmas stocking pinned to her workstation wall. Ever so gently, she eased herself from her chair, stood in front of the stocking to shield it from view, and began to look inside at the jumble of interesting gifts.

Mandy looked up from the warrant she was entering just in time to see Lizzy's hand reach toward the stocking. "What do you think you're doing, Elizabeth Lauren Godfrey?"

Lizzy jumped and plopped back into her chair with a thud and a frustrated but mischievous grunt. "Mandy! I was just taking a little peek. I can't stand it."

"Little missy, you'll wait for the party just like the rest of us." Mandy looked at her sternly, then changed her expression to one of false agrievement. "I can't believe you tried to look early. I'm just so ..." she sniffed and dabbed at her eyes with a tissue. "I'm shocked. Shocked and deeply saddened."

"Um, ladies." Justine's voice came from the other side of the room. "I must confess. I kind of looked in my stocking yesterday. Just the stuff at the top, though." The women laughed uproariously, and two more in the group admitted to peeking when no one was looking.

Lizzy looked at Denae, who sat in front of her, and grinned. "I guess we can't always be angels, huh?"

Denae returned her grin with a look of consternation. "This is the last year I get the angel stocking." She cleared her throat and addressed everyone. "I mean it, ladies. This is way too much pressure. It's someone else's turn next year." The women laughed together, enjoying the annual Christmas joke. Denae had been given the angel stocking for three years in a row, after a customer commented about how nice she was. When Denae was told about the praise later, she'd retorted, "I am *not* nice and I am not an angel." Denae laughed with them, but shook her finger to prove she meant business. "I'm serious now. If somebody puts Miss Angel in my area next year, I'll move her pronto."

Everyone laughed and returned to their work lighthearted. The stockings were tradition, as was the public chastisement of the first person caught peeking. The Christmas season was now officially in full swing.

~ * ~

The day of the circuit court records Christmas party arrived with much excitement. Baklava, colorfully decorated cookies, chips, salsa, and a variety of other treats and Christmas goodies covered the back room table. The women gathered together to exchange gifts before eating. Anticipation grew as Sandra rose to begin. Names were drawn in October and so far, no one knew who drew what name.

"This year, I got..." Sandra paused dramatically and looked around, drawing out the suspense. "Justine!" The ladies clapped while Sandra presented Justine with an elegantly wrapped gift.

They continued in this fashion until Lizzy was presented with a gift from Denae. She shook the box gently and put the gift up to her ear. "Hmm...could be the million dollars I asked for." She grinned. "Or maybe the key to the mansion." They all laughed while she pulled away the wrapping paper. "Oh, Denae, thank you! You know how I love Philosophy™." Lizzy looked at the gift box containing a bottle of shower gel and body emulsion, both in the Unconditional Love™ scent. "I absolutely adore these." She got up to give Denae a hug. "Thank you so much."

The ladies finished their party by enjoying the feast awaiting them. Lizzy sighed with contentment as she tasted a delectable piece of baklava. *Thank You, Lord,* she prayed inwardly. *Thank You for these wonderful people You've surrounded me with. Thank You for using them in my life to bring me back when I was so low. Bless every one of them in a special way.*

~ * ~

Tucker blinked to wakefulness when a shaft of sunlight pierced through the blinds. He stretched luxuriously, but then remained where he was, enjoying the comfortable bed. Like any red-blooded American man, his interpretation of taking it easy differed significantly from that of his doctor, and he had overdone during the past few weeks. The doctor ordered him to take a week of rest, while continuing his physical therapy at home. *Thank goodness this is Christmas week,* Tucker thought. *The work load is always lighter, so I won't get too much further behind.* He'd been glad enough to rest yesterday. His body complained about his thoughtlessness during the previous weeks and demanded sleep almost the whole day.

This morning, Tucker awoke feeling much better. He stared at the ceiling, trying to decide what to do with himself. Since cooking was a hobby in which he rarely had time to indulge, he industriously planned to make a triple batch of his favorite peanut butter chocolate chip cookies. He rose, took care of Porter's needs, and headed for the kitchen. Baking proved to be somewhat challenging since his left hand was still weak, however he had fun in spite of the inconvenience. He was just sliding the first pan into the oven, when the doorbell rang. He closed the oven, set the timer, and hurried to the front door.

"Mom, hi."

Emilie Bates gave her son a bear-hug and followed him into the kitchen. She groaned at the sight of bowls in the sink and ingredients still strewn all over the counter. "What in the world..."

"Trying my hand at making some cookies, Mom." Tucker glanced around the room, trying to avoid his mother's accusing stare as long as possible. No matter how old he was, that look, loving but stern, always made him feel seven years old again. "I feel great."

Emilie informed him in no uncertain terms, if she came in and caught him at work again, she would plan to stay with him and enforce the doctor's instructions. She waved him off to bed and took over the project.

Tucker awakened the next morning. *Guess I was more tired than I realized*, he thought. *I can't believe I slept right through another day*. Porter, who was snuggled up beside him, jumped off the bed and sat with tail wagging. "All right, buddy, all right." Tucker laughed while he patted the dog on the head. "I'll take you out. Just let me stop by the bathroom first."

Tucker enjoyed feeling the fresh cool air on his face while he walked Porter around the yard but was glad for his winter jacket. When business had been seen to, they returned to the house. He made his way to the kitchen and found the finished cookies neatly stored in a plastic container. A note informed him his mother would return that afternoon to clean and do some more cooking for him. Tucker opened the refrigerator and stared blankly into its depths for several minutes, trying to decide what he wanted for breakfast. He finally settled on a glass of milk and a handful of cookies.

He took his food to the living room, plopped down into the recliner, and clicked on the TV. Porter sat attentively on the floor right next to the chair. Tucker grinned at his polite begging but then turned his attention back to the reporter. When the news was over, he went to his library to select a movie. Once again, the good night's sleep had revived him. He looked over the movie titles he owned feeling disgruntled. Sitting around during the day was not in his nature. He thought of his mother and with a sigh, grabbed his *Lord of the Rings Extended Edition* set and returned to the living room. He put the first disc of *Fellowship of the Ring* into the DVD player and returned to the recliner. "Might as well have a *Lord of the Rings* marathon as long as we're confined here, Porter." The dog looked at him sympathetically and jumped into his lap. He didn't care what they did. He was just glad to have his dad home with him. Tucker was still dutifully resting in the chair with Porter in his lap, when Emilie Bates arrived. He paused the movie and went to greet her.

"Good morning, son," she said cheerily and came through the door with several shopping sacks. "I've got enough here to fix you up for the rest of the week, so you won't have to cook a thing. Besides, you and Porter had better be planning to be at the house tomorrow evening for Christmas Eve and then for Christmas Day, too. Dad said to be ready for a chess match."

"Morning, mom." Tucker's voice contained a bit of an edge. "I appreciate this, but I really don't think it's going to hurt me to do a little cooking."

Emilie put the sacks on the kitchen counter and then came over to where Tucker had taken a seat on a bar stool beside the island. "You, my dear, look like a little boy pouting," she said pointedly.

"I feel fine. This is ridiculous." Tucker looked at her sourly. "It's driving me crazy. My people didn't elect me to sit on my duff, Mom. Plus, all my clients are on hold, too." He sighed and ran a hand through his dark brown hair. "I've already had so much down time. I need to be at work."

Emilie sat on the stool beside him. "Son, you know we all love you and I know Dr. Thompson is only concerned for your health. He truly has your best interests at heart. Your body went through incredible trauma, and if you don't handle this correctly now, you may pay a serious price later." She looked at him lovingly and took his hand. "How many times have we had talks like this?" She chuckled, remembering. "Your broken leg in elementary school. The asthma you developed in high school. Mono in college. What were you, allergic to school?" Tucker's lips curved ever so slightly, though he didn't want to laugh. "Honey, I know this is just as hard for you now as it was then." Emilie looked at him intently. "But obeying the authorities God has set above you is part of your responsibility to Him. He knows all about the people you represent and your clients, and He will take care of them. He also knows *your* needs. Don't buck Him, son. Surrender yourself to His will."

Tucker looked at her with a petulant expression but tried to have the right attitude. "I know, Mom, I know. It's just so frustrating."

Emilie stood and hugged him. "Let's pray right now." They both bowed their heads, and Emilie asked the Lord for wisdom. "Oh, Father, I pray You would be especially close to Tucker right now. Please give him the patience he needs to rest and give his body time to heal. We thank You and praise Your name that he was not killed, and we pray that the man who was driving the truck will get the help he needs. Please help Tucker to use these days to rest and draw closer to You."

While she prayed, Tucker felt the anger and aggravation drain away, and he was able to truly surrender his own will to his Lord. When Emilie finished, Tucker prayed as well and both felt a sense of peace and serenity when they finished. "Mom, while you're doing all my housework, I'm going to do some Bible study." Tucker slid off the stool, and gave her a hug. "I'll finish my movie later."

"Good plan." She squeezed him back tightly. "Oh, and I almost forgot." She retrieved one of the sacks from the counter. "These are all the cards and letters you got while you were in the hospital. I talked to Cora yesterday, and she asked me to bring them since I was already coming. I know you've read most of them already but I thought you might like to go through them again."

"Thanks, Mom." He took the sack and headed off to his library, which also served as an office. The room's decor resembled his senate office, but also featured a cozy leather recliner and a lamp in one corner. He grabbed his Bible and made himself comfortable, intent on spending some serious time with God.

Tucker enjoyed a wonderful afternoon of study and felt spiritually and mentally refreshed. He realized how hurried and busy his life had become and determined he would make time for his Lord, no matter how many other things demanded attention. By the time Emilie left early that evening, the house was sparkling clean, and the refrigerator was well stocked with foods he could easily heat up in the microwave.

After a supper of lasagna and salad, he decided to sit in the living room and read through the cards and letters. He was touched at the outpouring of love and support he received. The fact that people took the time to write never ceased to amaze him. One card in particular caught his attention. The general look of the card was vaguely familiar. The photo on the front featured a perky looking Meerkat and the caption read, *Hoping You'll Be up to a Good Forage Soon*. Tucker grinned. He immediately recognized the correlation to one of his favorite shows, *Meerkat Manor*, which once aired on Animal Planet. He flipped the card over and saw the familiar stamp. *That's where I've seen this kind of card before. This is the same artist who made the flag card I lost*. He made a mental note to check the web site later to order a framed print of the flags for his office. He opened the card and saw the signatures of multiple members of the circuit court records office at the Riponville County Courthouse. They all wished him well and said they were praying for him. He felt such warmth and goodwill in the messages written and sensed these people knew the Lord in the same way he did.

That night, Tucker went to bed with a smile on his face and peace in his heart. He determined to enjoy this time of rest and use it as an opportunity to grow spiritually. He always looked forward to the family gatherings during the Christmas season. "Porter, I surely am thankful I did my shopping early this year," he said while he turned off the bedside lamp. "I'd have been in a world of trouble this year if I hadn't." Porter licked his hand in agreement, then curled up next to him and both were soon asleep.

~ * ~

Lizzy and Rose made the trip to Bamptonshire to spend Christmas Day with Deborah, Marshall, and the girls. "Aunt Lizzy," both nieces shouted in unison when their aunt walked through the door.

Kate grasped one hand and Millie the other. "Come see our new horses," Millie said, her eyes shining.

Lizzy went with them to their room and gave proper admiration to the new Breyer figurines each girl received for Christmas. After allowing the girls to show off what each horse could do, she smiled and winked at them. "Girls, you know, Grandma and I brought you each a gift, too."

"Really?" Kate put down the bay-colored horse and stood before her aunt. "Can we open them now?"

"Kate." Millie looked at her sister sternly. "Mamma says we're not supposed to beg for gifts."

"No worries, girls. You can open them any time you want."

"Let's open them now, Kate." Propriety was forgotten, and Millie grabbed her sister's hand. The trio returned to the living room where Rose sat with several wrapped gifts in her lap.

Deborah smiled at her twins' excitement "Yours are on the couch, Lizzy. And yours, ladies, are under the tree."

Squealing, the girls scrambled to snatch up matching boxes. They sorted out whose was whose, then sat cross-legged on the floor by the fireplace and tore open the boxes.

"Oh wow. Mama, look." Millie held up the light gray sweatshirt with a beautifully embroidered Friesian stallion on the front. "A horsy shirt." Kate opened her gift to find another of the same.

"What do you say, girls?" Marshall asked.

"Thank you, Grandma. Thank you, Aunt Lizzy," Kate and Millie chorused.

Lizzy went to hug them close. "You're welcome. I hope you both enjoy them."

The family opened the rest of their gifts, then enjoyed a sumptuous Christmas dinner and a lazy afternoon together playing board games. After supper the family piled into the den and settled comfortably in front of the fireplace.

Marshall took his iPad, opened the YouVerse app, and tapped to the second chapter of Luke. The group was solemn as he read the story of Christ's birth. When he finished, he asked, "Does anyone have anything to share about how God had worked in your life during the past year?"

"God has been so real to me at work lately," Lizzy said thoughtfully. "I see how many people are struggling with addictions and the bad choices they've made. God has really caused me to pray for them instead of just pity or look down on them. But for the grace of God, any of us could be there."

Deborah nodded. "I've had the same experience participating in the Kairos ministry. Girls, remember that's where we prepared the cookies for the ladies who are in prison." Millie and Kate nodded. The adults continued to share various instances where God encouraged and enlightened them and how He provided for them in special ways. The girls, who were suddenly silent and shy, chose not to share.

"Let's thank the Lord for sending His son, Jesus." Marshall reached his hand out to Deborah and everyone joined hands. "Father, we praise You for sending Your son to die for us. Thank You for making a way for sinners to one day enter Heaven's gates. We acknowledge we are nothing without You, Father. Thank You for Your amazing love that saved us and reconciled us to You. Help us to honor and glorify You in everything we do. In Jesus name I pray, amen."

He looked up and smiled at the girls. "Millie, would you get the movie?"

His daughter nodded and went to the DVD cabinet. She came back with *The Nativity Story*. The movie began and Millie and Kate snuggled close to Lizzy on the couch. She put an arm around each of them, her heart so full she felt she might explode. *Thank You, Father, for my wonderful family. Bless them and keep them safe.*

~Seven~

"Mr. Greene, this is just routine, I assure you." The detective's voice was polite and respectful. "I'm sure you know the spouse is always a primary suspect. If you're willing to cooperate with us, we'll just get a quick interview, finger-print roll, a DNA swab, then we can rule you out."

Carl was not thrilled with this turn of events, but if he resisted, he would look guilty. He thought since January passed with no contact from the authorities, he was home free. *Better to cooperate fully, though, while keeping an air of innocence and playing the role of the still-grieving hus-band.* "Of course, officer, I understand. I can come now if that's convenient for your department."

"That would be fine. Just come to the Sheriff's De-partment and ask for Detective Howard."

"Will do. Thank you, sir." Carl tapped off the phone and threw it in his briefcase. He slammed the lid closed and stormed out of his office.

This had better be the end of this whole affair. It's getting out of hand. Not only did I have to sit through that ridiculous memorial service that made Marcie out to be some kind of angelic being, now I have to talk to the police. She's still trying to yank my chain even though she's dead.

After arriving at the sheriff's department, Carl was es-corted by an emotionless deputy to a small interview room. Detective Howard arrived moments later and took a chair op-posite him. Carl squirmed inwardly while the detective stud-ied him. Was there something that had been unearthed? No, he'd been too careful. There was no way he'd ever be found out.

"Carl, we appreciate your cooperation today. This is a huge help to us. I know your day has been interrupted, and I'm going to make this as short and painless as possible."

"I appreciate that, sir, but I'm happy to help." Carl's voice broke as he choked back a sob. "I just want to find out what happened to my Marcie."

Detective Howard nodded and jotted a note on his pad. "Let's start off with where you were November 2nd and 3rd." He pulled out his phone and checked his calendar. "That's Tuesday and Wednesday, November 2nd and 3rd," he confirmed.

"Hmmm, let me think." Carl had planned for this question. "I was home during the early afternoon on Tuesday, but left around four for a convention. I didn't want to have to drive early Wednesday morning to get there, so I planned to stay over. I can get you copies of the hotel reservations if you need them."

"Yes, please do, that would be helpful." Detective Howard jotted notes on his pad.

The interview continued, and Carl indicated he had no idea how Marcie could have been found in the forest. He relayed the story of her being out of the country. "She was so excited about the trip. She turned back and waved to me before she went into the plane." Carl looked dejectedly at the man opposite him. "I just don't understand how this could have happened when she wasn't even in the U.S."

After nearly an hour, Detective Howard thanked Carl and assured him they would keep him informed of any developments. "Now, we need to roll your fingerprints and obtain a buccal swab for DNA identification purposes, then you're free to go. This is just routine. Do we have your permission?"

"Yes, of course."

"We'll need you to sign this consent form and let us make a copy of your driver's license." Detective Howard slid the form across the desk, and Carl signed without hesitation. After his license had been copied, Detective Howard shook Carl's hand. "Thank you, Mr. Greene." He opened the door. "We appreciate your cooperation. My condolences for the loss of your wife."

"Thank you, Detective. Please..." Carl's voice broke. "Please find who did this to my Marcie."

Detective Howard escorted Carl to the forensics lab for the buccal swab and fingerprint roll, then returned to his office. He sat down and looked thoughtfully at his notes.

Carl's explanation for Marcie's absence during the days after her death was a trip to Ireland, which matched what her parents told him. The detective tapped his pen absently on the desk. *But all is not as it seems. I feel in my bones something is not right. Just gotta figure out what's wrong with this picture.*

~ * ~

"This is going to be great," Lizzy whispered to her coworker Delane. They stood between the rows of files where they hoped they would not be overheard. "She's not going to suspect a thing because she hasn't been here long enough to know what we're up to. Plus, with all the hubbub from Christmas, she won't expect much for a February birthday."

Delane laughed quietly and nodded. "I think we can pull off a total surprise. Let's send out an email and get everyone to sign up to bring something."

"Right. I'll get on it." Lizzy returned to her desk and began to type out a message on her computer.

> *Ladies, Justine's birthday is next Tuesday. Since she's never experienced one of our parties extraordinaire, let's go all out. But keep it a secret! Please sign up to bring something and try to keep your lunch hour free on Tuesday, so we can all celebrate together. Here's the plan. I'll invite Justine to go to out to eat that day so I can get her out of the office. As soon as we leave, you get the room decorated and the party set up. I'll bring the cake.*

Lizzy clicked send and sat back in her chair with satisfaction. *This is such a wonderful office*, she thought fondly. *We're all like a bunch of sisters. Thank you, Lord, for bringing me here. You used these women in such a wonderful way in my life. I could never have healed completely without them. Your ways are so wonderful and so perfect. Thank You.* A tear of gratefulness formed while she returned to the inmate correspondence on her desk. Emails began to trickle in while Lizzy worked her way through the stack of letters. Soon all the supplies and food for the party were covered. *It's going to be great*, she thought with satisfaction. *Justine will be totally surprised.*

~ * ~

"... and I just can't believe we were almost there, and I didn't have my purse," Lizzy huffed in exasperation. "I must have left my brain at home in bed this morning."

"No problem, really," Justine reassured while they re-entered the office. "We'll still have time to eat."

"Would you go check in the back room? I may have left my bag back there during my break. I'll check at my desk."

"Sure."

When Lizzy was certain the other woman would not look back, she crept softly along after her. She was directly behind Justine when her co-worker went through the door and heard, "SURPRISE!"

Justine jumped and gasped, then began to laugh. "You guys," she exclaimed with a huge smile. "Oh my word, I had no idea."

She cheerfully punched Lizzie in the arm. "Forgotten purse, huh? You played me, girlfriend."

"Guilty as charged." Lizzy gave her a wicked grin. "But the plan worked, didn't it?"

"It did." Justine nodded in acknowledgment. She looked at the table laden with goodies, the festive balloon, and flowers. "This is so great!" she exclaimed. "Let's dig in."

"Oh, and just for the record," Lizzy said. "No lies were told today. My purse *was* under my desk, and I never said I forgot it." The group laughed approvingly.

They enjoyed the buffet with much fun and laughter. All were pleased that the party went off without a hitch, and their newest office member's birthday was properly celebrated.

~ * ~

Bill Carson sat at his computer, rubbing his chin and looking over the document his daughter had prepared regarding her funeral desires. *How odd that she prepared this on the very day she died.* He remembered how touching the service was, and the wonderful people who expressed their love and appreciation for Marcie. The sanctuary was decorated for the Christmas season when they held her memorial. *The holidays will never be the same.* Bill sighed. *I hope we'll be able to enjoy the season again someday.*

They had never identified the song, "The Cloud of My Thoughts" and the title still puzzled him. *Lord, what is it? There's something going on here. I can't get this out of my head. Guide my thoughts, Lord. Help me to understand what you're trying to show me.*

Martha's voice penetrated his thoughts. "Hon, do you want a snack? I'm going to fix something during these commercials."

"No, thanks. I'm still full from supper." Bill continued to stare at the document on the monitor. Blaring from the TV in the den came the words, "Upload all of your documents to the Cloud today and enjoy peace of mind."

The Cloud. Wait, "The Cloud of My Thoughts". Could Marcie have meant the electronic kind of cloud? Could the title have been a clue? He went to the kitchen and explained his idea to Martha.

"Bill, it could be." She turned slowly from her bowl of popcorn. "Marcie told me once that she was keeping a journal stored in a place Carl wouldn't look. I always thought it odd she used the term 'stored'. If she had a physical diary, wouldn't she have said 'hidden' or 'tucked away'?" Martha thought for a moment. "But honey, how will *we* ever find it? From what I see on TV, there are thousands of cloud storage options."

"We're going to pray for divine assistance, that's what we're going to do," Bill said firmly. "I have no idea where to look, but I'm going to call Detective Howard and see what he thinks. Maybe he'll have an idea of how to find her cloud journal, if there really is one."

~ * ~

Tucker slipped into the busy courtroom as unobtrusively as possible. His day in court had arrived. The gallery was filled with nervous frightened people, while at the front, assistant district attorneys busily completed paperwork, made deals with defense attorneys, and rushed about on one errand or another. In the jury box, news cameras on tripods stood waiting, while cameramen hung out beside them looking bored. When confronted with the results of his blood-alcohol test, the truck driver agreed to plead guilty to driving under the influence. He also faced charges of cocaine possession and reckless driving. Tucker took a seat and watched the general hubbub of plea court gearing up. Ethan Leech, a prosecutor friend, came into the room and greeted Tucker warmly.

"Extra crazy today," he noted, watching the people milling around. "Good to see you, Tucker."

When his friend walked toward the front to speak with the courtroom coordinator, Tucker noticed an attractive woman sitting at the desk just below the judge's bench. She appeared to be busy with paperwork, but Tucker immediately observed her pleasant demeanor. People continuously asked her questions and handed her papers, yet she never seemed to be irritated at the interruptions and gave each person a friendly smile. At one point, the woman looked around the courtroom briefly and caught his eye. His heart quickened when she gave him a quick smile and then went back to her work. *I wonder who she is, and if she's available,* he thought. *Nah. I'm sure she's married.*

Tucker continued to watch while the morning preparations progressed. Around ten a.m., the bailiff announced the judge, who took her seat at the bench. The truck driver's name was first on the docket. Tucker approached and stood beside the assistant district attorney. The cameramen now stood attentively, capturing the moment for the day's newscasts. While the formalities of the proceeding progressed, Tucker could observe the clerk up close. She processed paperwork busily at her computer. He noticed she wore no wedding or engagement rings, just a small silver Irish Claddagh ring on the pinky finger of her left hand. Her shoulder-length dark hair set off her beautiful features. Her face and demeanor showed a confidence which seemed to send out gentle waves of calm. Tucker found himself fascinated and was sure he had seen her somewhere before. When his turn to speak came, he nearly stumbled over his words.

"Your honor." He pulled his mind back to the moment at hand. "This man nearly took my life. My car was totaled and I still don't have complete use of my left hand." Tucker noticed the clerk stopped typing and was watching him while he spoke. Briefly their eyes met. Compassion and concern were in her eyes, and again he felt that gentle calm.

"I have forgiven this man for the wrongs he has done toward me," Tucker continued, focusing his attention back on the judge. "But I still believe punishment is in order. I also truly hope he can get help for his drug and alcohol problem. If he doesn't change his ways, next time someone might be killed."

"Thank you, Senator, for being in court today." Judge Victoria Lily nodded to Tucker. She allowed the defense attorney to speak, then sentenced the truck driver to a year in prison, plus five years of probation, during which he was to receive drug and alcohol treatment.

Lizzy took the case paperwork from the judge, then handed the bundle to the probation agent sitting to her right. The assistant district attorney handed her paperwork for the next case. She published the plea on the record and placed the defendant under oath. While she took her seat, she made a quick perusal of the courtroom and noticed the senator leaving. He glanced back at her when he reached the door, and for a moment their eyes met again.

Lizzy sighed deeply. *What a handsome man. Not like a model, though—a peaceful- strong handsome. He seems like a kind man, too. I wish I could get to know him.* The sound of papers hitting her desk brought her back to reality. *Gotta focus on what's in front of me, not on "What-ifs"* she scolded herself.

During her drive home, she thought of Tucker again and fussed at herself. *You've got to get a grip, woman. Don't go there.* She reflected on what she knew of his background. *We're from two different worlds. Even if he is a Christian and isn't in a relationship, it would never work. Get him out of your mind. Don't let a fantasy steal your contentment. You know better. No man alive wants second-hand goods.* But later as she drifted off to sleep, the memory of his brown eyes made her feel a longing so intense that it surprised her.

~ * ~

You can't watch somebody board the plane at our airport. Lucas Howard woke in the middle of the night out of a sound sleep. He sat up, his mind instantly alert. *You'd have to go through security, and they only let the passengers through. It's not like the old days where you could watch from the gate windows.* Lucas climbed out of bed, careful not to wake his wife, and made his way to the desk in the living room. Quickly, he jotted down his thoughts. He returned to bed with a plan to begin calling airlines first thing in the morning.

~ Eight ~

Mesmerized by the pornographic pictures on his computer, Carl Green failed to hear the knocking on his front door. The obnoxious ringing of the doorbell, followed by another insistent round of knocks, startled him, causing him to spill the tepid cup of coffee on his foot.

His erotic fantasy ended abruptly. He cleared his cache, then returned to the desktop's home screen. *Doesn't anyone value privacy?* Still, he had to play nice, just in case anyone suspected him of anything. And porn on his computer wouldn't help his good-guy image.

"May I help you?" he asked solicitously, eyeing the officers on his front porch. He shivered slightly as a feeling of foreboding hit him.

"Alastair Carlton Greene?" a burly six-foot-five deputy asked.

"Yes, sir, I am. What can I do for you gentlemen today?"

The deputy stepped forward and began to snap handcuffs onto Carl's wrists.

"Mr. Greene, you're under arrest for the murder of Marcie Carson Greene."

As the other officer immediately began to recite the standard Miranda warning, Carl's mind tumbled with a scramble of thoughts and emotions. *How did they find out? What did I forget? What did I miss? How on earth? How could they have traced anything to me?* The officers escorted Carl to their patrol car, assisted him into the back seat, and drove off down the long gravel driveway, leaving a cloud of white dust behind them.

Carl was silent during the forty-five-minute drive to Riponville. He attempted to calm himself and to think rationally. *I can beat this. There's no proof. I bleached down the shovel and the cart so there were no prints or blood. The rainstorm came after I took care of things, so there wouldn't even have been footprints. I'm sure I didn't say anything incriminating during the original interview.*

He began to think through the actual murder, intent on reviewing his clean-up procedures, but the memory of the experience overwhelmed him with a feeling of power. The scenes played through his mind like a thriller movie. Carl had considered using his .45 ACP Smith & Wesson pistol to kill Marcie, but in the end, felt the weapon would make things too messy. And too loud. He did use the gun to force her to write out her funeral plans. She was horrified, of course, and her fingers shook so that she could barely type. He got off on the fact that he could stand there holding the gun to her head, forcing her to plan her own funeral. The feeling was more exciting than any physical sensation he'd ever known. When she finished, he took her out into the woods behind the shed. First, she pleaded for mercy while he dragged her along. When she began to struggle and scratch at him, he snatched the zip ties from his back pocket and bound her hands and feet tightly so he could finish the job.

Stupid witch. Thought she could beg for mercy and then scratch him. God gave her to him to please him and to obey him. Her lack of submission, her constant shortcomings, and her dismal failures only proved what he must do. No woman so flawed could be allowed to survive and corrupt others. *I was only doing God's will.* Carl smiled as the police cruiser sped into town. *She was never going to be the kind of Christian woman she should have been. The kind of woman I deserve. I just don't know why I keep getting these duds. I'd have dispatched Beth, too, if she hadn't up and left. The little harlot. Her independent spirit and rebellion will eventually do her in.*

For a moment, he was lost in another fantasy of murdering his first wife, Beth, some night when he might get lucky enough to catch her alone. He'd tried to finish her off years earlier, before she spread her lies and corruption to others. But apparently, she'd wised up and always managed to have someone around. In spite of his stalking, he never found the right time and place. He would not take the risk of people thinking him anything but the fine, gentlemanly 'Brother Carl' he was at church and so never considered approaching her in public. He gave up on her, should the opportunity ever present itself, he would not hesitate to teach dear Beth the lesson she deserved.

When he eventually decided it was time to re-marry, he abruptly ended his relationship with Charlene, the woman he'd picked up at a bar long before Beth left him. Charlene did not want to break up and begged him to marry her, but he disdainfully slapped her and walked away, telling her never to contact him again. There was no way he would make some slut his wife.

He began scoping out women at church and met Marcie at a small-group meeting. Her soft demeanor and giving gentle spirit drew him at once. She was attracted to him as well, and nature took its course. He quickly wooed and won her, using every ounce of his charm. He impressed her with his spiritual knowledge and made sure she observed him reading a well-worn Bible often. They were married at the church and for a few months, she genuinely satisfied him. But then, just like Beth, she began to resent him. All he wanted was a submissive, hard-working woman who didn't have to be coddled and who understood that he was in command. Why did he have to suffer so? At least he had been able to get rid of Marcie before she started spreading lies about him all over town.

Carl's self-righteous thoughts continued while he was booked into the Riponville County Jail. While his fingerprints were taken, his thoughts turned to attorneys. *I don't know that I need a lawyer. This is an open-and-shut case, and there's no way they'll pin this murder on me. Besides, if I get in over my head, I can always call Thomas. He owes me big time.* He pictured his attorney friend squirming when he found out Carl knew all about his gambling addiction. *I know Mr. Upright Church Man wouldn't want his family and friends knowing about that. If I need an attorney, I've got one, no problem.* He smiled jauntily for his booking photo and walked into his cell, confident he would not be there for long.

~ * ~

Lizzy found a space in the busy parking lot and grabbed her purse. She exited the vehicle, carefully clicked the lock with her key fob, and made a mental note of what row she was on. She walked briskly to the store's entrance, going over her small list of needed items and enjoying the scent of spring in the air. She found all she needed and was back in the parking lot within twenty minutes.

~ * ~

Tucker looked at the line-up of movies on Blu-Ray. He'd tried for the past ten minutes to decide which would most suit Cora for her birthday. She loved old romantic films, so he finally decided on *The Shop Around the Corner*. He browsed a bit longer and selected a couple features for himself as well. He finished his shopping trip in the pet section, where he grabbed a box of Wellness™ treats for Porter.

He paid for his purchases and made his way outside. When he approached his vehicle, he saw a woman pointing her key fob at the front of his car, pressing the button firmly. When nothing happened, she approached the driver's side and tried to insert the key into the lock. Suddenly, the car's alarm system began to blare loudly. The woman jumped and dropped her keys on the ground.

Tucker approached as she grabbed up the keys and began frantically pressing the buttons again. "Hey, what do you think you're doing?" he asked in a firm, authoritative tone.

Lizzy nearly dropped her keys, her purse, and her shopping sack this time. She whirled around to face him. "Oh," she gasped, her voice shaking. "I don't know what's going on."

It's her! Tucker thought with amazement. *It's the woman from the courthouse. Why is she trying to steal my car?*

"I don't know what the problem is." She punched the useless buttons again. "This crazy thing worked just twenty minutes ago."

Tucker summed up the situation immediately when he looked further up the row of cars and spotted an identical burgundy Honda Accord. He calmly removed his keys from his pocket and effectively silenced the obnoxious alarm.

Lizzy stopped still and looked at him intently. "Hey, how did you make the noise stop?" Her voice went from frantic to suspicious in the space of two seconds. "Just how is it that your keys work on my car?"

"Your car?" He raised one eyebrow Mr. Spock style.

"Yes, my car." She glared at him. "The one I'm paying every month for, thank you very much. The one I nearly break my back on trying to keep looking new. The one with a courthouse parking sticker right on the front wind ..."

Tucker's eyes brimmed with barely controlled mirth, and he tried desperately not to smile. Lizzy stared intently at the spot on the driver's side windshield where her parking sticker should be. He watched her bravado deflate faster than a balloon.

"This is your car," she stated flatly.

"Yes, actually, that is correct." Tucker's tone was gentle, but had a hint of a smile. "I take it you own the burgundy Honda up the way there?"

Lizzy looked and nodded. She did not often blush, but this time she felt her face growing warm. *What a total and complete dork I am*. She mentally chastised herself. *And in front of Senator Bates of all people*.

Her embarrassment gave way to annoyance. "What in the world are you doing in a parking lot in Riponville?" she asked frostily. "Shouldn't you be at some legislative meeting or doing some big important senatorial thing in the capital?"

Tucker's laughter could no longer be contained. She'd acted so flustered to start with, that he began to feel sorry for her. But her sudden ire, in spite of the fact the mistake was her own, finally did him in.

After a moment, he saw a smile on Lizzy's face just before she burst into laughter as well. When they finally caught their breath, she said, "I'm so sorry, Senator Bates. I had absolutely no call to fly at you like that when I'm the one who was in the wrong." She extended her hand in a truce. "I do apologize."

Tucker's eyes met hers while he shook her soft hand. He was surprised that his heart did a little jump. He remembered the day in court when he watched her work. She was so capable, doing her job efficiently with a smile and a kind word for everyone. He wanted to meet her then, but the opportunity never presented itself.

He reluctantly released her hand and smiled. "You seem to have the advantage, ma'am. You obviously know who I am, but I don't know who you are."

"You aren't going to press charges for auto breaking are you?" A twinkle of mirth flashed from her eyes. "If that's the case, I'll not be giving you any further information."

"No, ma'am." He grinned. "If you give me your name, I won't report a thing."

"Elizabeth Godfrey." She extended her hand again. "Very pleased to meet you."

Tucker felt shock ricochet through his system. "Elizabeth Godfrey?" he said softly, as though to himself. He was so surprised he did not even take her hand.

"I generally go by Lizzy, at least that's what most people call me." She looked at him curiously. He seemed suddenly preoccupied and was apparently no longer listening. *Now I've gone and done it*, she thought and immediately retracted her hand. *I shouldn't have been so informal with a public official.*

"Senator, again I do apologize." Her tone became brisk as she pulled all her professional experience to the surface. "I know you're a busy man, and I'm keeping you. Thanks for not being too upset. I'll be more careful in the future."

Tucker still seemed in a daze, so Lizzy turned and headed for her car. *I am such an idiot. Such a total, blooming idiot.*

"Ms. Godfrey, wait...please."

Lizzy turned back obligingly, wondering just how much trouble she'd gotten herself into. All signs of preoccupation vanished as he met her halfway and looked at her intently. "Did you send me a card after the election last fall? It was a beautiful picture of a field of flags against a stormy sky."

"I did. "I can't believe you'd remember that. Surely you receive thousands of cards and letters."

Tucker's thoughts were still in a jumble. This was the woman he decided he didn't want anything to do with. The woman with a past and a load of baggage. The woman he decided was a whimpering, simpering, perpetual victim. And yet she was the same person he saw in court, who drew his attention like never before. A woman he could not get from his mind. She was this adorable lady before him who appeared in every way confident and in-charge. She did not exhibit the slightest evidence that she thought herself any kind of victim. He was at a loss to think clearly.

"I'm sorry," he finally blurted out when he realized he was staring at her. "I didn't mean to be rude."

"I'm sorry I tried to drive off with your car." She grinned. "By the way, you have excellent taste in vehicles." The impish glint was back in her eye.

Tucker relaxed with a laugh. "Likewise." He smiled back at her, thinking her brilliant blue eyes were so warm, yet full of fun. He was sorely tempted to ask her if he could call her, but squelched the impulse. *Not until I sort things out*, he thought firmly. *I've got to think this through.*

"By the way, how's your hand?"

"It's doing quite well." He was touched by her concern. "I'm doing physical therapy at home. Not much fun at first, but I am getting more flexibility back. I'm just thankful I'm not left handed."

"I'm glad to hear things are healing well." Then almost shyly, she added, "You've been in my prayers."

They parted with the usual pleasantries, and Lizzy drove home deep in thought. *I don't know what to make of that. Who would have ever thought I'd run into Tucker Bates in a parking lot?* She shook her head, a lopsided smile on her face.

When Lizzy walked through the back door, she heard the TV blaring. "The victim's body was discovered by hikers in November. The suspect was arrested without incident and remains in the Riponville County Detention Center with no bond." The local news anchor then proceeded on with her next story.

Wonder what that was about, Lizzy thought with interest. *I guess I'll find out soon enough. We'll probably get the warrant in the office soon. I think I'll check that out.*

After petting the dogs, she called a greeting to her mom who was down in the basement, then headed to her bedroom to change into something more comfortable for the evening. She intended to check the television station's web site to investigate the news item further, but became so engrossed in a book, the news story never entered her mind again.

~ * ~

"Oh, Jack, baby, what's going on with you?" Lizzy looked around her bedroom in dismay.

Over the past months, she noticed the animal's increasingly pickiness about his food. The cat who once asked for a snack during the night with loud purring and a gentle touch of his paw on her cheek, now left much of his dinner in the bowl. This evening, Lizzy's mother met her at the door, her face a mask of concern.

"Honey, something is wrong with Jack. He's yowling and won't let me touch him. He's in your bedroom."

Lizzy had immediately dropped her purse and satchel on the kitchen table and headed for her room. "Jack? Jack?" Lizzy called softly. "Where are you, baby? Come here sweetheart."

The cat did not appear. She quietly searched the room. When she opened the door to the aquarium stand, she saw him hunched in the corner. Eyes were wide with alarm the cat hissed and drew away. Lizzy slowly sat cross-legged on the floor and began to talk to him soothingly. After many minutes passed, the cat darted from his corner and went under the bed. Tears began to form in Lizzy's eyes. *Something is wrong. I've got to get him to the vet*. But there was no catching Jack. Afraid of making things worse, Lizzy decided not to chase him. With a heavy heart, she finally went to bed and tried to sleep.

Morning dawned to find Jack snuggled up beside her. "Oh my baby boy," Lizzy exclaimed softly. She gently stroked the cat, and he purred madly as if nothing was amiss. Lizzy felt relief, but knew she must find out what was going on.

She dropped Jack off at the veterinarian's office before work, where she was told they would do blood work and a general exam. She could pick him up at noon. Giving him a quick pat and a kiss, she left the cat in the care of the professionals. The morning crawled by, and Lizzy was relieved when lunch time finally arrived.

"He's thin," the veterinarian stated. "But we won't know for sure what's going on inside until we get the results of the blood tests. I'll call you as soon as they come in."

"Thank you." Lizzy was disappointed she must wait even longer to know the story. She paid the bill and transported a deeply unhappy Jack back to the comfort and safety of home.

Two days later, the phone call came. Her world shattered as she heard listened to the vet deliver the diagnosis and options—kidney disease. She could do nothing but try to make him comfortable. Prescription food and fluid therapy were the only options for treatment.

Lizzy tried to keep the tears from flowing. "I'll stop by tomorrow to buy the food. Can you show me how to administer the fluid therapy?" she asked. "I hate to get him upset bringing him in so often. He hates to leave home."

"Absolutely," the veterinarian said kindly. "Why don't you stop by tomorrow after work? I'll have everything ready for you, and I'll show you what to do. We'll try to help you keep his quality of life as optimal as we can."

"Oh, thank you. I want to do whatever I can to make him comfortable until it's time." Tears welled up while she tapped the phone off. "Oh, my sweet Jack," she sobbed, looking at the cat sprawled out in her recliner. "I don't want you to go. You're my sweet, lovey boy." She knelt beside the chair and stroked the cat lovingly while the tears streamed down her face. She buried her nose into his fur, as if trying to imprint his every essence into her brain so she would have him with her forever.

Rose joined her and gave her a gentle hug. "Honey, I know. I love him, too." Her own tears began to fall, and the women sat together with Jack for many moments, coming to grips with his diagnosis.

~Nine~

"Mr. Greene, we found your DNA under Marcie's fingernails." Detective Howard leaned toward the table between them, his expression pleasant and non-confrontational. "This is your opportunity to tell us your side of thestory. What happened?"

"Oh for Pete's sake, she was my wife. Of course she had my DNA on her." Carl felt blind rage welling up within him. He was already furious that the magistrate judge refused to set bond. He'd never expected to be in jail this long. Now he would have to get Thomas to file for a bond hearing. Almost as quickly as his rage flared, his good sense took over, and he warned himself to calm down. *Don't lose it, man. Don't lose it.*

He looked around the small interview room as if trying to hold back tears, then stared down at his orange jumpsuit. "I'm sorry, Detective. I didn't mean to crawl all over you. You're just doing your job. I'm having a hard time coming to terms with the fact you all think I could have killed my..." His voice trailed off and an actual tear trailed down his face. He took a short gasping breath, then continued in a pained whisper. "I can't believe I've been arrested for Marcie's murder. I loved her so much. I miss her and our home. I keep picturing her there in the kitchen, and then I remember and..." Carl took a deep, rattling breath and tried to compose himself.

Detective Howard leaned back and looked at Carl thoughtfully, then turned to his notes. "When you were first interviewed you said Marcie was on a trip to Ireland. You mentioned you watched her board the plane, and she turned back and waved to you." He leaned back in the chair and raised one eyebrow. "Mr. Greene, we found no evidence of a trip planned or taken. No bank or credit-card transactions. No airfare. No Marcie Greene or Marcie Carson on any passenger list during the dates you said she planned to travel.

No reservations for hotels or inns in Ireland. No evidence, Mr. Greene. None."

Carl's creative brain immediately came up with the answer. "Her parents were the ones who told me she was planning a trip." He paused, appearing to think things through. "They must have made up the story. They never liked me." Carl stared at a pen mark on the table and shook his head. "I'll bet they were planning to take Marcie away from me. I told her repeatedly she was the only one who really understood me. I tried to make her realize her parents had the wrong idea about me, and I didn't know why because I loved them like my own folks. I don't know why they hated me so much." He ended with a sob and put his face in his hands.

Detective Howard cleared his throat, unmoved by Carl's show of sorrow. "So I assume you were being untruthful when you said you watched her board the plane. I'm still puzzled as to why your DNA would have been under her fingernails. If she didn't go away on a trip, then you must have been with her not long before her death."

Carl gave an aggravated sigh and shook his head. "I never said I watched her board the plane." His tone was condescending and cold. "You can't get to the observation windows without going through security and only passengers can go through security, so I couldn't have watched her, now could I? I don't appreciate your putting words in my mouth, sir."

Detective Howard let that pass, knowing Carl's previous statement was on video. He waited silently for several moments, then started jotting notes in his folder.

Finally, Carl could take the awkward silence no longer. "Okay, Detective. It's time for the truth." He stared at the table and gave a small shudder. "Marcie and I did have a fight right when I was ready to leave for the convention. Her parents were begging her to get away from me and were filling her mind with a bunch of lies. I took her arm to try to pull her into a hug good-bye, but she scratched me and ran off into the woods." Carl allowed a few tears to flow. "I promise you, Detective, she was alive when I last saw her. I had to leave for my convention, so I couldn't go after her. Besides, I figured she needed time to cool off."

"Thank you, Mr. Greene. That will be all for now." Detective Howard tapped the window, and a guard opened the door. While Carl was escorted back to his cell, Detective Howard smiled to himself. *We've got him. His story is starting to unravel.*

~ * ~

Lizzy sat in the courtroom entering case dispositions. She knew the judge would break for lunch soon. In an effort to save money, Lizzy didn't eat out often, so she sat trying valiantly to convince herself to eat her lunch from home. She mentally shook her head. *Nope, today I can't do it. I just cannot eat that salad in the fridge. If I can't have something delicious downtown somewhere, I think I'll probably die and then where would we be?*

When the judge announced court was in recess until 2:30 p.m., she grabbed her sunglasses and her purse and headed out the door. Her favorite bakery/deli was only a few blocks away. Lizzy took a deep cleansing breath while she walked briskly along. *I guess I'll just take the food back to the office to eat.* A touch of sadness dampened her cheery mood. *Eating in a restaurant alone always feels so weird.* She placed her order to go and was waiting off to the side of the counter, when she heard her name. She looked around and, to her complete surprise, saw Senator Tucker Bates sitting at a nearby table.

"Hi, Lizzy." He smiled warmly. "Do you have a working lunch today?"

Oh great. How do I answer without looking pitiful?

"Hello, Senator." She tried to sound confident. "No working lunch. I was planning to take my order back to the office. I'll probably just read a book or something."

Oh, no. You're not going to slip away from me that easily. Not again. Tucker rose and came to stand in front of her. "I would be honored to have you join me."

Lizzy felt rescued and safe at the look in his eyes, but she cautioned herself inwardly. *He just feels sorry for me. But hey, even so, I'm not going to miss this chance.*

"Thank you. I'd love to." She spoke lightly, trying not to reveal how jittery she had suddenly become.

Tucker gave the cashier a dazzling smile and said, "The lady has decided to dine-in instead." He waited at the counter until the order was ready, then carried it to the table and pulled out her chair.

There's nothing like a real gentleman, she thought while he seated her.

She looked at him when he resumed his place across the table. "Thank you, Senator."

"Please, call me Tucker." Mischief sparkled in his eyes. "Since you tried to steal my car, I think we should be on a first-name basis, don't you?"

Lizzy burst out laughing, and the joke eased her tense nerves. They talked non-stop throughout the meal and discovered they shared the same views on a number of issues and enjoyed many common interests.

During their conversation, Lizzy noticed Tucker seemed to drink in her every word, his expression one of rapt interest. So many times in the past, she felt guys she dated had their minds on other things. More than once, she turned down a second date because she sensed the guy cared nothing for her as a person.

All too soon, Lizzy realized her lunch hour was over. "I'm sorry, Tucker, but I've got to get back. Court will be starting up in about twenty minutes."

Tucker nodded, but did nothing to hide his disappointment. "May I walk you back?"

Lizzy smiled. He seemed so vulnerable at that moment, and her heart warmed. "Of course." She gave him a gentle smile. "Thank you."

They continued on to the courthouse, and he walked with her to the courtroom. "I really enjoyed this, Lizzy. Do you think we could get together again?"

"I'd like that." She met his warm gaze with one of her own. She jotted something on a scrap piece of paper and handed it to him. "Here's my email address and phone number," she said shyly. With a huge smile, Senator Tucker Bates thanked her, told her to have a wonderful afternoon, and exited the courtroom to return to his office.

I'm not believing this just happened. Lizzy was unable to keep the smile off her face. *I hope I can actually work this afternoon. I never thought I could feel this way again after what happened. I guess I shouldn't be surprised, though. When the Lord heals a heart, He does a thorough job.*

She booted up her laptop. Before organizing her papers for the rest of the day, she ran a quick background check on Tucker. Pleased to see only a speeding ticket from years ago, she allowed herself a moment to dream before focusing her concentration on the job at hand.

~ * ~

Tucker reached his office and sat down at his desk with a deep sigh. He'd been thinking things over after meeting Lizzy in the parking lot that day, and decided he would love to get to know her better. He was also convicted about his attitude toward those in abusive relationships. He went back to finish reading Lizzy's article online, and found the piece enlightening. He did further research on the subject, and talked to several counselors who worked at a safe house. He came to the conclusion that his views were horribly wrong on the subject. He now realized emotional and verbal, as well as physical abuse, were most serious and the damage done sometimes irreparable.

Tucker sat back in his chair and stared out the window, remembering the shock he felt when he saw Lizzy enter the deli. *I thought I'd have to wait for months. And suddenly, there she was, and I know without a doubt the Lord arranged our meeting.* He smiled to himself. *I've never met anyone like her. I wonder how long I should wait before I ask her out.* Deciding he needed to seek the Lord, he took a few moments to pray before returning to the work on his desk.

After several minutes in prayer, he felt a definite sense of unease with the idea of asking her out right away. *Even though she appears to have recovered from the abuse in her past, there's still something not right. I'm disappointed, Lord. I was ready to call her tonight. But I wouldn't want to do anything out of Your will, Lord. I feel such an attraction to Lizzy. I want her to know I would never hurt her, and she would be safe with me.* The definite feeling that he must wait persisted as surely as if he'd received a written message from God. Pragmatically, he put his feelings aside, resolving to continue to pray for Lizzy, but to watch and wait before pursuing any kind of relationship with her. *Your timing is more important than my desires, Lord,* he thought. *If You want us to become friends, You'll arrange everything when the time is right.*

~ * ~

Weeks passed and when Tucker never called or emailed, Lizzy felt disappointment cover her spirit like a shawl with weighted tassels.

"Honey, what's wrong? You've been so down the last few days." Rose sat down at the kitchen table while Lizzy ate scrambled eggs and toast. "Can I help?"

"Oh, Mom, I was such a fool." Lizzy shook her head dismally. "I told you about meeting Senator Bates a while back. I ran into him again at the deli several weeks ago, and we enjoyed a nice lunch. He asked if we could get together again, but then I never heard from him." She sighed with discouragement. Tears hovered for a moment at the corners of her eyes, then trickled down her cheeks. "He seemed so nice and Mom, I actually found myself drawn to him. I truly didn't think I could ever feel attracted to a man again after what I went through with Carl. I actually found myself hoping Tucker would call or email. But he didn't." She brushed her tears away, frustrated that she'd gotten so emotional. She broke off two small pieces of crust and tossed them to Nugget and Downton, who were sitting by her side with rapt attention. "I just feel like damaged goods, Mom. Like somehow he must have found out I'd been married before and didn't want me."

Rose reached over and squeezed Lizzy's hand tightly. "No, honey. God does not make junk. You may be wiser now than before you met Carl, but you have allowed God to work in your heart through all the horror you endured. I just have a feeling someday God is going to use your experiences to help others. Carl meant it for evil, honey, but God can use what happened for good."

Tears ran down her face again, unchecked. "You are my precious girl, Lizzy. I know this hurts right now, but God has a reason for Tucker not contacting you. Maybe it's not the right time. Or maybe he just wouldn't be right for you. You know how much you dislike politics. A relationship with Tucker would mean being a part of his lifestyle."

Lizzy blinked back tears, sniffed, and sighed deeply, staring at the honey bear on the table. "I never thought of that, Mom," she said after a moment. "I just couldn't be in politics, even on the sidelines. I realize we need good Godly men and women in the political realm, but I know I couldn't take the nastiness for long."

Rose nodded. "I think you would be unhappy. Let's trust the Lord in this like we have in everything else. He has a plan, and I feel in my bones, He is going to use you in a mighty way."

The women prayed together and dedicated their lives anew to their Lord Jesus Christ. "Teach me what you want me to learn from this, Lord." Another tear trickled down Lizzy's cheek. "I feel so badly right now—rejected and unworthy. But I know You want only the best for me. Please help my emotions to come in line. And thank You, Lord, for protecting me. You know I trust You, and I don't want anyone in my life who is not part of Your plan for me. Use me, Lord. Use what I've been through to help others."

Lizzy and Rose hugged before Lizzy glanced at her watch. "Mom! I'm going to be late for work if I don't get out of here." She quickly brushed her teeth, gathered her purse, and rushed to her car.

"Drive safely, honey. Better to be late than get in a wreck."

"I will, Mom." Lizzy smiled and waved good-bye as she backed out of the garage.

~Ten~

The trip to Clifton was only a one-hour drive, but traveling on the large interstate made Lizzy jittery. With Tucker's accident on her mind, she was ever more nervous, but the trip could not be avoided. She had been subpoenaed to testify before a state agency regarding a bondsman issue. She knew well that receipt of that subpoena meant her testimony was required. Before she started out, Lizzy set her iPod to an old-time radio show, hoping she could get into the story and calm herself. The familiar music, the sound of hoof beats, and the announcer's voice poured from the car's speakers.

"The man in the saddle is angular and long-legged. His skin is sun-dyed brown. The gun in his holster is gray steel and rainbow mother-of-pearl: its handle unmarked. People call them both *The Six Shooter.*"

Only June, and already it's so hot. Lizzy turned on the air conditioning, relishing the sudden blast of cool air fanning her face. *And I can't take this horrid humidity. Ugh.* She sat back, determined to relax and enjoy the show, starring her favorite actor of all time, Jimmy Stewart. By the time she crossed the Riponville County line, she was completely into the story, *Battle of Smoke Falls.* Just as Britt and Tom were closing in on the killer Dink Faulk, Lizzy noticed the acrid odor of diesel fuel begin to fill the car. She glanced into her rear-view mirror and noticed a large red pick-up truck bearing down on her. Her heart slammed in her chest, and her throat went dry.

Red truck. Carl. Danger. Death. The thoughts spiraled through her brain like swirling rain drops. The truck was nearly touching her bumper, and Lizzy clutched the steering wheel so hard her hands ached. She moved one hand and began feeling through her purse for her phone. *How did he find me?* Her thoughts tumbled frantically one over the other. *How? I've been so careful. Dear God, please protect me.* She remembered she'd put her iPhone phone in the cup holder beside her, but at highway speed, she was afraid to remove her eyes from the road to dial. Her stomach clenched, and her hands began to shake uncontrollably.

Memories washed over her of the incident that drove her to flee from Carl. She'd come home from work a few minutes late, which always made Carl angry. He expected her to have the house clean, and to be ready for him with dinner and whatever else he wanted, whether she'd worked all day or not. Carl stalked toward her and opened the car door. He grasped a fistful of her hair and dragged her from the vehicle. Stumbling and gasping with pain, Lizzy tried to stay on her feet. Carl released her hair, then grabbed her arm and pulled her along to a nearby tree.

"This will teach you to hang out at work when your place is here." He jerked her to her knees, grabbed another fistful of hair, and pulled her head back. "You are totally worthless. Worthless and a freak. You will hand in your resignation tomorrow, Beth." The name struck her like a blow. After they had been married for two months, the abuse began and Carl abruptly decided he no longer liked her name. "'Lizzy' sounds like a stripper name," he'd said with derision. "You have a Bible name. You shouldn't pervert it. From now on, your name is Beth."

Carl snatched a coil of clothesline lying near the base of the tree and tied her hands together, then secured her to the tree. "I've had about enough of your selfish ways." He slapped her savagely, stalked away, and went into the house.

Tears of fear, pain, and humiliation ran down Lizzy's cheeks. How could she have not seen Carl's true nature? Red flags of warning that were vague before their marriage, were painfully clear now. The verbal, emotional, and psychological abuse escalated ever since he changed her name, but this was the first time he'd ever struck her. Twilight fell, and the air began to cool. Lizzy shivered. Silence surrounded her, and she wondered if he would leave her there all night. The parking circle was behind the house, and she knew no one would see her, unless they drove down the driveway.

Lord, help me. She prayed silently, agonizing over her dreadful decision to marry this man. *I made such a horrible mistake. I've tried so hard to be what he wants. I've tried to be the kind of Godly wife You would have me be. But do I stay and keep letting him treat me like this? I took my vows seriously, but oh, Lord, I don't know what to do.*

Suddenly, the roar of an engine and the smell of diesel filled the air. She looked around in confusion, blinded by the bright lights. Her heart filled with a terror when she realized Carl's truck was coming straight for her. Lizzy began to strain against her bonds with every bit of strength she possessed. Repeatedly, from every conceivable angle, Carl aimed the truck at her, slamming the brakes just before crushing her body against the tree. Finally, head hung low, legs curled under her, she ceased to struggle. After some time, Carl's anger was spent. He parked the vehicle and returned to the house. As darkness overtook the sky, a steady stream of tears flowed from Lizzy's eyes. Her spirit had never taken such a beating. It was unfathomable to have the one who vowed to love and cherish her treat in such a fashion. Her head began to throb with a migraine. She had never known such misery.

Why, oh why did I think I needed to be married to be happy? she thought dully. *Why couldn't I have been content with God and my family who loves me?*

Lizzy stayed tied to the tree until morning. Carl approached just after dawn, untied her, and gently lifted her chin with a finger. "Beth, my darling Beth." His voice was tender and his tone sorrowful. "Why do you do this to me? I don't want to constantly have to correct you, but you just won't learn. God told you to submit to me. To obey me. I just want you to be happy being the woman you were made to be, honey."

Lizzy rose shakily and stood before him silently. "Go on to the house now," he said softly. "You're a mess. Good grief, you've even peed all over yourself. You stink. Go get cleaned up."

He walked with her to the house. "I've got to go to work, but tonight we're going to talk this out." The steely look in his eyes chilled Lizzy to the core, and she knew in that moment, talking was not what he intended. He would kill her; of that she was certain.

Though early-on Carl warned her never to talk to her parents about their life together and rarely let her see them, she secretly sought counsel from them when the abuse began. As soon as Carl's car left the driveway, she called them. After hearing about the episode of the previous evening, they agreed her life was in danger and insisted she come home. She quickly gathered as many belongings as she could stuff in her car and made her escape.

Lizzy's mind returned to the present. Sweat trickled down her temples, and she glanced in the rear-view mirror again. After a few moments, the truck roared into the left lane and passed her, leaving a cloud of exhaust. Within minutes, the vehicle left her far behind.

Wrong license plate. That fact took a moment to register in Lizzy's frantic brain. *No bumper stickers. It's not him. Oh, Lord, praise Your name, it's not him*. Lizzy's entire body shook with sobs of relief. She noticed a rest stop just ahead, so she pulled over and parked. She drank deeply from her water bottle, then fumbled in her purse for a tissue. She dabbed the sweat from her forehead and the tears from her eyes.

Thank You, Lord. Thank You. You rescued me from a horrible pit and set my feet on a rock. Thank You for giving Mom and Dad the wisdom to tell me to escape when I did. I don't know if I'd have possessed the strength on my own. Thank You for the people You've put in my life to aid in my healing. Lizzy sat for many minutes, not caring if she was late for the hearing.

When she felt more composed, she went into the facility to care for her needs and attempt to repair her makeup. *Glad I keep an extra container of cover-up handy*. She ruefully surveyed the streaked mascara trailing down her cheeks. The only other woman in the facility washed her hands and left without speaking to Lizzy. Grateful not to have to explain herself, Lizzy did her best to repair the damage. Since she had a container of saline solution and a contact case in her bag, she took out her lenses and let them soak for a few minutes, hoping to remove some of the protein build-up her tears caused. *Guess that's the best it's going to get,* she thought ruefully after replacing the contacts. Though her eyes felt refreshed from the rinse, they still sported bloodshot veins. *Hope the redness goes away before I get to court.* When she returned to the car, she tapped the worship playlist on her iPod before pulling out of the rest area and back onto the interstate. She sighed deeply. *The fear still gets me, even after all this time.* She was confused and disheartened. *I thought I was past all this.* She shook her head and began to sing along with Jamie Grace and *You Lead, I'll Follow* while she continued her journey.

~ * ~

Shawn Stokes stretched and reached to tuck a stray strand of hair behind one ear. Another load of case files sat on her desk, expertly prepared for her perusal by criminal investigator, Sybil McInyre. The assistant district attorney opened the first folder, typed the case number into her computer, and began to look over a scan of the arrest warrant. Alistair Carlton Greene. *Another murdered spouse,* she thought dismally. *What is with these people?* She thought back over her years as a prosecutor. Never had she seen so many instances of domestic violence as she had in the past five years. Despite efforts to stem the tide with education and assistance to victims, the epidemic of violent incidents seemed to grow daily. While she looked through the reports and other available evidence collected by law enforcement, a smile began to grow on her face. *We're gonna nail this guy for sure.* She looked at the DNA report. *No way can anyone talk him out of this. Thank goodness we had cold weather and those hikers found the victim as soon as they did.*

Shawn sat back and stared at the wall, her mind already churning with ideas of how she would proceed at trial.

There was a lot of work to be done between now and then, but Shawn always tried to get an overall feel for the case before digging in. She called Sybil over, and the two began to plot their course.

Shawn was still thinking about the facts of the case while she drove home that evening. *I can't believe they found her journal. What a lucky break.* A look of determination touched her face while she pulled into her driveway. *I'm going to thoroughly enjoy putting this guy behind bars for life. This one will not get away with murder. I just hope a conviction will bring some sort of peace and closure to the victim's family.*

She pulled into the garage, and a handsome man opened the door leading into the house. Shawn grinned at him, got out of the car, and walked over to greet him with a hug and a kiss. "You beat me home." She looked at him with eyes sparkling.

Ashton Stokes chuckled, his arms still around her waist. "I know that look, sweetheart. You got a good one today, didn't you?"

Shawn nodded and returned to the car to retrieve her bag and briefcase. "Boy, did I ever. Abusive guy murdered his wife." She shut the car door and followed her husband into the kitchen. A beautiful tri-colored collie bounded to her side, and she knelt to hug him affectionately. She looked back at Ashton, her face alight with purpose. "You should see all the evidence. No way is this guy going to be acquitted. Might even get him to plead guilty. Just depends on how much of a narcissist he is, I guess."

Ashton leaned against the sink, enjoying watching his beautiful wife. He loved to see her so excited about justice being served. Not only was prosecuting cases her job, it was her passion and calling. *The victim's family has no idea how tenderly they will be taken care of through this process. My girl is tough on crime, but so loving with the families.*

"I'm proud of you, babe." He gave her the grin that had melted her heart eleven years ago and still melted it a little more each day. Arm in arm, they proceeded to the living room to relax, discuss the day, and decide what they wanted for dinner.

~Eleven~

"Thomas, you know I can't afford that. I lost my job, remember?" Carl stood at the pay phone and clenched his fist. The guard looked on disinterestedly while Carl lowered his voice to just above a whisper. "Thomas, I don't think you'd want your sweet trusting wife and your church friends finding out about those debts you owe, would you?"

In a moment, Carl responded. "Don't pull that with me. I know all about your little side line. Just so happens some of the guys you owe are friends of mine who grumble when they don't get paid." The man on the other end of the line was silent. Carl grinned and spoke again, this time with a friendly tone. "So, Thomas, how much was that fee, my friend? I need your help, man. I need a good attorney, and you're the first person I thought of. $100? Awesome. I think I can handle that. Now how quickly can we get a bond set? I've got to get out of here."

~ * ~

Thomas O'Brien's hand shook while he placed the handset on its cradle. A feeling of dread mixed with fear spiraled through him. Anxiety clogged his throat and finally landed with a thud in the pit of his stomach. *How did I let things go this far?* The attorney stared at his desk calendar, a cold sweat beginning to form on his forehead. *Why did those guys have to talk? They said no one would know. What am I going to do?* Panic edged in while his mind scrambled frantically for a solution. He couldn't take on any more cases. He could barely keep up with the ones he had. *I'll have to take Carl's though. No way out of that one*. He clenched his jaw bitterly. *And all this time I thought he was a good guy. You just never know about people.*

He considered buying another lottery ticket, but remembered he'd spent the last few dollars in his checking account that morning at Starbucks. All his credit cards were maxed out, and he rarely carried cash. *I wonder if Meredith has any cash at home. Yes, I'll bet she does. Just gotta sneak it out of her purse.* Relief spread over him, and his tense muscles began to relax. *I know I'll win this time. Then I can pay off all the debts and be home free.* He took a deep cleansing breath. *And then I'll quit. After this, no more casinos, no more poker games, and no more lottery. I can quit. I can do this. I can quit any time and now is certainly the time.*

~ * ~

The next night Thomas snuck to the spacious three-car garage with his tablet. Hands shaking, he pulled up the lottery site. His heart began to beat faster as the rush of a possible win filled his mind. He pulled the ticket from his pocket. *I know this is the one. This is it. This is going to fix everything.* He focused on the screen, then looked at his ticket in disbelief. Not one number matched. *No. Not possible. I was so sure. Something just told me I would win, and all these issues would be resolved.*

He put the tablet down on the work table and went to stare out the window. All the fear and despair of the day before came back in a wave. The burden of debt and the fear of discovery weighed so heavily on him, he felt he would suffocate. *I could sell my home theater. Should bring in enough to keep those loan sharks at bay for a while. But what about Meredith? What will I tell her*? He could come up with no believable reason to explain parting with the star attraction of his man cave.

He slumped down in a nearby lawn chair and stared resentfully at the sleek Mercedes convertible parked next to the four-door Lexus. *Stupid cars. Stupid payments.* He put his head in his hands, feeling sick inside. *I've got nowhere to turn. Double mortgage on the house. Car payments. Credit cards maxed out. And that's not even counting what I owe the guys and the freakin' loan mafia.* He clenched his fists. *If only I could find a little cash, I know I could turn things around. I'm really good at poker. I know I could win everything back this weekend if I just had some money to get a game started.*

Suddenly, he sat up straight. Celia. Celia just sold her old saddle in order to buy a new one for her hunt seat shows. She said they paid in cash. *Wonder where she put it?* He stood and paced back and forth beside the cars, his thoughts a war between sanity and addiction. *She's your **own daughter**. Your own flesh and blood. You can't steal from your own little girl.* He thought of Celia's generous spirit. *But she'd understand,* he reasoned. *And besides I wouldn't really be stealing.* He would just borrow the $350 for a while and would pay the money back with interest out of his winnings. How would he get it, though? Wait, wasn't Celia at an overnight birthday party? If he could just be sure Meredith didn't catch him. Much encouraged, Thomas returned to the house and gave his wife a loving hug before relaxing in the recliner with the newspaper.

~ * ~

"Sweetheart, I've got to run to the store." Meredith stood in the great room and looked back toward the spacious kitchen with aggravation. "I thought I had buttermilk for these cupcakes, but I can't find any."

"Can't you wait 'til tomorrow?" Thomas moved his newspaper slightly and looked over at her sympathetically.

"No." Meredith took off her apron and tossed the garment on the granite countertop. "I promised these for the bake sale at church, and I have to drop them off in the morning." She ran a hand through her short hair. "It can't be helped. I've just got to improve at making shopping lists." She shook her head in frustration, then grabbed her Dooney & Bourke™ bag and walked to the door. "Won't be long, hon."

"Be careful. See you in a bit."

Thomas waited until he heard his wife's Lexus start, then he casually strolled to the large picture window in the great room. He admired the lake view and felt a moment of pride at their luxurious home and property. Out of the corner of his eye, he saw Meredith start down the driveway. *What a lucky break!* As soon as she pulled out onto the road, he rushed upstairs to Celia's room.

Now where would a sixteen-year-old hide cash? He checked all the obvious places: the bedside table, under the mattress, in her jewelry box. But he found nothing. He glanced up at all her trophies and ribbons and felt his heart swell with pride. His little girl was beautiful, accomplished, and good at everything she tried. To top it all off, she was as sweet as she was pretty.

My baby Celia is so talented. He smiled at her equestrian trophies. *She took to horseback riding like a duck to water.* He stared at an 8 x 10 photo of Celia with her thoroughbred gelding. Celia's strawberry-blond hair glistened at the edges of her helmet. One hand grasped the reins while with the other, she patted Diamond's glossy black neck. Her smile was wide and filled with joy. Blue, red, and yellow prize ribbons were attached to Diamond's bridle.

My little girl. That's ***my*** *little girl.* Something caught in his chest, and he stumbled back in horror. *What am I doing? What on earth is wrong with me?* ***Stealing*** *from my* ***daughter****? What kind of monster have I turned into?* He bumped into the bed and sat abruptly. He ran his hands through his hair as the ugliness of his addiction reared its abhorrent head. *Oh dear God, how could I even think of doing this?* He sobbed, begging God for forgiveness.

Finally, feeling drained, he sighed and looked up once more. He rose and looked around the room, admiring the pictures and treasured objects that represented his daughter's life. Her favorite teddy bear, still given the place of honor on her bed. Photo collages of friends and pets. Her cheerleading debut portrait. He smiled and reached up to grab one of Celia's trophies from the bookshelf. A gentle shower of twenties floated lazily to the floor around his feet.

Of course. She'd hide the cash among her prized possessions. He gazed at the money. Visions of bills and loan sharks flooded his mind. *I'm not stealing from my daughter. I'm just borrowing a little money. I'll have the cash back under the trophy before she even knows it's gone.*

He gathered up the bills, carefully replaced the trophy, pulled out his cell, and dialed. “Hey, Sam, it’s Thomas. Wanna get a game up for tomorrow?

~ * ~

The courtroom buzzed with pre-hearing conversation. Defense attorneys chatted with assistant district attorneys, while victim advocates gently counseled those who wanted to be heard. The court reporter prepared her equipment, and the bond coordinator examined her docket one last time.

“All rise,” announced the bailiff. “Court is now in session, the honorable Victoria Lily presiding.”

About three feet from the bench stood a large monitor on a portable stand. Defendants in the Riponville County Detention Center would appear for their bond hearings via closed-circuit television. After several names were called and bonds were set by the judge, the docket assistant called the next defendant. “Alastair Carlton Greene.” The sergeant at the detention center disappeared into a small room, then Carl came out and stood at a podium. He could see the judge and his attorney while they watched him on the monitor.

“Go ahead, ma’am,” Judge Lily instructed the assistant district attorney.

“Your honor, this is Alastair Carlton Greene, who goes by Carl Greene, here with his attorney Thomas O’Brien,” Shawn began. “He has been in the Riponville County Detention Center since April second on the charge of Murder in the First Degree. No bond has been set. He has one prior juvenile charge out of Michigan for Assault with Intent to do Great Bodily Harm. He served one year in the juvenile detention facility in Michigan. As to the facts, on November fifth of last year, the victim was found deceased. There were outward signs of trauma to the victim’s neck area, and the autopsy revealed internal signs of manual strangulation. Evidence also shows that her hands and feet were bound with zip ties, and her body had been wrapped in a canvas tarp. Physical evidence shows the accused did, with malice aforethought, kill his wife Marcie Carson Greene. This incident is believed to have occurred somewhere on the property located at 5656 Lightview Road in Riponville County and owned by the accused. The victim's body was found about a mile into the Thirskton State Forest, which is one tract away from the aforementioned property. Your honor, Mr. Greene has lived in three states at various times and maintains contacts all over the country and in Europe. He has a current passport. We believe him to be a serious flight risk and a danger to the community. We ask that he remain in the detention center on no bond."

"Thank you." Judge Lily looked at Thomas. "Go ahead, sir."

Thomas cleared his throat. "Your honor, Carl Greene is forty-one years of age and has a Bachelor of Science Degree in Architectural Studies. Up until his arrest, he worked for the firm Bartram and Phelps. Mr. Greene is a respected member of First Baptist Church of Riponville. He has had no prior record other than the juvenile charge just mentioned. Mr. Greene is a pillar of this community, your honor, and in spite of the district attorney's claims, is not a flight risk. He is a man of dignity and honor and is not any danger to Riponville County." Thomas racked his brain desperately, but he could think of nothing else affirming to say about Carl. He knew his words were empty, though he'd presented them with as much confidence as he could muster. "Your honor, we request a surety bond of ten thousand dollars."

Judge Lily thought for a moment. "Based on the matters presented, the court finds the defendant, Alastair Carlton Greene, to be a flight risk and a danger to the community, therefore he shall remain in the Riponville County Detention Center with no bond until trial. She wrote "denied" diagonally across the proposed bond order before her, signed the document, and passed it to the bond coordinator.

~ * ~

"Hi, Shawn, how are you?" Lizzy took the filing from the prosecutor.

"Oh, just trying to keep my head above water as usual." Shawn sighed and grinned. "I don't see us going paperless anytime soon."

"I know what you mean."

Delane came to the counter just as Lizzy began to peruse the document in preparation for clocking and filing. "Lizzy, let me take that for you. Your mom is on the phone and needs to talk to you. She sounds pretty upset."

"Okay. Thanks, Delane. Good to see you, Shawn." Lizzy handed the *Notice to Seek Life Without Parole* to Delane and hurried to her desk to take the call.

Delane briskly verified the information on the document. "Everything is in order. Alastair Carlton Greene. Wow, he has a pretty lofty name."

"He's one bad dude, though." Shawn grimaced. "Murdered his wife. I hope we can put him away for good."

"Oh my word, that's horrible." Delane shuddered. "You'd think as long as I've been working in this office, nothing would surprise me anymore. But this kind of thing still gives me the creeps. So sad."

"That's for sure. Seems like we just keep getting more and more of these domestic violence cases. I read somewhere that one in three female homicides are committed by their current or former partners."

"Oh my. Those are horrible statistics." Delane shook her head in disbelief. "Shawn, did you need any copies?" she asked, trying to shake her pensive mood.

"Yes, two please."

Delane prepared and clocked the document, then went to the copy machine. "Good luck with this one, Shawn," she said encouragingly when she returned to the counter. "I hope you get this guy."

"Thanks, I hope so, too." Shawn put the copies in her file and waved to the rest of the office. "Have a great day."

~ * ~

"Mom, what is it? Are you okay?" Lizzy's voice was laced with concern.

"Oh, honey, I hate to bother you at work, but Jack is really low. Lizzy, I think it's time—he can hardly breathe."

Lizzy struggled for composure. "Okay, Mom, I'll see if I can come home and take him."

"Be careful driving, honey. I know you're upset."

After a quick conversation with Sandra, Lizzy was out the door and hurrying to her car. Traffic was light, so she arrived home quickly. As soon as she saw the suffering cat, she knew. The look in his once expressive eyes was now far away and withdrawn. A huge area of swelling had developed on his chest and hung below his stomach. His mouth was partly open, and his nostrils flared as he tried to breathe.

Lizzy gently stroked his black fur. *He used to have such a glossy coat. Now it's so dull and lifeless.* He turned to her then and gave her a look as if to say, "Mama, its time. I'm tired. I hurt. I want to go."

With a trembling sigh, Lizzy gathered him up as gently as possible and placed him on a soft blanket in the cat carrier.

"I'll drive, honey." Rose gathered her purse and keys. "You're too upset."

With a nod, Lizzy agreed and the women headed out to the car.

~ * ~

That night, Nugget and Downton followed Lizzy around the house looking forlorn. Their soulful eyes pleaded with her to help them understand why their buddy Jack was gone. She gathered them together in a group hug, and each comforted the other as best they could. In the days that followed, Lizzy was surprised to see how the dogs mourned the loss of their kitty.

Saturday morning, Lizzy reluctantly packed up Jack's supplies: his prescription food, his medicine, and the extra bags of fluids. "At least these things bought him another six months," she said sadly while she prepared to drop the items off at the veterinarian's office.

Rose opened the car door for her. "You were a wonderful nurse to him, honey." She gave Lizzy a tight hug, and both women's tears began to flow. Rose held her gently before Lizzy pulled away and gave her mother a wobbly smile. She started the engine and cranked up the air-conditioning to cool down the oven-like temperature inside the vehicle. Lizzy paused to dab her eyes with a tissue before she climbed into the car and backed out.

~ * ~

A week passed during which Lizzy and Rose decided they needed another cat. On Saturday morning, Lizzy headed off to the Humane Society to see if she might find a match for them. Rose's health issues precluded her from joining Lizzy for the outing, but she assured her daughter she trusted her to find the right animal.

Lizzy entered the facility and looked around. Happy photos of dogs and cats with their adopted human parents adorned the walls, along with product posters for flea control and heartworm products. A display of collars and leashes sat to one side and upbeat instrumental music played in the background. Lizzy smiled and made her way to the front desk. "I'm hoping to find a new kitty," she told the receptionist. "I lost my sweet Jack to kidney disease last week."

"I'm so sorry." The receptionist was instantly sympathetic. "Let me call Greta and she'll show you to the cat room."

Greta came into the room a few minutes later. She gestured to Lizzy. "This way, ma'am." Lizzy followed her down a short hallway. "Here we are." Greta smiled gently. "Feel free to look around and take your time. I'll be right here if you have any questions."

"Thank you." Lizzy entered the room slowly and began methodically looking into each cage. Eager feline faces looked at her pleadingly, and some meowed politely. *I want them all*. Lizzy gripped her purse tightly. *How am I ever going to choose?* When she came to the last few cages, she was torn. *I wish I could take every one, and yet I haven't felt a special connection yet. Maybe I'll have to come back another day*. She crouched down to peer into the last cage.

"Those are brothers." Greta came forward with a smile. "They were just put out for adoption this morning. They're only eight months old."

Lizzy took in the long lush coats, one a beautiful seal color and one a gray tabby. *They've got the 'M' marking in the fur on their foreheads. And look at those giant paws*.

"Maine Coons, aren't they?" Lizzy asked.

"Yes, ma'am. They even have their papers."

"Why on earth would anyone give them up?"

"I'm not sure of their story, ma'am. Would you like me to take them to a visiting room so you can interact with them a bit?"

Lizzy gazed at the beautiful siblings, and they stared back, their eyes mesmerizing. As the threesome considered each other, both cats began to rub the front grill and knead their paws. "Yes, please." Lizzy's heart began to beat faster. "Yes, I'd like that."

Once in the comfort of the visiting room, the cats gingerly inspected their surroundings while Lizzy sat cross-legged on the floor. After only moments, both cats came to her side, so she offered a hand to each. They sniffed her fingers and her jeans thoroughly, appeared to consult together, then began to rub their heads against her knees.

Lizzy stroked them gently. All in a moment, she knew. *These are the ones. These are our new babies*. She rose slowly so as not to startle the striking felines, then opened the door and Greta came over.

"I want them." Lizzy grinned. "They're the ones for sure. These guys are coming home with me."

"That's wonderful, ma'am." Greta smiled widely.

"I have a kennel in the car. I'll go get it." Lizzy looked thoughtful. "Although I hope it's big enough. These guys are bigger than my cat was and there are two of them."

"Why don't you bring it in, and we'll see? We have cardboard carrying boxes if you need an extra."

Lizzy left her references and went to the car, while Greta went to the computer to prepare the necessary paperwork. When Lizzy returned, they re-entered the visiting room. The brothers looked at them with questioning expressions and soft meows. *This could be interesting.* Lizzy placed the cage on the floor and opened the door. *Jack hated this thing.*

To her complete amazement, the cats went right to the cage. The seal cat entered first, turned around, and settled down on one side. The tabby followed suit. Both looked at Lizzy as if to say, "What's the hold up? C'mon, let's go home." Lizzy grinned and was surprised to see tears in Greta's eyes.

"I'm sorry, ma'am. But I've never seen anything like that. I was hoping they'd go to a good home. There's just something about them that's special."

Lizzy patted her on the shoulder. "I'll bet this is a hard job. I know I couldn't do it."

Greta nodded and sniffed, then got down to business. "Here's their information. They were eight months old last week. In this packet, you'll find their registration papers, their neuter certificates, their shot records, and their rabies certificates. Oh, and they've been declawed in the front, so they should stay inside."

"Oh, no worries there. I don't keep cats outside. Just too many opportunities for heartache," Lizzy said firmly. "But they'll have to get used to two sisters. I have a Pomeranian and a Sheltie."

"Their info card says they get along with dogs, so I think you'll be fine."

Greta handed Lizzy the packet of papers and her receipt for payment. "You're all set, ma'am." She smiled. "We never got names on them. What are you going to call them?"

Lizzy looked at the cats for a moment, then grinned when the thought hit her. “Greta, I’d like to introduce you to Sherlock and Watson.”

Greta laughed. “Great names. Perfect.” She knelt down one last time and stroked the cats gently before closing the pet taxi. “Good luck, guys. I’m so glad you found a new mom.”

~Twelve~

One year later…

The morning of Wednesday June 3rd, dawned with the threat of rain and thunderstorms. Channel 5 AccuWeather forecasted a seventy percent chance of rain. Shawn Stokes finished taking one last look over her notes and glanced at her criminal investigator, who was putting files into boxes. "Sybil, I think we're ready. We've spent a solid year preparing for this case."

"I agree. We've put in a lot of hard work. We're just a few steps away now."

Shawn turned to the window, watching the gathering clouds. She remembered the pre-trial conferences, preparing for a grand jury indictment, reviewing the evidence, interviewing and vetting witnesses, crafting arguments, and the myriad of other details that led to this day. She helped Sybil load the boxes onto a hand truck, then shrugged into her suit jacket and stepped into the pair of heels she left by her door.

The two began to make their way to the courtroom. "Nasty day out there, but I feel good about this, Sybil." Shawn held the elevator while Sybil pushed the hand truck inside. "I hope we can put this abuser away for life."

The elevator closed, and Sybil punched *three* on the panel. "Carl Greene is as bad as they come. Honey-sweet on the outside, poison on the inside."

"Ashton said he'd be praying for us today. I'm glad for the spiritual support."

Sybil nodded. "Me, too."

When they entered the courtroom, they noticed several spectators on the defense side already seated and waiting. "I'm surprised he has anybody here," Shawn murmured while they placed the files on their table.

"Don't forget what a smooth operator he is." Sybil kept her voice low. "He's got a lot of people fooled. Abusers are usually only known as abusers to their victims. Most everyone else thinks they're fine upstanding people."

The courtroom clerk and the court reporter were just getting their laptops and equipment set up, when Thomas O'Brien arrived and sat at his table. The deputies brought Carl from the holding cell and seated him beside his attorney. Dressed in an expensive designer suit, tie, and wing-tip shoes, Carl Greene appeared to be the epitome of class and grace, all in one good-guy-law-abiding-citizen package. His hair was styled neatly, his expression serene and peaceful. He'd added a pair of glasses to his look, feeling they lent him an air of dignity and intelligence.

The bailiff emerged from a side door and announced, "All rise. Court is now in session, the Honorable Judge Anthony Blake presiding."

Everyone in the court room rose to their feet and remained standing until the judge entered and said, "Please be seated."

"Mandy, please have them bring up thirty-five," Judge Blake quietly instructed the clerk.

Mandy immediately emailed the request to the jury coordinator, who would draw thirty-five names from the pool of jurors summoned that week for the proceedings. After she hit *send* and perused the trial docket to see what other cases were set for the day, she turned to the indictment for the current trial.

She froze. Alistar Carlton Greene. Slowly and unobtrusively, Mandy glanced at the defendant, and her stomach lurched.

Oh my word, she thought. *It's him. How did we all miss that it's him? I don't think Lizzy even knows about this.* While they waited for the jurors to arrive, she maximized her email window and tapped out a message.

Lizzy, you won't believe what I just found out.

Lizzy's response immediately popped up.

What? What's going on?

Mandy typed her reply.

The first trial up on the docket is for a defendant named Alistar Carlton Greene. I didn't notice when I pulled the paperwork for court. I think it's your ex. And he's on trial for murder.

Back in the office, Lizzy's pulse quickened when she read the message. A sick feeling began to spread over her. "Oh no," she gasped aloud. "This can't be happening."

Quickly, she typed another message to Mandy.

What's the warrant number on the case?

Mandy replied with the number and said she had to go because the jurors were coming into the courtroom. Lizzy entered the warrant number into the computer, pulled up the case, and clicked to view the arrest warrant. The mug shot of the familiar face leered at her from the upper left corner of the document.

It is him, she thought. *Oh, dear God, no.* In horror, she read the description of the offense.

> *The affiant has documented evidence that the defendant did with malice aforethought kill the victim, Marcie Carson Greene, by means of manual strangulation. This incident did occur at 5656 Lightview Road in Riponville County.*

Lizzy's emotions were in a whirl while she pulled back from the computer. *That poor woman. Oh dear Lord, that poor woman.* Her stomach clenched and she felt a chill rush through her body. *That could have been me*. She felt as though she'd been struck and she flinched slightly. Tears pricked her eyes, so she grabbed a tissue before heading to her supervisor's office. Sandra was not only a manager but a friend and mentor. Her Godly advice and counsel were instrumental in Lizzy's healing.

"Sandra, do you have a minute?" Lizzy was barely able to hold back her tears.

Aware something was seriously amiss, Sandra said, "Of course. Come in."

Lizzy shut the door behind her and sat in one of the chairs before the large walnut desk and sobbed uncontrollably.

"Lizzy, what on earth is wrong?" Sandra's beautiful features were covered in concern. "Here, let me get you the tissue box."

Lizzy dabbed her eyes. "The ex is on trial for murder today. I didn't know anything about it. Mandy just emailed from the courtroom. It's definitely him."

Sandra's eyes widened in alarm. "Oh, no."

"Sandra, I feel so responsible."

Sandra came around the desk and wrapped her in an embrace. "No, Lizzy." Sandra said firmly. "Don't let Satan put that burden on you. Don't you do it. This is a terrible thing and if Carl is guilty, I trust the Lord will allow him to be convicted. But no guilt lies at your door, my friend. No guilt at all. Just you remember that." She gently squeezed Lizzy's hand. "Understand?"

Lizzy squeezed back. "I will try to remember that. I was just so horrified when I heard." She sat back as the realization hit her. "Oh, Sandra, that could have been me. If I hadn't escaped when I did, I have no doubt he would have killed me." She bowed her head and whispered, "Thank you, Lord, for rescuing me."

Sandra patted her shoulder gently. "That's right, He most certainly did rescue you. You're safe now and much the wiser for the experience."

Lizzy stared at the desk. "You know," she mumbled. "In a way, I'm relieved." She twisted her hands together in frustration. "I didn't just imagine the threat. Some people acted like I made up the drama when I told them the reason I left. Especially the people from the church we attended.

Even the pastor seemed to think I was just looking for a reason to leave Carl. I mean, I guess now I'm realizing that I wasn't crazy. He really would have killed me. And somehow I feel validated." Lizzy sighed deeply. "But a woman has died. I feel guilty for even thinking of myself."

Sandra shook her head. "No, Lizzy, I don't agree. You can't take a burden of guilt because your worst fears for yourself were realized in someone else's life. You're processing a lot right now. Give yourself permission to let it out."

Lizzy thought for a moment. "I would have done anything I could to save her, but I didn't even know her name."

"Of course you would have." Sandra looked at Lizzy intently. "Do you want to watch the trial? You're welcome to take personal leave time if you want, just please make sure any priority work is finished first." She paused for a moment, deep in thought. "You know, God knew this day was coming, Lizzy. Maybe He has you here for such a time as this."

Lizzy's head was bowed, her dark hair falling in a curtain around her face. She was silent for a few moments. "The evil that is Carl Greene is ugly, wicked, and frightening," she said, finally looking up. "I'm afraid to be in the same room with him."

"I understand completely. But if you change your mind, let me know. I'm not trying to talk you into going, but you might find being there would give you some sense of closure." Sandra patted her shoulder again. "Think about it. I'll support you whatever you decide. And if you need to talk further, you know my door is always open."

"Thanks, Sandra. You are such a blessing to me." Lizzy rose and opened the door. She shared the news with her coworkers, and each gave her a hug and promised to pray for her, knowing the trial would bring back many difficult memories. Several offered to cover her work duties if she decided to go to the courtroom.

"I wonder why they didn't have you testify, Lizzy." Justine looked puzzled. "Seems like after what you went through, your story would prove the kind of person he is."

"You know about opening the door to prior offenses," Lizzy replied. "Most of the time that information can't be admitted unless the defendant testifies. Carl is too smart to do anything that would make him look bad. He for sure wouldn't want any prior record to be brought out. Besides, with me, there was never anything I could go to the police with. There were plenty of threats, but no real evidence. Even when I left, there was no proof of what he did to me. I tended to my own scratches when I got to my folk's house and never went to the hospital. I couldn't find any charges on him in our system. For all I know, Carl may not even have a record."

The women sighed in understanding, each silently thanking the Lord that Lizzy escaped when she did. Elsie, the eldest member of the office who was lovingly known as the office mom, came to Lizzy's desk and gave her a hug.

"God rescued you out of there, honey." Tears brimmed in her eyes. "I'm so glad He brought you here to us. We love you, Lizzy."

Lizzy returned her hug, silently praising the Lord for the wonderful people with whom He had surrounded her. Mandy emailed later that day. Due to a family emergency, Judge Blake rescheduled the trial's opening arguments. The jurors had been chosen and would return Monday morning to fulfill their civic duty.

~ * ~

A cold sweat spread over Lizzy's body while her brain slowly came to wakefulness. Fear gripped her in a tenacious hold while she struggled to escape from the nightmare. Carl had been chasing her through the woods. His gun was raised, and he took shots at her every few minutes while she careened wildly through the trees. She tugged the covers tightly around her in the darkness of her bedroom. She was afraid to move. Everything was still except for the faint blowing of the air filter and hum of the fish tank pump. She could feel Nugget and Downton snuggled close to her on one side and Sherlock and Watson on the other. Terror squeezed her like a vise. Carl was in the house. She could feel it. He was waiting down the hall. Waiting for her to come out of the bedroom. Somehow he'd broken in without triggering the alarm and now sat silently in the dark waiting to snatch her away. Lizzy shook all over, and the grasping claws of panic threatened to overcome her. Her breath came in short gasps. In desperation, she began to quote scripture.

"God has not given us the spirit of fear," she whispered. "But of power and of love and of a sound mind. Greater is he who is in us than he who is in the world. I will never leave you nor forsake you." Gradually, reason and discernment penetrated the fog of fear. "Lord Jesus Christ, protect me," she prayed. "Protect me from the spirits of Satan, who seek to destroy me." Her voice became stronger. "In the name of Jesus Christ, I pray you would surround me with a hedge of protection. Protect Mom, my babies, me, and our home from anyone with ill intent against us." Peace began to trickle into her soul, and she felt herself relax a bit. She reached to turn on the bedside lamp and sat up slowly. The dogs looked at her sleepily, then returned to their slumber.

Lizzy put on her glasses and looked for her iPad before remembering she'd left the tablet in the living room to charge overnight. She retrieved her Bible from the bedside stand and flipped to the book of Psalms.

After reading through several chapters, she found the strength to crawl out of bed, open her door, and proceed down the hall to the bathroom. After attending to her needs, she glanced into the mirror while she washed her hands. Her hair was damp with sweat and clung to her head. Dark shadows hovered under her bloodshot eyes. Her sleep T-shirt and pajama bottoms were rumpled and soaked with perspiration. *I look a fright*, she thought morosely.

Heart racing, she padded silently down the hall. She felt her way to the corner, then to the light switch. Holding her breath, she flipped all the living room lights on at once. She looked around, exhaled, then proceeded to check every other room in the house just to reassure herself. All was still. Her mother's even breathing told her nothing was amiss in her room. After a huge sigh of relief, Lizzy returned to her bedroom. She was beginning to shiver, so she changed into another set of pajamas and tossed the sodden ones in the laundry basket. Afraid she would return to the nightmare, she climbed back into bed, but sat up reading the Psalms for nearly an hour. Finally, complete peace covered her. She put her Bible away, removed her glasses, and crawled back under the covers.

"Thank you, Lord," she breathed softly when she closed her eyes. "Thank You for Your word and for peace and safety."

~Thirteen~

The sound crashed through Lizzy's consciousness. She started violently and sat up. She looked around the room fearfully, remembering the night's terrors. The insistent buzzing that awakened her gradually identified itself in her brain. *The alarm. It's time to get up.* She reached over and slapped the clock off. *Oh my word, it is entirely too early. I feel like I was hit by a bus.* While she showered and prepared for work, her thoughts spiraled downward into despair. *To have such an intense dream and panic attack after being gone from that house of horrors for over ten years...* Her hand shook as she struggled to apply mascara. *I really am damaged goods. Am I ever going to be whole again?* Tears pricked her eyes while she finished her beauty routine.

Despite her attempts at a cheerful demeanor, Rose Godfrey saw through Lizzy's façade the minute her daughter entered the kitchen. The blood-shot, puffy eyes pierced her heart like a knife. "What's wrong, honey?"

"I had a horrible nightmare last night. And then I was sure Carl was in the house. I was so scared, Mom. I was scared to even get out of the bed to go to the bathroom."

"Oh, honey, I'm so sorry." Rose Godfrey enveloped her daughter in a hug and held her gently for a moment.

"I just don't understand." Lizzy finally pulled away and went to open the refrigerator. "I thought I was past all this now." She took out a container of strawberries and went to the counter to slice some into a bowl.

"Honey, I'm sure this has all come back up because of the trial." Rose sat at the table, her hands wrapped around her mug of coffee. "You don't need to feel so badly. I think this is normal. Knowing he murdered someone stirs everything up again."

Lizzy sat dejectedly and stirred a carton of vanilla Greek yogurt into the berries. She thanked the Lord for her food and began to nibble at her breakfast. Nugget and Downton sat by her chair, but she was so preoccupied she didn't even notice. Downton put a paw gently on Lizzy's leg. Her soulful Sheltie eyes gazed at her mom, pleading to be able to help.

Finally, Lizzy looked down. "I'm sorry, babies." Lizzy patted their heads. "I forgot your morning flakes." She rose, opened a box of corn flakes, and took out one flake for each of them. The dogs consumed the treat in one quick bite but continued to watch her with concerned expressions. Lizzy gave them a wobbly smile. "You girls are so sweet. You always know when I'm upset." She knelt to give them a hug before returning to her breakfast.

After she finished eating and put her dishes in the dishwasher, Rose said, "Lizzy, honey, let's pray together."

"Okay, Mom."

Rose stood beside her and grasped her hands. "Dear Father, we come before You this morning asking You to speak to Lizzy's heart. Comfort her, Lord, and help her not to fear. Help her love for You to overcome any fears from the past. Release her of this oppression, Father, and help my Lizzy to know how much You love her."

Tears filled Lizzy's eyes and she hugged her mother tightly. "Thanks Mom." She sniffed and reached to pluck a tissue from the box on the counter. "I love you."

"I love you, too, honey. So much."

Later, as Lizzy brushed her teeth, Sherlock and Watson strolled into the bathroom and began to rub against her legs. She gave them a quick scratch under the chin and a kiss on the head when she finished. "You guys are sweet, too. You know I need a little extra love this morning." She swallowed hard while she grabbed her purse and her iPad and headed out the door.

As she began her morning commute, she turned on the radio which she always left tuned to her favorite Christian station. Jesus Culture was in the middle of their song "One Thing Remains", singing of God's never failing, everlasting love. Lizzy began to sing along, but her voice broke and she blinked rapidly, trying to stem the rising tide of feelings. While she guided her vehicle through drive time traffic, song after song played that spoke of God's love and care. When the chorus of Amy Grant's "Better Than a Hallelujah" began to play, Lizzy's control slipped and the tears flowed in earnest. Amy sang of brokenness, and the fact that one's heartfelt cries to Almighty God are better than a hallelujah.

Realizing her precarious emotional condition, Lizzy pulled over into a parking lot, stopped the car, and sat sobbing. Feelings of being unworthy and damaged poured out, while the knowledge of God's mercy, grace, and love poured into the void. The bad was gradually replaced with the good.

"Thank You, dear Jesus, thank You," she gasped, choking on sobs which turned to those of joy. "Dear Jesus, thank You. Wash me clean. Never let me depend on anyone but You. I think this has been brewing ever since Tucker didn't call. I thought that when he discovered I was a victim, he would want nothing to do with me." The pain of rejection hit her again, but this time she handed the feelings right over to her Lord. "I want to be whole, confident, and balanced in You alone, Lord. Not because some guy comes along who feeds my ego." She shook her head. "That's not real healing. I need to be content. My feelings of self-worth should stem from what You have done for me and because You love me, in spite of my failures and humanness."

Lizzy sat in wonder while peace enveloped her entire being. Just then the song "Faithful" performed by Chris Tomlin began to play.

"Lord, you planned this morning's playlist just for me, didn't You?" she whispered in awe. "Thank You for these artists. Thank You for giving them the talent to write songs that honor and glorify you. Songs that preach Your truth to hurting souls like mine." Lizzy leaned back to listen and a feeling of warmth and belonging flooded through her. The song spoke of God's unwavering presence with us in every season of our lives.

My faithful Lord and Savior, Jesus Christ. Lizzy smiled and searched her purse for a tissue. *How could I have ever doubted Your love?* With a deep, cleansing breath, Lizzy dabbed at her eyes, blew her nose, and prepared to continue on to work.

~ * ~

Lizzy was excited like never before when she entered the church lobby. After her amazing experience with God Friday morning, meeting with her brothers and sisters in Christ meant all the more. She missed having her mother with her, but Rose's physical condition now kept her confined to the house most of the time. She greeted several friends from her small group while she entered the sanctuary of Ripon Falls Community Church, then found a seat near the back. She turned on her iPad and checked her email while she waited for the service to start. Finding nothing but ads and junk mail, she turned to the church bulletin.

Her heart skipped a beat when she saw the title of the new sermon series *God's Unbroken Promise Through Broken People*. Hope burgeoned in her heart while she considered the possibilities. The lights dimmed indicating the beginning of the service, and a video played with general church announcements and reminders. Then a slide came up.

You are washed in the blood of Christ
and born again as a child of God.
Don't let the voices of shame and regret
push you away from Jesus.

Lizzy's heart caught in her throat. Then she smiled. *Lord, You're not finished with me are You?* She thought with delight. *I get it! You got my attention Friday and I think there's more to come.*

After several songs of worship, Pastor Williams approached the podium and read from Genesis 16, the story of Abram, Sarai, and Ishmael.

"God promised to make of Abram a great nation," he began. "But Abram waited for many years, and the promise was not fulfilled. Our first point today is *The Problem*. Abram and Sarai had no children. So Sarai felt she needed to

take matters into her own hands, rather than wait on the Lord. She came up with her own solution by giving her servant Hagar to her husband as a concubine, a practice that was common in those days.
Think about it, church. What problem might you be facing in life for which you are considering your own solution? What have you taken into your own hands in the past?"

Lizzy thought of the time before her marriage to Carl. *I was so sure I needed to be married,* she thought dismally. *All my friends were married and were always asking when I was going to settle down.*

She took out her pen and began to jot notes on her bulletin.

1. Pressure to marry
2. Felt as older single, I would never get married
3. I wanted love and acceptance from other people - more important than God

Pastor Williams continued. "Our second point is *The Solution*. Sarai's solution was to have a child through Hagar. Abram listened to his wife's voice, rather than God's voice, and ultimately, took action outside God's plan."

Lizzy continued to examine herself and note her thoughts.

1. I didn't have many dates after college. I thought Carl must be *the one*.
2. I thought he was the answer to all my dreams of home and family.
3. I thought I needed to be married to have a "real life".
4. I felt validated by his supposed love and acceptance and in my insecurity greedily took in his early flattery.
5. I went ahead and married him in spite of the red flags and lack of peace.

Oh, Lord, what was I thinking? Why did I think my solution would be better than waiting on You? You tried so hard to warn me. You let me know Carl was not for me. But

I let him completely manipulate my thinking. She remembered the countless times he quoted scripture to her out of context but with such convincing arguments, she fell for his lies. With effort Lizzy pulled her attention back to the sermon.

"The results of course, were immediate suffering and the revelation of the true character of those involved. Hagar revealed her pride. She bore the promised child when Sarai could not conceive. Sarai was irate, jealous and turned on Abram in her anger, even though she was the one who came up with the solution. Abram was ambivalent and took no action.

"But you have to expand the story. Much of the fighting and conflict today in the Middle East was predicted in scripture because of this story. But the story does not end there, folks." Pastor Williams smiled and his voice became excited.

"When we expand the story fully, we see God is sovereign and works out His promises even through our messes. So church, here's what we all need to think about: Are you sleeping with Hagar?" He paced to one side of the stage, looking out at the congregation earnestly. "Are you trying to get ahead of God and find your own human solution? Have you measured your acceptance before God based on your moral or religious performance, trying to earn God's favor by works rather than accepting His grace? Do you value efficiency over effectiveness? Do you feel God is too slow, so you need to jump in and do more? Do you seek immediate satisfaction over true satisfaction? Brothers and sisters let's remember, we are to seek first the kingdom of God and His righteousness, then all these things will be added unto us." He smiled and returned to the podium. "Ladies and gentlemen, before we make a decision, let's ask ourselves: Are we getting ahead of God? Is His hand on this issue or have we come up with a human solution? Are we waiting on God's timing with contentment or are we forging ahead with impatience? Let's ask God to guide us through this life."

While Pastor Williams began his closing prayer, Lizzy prayed inwardly. *Oh, Father, I see now. I see how I was deceived and fell for Satan's trap. I see how I was fooled into thinking Carl was right for me. Oh Father God, help me to never forge on ahead of You. Help me to always stay right in the palm of Your hand. Give me wisdom and contentment in You. Thank You for loving me and finding me valuable in spite of my brokenness and past mistakes. I love You, dear Lord Jesus. I love You.*

Lizzy rose with the congregation while they began to sing the final song. She could barely whisper the words, and tears started to spill down her cheeks. When the music ended and she made her way out of the sanctuary, her heart was full. "Thank You, Lord," she said while she drove out of the parking lot. "Thank You for the sermon today. I needed to hear that. Help me to never again get ahead of Your plan for me."

~Fourteen~

Fourteen jurors filed into the jury box. Twelve would decide the fate of Alastair Carlton Greene. The two alternates would hear the case and be available should one of the regular jurors become ill or have an emergency. The men and women were seated, and Judge Blake instructed Deputy Clerk Mandy Carrington to put them under oath. Mandy stood and faced the jury.

"Please stand and raise your right hands." The jurors stood, their solemn expressions indicating they understood the seriousness of their role. "Ladies and gentlemen, the correct response to this oath is 'I will'. You shall well and truly try this case, the State versus Alastair Carlton Greene, indicted for Murder in the First Degree, and a true verdict render according to the law and the evidence, so help you God. Please say 'I will'."

The jurors responded in unison, "I will."

Mandy took her seat, and a bailiff escorted the jurors to a deliberation room. Several pre-trial motions were heard, and issues decided. After the *Jackson v. Denno* hearing, during which Judge Blake ruled Carl's statement to have been voluntarily given, and therefore admissible during the trial, the jury returned to the courtroom.

Judge Blake nodded to Assistant District Attorney Shawn Stokes. "Is the state ready for opening statements?"

"Yes, your honor." Professional in her navy skirt suit, white blouse, and heels, she rose and confidently went to face the jury. "Ladies and gentlemen, the defendant you see before you is a cold-blooded killer." Shawn absently trailed her hand on the railing of the jury box, allowing her last words to make the desired impact before continuing.

"Carl Greene was not driven by greed or by passion. He had nothing material to gain from his wife's death. You will not hear about insurance policies or trust fund inheritances. His desire was for power over and control of the woman he promised to love and cherish. Carl Greene got off on tormenting his wife psychologically and physically abusing and humiliating her as well." She made eye contact with each juror while she spoke.

"The evidence will prove Carl Greene did, with malice aforethought, plan and implement his wife's murder. Testimony you will hear during this trial will show that Carl Greene abused his wife since the beginning of their marriage, and in a final show of dominance, bound her hand and foot and strangled her to prove just how helpless and inferior she was. At the conclusion of this trial, you will be fully convinced beyond a reasonable doubt that Alastair Carlton Greene is guilty of murder. Thank you."

~ * ~

Lizzy sat at her desk staring out the window watching traffic pass by. On the one hand, she wanted to watch the trial. She was curious to see what evidence the state would present, and she wanted to see if Carl's true nature would finally be revealed for all to see. On the other hand, the thought of being in the same room with him made her feel nauseated. *What if he sees me? I know there are deputies there to protect us, but still...* She'd completed her priority work, and Denae had offered to help if she wanted to go. She sighed, filled with indecision. She remembered her bailiff friend, Billy. *Billy is assigned to that courtroom. If he's in the back, I could get him to save me a seat right by the door. Then I'd be directly behind the defendant's table. With all the people in the gallery in between, Carl would probably never see me. His focus will be up front on the witnesses and the attorneys.*

Lizzy rose and walked into her supervisor's office. "Sandra, I've finally decided. I'd like to watch the trial."

"Okay, Lizzy, that's fine." Sandra rose from her desk and came around to give her a hug. "I'm proud of you. You're a strong, brave woman, and I have a feeling God is going to use this to help you truly move on." She smiled encouragingly. "I'm excited about what He's going to do in your life, Lizzy."

"Thanks, Sandra. I feel peace about my decision. But don't worry, I won't let my work get too far behind. Denae said she'd help if need be."

"I know you won't, Lizzy. I'm not worried at all. Just keep track of your time and turn it in as personal leave."

"Will do." Lizzy left the office and made her way to the third floor. On the way, she stopped by the restroom and took a moment to pray. *Lord, keep me safe. Keep us all safe. Carl is a ticking time bomb which has already gone off more than once and could again if things don't go his way. Protect everyone in the courtroom, and Lord, please let justice be done.* With a deep breath, she checked her makeup and made her way to Courtroom Ten.

~ * ~

Lizzy took her seat in the back just as Shawn finished questioning Mike Branson about the day he and his son Frank discovered Marcie's body in the Thirskton State Forest. The 9-1-1 call center operator testified, and a recording of Mike's phone call was admitted as evidence and played for the jury. After Chief EMS Officer John Freeman left the stand, Shawn looked behind her. "The State calls Riponville County Coroner Doctor Ellis Michaels." The witness came forward.

"Please place your left hand on the Bible, and raise your right hand," Mandy instructed. Ellis complied. "Do you swear or affirm to tell the truth, the whole truth, and nothing but the truth, so help you God?"

"I do."

Mandy gestured to the witness chair. "Thank you. Please be seated and state your name for the record."

Ellis took his place and stated his name into the microphone. Shawn asked him a few routine questions about his education, training, work, and experience, and the defense stipulated that he qualified as an expert witness. "Dr. Michaels, did you bring with you today a pathology report on the death of Marcie Carson Greene?"

"Yes."

"Did you yourself perform the autopsy?"

"Yes, ma'am, I did."

"When did the victim die?"

"Between the hours of three and eleven p.m. on Tuesday, November 2nd."

"And what was the cause of death?"

Ellis looked at his report. "The victim died by strangulation."

Shawn produced several photographs enlarged to 8"x10" size, which the court reporter marked for identification with small stickers. Shawn handed the first photo, a close-up of Marcie's head and neck, to Ellis.

"Dr. Michaels, do you recognize this picture?"

"Yes."

"How do you recognize it?"

"This is a picture taken at the scene where the victim, Marcie Greene, was discovered.

"Did you take the victim photos?"

"No, ma'am. They were taken by a member of the forensics team assigned to the scene."

Shawn looked at the judge. "Your honor, the State moves to admit State's Exhibits 2 through 5 into evidence."

Defense attorney Thomas O'Brien rose. "Objection."

Judge Blake leaned forward and stared at him. *I wonder what kind of defense he has planned this time? He's got that deer in the headlights look. Not a good sign.* "What is your objection, Mr. O'Brien?"

"The probative value of the pictures is outweighed by the potential prejudice to the jury."

Shawn spoke up. "These photos will assist the coroner in his testimony by showing the injuries sustained, your honor."

Judge Blake's decision was swift. "Objection overruled. Ms. Stokes, you may proceed."

Shawn placed the first photo on the overhead, and the image appeared on a drop-down screen across from the jurors. "Dr. Michaels, what are the marks we see here, and here?" She used a laser pointer to indicate the bruising on Marcie's neck.

Ellis cleared his throat. "Those are the bruise marks left by the fingers of the person who strangled her."

Shawn placed another photo on the projector. "And these?" She indicated more marks on the back of Marcie's neck.

"Those are bruising caused by the thumbs."

Shawn looked at him. "So in your opinion, what was the cause and manner of the victim's death?"

"Based on the bruise marks and the distance between them, strangulation by hands."

"What other findings indicate death by strangulation, Dr. Michaels?"

Ellis looked at his report again. "X-rays showed a fracture of the Hyoid bone, which is consistent with manual strangulation. Also consistent is the fact that the Strap muscles in the neck showed evidence of hemorrhage." Ellis continued to testify as to other facts and details of his report, including a slight postmortem fracture of the Ilium. Shawn admitted several other photos into evidence, as well as a diagram illustrating the victim's injuries.

Lizzy felt as though she were in a dream. To see pictures of the woman, lifeless and cold on the screen up front, brought back memories she thought long forgotten. *That could have been me*. She shivered and crossed her arms in an effort to warm herself.

After an hour on the stand, Shawn thanked the coroner and indicated she had no further questions. Thomas did not wish to cross-examine, and Dr. Ellis Michaels was excused.

"The State calls Ms. Sally Patmore," Shawn announced. A young woman wearing tan slacks and a polo shirt with *Forensics* embroidered on the front left side came forward and was sworn in. Shawn established Sally's credentials as she had with Ellis. She walked over to the court reporter and handed her a small manila envelope with an evidence seal across the flap. After the exhibit was marked for ID, Shawn handed the envelope to Sally.

"Ms. Patmore, do you recognize the object in this envelope?"

Sally broke the seal, opened the envelope, and drew out the square flat object within. "Yes, ma'am. This is a ZarPro™ Blood Lifting Strip containing a bloody fingerprint." Sally looked at her expectantly.

"Did you collect this fingerprint?"

"Yes, ma'am. I lifted the impression from Marcie Greene's neck."

"What did you do after you lifted the print?"

"I sealed the strip in this envelope."

"How do you know this is the same strip you collected?"

"My initials are here, and this is my handwriting." Sally indicated the handwritten label on the front of the envelope.

Shawn questioned Sally as to the chain of custody involved during analysis of the print, then looked at the judge. "The State moves to enter State's Exhibit Six, the bloody fingerprint, into evidence, your honor."

When Thomas made no objection, Carl's blood began to run cold. *A **bloody** fingerprint? Seriously? No freakin' way. How on earth did that happen? I wasn't bleeding when I killed her.* He thought furiously, trying to make sense of this unexpected development. When they went over the evidence together, Thomas showed him a fingerprint card, but Carl was sure he never mentioned blood. He assumed Thomas meant prints from his home, which would obviously have every right to be there and so would be excluded.

Suddenly, with sickening clarity, he remembered one small seemingly insignificant detail. He'd opened a drink the week before the murder and cut his pointer finger. The wound was healing, but the pressure of his hands around Marcie's neck must have caused the cut to open again. He remembered the stinging feeling in his finger when he washed down the wheelbarrow and shovel with bleach.

Curses and blind fury welled up within Carl just when the judge declared the court would be in recess for lunch. He was escorted back to the holding cell where he stood in the corner, his jaw clenched so tightly his head began to ache. *How could I have been so careless? Why didn't I use gloves?* He finally sat down and tried to breathe deeply. Thomas would get him off. The attorney's reputation, and quite possibly his relationship with his wife and daughter, depended upon it. *Fingerprint or no fingerprint, Thomas has a job to do. And so help me, he'd better get this right.*

When court reconvened after lunch, Shawn continued to question Sally Patmore about other evidence: hairs not belonging to the victim found on her sweater, the zip ties used to bind her, fibers of fabric not consistent with the clothes found on her body, skin tissue from beneath her fingernails, and evidence of duct tape residue removed from her lips and cheeks. Shawn then handed her a small envelope. "Ms. Patmore, to you recognize this item?"

"Yes, ma'am. This contains a receptacle holding the buccal swabs I took from Mr. Greene after his initial interrogation with Detective Lucas Howard."

"And how do you recognize this?"

"My name is on the envelope, and this is my handwriting." The witness pointed to the label portion of the envelope, which also contained the date, the name and address of the subject, and his driver's license number.

"Did the defendant voluntarily allow these swabs to be taken?"

"Yes, ma'am. Here is his consent form. A copy of his driver's license is stapled to the form." The witness produced a form signed by Carl Greene indicating his voluntary agreement to the procedure.

"Your honor, the State moves to admit State's Exhibit Eleven A, the buccal swabs, and State's Exhibit Eleven B, the consent form, into evidence.

"Granted."

Shawn placed the exhibits on the evidence table. She had no further questions, and Thomas did not wish to cross-examine, so Sally was excused.

Shawn checked her witness list, then looked at the judge. "The State calls Jennifer Holm." After the witness was sworn in and established as an expert, Shawn began. "Ms. Holm, was a comparison run on the DNA from Mr. Greene's buccal swabs against the DNA from the blood in and around the fingerprint, as well as the skin tissue under the victim's fingernails?"

"Yes." Jennifer produced a form and handed it to the prosecutor. "This report indicates that the probability of the DNA found belonging to someone other than the defendant is one in three point four five billion." Shawn admitted the DNA report into evidence and indicated she had no further questions.

Thomas rose and walked to face the witness. "Ms. Holm, has there ever been a time when DNA test results from your lab were proven to be inaccurate?"

"Yes, sir. If proper storage procedures were not followed, or contamination occurred, the results could be inaccurate."

Thomas nodded. "So it is possible that the DNA results on the defendant, Carl Greene, were actually incorrect?"

Jennifer shook her head. "No, sir. All proper procedures were followed during the collection, storage, and testing of both the buccal swabs and the blood from the finger print."

"Thank you." Thomas took his seat. *Had to try*, he thought glumly. Shawn had no additional questions, and Jennifer Holm was excused.

"The state calls Detective Lucas Howard." Lucas took the stand and Shawn established his qualifications, experience, and current work duties. "Detective Howard, you have questioned the defendant Carl Greene several times, is that correct?"

"Yes, ma'am."

"Can you identify this document?"

Shawn handed the detective two sheets which were already marked for identification. He looked the paperwork over and nodded. “This is my report from the interviews with Mr. Greene, and this is his statement.”

“When you asked Mr. Greene where he was on November 2nd and 3rd, what was his answer?”

Detective Howard looked over his report. “He stated he was off the afternoon of Tuesday, November 2nd, and that he left for a conference the evening of the same day.”

“What did the defendant say happened before he left for the conference?” Shawn asked.

“He said he and his wife, the victim Marcie Greene, fought and when he tried to hug her before he left, she scratched him and ran off into the woods.”

“What did he say her condition was when he last saw her?”

“He stated that she was alive, but he didn’t have time to go after her and thought she needed time to cool off.”

“Did you receive proof of the trip and the conference the defendant attended?” Shawn asked.

“No, ma’am. The defendant initially said he would provide that information, but later said he lost the receipts for the trip mileage and the conference reservations. He said he must have thrown them away in the trash from a fast-food meal he bought on the way.”

“The State moves to admit State’s Exhibits Thirteen and Fourteen, the report and the statement, into evidence.”

Thomas made no objection, and Judge Blake nodded. “Granted.”

After about fifteen more minutes of questioning, Detective Howard was excused. Shawn called the expert who had taken Carl’s prints the day he was first interrogated. The fingerprint examiner stated that based on sixteen points of comparison, the fingerprint taken from the victim’s neck was a conclusive match to the right forefinger print of the defendant Carl Greene. The fingerprint rolls and the report were admitted into evidence and the witness was excused.

Shawn checked her notes. "The State calls Mr. Hugh Phelps." A handsome man with salt and pepper hair, dressed in a Versace suit, walked forward and was sworn in.

"Mr. Phelps, where do you work?" Shawn asked.

"I'm a senior partner in the architectural firm Bartram and Phelps."

"And do you employ Carl Greene?"

"We did up until the date of his arrest. He was terminated at that time."

"Do you maintain employee attendance records, Mr. Phelps?"

"Yes, ma'am, we do."

"And how do you keep those records?"

"Attendance is tracked by a software program."

"How long do you retain your attendance and employee records?"

"They are retained for the entire time the person remains an active employee, plus five years."

"What does the software keep track of?"

"Attendance, sick and personal leave requests, and actual leave time taken."

"Have you reviewed those records as they relate to the defendant?"

"I have."

"According to those records, did Carl Greene take the afternoon off on November second two years ago?"

Hugh opened a leather folio and removed a document. "Carl did not come to work at all on November 2nd. We called his cell phone that morning around nine o'clock, but received no answer. His wife, Marcie, answered the home phone. She indicated Carl told her he was taking the day off and had gone to the hardware store for some supplies he needed."

"According to your records, had Carl requested time off for November 2nd?"

"No ma'am."

"Mr. Phelps, was Carl scheduled to attend a conference associated with your firm on Wednesday November third?"

"No, ma'am. No one from our firm was attending any architectural conferences of which I was aware."

Shawn reached out to take the document from the witness. "Thank you, Mr. Phelps." Shawn moved to admit State's Exhibit 16, the employment record, into evidence and Thomas had no objection.

The judge glanced at Thomas, who rose and approached the witness. "Mr. Phelps, how secure are your employee records?"

"The program is password protected and is stored on our company's network server."

"Who has access to entering data?"

"Each employee has a password to the login features, as well as the leave request area. Only our accounting manager has access to the entire program.

"Can information be changed after an employee has entered their login? For example, if someone was actually at work, but another employee wanted to alter the record to make it look as if that person was absent, could that be accomplished?"

"No, sir. Employees only have access to their individual accounts."

"But if employee one had given employee two their password, couldn't data be compromised?"

Hugh thought for a moment. "I suppose that is possible. However, sharing of passwords in our company is grounds for immediate termination. I can't imagine why someone would risk their job."

"Thank you. No further questions." Thomas sat down. *A break. Finally! That could possibly put some reasonable doubt into their minds.*

While Hugh Phelps left the stand, he glanced over at Carl, who gave him a look of hatred just when his body blocked the jury's view. Hugh Phelps shook his head. *You just never know about people*, he thought while he left the courtroom.

Shawn called Edith Dockery to the stand. The woman came to the front and was sworn in. Shawn brought forward another document, which the court reporter marked for ID.

"Ms. Dockery, can you identify this document?"

"Yes, ma'am. That's a receipt from my store."

"What is the name of your store and where is it located?"

"Dockery Hardware on Shire Road in Riponville."

"And what does the content of this receipt reflect?"

Edith focused on the slip of paper. "The receipt shows that on Tuesday, November 2nd, a purchase was made consisting of a package of zip ties, a canvas tarp, a roll of duct tape, and a gallon of bleach."

"What time was the purchase made?"

"According to this receipt, at 9:35 a.m."

Shawn used a pencil to draw the witness's attention to the bottom. "And what does this portion show?"

"The purchase was made by Alastair C. Greene and paid for with his MasterCard™." Shawn paused for a moment to let the information sink into the juror's minds, then took the receipt from the witness. "Thank you, Ms. Dockery. No further questions." The receipt was admitted into evidence, and Edith Dockery was excused.

Several more witnesses were questioned and cross-examined, before the judge adjourned for the day. The jurors were instructed not to discuss the case with anyone or research the case in any way. Lizzy quickly left the courtroom while the jurors were filing out, not wanting to take any chance Carl might turn around and spot her.

She drove home feeling drained and vaguely frightened. The trial was awakening memories she thought long buried. Though she knew she'd made the right decision to attend, the experience was exhausting and upsetting.

~Fifteen~

The trial continued the next morning at nine, and Lizzy took her seat in the back. Before the jury was escorted into the courtroom, a brief in camera hearing was held during which Shawn established the validity and proof of ownership for the next group of exhibits she planned to introduce. Though Thomas objected, Judge Blake ruled the exhibits admissible. While the court reporter marked three documents for ID, the jurors filed in and were seated in the jury box.

Judge Blake looked at Shawn. "Ms. Stokes, you may call your next witness."

"Thank you, your honor. The State calls Mr. William Carson."

Martha gave her husband's hand a squeeze before he rose, and walked to where Mandy stood. "Please place your right hand on the Bible and raise your left hand." Bill complied and looked at her attentively. "Do you swear or affirm to tell the truth, the whole truth, and nothing but the truth, so help you God?"

"I do," Bill answered firmly.

"Thank you." Mandy smiled at him slightly, willing him to understand, though she must remain neutral, she felt his pain at this emotional time. She gestured to the witness stand. "Please be seated, and state your name for the record."

Bill sat and adjusted the microphone before stating his name. "Mr. Carson, what was your relationship with the victim?" Shawn asked.

"I'm her father." Bill looked around and breathed deeply as he took in the courtroom scene. The crowd in the gallery, some people in support of them, some in support of Carl. One bailiff at the back, and a woman sitting beside him next to the door. A bailiff by the side door, and another by the door to the holding cells. Shawn, professional and solemn, ready to win her case and further the cause of justice.

Thomas and Carl, joined in their efforts to gain a murderer's acquittal.

I can't believe I'm doing this, he thought. *I can't believe I'm testifying during the murder trial for my precious girl.* Memories of Marcie's childhood flashed through his mind, and he wondered for a moment if he could continue. His eyes met Carl's and his resolve returned, strengthened ten-fold. *I cannot let that monster get away with murder.* He gathered his wandering thoughts and returned his gaze to Shawn.

"Mr. Carson, what is your mailing address?"

"7 Valinor Road, Riponville."

Shawn handed him two documents. "Mr. Carson, do you recognize these?"

Bill took the sheets from her and looked them over. "These are Discover™ card statements."

"And to whom does the account belong?"

"It belonged to my daughter, Marcie."

"To what address was the statement mailed?"

"It was mailed to my address, 7 Valinor Road."

"Your honor, the State moves to admit State's Exhibit 18 and 19." Thomas made no objection, and the exhibit was entered into evidence. Shaw continued to question her witness. "Mr. Carson, why would your daughter have her credit card statement mailed to your address? Did you pay her bills?"

Bill Carson shook his head. "No, ma'am. I did not pay her bills. About a year ago, Marcie told me she opened a private Discover™ account and used our address. She stated she would give me the cash to pay the bills."

"Mr. Carson, did your daughter tell you why she wanted to do this?"

Bill choked up a bit. "She said she strongly felt the need for a private account, but she would not tell me why."

"And did Marcie give you the money to pay the bill each month?"

"No, ma'am, not each month. There were only two times, about a year apart, when she had any charges due.

Both times, she gave me a one-hundred-dollar bill to cover the balance."

"Thank you, Mr. Carson. No further questions." The witness was excused when Thomas indicated he did not wish to cross-examine. Bill walked back to sit beside Martha in the gallery.

"The State calls Atticus Carmichael," Shawn announced. A tall man carrying a three-ring binder approached. Mandy administered the oath, and he took his seat in the witness chair. Shawn walked forward. "Mr. Carmichael, where are you employed?"

Atticus adjusted his glasses. "I work for Solutions CloudSpace managing customer accounts."

"If I wanted to prove ownership of an account with your company, how would I do that?"

"We would need the email address from when the account was created, the name of the individual who placed the order, the date and order number, and the payment option used."

Shawn handed her witness one of the documents previously marked for ID. "Mr. Carmichael, can you identify this document?"

Atticus took the sheet of paper and looked it over. "Yes, ma'am. This is a confirmation email for an account set up with Solutions CloudSpace by a Marcie C. Greene."

"Can you verify that the information in this email matches the information on file with your company?"

Atticus opened his binder, removed a sheet of paper, and compared the information. "Everything but the payment option used, ma'am. I don't see that listed. The email just indicates the amount paid."

Shawn retrieved State's Exhibit 18 from the evidence table. "This is a Discover™ card statement previously admitted, which lists Ms. Greene as the account owner." She pointed at the sheet with a pencil. "I'll direct your attention to the only charge on the statement, $99.95 from Solutions CloudSpace. Does this match your information, sir?"

Atticus Carmichael carefully looked over the statement, checked the information against his company's document, and nodded. "Yes, ma'am. This is the payment option used to set up the account. The last four digits of the credit card number match the card number we have on file."

"What is provided with a charge of $99.95?"

"That package includes one terabyte of cloud storage for one year."

Shawn handed Atticus State's Exhibit Nineteen. "This is an additional Discover™ card statement from Ms. Greene's account. Can you identify what this charge from Solutions CloudSpace would have been for?" She pointed at the sheet before handing it to the witness.

Once again, Atticus Carmichael compared the document to his information. "This is a yearly renewal of her cloud storage account. She checked our auto-renew option, so this charge was generated one year from the date her account was set up."

"Mr. Carmichael, what documents were stored in Ms. Greene's cloud account?"

Atticus flipped to another page. "As requested in the subpoena, we have generated a list of the files stored in that particular account, as well as the contents of those files." He handed Shawn a document. "You will see on this sheet one listing named 'My Thoughts'. That was the only file folder found in the account." He removed a small stack of printouts from his binder. "Within that folder were twenty-three other files, each named by date. These are printouts of each of those twenty-three files."

After they were marked for ID, Shawn took the papers over to Thomas. He nodded, his heart sinking. He'd read them when he received discovery and knew full well what the printouts contained. Funny thing was, so did Carl, but he'd laughed it off and said his wife always was a drama queen. He seemed to have no idea the impact Marcie's words would most likely have on the jury. Thomas sighed inwardly but tried to keep his expression professional and optimistic.

Shawn turned to face the judge. “Your honor, the State moves to admit State’s Exhibits 20 through 45.”

Thomas rose. Though his objections to allowing the jury to see Marcie’s files were overruled during the in camera hearing earlier that morning, he felt he must try again. “We renew our previous objections, your honor.”

Judge Blake looked at him. “Noted and denied. The exhibits will be admitted.”

Shawn placed on the evidence table the confirmation email, the Solutions CloudSpace account data sheet, the second Discover™ statement, the Solutions CloudSpace file listing, and most of the printouts. She held onto eight of the individual file documents, turned to face the witness stand, and smiled. “Thank you, Mr. Carmichael.”

Thomas rose and addressed the witness. “Mr. Carmichael, does Solutions CloudSpace ever get customer accounts mixed up? In other words, could one person’s documents end up in another person’s account?”

“No, sir. Not from our end.”

“But a customer could share their account name and password, could they not?”

“Yes. Sharing of account information is completely at the discretion of the account holder.”

“Thank you. No further questions.” Thomas sat down and tried not to look too happy.

Shawn rose. “A few additional question of this witness, your honor?” Judge Blake nodded. “Mr. Carmichael, in our subpoena we also asked if you could produce a listing of each time Ms. Greene’s account was accessed and the computer IP address from which that access came. Were you able to generate that information?”

“Yes, ma’am.” Atticus removed a sheet from his binder and handed it to Shawn. She had the court reporter mark the paper for ID, then handed it back to the witness. “And what does this report indicate?”

“Access occurred from only one computer. The IP address is listed beside each entry, and all IPs are identical.”

Shawn retrieved State's Exhibit Nineteen from the evidence table. "Mr. Carmichael, what does this document reflect here?" She used a pencil to point out a number in the upper-right corner of the email.

"That's the IP address of the computer from which the account was set up."

"What conclusion would you draw from these two documents?"

"The IP address on the email matches that of our access report. Access was made each time from the same computer."

"Thank you. Move to admit State's Exhibit 46, the access report, into evidence."

Thomas was chagrined. He considered bringing up the possibility that another person in the house had used the same computer to access the cloud account, but in order to set a foundation for the idea, Carl would have to testify as to the residents of the house. *Too risky. I know only Carl and Marcie lived there. Besides, Carl stated in no uncertain terms, that he did not want to testify in his own defense, so what's the use?* Thomas made no objection, and the exhibit was admitted. Atticus Carmichael was excused, and Shawn addressed Judge Blake. "Request to publish State's Exhibits 23 through 30, your honor."

The judge nodded. "Granted."

Shawn placed a sheet of paper on the projector, and a journal entry appeared on the screen. She looked at the jurors. "Ladies and gentlemen, I will now show you and read aloud some of the entries in the file entitled 'My Thoughts', written by Marcie Carson Greene."

"June 4th. What a wonderful man I've married. I had doubts before but I know I made the right decision. Carl just wants the best for me and tries to correct my faults. I don't know how or why he fell in love with me. I have so many areas that need work. I hope I can be what he needs me to be. With God's help, I will."

An intense feeling of sadness washed over Lizzy while she listened. *I remember feeling the same way. Marcie's words could have been my own.* She wished once more she could have warned the unfortunate woman.

Shawn removed the printout and replaced it with another. "August 30th. I don't understand. I bought a cute little butterfly utensil holder for the kitchen, and Carl is so angry. He said he doesn't work his butt off so I can waste his hard-earned money on stupid crap. He won't talk to me at all, even though I said I'm sorry over and over. He loved it when I bought things for the house before we got married and even gave me money to buy them. Oh dear God, help me to not be so stupid again. I feel sick that I've made him so furious. I know that's not what a virtuous wife would do. Help me to be the kind of woman I need to be, Lord. I'm going to return the utensil holder tomorrow. I just hope that will appease Carl."

"October 14th. I'm losing it. I couldn't find my car keys yesterday. I looked everywhere, even in purses I haven't used in years. When Carl came home, he started to help me look. Then he said, 'Marcie, come on. Is this some kind of plea for attention? The keys are sitting on the kitchen counter.' And they were. I don't understand how I could have missed them sitting right there in plain sight. I know I looked in the kitchen a dozen times today. I feel like such an idiot. Carl was really disappointed in me. How could I be so stupid?"

"October 20th. We went out to dinner with Tilley and Dan last night. Carl had the best time making fun of me for 'losing' my keys. He made a huge deal about the fact that they were sitting right there the whole time. He would not let up about it. I tried to laugh at myself, but he just kept on and on. Tilley looked upset. It was so awkward and humiliating. When I said something about it after we got home, he slapped me and said to quit being so sensitive. He said his friends got a good laugh out of my ineptness, so at least I was good for something."

"April 11th. Our anniversary was yesterday. We've been married for a year. Carl slapped me again last night because I didn't have the porch swept off when he got home from work. I had a horrible migraine, too, and he was furious because I didn't want to go out for our anniversary. I was so scared he would hit me again, so I went to bed and pretended to be asleep, hoping he'd leave me alone. He came in and told me I was one sorry excuse for a wife but then left me alone."

"April 11th. Married two years now and I've never known such misery. Carl hit me again today, this time with his fist. He ranted and raved and went on and on before he struck, but I don't even know what I did wrong. Then we had supper. I'd prepared fried chicken, mashed potatoes, and green beans. He's always said before that was his favorite meal, but tonight all he could talk about was calories, saturated fat, and carbs. He picked up the plate and threw it across the room. Then he grabbed a piece of the broken plate and jabbed it at me. Thank goodness he calmed down before he did more than cut my arm. Even so, it took a while for the bleeding to stop. I'm so scared. He just won't let up. Nothing I do is right. I've tried so hard to be a godly Christian wife and live a life pleasing to God. I made a vow to Carl, and I know there must be something I'm missing, something I'm not doing right. God show me, please. I don't know what I'm doing wrong. I don't understand why Carl is so unhappy. He acts like he despises me. Last night, he said I'd better watch out because he'd had just about enough. But then this morning, he kissed me and said he loved me. I feel like I'm going crazy. I wish I'd listened when Anna told me what his first wife said. I was warned, and I didn't pay attention. Oh, dear Lord, why didn't I listen? Now I'm trapped with a monster."

In the back of the courtroom, Lizzy froze. *What was that?* She looked at the words on the screen again to be sure she'd heard correctly. She remembered the odd call as if it was yesterday. The display on her cell phone that day five years ago indicated an unknown number. She answered, expecting the caller to have dialed incorrectly. "Hello this is Lizzy."

"Hi, I'm trying to reach Elizabeth Godfrey."

"This is Elizabeth."

"Oh, I'm so glad I found you." The woman's voice was both relieved and hesitant. "My name is Anna Coyle. I know this is going to sound strange, but were you once married to a Carl Greene?"

Lizzy's stomach lurched. *What on earth?*

"Yes, I was," she choked out. "We've been divorced for about seven years now."

"The reason I'm calling is because a friend of mine has been seeing him, and they're getting quite serious. I've hung out with them a couple of times, and I just have a feeling something isn't quite right. He really acts like he doesn't want me around. I Googled him and found out about you. He was really unhappy when I asked him about his first marriage. And from the look on my friend's face, she clearly had no idea he'd been married before."

"Wow." Lizzy was silent for a moment while a myriad of feelings and emotions raced around in her mind. "Anna, please warn your friend. Carl is an abuser. Your friend needs to get out of the relationship right away." Lizzy continued to share with Anna some of the things she'd gone through, desperate to warn this unknown woman about the misery which was sure to follow if she stayed with Carl.

"Thank you, Elizabeth." Lizzy was relieved to hear how serious Anna sounded. "I'll talk with my friend and tell her what you've said."

"I'll be praying for her." Lizzy's voice was shaky. "She must not continue to see him. Abusers go from bad to worse. Please, please tell her to break it off."

Lizzy prayed fervently, but received only one more phone call from Anna. Though she had presented the information Lizzy shared, Anna's friend was not convinced. "She said she just couldn't believe he would do things like that." Anna sounded defeated. "She said he is so spiritual and close to God. She felt what you said was just sour grapes from a relationship gone wrong. Carl apparently gave her an earful about you, most of which I suspect was false information."

"No doubt." Lizzy felt tears prick at her eyes. "She's got to get away from him, Anna."

"I did my best, but she was not convinced."

"Carl is excellent at manipulating and controlling. He did a number on me, that's for sure. Even though there were all kinds of red flags before I married him, he still managed to manipulate me into going through with it." Lizzy sighed deeply. "I let a guy who I'd only known for a few months override the gut feelings of my parents and family, who'd known and loved me my whole life. But Carl had me so messed up mentally, I didn't know which end was up."

"I'm glad you got away from him. We'll just have to pray for Marcie, that somehow she'll see the truth before it's too late. We can't force her to make the right choice." Anna became brisk. "Elizabeth, thank you for talking with me. I appreciate what you did to try to help."

Lizzy's mind returned to the present while Shawn continued to present entries from Marcie's journal.

"July 23rd. He's at me about my clothes again. The weather is so hot, but he insists I wear big bulky sweaters and baggy jeans. Anything that fits correctly, he says is 'body-hugging'. He says I've gained weight, and I can't wear what I used to wear. But that isn't true. I might weigh a little more, but not that much. He got so angry at me yesterday when I tried to wear a double-layer long-sleeved T-shirt with my jeans instead of a sweater. He hit me and then grabbed my hair and dragged me to the dresser to get the sweater. He said he knew I was hoping people would stop by the side of the road, so they could see my boobs through the T-shirt. He said I might as well go out and get a pole and dance in the front yard for all to see. He said he failed to understand why God didn't strike me dead for being such a tramp. But it makes no sense. You can't see anything through that T-shirt and it's about three sizes too big. I don't know what to do. I want to please him, but nothing I do is right. I hate my body. I feel like I'm going crazy."

Why? Why didn't she listen? Lizzy felt a surge of frustration with Marcie but just as quickly was ashamed. *Would I have reacted any differently? If I was warned beforehand, would I have listened? Probably not. Carl is truly a master manipulator and a consummate actor. He led me to believe what he wanted me to believe, and I was completely convinced his word was the absolute truth.*

Shawn put another entry on the projector and read aloud. "October 30th. Carl said yesterday he didn't know why I'd turned into such an old frump. He yanked my hair and said to go get it cut into some kind of decent style. So I went to the hair stylist and had her give me a really cute chin-length cut. When I came home Carl went nuts. He screamed, shouted and asked if I was happy now that I 'look like a man.' He slapped and punched me so many times my cheeks are still red and bruised. I wanted to go to the hospital because I was afraid my cheekbone was broken, but he wouldn't let me, and he took my phone, so I couldn't call 9-1-1. Oh, dear Lord, why is this happening to me? All I ever wanted was to make him happy. I stood in the laundry room after he left for work this morning, and I could literally feel my sanity slipping away. I am so frightened. He's going to kill me, or I'm going to lose my mind. If I had the guts, I'd drive the car off the road into a ravine and end it all. But it would be just my luck I wouldn't die, and then he would be my caregiver. I can't even imagine how horrible that would be."

Shawn removed the last sheet from the projector and said, "The State calls Ms. Tilley Bonneville."

Billy stepped out into the hall to call the witness, who had been asked to wait outside. The short blonde-haired woman dressed in a print blouse, khakis, and croco heels followed him into the courtroom. After Tilley was sworn in, Shawn walked forward. "Ms. Bonneville, where are you employed?"

"I'm a teller at Riponville Central Credit Union."

"And how many years have you worked there?"

"Let me see." Tilley thought for a moment. "It will be fifteen years next month."

"Ms. Bonneville, how did you know the Greene's?"

"I met Marcie in our church small group. We became dear friends in short order. I met Carl when he and Marcie started dating. I was the maid of honor in their wedding."

"Ms. Bonneville, what do you recall about October 20th, four years ago?"

"That was the night my husband Dan and I went out to dinner with Carl and Marcie."

"And how would you remember? That was a long time ago."

"I write in a daily journal." Tilley smiled. "I like to keep track of things."

"I see." Shawn nodded. "And was that particular dinner memorable in some way?"

Tilley cleared her throat and began to blink back tears. Mandy reached over to hand her a box of tissues. "Yes. I could remember it, even if I hadn't written everything down. Carl was acting horribly. He kept making fun of Marcie for losing her keys when they were right there on the counter. I could see them possibly laughing together about it, but he was really belittling. I was so embarrassed for her. Marcie tried to laugh about it at first, but he wouldn't drop the subject. It was awful. I mean, we were in public, and he was talking really loud. People were starting to stare at us."

"And what do you remember about April 11th two years later?" Shawn consulted her notes. "That would be the day after their two-year anniversary."

"I went out to their place to take them an anniversary gift. When Marcie answered the door, I was horrified." Tilley's eyes began to fill again, and she reached for another tissue. "She had a black eye. I asked her if she was okay and if she needed to go to the doctor. She acted scared and said no, she was fine, that she just stumbled and hit the corner of a table. She gave a funny little laugh and said she just needed to stop being so clumsy."

Tears filled Lizzy's eyes, and she unobtrusively felt in her purse for a tissue. Oh how she understood Marcie's pain. The agony of her years with Carl rose up in her mind as if they had just happened. Her anger and bitterness over what he'd done to her made her taste bile. She wanted to scream and cry out. Silently, she rose and exited the courtroom. She made her way to the restroom and closed herself in a stall. Sobbing, she stayed there, the storm of anger and hurt crashing over and over onto her soul like surf on a rocky shore.

When she was finally spent, she looked upward. *Dear Lord Jesus, I thought I forgave him years ago. Where did all this emotion come from? I hate him, Father.* She clenched her hands into fists. *I hate him for what he did to me and for what he did to poor Marcie. I wish somebody would do to him what he did to us. But I know it's wrong to hate anyone. Father help me. Give me the right spirit, for I surely do not have the strength on my own.*

After ten minutes, she felt more composed. She repaired her makeup, and returned to the courtroom. *I am going to see this through.* She was resolute. *I'm going to finish this.*

More witnesses testified, and more evidence was admitted that afternoon. "I can't imagine what the defense could say tomorrow that would give those jurors any reasonable doubt," Lizzy told Sandra before leaving for the day. "The evidence they have on Carl is pretty damning."

Lizzy considered her feelings later that night in the safety and security of her home. *I guess forgiveness is not just a one-time thing,* she thought while she prepared for bed. *I thought I'd forgiven Carl, but clearly I need to continue to forgive if I'm to go forward without bitterness. Father God, please help me. Renew a right spirit in me, Lord. I cannot do this in my own strength.*

She hugged Nugget and Downton close, then held Sherlock and Watson in turn, stroking their thick fur, and enjoying their delighted purring. The group snuggled down in bed, but Lizzy spent some time in the Psalms before turning in for the night. While she drifted off, she begged the Lord once more for peace in the storm.

~ * ~

His turn would come any minute, and Thomas wished his hands would stop sweating. He was well aware his client was guilty as sin. *I'm just here to protect his rights*, he comforted himself. *Everyone is entitled to representation and a fair trial, right? I've got to make Carl feel that I've tried to get him off. Then he won't say anything about the gambling. He's a reasonable guy. He'll see I've done my best, considering what I had to work with. Defending the guilty is no easy task. Good grief, even the mental evaluation came back normal. I have nothing to work with.*

"Your honor, the State rests," Shawn said, confident her case was won.

The jury was escorted out of the courtroom, and Thomas rose. "Your honor, the defense moves for a directed verdict. Insufficient evidence."

"Denied." Judge Blake rose. "We'll take a quick break."

The judge returned in about fifteen minutes and instructed the bailiff to bring in the jurors. They filed back into the jury box, and everyone in the courtroom waited expectantly for the defense to begin. Thomas O'Brien took a deep breath and adjusted the papers before him. *Show time*. He rose with faux confidence he was sure everyone could see through. "The defense calls Pastor Boyer Allendale."

The witness rose and began to make his way forward. Lizzy tried to squelch nausea at the sight of her former pastor. The betrayal still felt as fresh as if it had happened yesterday. The day she fled from Carl's house of horrors, she'd called Pastor Allendale to explain the reason for her flight. He had been most sympathetic and agreed she'd done the right thing. Several days later, Pastor Allendale's wife called and invited her for dinner. She shared with the couple how Carl had abused her, and felt they truly understood and supported her.

Two weeks later, Lizzy was having lunch with her friend Suzie. When Lizzy explained her situation, Suzie suggested the couple go to her pastor for counseling. Suzie said the Reverend Jackson Canes had helped her family so much, and she was sure he could assist Lizzy and Carl as well. Feeling she needed to try, Lizzy contacted Carl to see if he would be willing to meet with Reverend Canes. She also called Pastor Allendale, telling him she would feel more comfortable if he was present. Both men agreed, and the meeting was set for that Thursday.

Lizzy felt sick the day of the session. Though she truly hoped Carl might change, she felt frightened about the prospect of being in the same room with him. She prayed for strength but approached the meeting with trepidation. The session began harmlessly enough, with the Reverend Canes asking for basic information. Then he asked Lizzy why she left. Though she promised herself she would not cry, she could not hold back her tears while recounting the incident when Carl tied her to the tree and left her all night.

When she finished, Carl jumped in. "Oh my. Oh, Lizzy." His voice was laced with pain and disbelief. "How can you make up these stories? I never did anything like that, Lizzy." His voice broke and he whispered, "I've never abused you, Lizzy. I love you, honey."

There he goes again, claiming he didn't do things I know he did. Lizzy stared at the reverend's desk with expressionless eyes. *But they'll see through this. They're professionals. They'll recognize his con job.*

Pastor Allendale, the man who had shepherded her with understanding and kindness, turned toward the man who filled her days with horror. "Oh Carl." His tone dripped with sympathy, and his expression was filled with compassion. "We know you've never abused her."

Shock ricocheted through Lizzy's entire being. *What? What did he just say?* If the man had stabbed a butcher knife into her back, she could not have been more wounded. The rest of the session was a blur until the end. The Reverend Canes looked at Lizzy pointedly. "The sooner you return to your home the better. Now, I think you need to give each other a hug before you leave today."

The words pummeled Lizzy like a boxer duking it out with a punching bag. *It makes my skin crawl just to be in the same room with him. Hug him? Go back to him so he can kill me? You've got to be kidding!* She made a beeline for her car as soon as they were dismissed and never looked back.

Lizzy bit her lip and her mind returned to the present. Her former pastor was now on the stand.

"Pastor Allendale, thank you for being here today." Thomas smiled at him. "Do you know the defendant, Carl Greene?"

"I do."

"And how do you know him?"

"He is a parishioner at our church."

"How long have you known Carl?"

"Let's see. He's been attending Faith Freedom Church for about fifteen years now. I've known him ever since he joined."

"Pastor Allendale, how would you describe Carl Greene?

"Carl is a pleasure." The portly man smiled, and his face seemed to glow. "He never misses a service, unless he's out of town. He is always congenial and uplifting. He gives regularly and generously to our ministry. He is responsible and hard-working. Carl Greene is a good Christian man."

"Have you ever known Carl to be violent?"

The pastor shook his head firmly. "Never. Carl has always been kind and gentle, and it is a privilege to know him. I would trust him with my life."

"Thank you, sir. No further questions." Thomas took his seat.

Shawn rose for cross-examination. "Pastor Allendale, thank you for being here today." She smiled at him. "Can you tell me how gentle and kind Carl Greene is when you aren't there?"

"Uh, well, no. I guess I can't." The witness looked uncomfortable and shifted in his chair.

Shawn took a step closer. "Does your determination as to the character of a person relate directly to the size of their donation to your church?"

Boyer Allendale convulsed in a spasm of coughing, and Thomas shot out of his chair. "Your honor, I object. Relevance."

Judge Blake looked at Shawn. "Goes to the manner by which the witness determines a person's character, your honor." Shawn's voice was firm. "The witness mentioned giving."

"Overruled." Judge Blake looked at Thomas. "The witness may answer the question."

A trickle of sweat ran down the pastor's face as his coughing fit seemed to worsen. Concerned, the bailiff handed him a cup of water. Shawn waited until he was settled. "Are you okay, sir?"

"Yes, ma'am. Thank you. Just got a little tickle in my throat."

"Please answer the last question."

"No, of course I do not judge a person's character by their giving record." Bug-eyed, his face red with indignation, the pastor took a breath, struggling to regain his composure before answering. "That's an absurd notion."

"Did you ever spend any time with Carl and Marcie outside of church services and functions?"

"No, no, I don't believe I ever had the pleasure."

"How could you know how congenial, uplifting, kind, or gentle Carl Greene was outside of the one hour a week you saw him?"

Boyer Allendale mumbled something into the microphone and coughed again.

"I'm sorry, Pastor Allendale, could you repeat that please?" Shaw looked him in the eyes.

The witness shifted in his chair. He loosened his tie a bit and cleared his throat. "I guess I can't know that, ma'am."

"Thank you, sir." Shawn returned to her seat, and the witness was excused.

Thomas continued to question a total of ten character witnesses, knowing there was no other defense for his client. His witnesses painted a glowing picture of Carl but Thomas' heart sank with each testimony. Everyone sounded rehearsed.

Shawn asked the same question of each witness on cross: "Have you spent time with Carl and Marcie socially or in their home?" Not one had done so. Thomas drew on every bit of acting ability he possessed during his closing arguments, trying his best to convince the men and women of the jury that his client was an honorable, decent man who loved his wife and mourned her loss. *We've got no chance...no chance at all*. Thomas slumped in his seat. *This guy is going down in flames, and he's going to take me with him.*

While Judge Blake began his charge to the jury regarding the law as it related to Murder in the First Degree, Lizzy's mind began to wander. *How long will they deliberate? Will they see the truth of Carl's guilt?* She could read nothing from the juror's faces. Each wore a similar serious expression. *Will I finally be able to relax and stop looking over my shoulder, knowing he's in prison for life? I don't feel unsafe most of the time. But still, I keep an eye out nonetheless. I know he'd try to kill me, too, if he thought he could get away with it. I've always felt I need to stay watchful and careful.*

Judge Blake's next words interrupted her thoughts. "Ladies and gentlemen, Carl Greene has pled not guilty to this indictment. That plea puts the burden on the State to prove the defendant guilty. A person charged with committing a criminal offense in this state is never required to prove themselves innocent. I charge you that it is a cardinal and important rule of the law, that a defendant in a criminal trial will always be presumed to be innocent of the crime for which an indictment has been issued, unless and until guilt has been proven by evidence satisfying you of guilt beyond a reasonable doubt."

Lizzy snapped to attention. *The Reasonable Doubt Charge*. She knew the judge was duty-bound to present this information to the jury, but inwardly she cringed. *How could anyone have one iota of doubt after the evidence Shawn presented? Surely they won't acquit. They can't.*

"Reasonable doubt is the kind of doubt that would cause a reasonable person to hesitate to act," Judge Blake continued. "Reasonable doubt may arise from the evidence which is in the case, or from the lack or absence of evidence in the case. You, the jury, must determine whether or not reasonable doubt exists as to the guilt of this defendant. The State has the burden of proving each and every element of a crime beyond a reasonable doubt. Reasonable doubt you may have in your deliberations should be resolved in favor of the defendant."

Dear Father in Heaven, please guide and direct this jury while they deliberate. Lizzy twisted the tissue in her hands. *Father please let justice be done here today. Help them to be sure. Please, Lord, don't let Carl get away with his heinous evil deed. Please be with Mr. and Mrs. Carson. I can't even imagine what they're going through right now. Give them strength as they see this trial through to the end. And Father, give them grace to go forward when this day is done, and help them to find peace and closure.*

~ * ~

In one short hour, the jury filed back into the courtroom and took their seats. "Ladies and gentlemen, have you reached a verdict?" Judge Blake looked at the foreman who nodded soberly.

The bailiff took the indictment and the verdict form from the foreman and handed them to the judge. After glancing over them, Judge Blake handed the paperwork to Mandy. "Will the defendant please rise?"

Carl and Thomas rose. Carl tried to control the urge to smirk. No way was he going to be convicted for Marcie's murder. No way. He had the final say and would go through life content in the knowledge that she did not best him in the end. He could already taste victory.

"Madam Clerk, please publish the verdict," Judge Blake said.

Carl's attention was drawn back to Mandy while she slowly rose. She looked the documents over briefly and began. "Your honor, in the case of the *State versus Alastair Carlton Greene* indicted for Murder in the First Degree, the verdict is guilty." She glanced up at the jury. "This is your verdict, so say you all?" The jurors nodded grimly.

Thomas leaped to his feet. "Your honor, I request the jury be polled."

Judge Blake nodded to Mandy, who proceeded to call each juror by name to state their individual verdict aloud for the record. When the process was complete there was a moment of silence in the courtroom.

"You freakin', stupid moron." Carl's voice started in a whisper and ended in a furious shout. "You incompetent fool. I'll tell everybody your dirty little secret. You can count on it." The spectators in the gallery erupted in gasps and a buzz of whispered questions.

"Order," Judge Blake thundered. "There will be order in my courtroom. Mr. O'Brien, please control your client."

Carl's eyes bulged behind his fashion glasses, frantic orbs of fury and hate. "Don't you tell me to be controlled, you sorry excuse for a public official. This trial was fixed. I know you guys are all on the take. But you're not going to get **me**." He grabbed his chair and made a lunge for the bench.

The courtroom erupted in chaos as deputies closed in immediately and wrestled Carl to the floor. In minutes, he writhed beneath them, powerless, with his hands cuffed behind his back.

"Order," Judge Blake shouted once again, looking out at the gallery. "This courtroom will come to order or every one of you will spend the night in jail." With the exception of a few worried whispers, the crowd became quiet. "Ladies and gentlemen of the jury, I'm sorry you had to witness this display today. We appreciate your service to our county and for bringing a conclusion to this case. The bailiff will escort you out, then you are free to go."

The shell-shocked jurors quickly filed out of the courtroom. Judge Blake looked at Shawn, then at Thomas. "Please approach the bench for sentencing."

The two slowly came forward and were joined by Carl, now with his feet shackled as well. The deputies kept a careful eye on him, ready with their Tasers. Shawn handed Mandy a sentencing sheet. The deputy clerk quickly filled in the date and judge code, and handed the document, along with the indictment, to the judge. Judge Blake looked over the paperwork, then allowed Shawn to present Carl's prior record and work history. Lizzy was shocked to hear that Carl had been arrested in another state when he was seventeen. His assault on a police deputy put the man in the hospital for two days. Carl served one year in the Shawono Center for the charge.

When Shawn finished, Judge Blake allowed Thomas to speak. "Your honor, we cannot apologize enough for the unfortunate display seen here today." Thomas looked at the judge remorsefully. "Mr. Greene has been distraught by the loss of his wife. This final blow drove him over the edge. He has only the one conviction Ms. Stokes indicated. Other than that, his record is clean. I have here letters from his pastor, former employers, and from the various civic organizations." Thomas gave the letters to Mandy, who handed them up to the judge. "Carl has faithfully served our community over the years and is loved and respected by all who know him. I beg the court to consider the minimum sentence in this case." Carl glared at his attorney menacingly, and struggled against the restraints.

Thomas shot him a warning look and muttered under his breath, "Carl, get a grip. Get a grip, man."

Judge Blake slowly read the letters presented to him and sat for several moments afterwards, deep in thought. Finally, he cleared his throat. "Mr. Greene, please step forward."

Carl shuffled up a few steps.

"I have considered the jury's verdict and all the information your attorney has presented. I hereby sentence you to the Department of Corrections for the rest of your natural life, with no possibility of parole. May God have mercy on your soul, Mr. Greene." The deputies each took one of Carl's arms and proceeded to march him out the side door to the holding cell. Just before the door closed, the courtroom heard a shout.

"You're dead, Thomas O'Brien. You're a gambler and a fool and just lost big time. You'd better watch your ba..." The door closed, and the sound ceased abruptly.

Lizzy wept while she grabbed her purse and exited the courtroom to return to her office. She walked in and looked at her co-workers. "Guilty," she announced, tears flowing down her cheeks. "They found him guilty and he got life without parole."

Lizzy's teammates surrounded her in a group hug. "You won't have to look over your shoulder anymore, honey," Elsie said, giving her hand a squeeze. "I'm so glad the Lord allowed justice to be served."

"Me, too, Elsie." Lizzy sighed deeply. "Me, too."

Back in Courtroom Ten, the visitors in the gallery slowly disbursed while Mandy and the court reporter began to catalog and box up the trial exhibits. Thomas slumped down into his chair at the attorney table, head in hands. He felt trapped. *No doubt in my mind Carl will follow through on his threat; whenever I least expect it, he'll strike like the snake he is.*

Sweat trickled down his forehead, and he struggled to take a deep breath. His heart pounded laboriously, as if some unseen hand was trying to squeeze the life out. *A heart attack. Maybe that's how Carl's gonna do me in.*

The reality of his addiction suddenly came home to him like never before. *I'm addicted to gambling. I am an addict. I'm no better than the druggies I represent. I act like I'm such a big deal, but I'm just another addict. Oh, God, help me.* He clenched his teeth to hold back tears while he slowly gathered his papers and left the courtroom. He tossed his briefcase in the back seat of the Mercedes, then sat in the driver's seat sobbing.

Dear Father, in Heaven, You have my attention. I can't do this anymore, but I don't know how to stop. Please help me. The ugliness of his addiction glared at him, and suddenly he began to consider what could happen. He pictured the loan sharks harassing or even hurting his sweet Celia or Meredith. *Who knows what those guys would do to get their money. They're capable of anything. I have to tell my family. And I have to tell them now, before someone else does. They deserve to hear the truth from me.*

He started the car forlornly and began to drive home. He sat at an intersection, and the thought struck him. *I'm so tired of living a lie. The burden is too heavy. I can't take it anymore. I don't want to be this monster I've become. Lord, help me. Help my family. I pray they would be merciful and forgiving and support me while I get help.* New tears of resolve formed while he pulled into his garage and headed inside for a family meeting.

~Sixteen~

The remainder of June, as well as July and early August, passed in a blur. Lizzy's struggle to keep forgiving, despite the feelings brought to the surface during Carl's trial, continued. The morning of August 19th, Lizzy entered the office feeling discouraged. She turned on her computer, then reached to flip her devotional calendar to the correct date.

The author's title "Forgiveness" jumped out at her. She squirmed a bit inside. Many people she'd met seemed to equate forgiveness with forgetfulness and blind trust. Some even suggested she should have gone back to Carl regardless of the abuse. *I just don't think that's what forgiveness means,* she thought. *But what **does** it mean?*

She sighed with skepticism, but made herself read the entry. When she finished, she stared at the wall of her workstation, deep in thought. *Wow! I never thought about forgiveness like that. It's like if I let someone borrow money but then tell them they don't have to pay me back. Even though Carl would have killed me if I'd stayed, I have to let go of my anger and hate. Even though he did horrible things to me, I have to let them go. And my letting go and no longer expecting him to pay for the wrongs he did toward me, equals forgiveness.*

She sat back in amazement. How freeing the thoughts were. Tears pricked her eyes while she read the devotional once more. *Thank You, Lord. Thank You for these words today. Help me to truly forgive Carl and move forward. Help me to remember this definition of forgiveness every time those dark memories surface. Help me to truly let go.* With a smile of thankfulness, Lizzy began entering the neatly stacked bond forms on her desk.

~ * ~

Lizzy's cell phone rang with the familiar theme from the BBC *Sherlock* television show just as she was finishing her lunch. Chewing rapidly, she swallowed, then tapped the 'answer' button.

"Hi, Lizzy." Her sister's excited voice boomed from the phone. "You're not going to believe this."

"What on earth? Deb? What's up?"

"Remember my college roommate, Mickey? She got married a couple years ago, and they bought a ranch out in Montana. Her husband's name is Christopher. And this is so cool, Lizzy. Mickey called yesterday and invited our family to come out for a visit. And she specifically wants you to come, too. She said you'd been on her heart over the past few months, and she's been praying for you like crazy." Deborah paused for breath.

Lizzy was stunned. She knew Deborah and Mickey remained friends after school, but to find out this sister-in-Christ had been lifting her name up before the throne made her choke up with emotion.

"Wow, Deb." A tear escaped down her cheek. "I mean, wow. I was going to call you this weekend. Things have been so crazy, I realized the other day that I hadn't told you what's been going on here." Lizzy proceeded to fill her sister in on her close encounter on the road to Clifton, finding out about Carl's trial, and the resulting panic attack. She shared how the Lord got her attention through His playlist designed just for her, and the sermon the next Sunday.

"Honey, that is amazing," Deborah said with emotion. "You know, Mickey went through an abusive relationship during our junior year. She told me later God used your story to give her the strength to break things off with her abuser."

"I think I vaguely remember you mentioning that." Lizzy tried to recall the details.

"This is totally a God thing, Lizzy." Deborah's voice was breathless with excitement. "I know He has something special for us. Marshall and I haven't gone on vacation in the past few years, and the twins will absolutely love getting to ride horses."

Lizzy giggled, thinking of her horse crazy nieces. "They will be in Heaven on earth, that's for sure. How many horses do Mickey and her husband have?"

"Three of their own, I think, and a couple ponies, but they foster horses who were abused and try to retrain and rehabilitate them so they can be adopted out."

"Oh yes." Lizzy's grin was wide. "Millie and Kate will love the ranch. You may not be able to convince them to come back home."

"That is a risk I'm willing to take." Deborah laughed. "So can you get the time off? We were thinking the best time to go would be toward the end of September. Winter comes really early out there, but we can probably hit the fall colors if we go then."

Lizzy's thoughts were swirling. She had longed to visit the western states. This opportunity not only to see the beautiful landscapes of which she dreamed, but to also stay in a private home, seemed like more than she could comprehend.

"Lizzy, you still there? Hello?"

"Oh, yes. Sorry, Deb." Lizzy laughed. "I'm still in shock. You know, if you'd have asked me, 'Lizzy, do you need a vacation?' I'd have most likely said 'No, not really. I'm fine'. But I know in my heart God has arranged this to meet a specific need. I'm sure I can get off. I have a lot of personal time saved up. And I have some mad money in savings. Tell Mickey and Christopher yes, I would love to come! Hey, can you give me her email address so I can write and thank her?"

Deborah provided the information, and Lizzy promptly punched the address into the contacts app in her iPad. Only a few minutes remained before her lunch hour was over, but she quickly wrote a message to Mickey, thanking her for the invitation to visit and indicating how excited she was about the opportunity.

~ * ~

Lizzy smiled when she drove around a bend and her favorite mountain vista opened up before her. *Finally, time for Honey Crisp apples*, she thought with glee. *I love this drive. There's something about mountains and early apples that are good for the soul.* Deborah and the girls had planned to join her for the trip, but Millie came down with strep at the last minute. Though disappointed, Lizzy sensed God had something special for her.

She arrived at Mountain Top Orchard, got out of her car, and took a deep breath of pure mountain air. *What a beautiful day*. The sky was dotted with white fluffy clouds and the temperature at the summit was just cool enough to need a light sweater. Lizzy went to the apple barn to retrieve a couple of baskets. After receiving directions to the Honey Crisp trees, she headed out into the orchard. She felt an overwhelming sense of peace while she walked along the grass lined gravel path.

Thank You, Lord. You have begun a good work in me. And I know you have promised in your Word that you will complete that work. Help me to learn what you want me to learn and continue to grow. Help me to always be aware of Your love for me.

She stopped at a tree loaded with luscious fruit. She picked apples for several minutes, then put her basket down and stood perfectly still. A gentle breeze caressed her face and the beauty of the day seeped in and filled her heart. Across the path and up a small hill, she saw a pasture with several horses grazing. Bees buzzed busily around the wildflowers, which looked like colorful smiles here and there among the trees.

Lizzy closed her eyes, savoring the peacefulness. God seemed so close to her, and she felt as though His arms were wrapped around her in a loving hug. She looked around again, watching the horses in the field, their tails methodically swishing away the flies. She remembered the devotional she'd read the week before and pondered again the meaning of forgiveness. All at once, the thought hit her.

Nolle prosequi. Forgiveness is like 'nol prossing' a case. I'm not going to pursue prosecution any more. That's done. The case has been dismissed. I have forgiven Carl and I no longer have to pay any heed to the memories that seek to drag me back into bitterness and misery. Tears began to fall while she pondered the thought. *Thank You, Lord. Thank You.* She went back to picking apples, lighthearted and joyful at her newfound revelation.

That night, Lizzy sat at her computer and typed out a statement.

"I, Elizabeth Godfrey, do hereby nol prosse my case against Carl Greene. I forgive him, and I will no longer allow what he did to me to rule my life. I will not allow his evil to drag me into bitterness and cynicism. From this day forward when memories of his cruelty come to mind, I will remind myself his case has been 'nol prossed', and that God rescued me and loves me with an everlasting love. I will ask my Lord Jesus Christ to turn my thoughts to healthy things, and I will no longer dwell on the darkness of the past. I will no longer allow Satan to harass me in this way. I will press forward, I will serve my Lord, and I will live in obedience to Him. I will do His will and will trust Him to protect me from any relationship which should not be. The evil of the past has no place in my life now. My Lord has rescued me. He lifted me out of the miry clay and set my feet on a rock."

Lizzy printed out the statement, signed and dated it, and placed the paper in a file. *Now, that's done. Time to move on for good.* Lizzy smiled firmly while she shut the file drawer and went to share her thoughts with her mother. While the women talked, a thought came to her that had been skittering around the edges of her mind ever since the trial.

"Mom, I keep thinking that I should contact Marcie's parents to let them know I've been praying for them. I felt so sorry for them during the trial, but it didn't seem like the right time to approach them. What do you think?"

Rose sat quietly for a moment before responding. "Honey, I think that would be a very thoughtful thing to do. I'm sure they would appreciate that."

Lizzy nodded. "I'm going to do it. The Lord keeps bringing the idea to my mind, and I think He wants me to follow through."

The next day after church and lunch, Lizzy looked up Bill and Martha Carson's phone number online and dialed. Her hands were a bit shaky, but she knew she was doing the right thing.

"Hello, this is Martha Carson."

"Mrs. Carson, my name is Elizabeth Godfrey. I go by Lizzy. I attended the trial for Carl Greene."

There was a pause, then Martha replied, her voice cold, "Okay. We really aren't interested in doing any news interviews."

"Oh, no, ma'am. That's not why I'm calling." Lizzy cleared her throat. This was more awkward than she'd imagined. "I ... I'm calling because I just wanted you all to know I've been praying for you. I was Carl's first wife."

Lizzy heard a gasp and what sounded like the phone hitting the floor. Her heart sank. *Oh no. Now I've gone and done it.*

In a moment, Bill's voice came on the line. "Hello, who is this please?"

"Mr. Carson, I am so sorry. I didn't mean to upset you. My name is Elizabeth Godfrey. I was Carl Greene's first wife and was present at his trial. My heart has been so heavy for you all, and I felt like the Lord was prompting me to contact you. I just wanted you to know I've been praying for you and your wife."

Lizzy heard a sniff, then Martha's voice came on the line again. "Bill, I'm on the other line. Lizzy, you were so kind to call us. I'm sorry I reacted the way I did. I was floored. We knew Carl had been married before, of course, but never imagined talking to you."

"I completely understand. I know this must seem strange. But for quite a while God has put it on my heart to contact you. I can't even imagine how you must be suffering and wondered if there was any way I could help."

Bill cleared his throat. "Lizzy, I think I speak for Martha in saying that we would like to meet you in person. I know it seems odd, but I feel God's leading. Would you be free to come over for dinner next Saturday evening?"

"Yes and I would love to meet you all also." Lizzy felt surreal while they made arrangements, and she wrote down the Carson's address. She hung up and went to Rose's bedroom where her mother was reading. "Mom, guess what? They invited me over for dinner!"

"See, honey?" Rose smiled. "God has a plan. Maybe you can minister to them in a special way."

"That will be my prayer." Lizzy smiled. *God's ways never cease to amaze me.*

~Seventeen~

Lizzy dined with the Carson's several times and even met Martha at the mall for a shopping trip. The two shared an unusual bond and connected in a way Lizzy would not have dreamed possible. They encouraged each other in the Lord, and Lizzy began to feel that in some ways, she was stepping in to minister to Martha in Marcie's stead.

The rest of September flew by, and before Lizzy knew it, she, Deborah, Marshall, Millie, and Kate stood in line, shoes in hand, waiting to go through the security check at the airport.

"Montana, here we come!" Lizzy looked at her nieces and grinned.

"Aunt Lizzy, isn't this exciting?" Kate craned her neck to see where they were headed. "I've never been on an airplane before."

"Me, either," Millie put in. "But why are there police up there?" She frowned a bit. "I'm scared, Aunt Lizzy." She pressed closer to her aunt for comfort.

Lizzy put an arm around her. "Those security guys are there to make sure nobody brings anything dangerous on the plane. They're there to protect us, honey." She crouched down and hugged Millie close. "You're going to love it, Mille. Wait 'til you see the clouds from the plane. They look like piles and piles of snow or cotton balls. And when we get close to Montana, I'll bet you'll be able to see the mountains and everything. Flying is so cool."

Millie's frown eased, and she began to share her sister's excitement. Deborah smiled and squeezed Marshall's hand. "They're both going to love the experience."

He nodded and smiled broadly. "Especially when they get to ride the horses."

Both girls turned to him with a squeal. "Tell us about the horses again, Daddy." Mille looked at her father expectantly and Kate put in, "And tell us about the dogs, too."

Marshall deferred to his wife who began to describe the C & M ranch to the girls. She was still giving them tidbits to anticipate while they boarded the plane and took their seats.

~ * ~

Mickey Sterling hugged her friend tightly. “Oh, Deb, it’s so great to see you.”

“You don’t know how much we’ve been looking forward to this.” Deborah hugged her back, then dug in her purse for a tissue to dab her eyes. “I don’t know why I’m getting so emotional. It’s just so wonderful to see you again.”

Mickey’s husband, Christopher, greeted Marshall warmly. “Welcome to Montana, folks. We’re so glad you could come. We may be a wee bit prejudiced, but we think this is about the best place on earth to live and work.”

Marshall shook his hand and nodded. “I see what you like.” He looked out the airport windows to the beautiful mountains in the distance. “I can’t wait to see more.”

Deborah drew back and motioned to Lizzy. “Mickey, this is my big sister, Lizzy.”

Lizzy stepped forward hesitantly, ready to shake the petite woman’s hand, but Mickey engulfed her in a hug. “Lizzy, finally. I’ve been wanting to meet you for years.” She drew back and smiled in welcome. “Deb told me your story when we were in college. I was in a bad relationship and God used your experience to give me the courage to break up with Lee. I have always been grateful to you.”

“I know we’re going to have a lot in common, Mickey.” Lizzy smiled, her heart full at Mickey’s words. “I’ve wanted to meet you, too.”

After Millie and Kate were introduced, the happy group headed to retrieve the suitcases from baggage claim and begin the journey to the C & M.

~ * ~

As soon as Mickey opened the back door, three dogs bounded out eagerly. “Oh, Mamma, what a cute little dog.”

Kate's gaze was immediately captured by the tiniest of the trio. She knelt down and put her hand out. Poncho, a tan and white Chihuahua, came forward to sniff, then gave her fingers an enthusiastic lick. He seemed to be smiling at her, and his tail whipped back and forth in excitement.

Christopher grinned. "Looks like Poncho's found a new friend." The Sheltie and the collie pushed forward for their share in the attention.

"Mickey, what beautiful dogs you have." Lizzy dropped to one knee and rubbed the canines gently on their heads. "I have a Sheltie, too. And a Pomeranian."

"I had Kip, the Sheltie, when we moved out here." Mickey smiled, then pointed to the tri-colored collie and the Chihuahua. "Kelsey and Poncho were rescues. Poncho is really Chris's dog, though. I've never seen a dog be so devoted. He remembers Chris was the one who found him and saved him from misery."

The Jacksons, Lizzy, Christopher, and Mickey made their way into the house. Lizzy set her suitcase down. "Mickey, I've got to hear the rescue story. Sounds like a good one."

"Let's get you settled in. But I promise I'll tell you the story tonight at dinner," Mickey said with a smile. She led the group upstairs and pointed out the guest rooms and bathrooms. "Take your time getting unpacked. It's only three o'clock now, so we've got a few hours before we eat. Feel free to take a snooze if you want to. I know how tiring air travel can be." Mickey tucked strand of curly auburn hair behind one ear and smiled at them. "I am so happy you all are here. You have no idea how much I've been looking forward to your visit."

~ * ~

Lizzy took the serving platter Deborah passed to her and helped herself to a baked potato. "Okay, guys, let's hear about the dogs."

Christopher nodded at Mickey. "You start, honey. I wasn't there at the very beginning of the story."

Mickey nodded. "I was on my way home from town with a load of feed, when I noticed a car pulled off to the side of the road. I thought someone might be in trouble, so I stopped. Turns out, a friend of mine from church was there and saw this horse that was about to die. Literally. He was nothing but skin and bones. We managed to get him back here and tied him upright in a sling. The next day, we returned to the scene with a deputy to serve the owner with a seizure warrant. The guy was dead in his house. They found out later he'd died of alcohol poisoning."

"Oh my word." Lizzy stared at Mickey. "Is that why the horse was in such bad shape? Because the guy had been dead for a while?"

"No." Mickey's face showed her disgust. "We found Kelsey in a shed. She was covered with sores and had obviously been there for weeks. Clearly, he was an abusive and unfit owner. Poor Kelsey was skin and bones just like the horse. All there was in there with her was a bucket with about an eighth of an inch of scummy water. No sign of food."

She shook her head at the memory, and Christopher picked up the story. "I found Poncho out in the back. The little guy was chained to a stake. I think the chain weighed more than he did. We couldn't believe some predator hadn't gotten him. We took them home with us and eventually got a court order that allowed us to keep the animals or adopt them out to appropriate homes."

Mickey smiled. "Poncho has never forgotten who rescued him. From that moment on, he's stuck to Chris like glue." As if to prove the point, Poncho, who was seated beside Christopher's chair, let out a whine, his adorable brown eyes begging for a treat.

"That is so sweet." Lizzy sniffed and dabbed the corner of one eye with her napkin.

"Mrs. Mickey, why were the dogs like that? Why didn't they have food?" Kate inquired. Her young eyes showed her confusion, not understanding why the animals would have been mistreated.

"Sweetie, some people just should not have animals. They are mean, unkind, and take out their frustrations with life on their pets."

Millie looked at Mickey earnestly. "What happened to the horse, Mrs. Mickey? Can we see him, too?"

"He doesn't live at the C & M anymore, Millie. Our veterinarian Andrew adopted him. But I'll bet he would love for us to come visit."

"Mama, can we?" Millie and Kate said in unison. They looked eagerly at Deborah.

"We'll see, girls. If he has time for us to come, I don't see why not."

Marshall took a sip of tea and looked at Christopher. "So, I understand from Deb you're a professional photographer. How does the ranch fit in with that?"

Christopher smiled. "First of all, our land gives me endless opportunities for shooting. I still go to other locations, but there is so much I can do right here at home. I'm also doing photography for some local organizations. After we rescued the horse and the dogs, we were contacted by a local equine rescue society about becoming a sort of foster facility for abused horses. We've been taking them in ever since. I take pictures while Mickey works to rehabilitate the animals. She has a real gift." Christopher gazed lovingly at his wife. "They use the pictures for brochures and presentations."

"The trick is not wanting to keep them all." Mickey shook her head. "I mean seriously; I have a hard time parting with them. We actually did end up adopting a couple of the more special horses. God used them to teach me some lessons I needed to learn during our first year here. I just couldn't say good-bye to them." She grinned.

Lizzy smiled and nodded. "I could never foster animals. I'd end up with a zoo."

Christopher finished his last bite, leaned back, and patted his stomach. "Delicious dinner as always, Mick. Thanks, sweetheart." He looked at Marshall. "You do know what this great meal means, though, don't you?"

Marshall smiled broadly. "Oh yes, I most certainly do. Do you want to wash or dry?"

Everyone at the table burst into laughter. "Ladies," Mickey said. "This not only means we don't have to clean up, this means we get to feed the horses. I don't suppose the girls would want to help, though." She pulled a serious face. "Barn chores are a lot of hard work."

"But we want to help..." Millie looked at her sister. "We can do it, can't we? We're strong. We can do it." Both girls looked concerned, fearing they might be left behind, but Mickey grinned at them.

"She was teasing you girls." Lizzy's eyes twinkled. "And besides, Mickey, I doubt you could keep them away."

"I know the feeling. I would have given just about anything to be around horses when I was their age. God has been so good to allow me to be surrounded by them now." She squeezed Christopher's hand, and they shared a loving glance.

~ * ~

Everyone gathered in the living room after the kitchen was cleaned and the animals fed for the night. Lizzy stood before the two-hundred-gallon reef aquarium in awe. "Mickey, this is incredible."

Mickey grinned from her place in the recliner. "That, my friend, is my pride and joy. Chris gave me the tank for my birthday a few years ago."

She rose and stood beside Lizzy. Both women gazed at the small slice of ocean life before them.

"What are those?" Lizzy pointed toward a cluster of what appeared to be brightly-colored flower-like growths. Their centers were orange, the outer part of each bloom was light blue, and each head was fringed with bright green sweeper tentacles.

"They're *Zoanthids* or *Zoas* for short. Aren't they gorgeous? They're a soft coral. When I bought them, there were only two heads on the frag plug. They've grown so well."

"What's a frag plug? Sorry, I'm completely ignorant about marine aquariums." Lizzy looked chagrined.

"It's a little round ceramic do-hickey with a plug on the other end. The pieces of coral are attached to the disc part with reef glue. You tuck the plug into holes between the rocks. Once the corals adjust to their new home, they begin to grow and expand." Mickey looked hopeful. "In time they should spread all over the rocks. Look over here. I have another variety that are lavender and green."

"How gorgeous." Lizzy took a step closer. "I love this pink flowery stuff." She pointed to another rock.

"That's called *Pulsing Xenia.*" Mickey laughed. "I have to pace myself and not get too many things in the tank. I could get carried away, but one thing I've learned with reef aquariums is you cannot rush things. You have to add creatures just one or two at a time and let everything acclimate for a couple of months. That's why there's only a few fish in there right now."

"Now those are clown fish, right?" Lizzy pointed at a pair of the distinctive orange and white fish swimming lazily together. "Is one of them named Nemo?"

"I thought about it." Mickey laughed. "But I decided to call them Ori and Nori. Had to stick with the Tolkien theme you know."

"Of course, I get it." Lizzy grinned. "I love those movies and books, too."

"We'll have to try to watch some of them while you're here. Plenty of time during the evenings when it's too cold to stay outside."

~ * ~

How could I have forgotten my shampoo? I had it right there on the counter ready to pack. Lizzy looked at the shower in the guest bathroom with dismay. She had a headache, brought on by the long trip the day before, and was in no mood for inconveniences. She saw a bottle of something called *Wen*®, but noted the bottle said cleansing conditioner. Knowing conditioner would leave her hair limp and lifeless, she tightened the belt on her robe and went in search of her sister. She knocked lightly on the door of the other guest room. "Deb," she whispered. "Do you have any shampoo? I can't believe I forgot mine."

Mickey was coming down the hallway and heard Lizzy's dilemma. "Did I forget to leave some *Wen®* in there for you?" she inquired.

Lizzy felt flustered. "Oh, yes, I mean no, you didn't forget. But I can't use conditioner in my hair. It'll be a limp, horrid mess." She laughed weakly, not wanting to hurt the feelings of her hostess.

Mickey grinned knowingly. "My friend, those were my exact thoughts the first time I tried *Wen®*, but I figured if the stuff didn't work, I could always send it back." She laughed and put a hand on her hip. "I fell in love with the stuff." "I think you'll be pleasantly surprised, but if you don't like it, we'll zip into town and buy you some shampoo."

Lizzy looked doubtful, but did not want to be rude. "Okay, I'll try it. Thanks, Mickey." She returned to her guest bathroom feeling a bit put out. *Great, now my hair is going to look horrid this whole trip. How could I have forgotten something as essential as shampoo?*

With a huff she got into the shower, dampened her hair, and grudgingly began to pump some *Wen Bamboo Green Tea Cleansing Conditioner®* into her hand. The delightful aroma immediately began to soothe her ruffled feelings. She applied the conditioner to her hair, massaged it in gently, and then rinsed with cool water as the instructions dictated. She pumped another portion into her hand, massaged the Wen® into her hair, and proceeded to finish with her shower before rinsing. *Mickey knows how to make a bath like a spa*, she thought with a smile, feeling much refreshed. *How could she have known Philosophy Cranberry Medley® is my favorite shower gel? She must be a mind reader.*

She finished her shower and dressed quickly, then went to scoop the hair from the shower drain. To her surprise, there was none to be seen. *Interesting*. Lizzy shook her head, then went to the vanity and picked up her comb.

The tool slid through her dark tresses with ease. *Hmmm. I usually lose some hairs when I pull the comb through.* She noticed another Wen product sitting on the vanity. *Hmm, Styling Crème. Apply one pump to wet hair. Okay, might as well go all the way.* She applied the product and proceeded to dry and style her hair.

When finished, she was flabbergasted. Her expectation of limp, greasy locks was banished. Her dark hair shone and contained just enough body to make her medium-length stacked bob look fabulous. Lizzy applied her makeup, all the while looking into the mirror with amazement. *I don't remember my hair ever coming together like this,* she thought with glee. *Wow. Just, wow!* She went downstairs and peeked into the kitchen. She cleared her throat, and Mickey turned from the bread dough she was preparing.

"I believe I owe you an apology." Lizzy laughed and pointed to her hair. "Honestly, I didn't believe you about Wen. I just knew I was going to look terrible and was pretty much pouting in the shower." She sat at the table, grinning from ear to ear. "First the scent got me, then the fact that there was no hair in the drain or in the comb."

"Told you." Mickey nodded with satisfaction. "Yes! Another *Wen*® convert."

"And how on earth did you know I love *Philosophy*®? You could run a spa here, you know."

"That was just a lucky guess." Mickey turned back to her dough and began separating the sticky mass into three loaf pans. "But we can't have a real spa until we have a masseuse. Believe me, after a long horseback ride, a massage would be so nice."

"You should look into that." Lizzy rose. "This would be a perfect resort. Now, what can I do to help with breakfast?"

~Eighteen~

"Mickey, this scenery is amazing." Lizzy enjoyed the gentle movement of her mount Fili while she, Mickey, and Deborah rode across the north pasture. She drew in a deep breath. The view and the peacefulness reminded her of her recent excursion to the apple orchard, with the added plus of riding a horse thrown in to enhance the experience.

"We love living here." Mickey reached to pat Kili's sleek black neck. "My dreams have come true."

Deborah looked around with a deep sigh. "This is just plain good for the soul. I'm glad we could have a 'girl ride'."

Mickey laughed. "I think Millie and Kate were disappointed they couldn't come along, but when Chris promised to give them riding lessons with the ponies, they were fine."

Deborah and Lizzy chuckled. "For sure," Lizzy said. "Their eyes were sparkling like Christmas lights."

Mickey nodded. "I hated not having them along today, but I felt better keeping them on ponies in the ring for a while until they learn how to ride."

"They're having the time of their lives." Deborah brushed a fly from her mount A. J's neck. "I told Marshall we'll have to line up riding lessons when we get back home."

Mickey nodded and tucked a strand of curly hair behind her ear. "I think it's good for young girls to have the opportunity to learn to handle a horse. There's something about knowing you can work with a horse that builds confidence like nothing else."

Lizzy slapped a fly away from Fili's ears. "Mickey, what kind of horses are these? They're gorgeous."

"Fili and Kili are my pride and joy." Mickey smiled gently. "They're part Friesian. I adopted them from a Friesian rescue when they were just youngsters."

"How amazing," Deborah said. "So you actually got to raise and train them? I remember in school you used to talk about wanting to work with horses. She was totally horse crazy, Lizzy. Completely. Even had horse sheets on her bunk."

Mickey nodded. "Affirmative. Was horse crazy. Still horse crazy." She crossed her eyes in a comical expression, and everyone laughed. "Best kind of crazy to be, though."

The women rode on, enjoying the gentle breeze and the beautiful fall colors around them. They made their way out of the pasture and up the mountain trail. After riding for about an hour, they emerged into a meadow dotted profusely with colorful wild flowers.

"This is my favorite place on earth," Mickey said while she halted Kili and dismounted. Deborah and Lizzy did the same. They tied the horses' lead ropes to nearby trees and gave each a few handfuls of grain. Within minutes, the animals were dozing happily in the sunshine.

Deborah and Lizzy spread their blanket nearby, and Mickey went to unpack the saddle bags. Soon a fine picnic was laid out before them. After thanking the Lord for the food, they dove in, enjoying the chicken salad on croissants, chips, apple slices, and turtle brownies for dessert.

Lizzy laid back on the blanket with a contented sigh. "I'm stuffed." She put her hands behind her head. "Mickey, I needed this, my friend."

Mickey smiled. "I know exactly what you mean. God has a way of getting rid of the mental cobwebs up here."

"I understand." Lizzy sat up once more and looked inquisitively at Mickey. "Do you mind sharing your story? I'd love to know more."

"I'd be happy to." Mickey looked out over the meadow thoughtfully. "Just to give you a little early history, my dad died before I was born. He was killed by a drunk driver so my mom raised me. They were wonderful Christian parents. Mom told me Dad prayed for me every day after they found out I was on the way.

"In spite of my parents' faith, I fought God most of my early years. I just didn't get spiritual things, and I think I was bitter because God allowed my dad to die. When I was fifteen, one of my best friends was killed in a car crash. That brought me up short." Mickey hugged her knees to her chest and looked at Lizzy. "Everything became so clear. If I'd been with her, I would have died, too, and I knew I would have gone to Hell. I knew I was a wretched sinner and needed a savior. I asked Jesus Christ to forgive my sins, and told Him I wanted to belong to Him. I finally accepted His gift of salvation offered for me when He died on the cross." Mickey's dug into her pocket for a tissue. "Sorry, I cry at the drop of a hat these days."

"Me, too," Deborah and Lizzy said in unison. The women laughed in understanding while they searched their own pockets.

"I went to a Christian college," Mickey continued, tucking a flyaway strand of hair behind her ear. "That's where I met Christopher. We literally ran into each other between classes the first day of our freshman year. I was afraid I was going to be late and was rushing to another building when I smacked right into him." The women giggled. "My books went everywhere and being the gentlemen he is, he immediately helped me gather them up." Mickey smiled fondly at the memory. "We were instant friends. We got along famously and saw eye to eye on just about every issue. You would have thought romance would be the next step, but for me love didn't happen. Even though he was truly my best friend, I just didn't have those kinds of warm and fuzzy feelings. Our relationship was more like a brother-sister thing."

Lizzy looked at her intently, wondering how they went from just friends, to the obviously loving relationship they shared now. "Go on, Mickey. This is fascinating."

"Unfortunately for him, Chris was totally in love with me and began to tell me so on a regular basis. I finally said I needed him to promise that he would not mention loving me again, because I hated having to hurt him. I told him we couldn't be friends, unless he made me that promise."

"Wow." Lizzy's mouth dropped open. "What did he say?"

"He was incredibly hurt. Then he got angry. I didn't talk to him for about a week. I was miserable, and he was despondent. He finally called and asked if we could meet. He told me he loved me with all his heart, but he would make the promise I required and would never mention it again."

Lizzy shook her head. "What an amazing guy. There aren't many who would do that."

Deborah, who already knew the story, nodded and grinned. "It was amazing. But wait, it gets better."

Mickey laughed, but then sobered. "During my junior year I met Lee, and there were instant fireworks. He was everything I'd ever wanted in a relationship, or so I thought. We began dating and at first, everything was great. Except he told me I could not associate with Christopher anymore. That was hard, but since I had a boyfriend, I knew things would have to change. Time went by, and Lee became more and more abusive and demanding. He constantly cut me down, both privately and in front of others. Nothing was ever good enough." Mickey's voice trailed off while she remembered the pain of those dark days.

Deborah patted Mickey's shoulder gently. "She was a mess, Lizzy. That's the year we were roommates. I saw this woman go from an outgoing, beautiful person, to one who was withdrawn, haggard, and miserable. One day, I came into our dorm room and found her in tears. That's when I told her your story, Lizzy, about when you finally got away from Carl. I knew I was sticking my nose into her personal business, but I couldn't handle seeing her so unhappy."

Mickey sniffed, then squeezed her friend's hand gently. "Thank the Lord you did, Deb. Lizzy, your story got my attention and made me realize my relationship with Lee was unhealthy. But I didn't break up with him until Christmas time." She gazed out over the meadow again, enjoying the breeze across her face. "He came to stay with Mom and me during Christmas break. I walked into the kitchen one day just in time to see him savagely kick our little poodle. I screamed for him to stop, and he grabbed me around the neck. He was going to strangle me, Lizzy. I was starting to choke when Mom came in and screamed for him to stop. He just grabbed me more tightly and threatened her as well, but she wasn't intimidated and was on the phone calling 9-1-1 in about two seconds. He tossed me to the floor, ran to his car, and drove off."

Lizzy snorted. "He and Carl could have been brothers. Did he bother you anymore after that?"

Mickey nodded. "Oh yes. He kept showing up at the door and calling saying he loved me, he was so sorry, he'd never do it again, *blah, blah, blah* ..." She looked at Lizzy. "I finally told him I'd report him for harassment and that worked. He didn't want anyone to think him anything but a saint and a fine, upstanding Christian man. He wouldn't take the chance that he might look bad in front of anyone. God used your story and your experience to give me the courage to break up."

Mickey looked puzzled for a moment. "When I look back, I don't know how I could have missed the signs. He was the quintessential abuser - controlling, wanted to cut me off from my friends and family, wanted me to look perfect all the time, even though I never pleased him..." her voice trailed off. In a moment, she continued. "I don't know why it took me so long to recognize his true character."

"It was the same with me, Mickey. Don't feel badly. I don't know why I didn't see the signs with Carl." Then Lizzy shook her head. "No. I did see them. I just didn't heed them. There were red flags everywhere, but he mesmerized and flattered me. I thought he was my last chance to get married, and I just ignored the signs."

"We've both lived and learned, haven't we?" Mickey asked gently. "But praise our dear Lord Jesus for His healing and restoration."

Lizzy nodded, her eyes moist. "I'm still experiencing that." She took a deep breath. "But please, continue. I want to hear about how you and Chris finally got together."

Mickey smiled broadly and put on her best southern accent. "Oh, my dear, it's the most 'especially awesome story. I can just see the headline: Southern Belle Meets

Maine Man and They Live Happily Ever After on Montana Ranch." The women laughed. "In reality, it wasn't quite that simple." She sobered. "My mom passed away about eight years after I graduated from college. I was devastated both personally and financially. She'd been sick for a long time. Chris came along and proposed a marriage of convenience."

"No way." Lizzy looked at her in amazement. "Seriously? In this day and age?" Deborah laughed at Lizzy's expression.

"Yes, seriously," Mickey said with a wry grin. "But God knew just what I needed. He worked in my heart through Chris's love, acceptance, and friendship, and He eventually exposed my problem. I never worked through the bitterness I held onto about Lee and didn't understand my need to forgive. God brought things to a head one day when I was cleaning stalls and "Hello My Name Is" by Matthew West came up on my playlist. I felt like all the walls came down, and I finally saw my sin. I confessed my bitterness to the Lord and asked Him to help me forgive Lee." She grinned. "I also realized I loved Chris madly. I don't know when my feelings changed. I think I'd loved him for a long time but was afraid to admit it. For some reason, I equated love with abuse and thought if I loved him, he would turn abusive."

The wind began to pick up and the ladies quickly packed away the picnic garbage. "Looks like we might have a storm coming. We'd better head back," Mickey said. They folded up the blanket and returned to the horses.

While they rode back down the mountain trail, Mickey finished her story. "We still didn't end up together right away after that, though. Some crazy stuff happened, and I thought he didn't love me anymore. But now, looking back, I can plainly see I needed the time to depend on God alone. He still had things to teach me, and I would have never learned those lessons if I hadn't gone through that difficult time."

The women rode in silence until they reached the gate to the north pasture. Lizzy rode through on Fili, then asked,

"So you and Christopher are good now? I mean, you surely do seem to be totally in love with each other."

"Oh yes." Mickey looked dreamily out over the pasture toward the house she shared with her husband. "We are totally and completely in love. God allowed me to marry my best friend and even though things were a bit precarious for a while, it was worth every moment. I'm amazed how God can take our mistakes and bad decisions and use them to mold and make us into something good."

~ * ~

The Nikon™ clicked repeatedly while Christopher snapped shot after shot. Looking through the view finder, his breath caught as Mickey's smiling face filled the frame of his zoom lens. Just in time, he reminded himself to get a few shots of Lizzy and Deborah as well while the horses cantered through the tall pasture grass toward the barnyard. The women were laughing joyously, clearly enjoying the moment. Christopher artfully captured close-ups and long-range shots.

"Did you get some good ones?" Marshall lounged against a fence post with his hands in his jeans pockets.

"I think so." Christopher grinned. "Although, I'm sorry, man, but I had to remind myself to get shots of everyone, and not just my wife."

"No apology necessary, I assure you." Marshall laughed, but nodded in understanding. "If I could take a decent picture, I'd be totally focused on my Deb, that's for sure."

Christopher lowered his camera and looked at Marshall. "Hey, I'd be happy to get some family shots of you guys while you're here. The girls are doing well on the ponies. We could get some great shots of them riding, too."

"That would be awesome, Chris. Deb is our family's shutterbug, but of course that means she's not usually in the pictures. I'd love some of all of us."

The horses slowed to a stop at the gate, and Christopher circled around them while he took a few more shots. "What are you up to, Christopher Gordon?" Mickey dismounted Kili and put a hand on her hip. The sparkle in her eyes, however, gave away her good humor.

"Why, honey, you know I only have a few pictures of you." Christopher's eyes glinted with mirth.

Mickey burst into laughter. "Ladies, my fine, award-winning wildlife photographer husband has now added people pictures to his repertoire." She took on a dry tone. "Problem is, they're mostly of yours truly. To the tune of about ten gigs on the computer."

Lizzy dismounted Fili and looked at Mickey in disbelief.

"I'm serious." Mickey unlatched the gate to allow Deborah and Lizzy to walk through leading A.J. and Fili. She followed with Kili and closed the gate behind her. "Used to be about fifteen gigs," she whispered conspiratorially, "But I got on the computer one night and deleted the ones I hated."

Lizzy and Deborah snickered. "I would have done the exact same thing," Deborah said while nodding in affirmation.

"So that explains the sudden expansion of storage space." Christopher came up behind Mickey and grabbed her in a hug. She laughed when Kili turned his head and blew disapprovingly through his nostrils.

Lizzy laughed outwardly, but inside she felt a stab of pain. *They are so in love*, she thought wistfully. *I can't imagine having that kind of relationship*. She gave Fili a pat while the group headed to the barn, then clipped cross ties to the horse's halters. She allowed the happy banter to flow around her while she removed Fili's saddle and bridle, but she did not join in. *How can I feel so cynical about romance, but then wish a good man would come along for me? How would I even begin to trust again? I can't imagine tolerating a man touching me again, and yet I feel such yearning watching*

Chris and Mickey. How can my feelings be polar opposites and yet both be so strong?

She carried the saddle, blanket, and bridle to the tack room and placed them on their racks. She was deep in thought while she returned to Fili, clipped a lead rope to his halter, and began to walk him up and down the barn passageway to cool him down. Mickey and Deborah noticed she'd become quiet but wisely asked no questions, allowing her to ponder her thoughts. Soon Millie and Kate descended upon them, eager to share the adventures of pony rides in the ring.

~ * ~

The days passed far too swiftly for Lizzy. This time away in such a beautiful place was a balm to her soul. She took several walks alone up the long drive and down the road, spending time praising her Lord and meditating on His goodness to her.

The day before they were to leave, Mickey and Lizzy sat in Adirondack chairs on the back deck enjoying the view of the horses grazing and the mountains beyond the pastures. Lizzy shared her complete story with Mickey, who sat silently, trying to absorb what she heard. "Oh, Lizzy, I had no idea how evil he was." Mickey's expression was sad. "When Deb told me a little about you during our college days, she didn't give me all the details. And now he's been convicted of murder. Wow." She shook her head and tears formed.

Lizzy nodded. "He is evil and so cruel. I've had such a hard time dealing with Marcie's death. I mean, I feel like somehow, I should have been able to do something. I knew Carl was in a relationship with someone. A friend of hers called me once, asking about him, and I told her some of the things he did to me. I wish I could have stopped Marcie from marrying him."

Mickey nodded in understanding. "I can see how you would feel that way, but I also don't see how there's anything more you could have done. I never heard anything more about Lee after college, so I have no idea if he is married and torturing some other poor woman. If I had the chance to warn someone, I certainly would, but the opportunity has never arisen." She tucked a strand of hair behind one ear and raised her cup of tea to take a sip. Then she chuckled. "I was never much of a hot tea drinker until I started watching *Downton Abbey*. Now I'm hooked."

"Me, too." Lizzy laughed. "I've done the same thing. Now I have a cupboard full of different kinds of tea. I even named my Sheltie Downton."

"Great name, especially for a Sheltie." Mickey grinned, then suddenly sat straight up, her face alight with inspiration. "Lizzy, I just had a thought. Keep yourself open to opportunities to share your story. The Lord might bring something along. Domestic violence is so widespread these days. You might just have the chance to warn other people by telling them what you went through. Who knows how the Lord might use you."

Lizzy sipped her tea thoughtfully, then wrapped her chilly hands around the warm sides of the mug. "That's a great idea. God taught me so much during the years since I left Carl. In fact, I really thought I was over that time until I sat in on his trial. Hearing of his cruelty to Marcie brought everything back big time. I finally realized forgiveness is not just a one-time thing."

She looked out toward the pasture, watching Fili and Kili dancing around in a sudden game of horsey tag. "I was in an orchard picking apples, when the thought hit me. Forgiveness is like the legal term *nolle prosequi*."

Mickey looked at her questioningly. "*Nolle* what?"

"*Nolle prosequi*. It's a Latin term and means the prosecutor is no longer going to pursue prosecution of the case. At work, we say a case is *nol prossed* when it's dismissed for various reasons. So basically ..."

Mickey interrupted and looked at her excitedly, her eyes bright with understanding. "I get it! You've dropped the case. You're no longer requiring payment for the wrongs committed against you. I love it. What a perfect description."

"I thought so, too. For some reason, thinking of Carl's crimes against me as being *nol prossed* has enabled me to let go more easily. God has been so good to remind me of the 'status of the case' every time the horrible memories come back. And I keep verses handy on note cards to remind me of God's love."

Mickey grinned. "Been there, done that, got the t-shirt." She laughed. "My verses got me through those horrible days when I thought Chris didn't love me anymore."

The women sighed contentedly while they watched the sun begin to set. Christopher came out and leaned down to give Mickey a kiss. "Whatcha doing?"

"Oh, just talking and fellowshipping. God is so good." Mickey squeezed his hand gently. "Where are Marshall, Deb, and the girls?"

"They went for a walk, but they just got back. Why don't we all come out here to enjoy the sunset before dinner?"

Lizzy sighed. "That would be the perfect end to the perfect vacation. Seriously you guys, this has been just what I needed. Thank you so much for inviting us."

"We're so glad you could come." Christopher grinned. "I think I speak for both of us when I say we hope you'll come again."

Mickey nodded. "You'd jolly well better come again. I've so enjoyed having you all here."

Christopher grinned. "It's settled, then." He turned to go inside. "I'll go let the others know where we are." Mickey and Lizzy found chairs for everyone. Clouds were scattered here and there and reflected the rays of the setting sun while it slowly disappeared behind the craggy mountain peaks. The group sat in awe of God's spectacular light display. When they began to shiver despite their coats, they opted to go inside and start supper.

The group sat at the table an hour later. "I remember you saying you've been rehabilitating horses here." Marshall took a crescent roll, then passed the basket to Deborah. "But Chris, you mentioned something the other day about taking the ranch in another direction. What are your thoughts?"

Christopher nodded while he helped himself to a scoop of veggie casserole. "We still want to continue our work with the horses, but we're thinking and praying about expanding a bit. Mickey and I went out to Oregon last year to visit a youth ranch. The work those folks are doing is amazing. They're helping animals and troubled youth, and we were really inspired. We're praying about maybe doing something similar with the C & M."

"You guys have got to read Kim Meeder's books." Mickey smiled. "She and her husband are the folks who started the ranch. But keep a box of tissues handy. She is an amazing author and tells the stories of the many lives who have been touched. What's so cool is how the abused and hurting animals end up helping abused and hurting people." Her eyes misted over, and she laughed. "See," she said, grabbing her napkin. "I cry just thinking about them."

Once the kitchen was put in order after dinner, Marshall, Christopher, and the girls went to the living room to start a game of Monopoly™. Mickey, Lizzy, and Deborah went to the barn to feed the horses.

When all the animals were contentedly munching their oats, Mickey looked at Lizzy and Deborah. "Lizzy, I feel such a need to pray for you right now. Let's talk to God."

The women joined hands in the middle of the aisle and Mickey began. "Lord, I feel in my bones You have something amazing in store for Lizzy. Help her as she continues to heal from the past. Help her to run to You when the dark thoughts and memories threaten to overwhelm her. Give her Your grace. Lead her to opportunities to share Your love with others, especially those who may have gone through similar ordeals. "Thank You, Father, for Your love. Thank You, because of Jesus, we can actually forgive those who have hurt us and despitefully used us. Bless Lizzy more than she could possibly imagine. In Jesus precious name I pray, amen."

Lizzy felt tears squeezing from the corners of her eyes when Mickey finished her prayer. The kindness and love of her newfound friend touched her deeply.

"Dear Lord, thank You," Lizzy prayed softly. "Thank You for rescuing me from that evil, wicked man. Thank You for my amazing family. Thank You for using the ladies in my office to aid in the healing of my heart and soul. Thank You for bringing me to where I am today. Oh, Father God ..." Lizzy's voice choked, and she dropped her sister's hand to snatch a tissue from her coat pocket. In a moment, she continued. "Oh my precious Heavenly Father, You have blessed me beyond measure. Thank You for what You showed me during Carl's trial. Thank You for helping me to let go of the past and move forward. Help me, Father, to be open to Your leading. Use what Carl intended for evil, for Your good. Work through me, Father God, to minister to others. Amen."

By this time, Deborah was crying as well. "Dearest Lord Jesus," she prayed, sniffing while she wiped her eyes and nose with a tissue. "Thank You for saving my precious sister. Thank You for rescuing her and protecting her. Thank You she got away from Carl when she did. Thank You that her story helped our dear friend Mickey to avoid a life of pain and heartache. Thank You for all you've done in Lizzy's life, and I pray You will continue to do a good work in her. Use her for Your glory, and may many lives be touched by her story of Your protection and grace. Amen."

The women shared a tearful group hug, then checked on the horses one last time before turning off the lights and closing the barn door. A brilliant full moon shone down on them while they started up the path toward the house.

"Lizzy, I can't wait to see what God has in store for you." Mickey giggled. "I'm so excited I can almost taste it."

"I'm catching your enthusiasm, my friend." Lizzy looked up at the velvety night sky, scattered with stars as far as the eye could see. "God is so vast. So amazing. I find myself looking forward to the future like never before. Thank you, Mickey. And thank you, Deb, for introducing us. I feel like I have two sisters now."

The women joined arms and laughed delightedly while they returned to the comfort of the warm house.

~ * ~

Later in the evening, Lizzy went to her room and grabbed her iPad. “Mickey,” she called while she came back downstairs and plopped down on the couch. “What are the names of those books you recommended? I want to buy them now so I can read them on the plane.”

Mickey gave her the titles and Lizzy went to Amazon.com. With a few taps, she downloaded the books to her Kindle app. “Awesome. Thanks, Mickey. I know I’m going to enjoy these. And I’ll be praying about your thoughts for the C & M.” She smiled gently. “I know God can use this wonderful place just like He’s used it in my life this week. The C & M has been a balm for my mind and soul.”

The Monopoly™ players were in full swing at the game table, and Marshall had just purchased Park Place, when he stopped, the dice still in his hand. “Everybody, I don’t mean to embarrass her, but I feel the strongest need to pray for Lizzy right now. Can we join hands?” Lizzy, Deborah, and Mickey began to chuckle, and Marshall looked at them quizzically. “What?”

Deborah went to stand behind him and put her hands lovingly on his shoulders. “Great minds do indeed think alike, hon. We just had a prayer-time for Lizzy out in the barn.” She smiled, and Marshall and Christopher laughed as well. “But Marshall, if you feel that way, let’s pray again, together. You, too, girls.” Deborah looked expectantly at Millie and Kate. “Shall we pray for Aunt Lizzy, girls?”

“Yes, mama.” Millie rose and went to sit beside Lizzy. Kate followed and sat on her other side.

The group surrounded Lizzy and joined hands. “Father, we come before You on behalf of our dear sister, Lizzy,” Marshall prayed. “I think we’re all feeling that You are going to do something amazing in her life. Lead her and guide her. We thank You for rescuing her from that evil man, and for the healing You’ve brought in her life. Continue to minster to her heart and soul, Father, and use her for Your glory and to help others."

Everyone said a prayer, even Millie and Kate, which made Lizzy feel as if her heart might explode with emotion. "Thank you all, so much." She wiped away tears. "Now you've got me excited to see what God has in store. The fact that He's brought me this far is nothing short of a miracle. Only God could make a person who felt lower than dirt, feel as if she is now a butterfly released from her cocoon. To God be the glory."

~ * ~

The following morning, hugs were shared all around when the newfound friends parted at the airport. Lizzy tearfully promised she would visit again, and Mickey hugged her tightly. "Email me, okay, Lizzy? We have to stay in touch."

"Oh, I will. You can count on it. And we'll stay up-to-date on Facebook, too." Wiping away tears, Lizzy followed her family toward security.

Once the first leg of the flight was underway, Lizzy opened her iPad and tapped the Kindle app. *Mickey was right*, she thought when she got halfway through chapter one of *Hope Rising*. *I'll need tissues for sure*. Lizzy read story after story of God's healing power, and her heart was stirred. She stopped halfway through and prayed inwardly. *Dear Lord, use me. Use me as You are using the folks out at Crystal Peaks Youth Ranch. Bring opportunities to share my story with those who need to hear. Help me to share the wonderful truth that the abused do not have to be victims forever, thanks to Your amazing healing power and love. Use me, Lord. Use me for your glory.*

~Nineteen~

Lizzy turned on her computer and scratched Watson under his chin while she waited for the machine to boot up. The massive cat lay sprawled in front of her monitor, purring and kneading his front paws. Mickey stroked his gray tabby fur and gave him a kiss on the head. “Okay, baby boy, gotta write to Mickey. Now you let me type.” The cat uttered a soft chirp, purring even louder. Lizzy grinned, double clicked to open Outlook, and began a new email.

Hi, Mickey. Hope you and Chris are well. The time has completely flown by. It feels like the Thanksgiving, Christmas, and New Year celebrations were all a blur this year. I’m keeping your enthusiasm in the forefront of my mind, though. God used you and Christopher to minister to me in such a special way, so I’m looking for opportunities to minister also. I want to be ready when God opens up situations where I can pay it forward.

Mickey replied later in the evening.

You’re open to God’s leading, and I know He will bring just the right opportunities for you. Just don’t forget to write and tell me everything when He does.

~ * ~

“Lizzy, one of the Grand Jurors needs to see you.” Justine looked at her with concern. “She seems really upset.” Lizzy had just verified all the Grand Jurors were present and faxed the attendance sheet to the accounting office to ensure they would be paid for their service. She retrieved the paperwork from the fax machine and hurried to the front of the office.

The young woman’s tears brimmed in her eyes, and her expression was nervous. “I’m so sorry, Ms. Godfrey. I just don’t know if I can work today.” Her voice caught while sobs started to choke her.

"Oh, dear. Sabrina, I'm so sorry. Can I help you in some way? Do you need to talk? There's a conference room just down the hall."

"That would be awesome."

Lizzy came through the secured door to stand beside the slender young woman. She led Sabrina to the unoccupied room, and they sat at a table. She noticed a small box on a stand by the door. "Let me get you a tissue, Sabrina," she said gently. She returned to sit beside the sobbing woman. "What happened?"

"My boyfriend has been so mean lately and today before I came here, he grabbed my hair and yanked so hard, he pulled out a handful." She turned her head, and Lizzy could plainly see the damage. "He's angry because I want to go to college. He wants me to stay here and work in a fast-food restaurant. He says I just want to go to college because I think I'm better than him. I sent in an application to a four-year university a couple states away and my acceptance arrived yesterday." Sabrina's tears intensified, and her dark hair fell in a curtain around her head. "He went crazy when he found the letter this morning on the counter. He grabbed me by the hair and dragged me to the door. He threw me out. Said I was a filthy little traitor. He called me a lot worse things than that, too. Then he dragged me back in, lit a cigarette, and started burning my arm." She pulled up her sleeve to reveal numerous round burns.

Lizzy knew, with absolute clarity, this was God's moment for her to minister. "Sabrina, you need to get away from him. Now." Her voice was firm. "I escaped an abusive man, and I promise you, they do not get better. They only get worse." Sabrina's sobs began to abate, and she looked at Lizzy intently. "The ex tied me to a tree and drove his truck at me for hours. Then he left me tied up all night."

"Oh my word." Sabrina looked at her in horror.

"It gets worse." Lizzy looked at her, willing the woman to get a sense of how serious this was. "I got away, but his second wife wasn't so fortunate. He murdered her and is now serving a life sentence. Sabrina, you need to get out, and you need to get out now."

The young woman's face was a study in confusion and fear. Lizzy could see the gravity of her present situation dawning on her. "First we need to get you to a doctor to look at those burns. But how else can I help you, Sabrina? Do you have a place to go?"

"Yes, I can go back to my parent's house. They never liked Freddie anyway. They'll be glad I'm leaving him."

"Good. Now, what about logistics? Does Freddie work? If so, it would be best if you got your belongings and were gone before he comes home. If not, go without your things. It's only stuff that can be replaced - you can't."

"He works second shift. He's usually left the apartment by the time I get back on these Grand Jury meeting days."

"Good." Lizzy rose. "Let's go back to the office. We need to contact the judge and get his official permission to excuse you from today's meeting. Then we'll talk to my supervisor about getting you to the hospital. We'll also talk to the deputies downstairs and see how they recommend we get your things from the apartment."

Sabrina rose shakily and reached to give Lizzy a hug. "Thank you, Ms. Godfrey. I don't know what I would have done if you hadn't been here today."

Lizzy hugged her back gently. "I'm so glad I could help. And please, call me Lizzy."

They returned to the records office where Sandra contacted security. Lizzy called the judge, who gave permission for Sabrina to be excused. The young woman was taken to the ER where her burns were treated. Lizzy used annual leave so she could stay with her for the rest of the day. When they were sure Freddie would have left for work, they called the deputy who volunteered to escort them to the apartment to gather Sabrina's things.

Once Sabrina was safely settled in her parent's house that evening, Lizzy returned to her own home. "It's been quite a day, Mom." She threw her purse on the kitchen table and greeted Nugget and Downton, who were bouncing up and down in excitement. She sat down with a deep sigh and shared Sabrina's story. She and Rose prayed together for the young woman's safety. Later that same week, Sabrina phoned to report that Freddie had called her in tears, repentant and begging her to come back. He vowed to follow her wherever she went until she returned to him.

Lizzy advised her to stay strong and to get a restraining order. "Be sure you don't give him any details about where you'll be living once you leave for college," she added. "Don't talk to him anymore. Block him from your phone, email, and social media accounts." Her voice broke for a moment. "You can't let him trick you into going back. And the best way to accomplish that is to have no communication with him."

Sabrina agreed. "Thank you again, Lizzy. I don't know if I would have had the strength to do this if it hadn't been for you. Thank God for you, Lizzy. Most people don't seem to care. You're different. In a good way, I mean."

"It's all because of the love of Jesus and what He's done in my heart. I'm nothing on my own. Any good comes directly from Him."

"I used to be a Christian when I was a kid." Sabrina reflected quietly for a moment before continuing. "I think I need to get back to that. I need some religion in my life."

"Oh, Sabrina, Christianity is a personal relationship with Jesus Christ, which is so much more than just religion. He has forgiven my sin and the wickedness that would have kept me away from God forever. My life would be nothing without His love and grace."

"You've given me a lot to think about," Sabrina said softly. "Thank you again."

"Call if you need me, okay? Any time at all. And keep me posted on how things are going, will you?"

"I will. Good-bye, Lizzy."

Lizzy tapped the phone off and sat back with a deep sigh. *Lord, this has been amazing. You used me. You really did use me to help someone. Wow ...* She sat deep in thought for a moment, then went to her desk and booted up her computer. *I've got to email Mickey and Deb and ask them to pray for Sabrina.*

~ * ~

Music played softly in the background while Lizzy found a seat in the sanctuary. She settled in and pulled a small container of Philosophy™ hand lotion from her purse. *Mm, I love that Fresh Cream scent.* She rubbed the lotion in, then opened her iPad. Minutes later, Lizzy looked up when someone came into her row.

"Are these seats saved?" The question came from a handsome man with a gentle expression.

"Oh, no. You're fine. I'm not saving them."

He took a seat at the end of the row, and Lizzy returned to the Kindle book she was reading. She always spent Sunday mornings before church this way. Since Rose could no longer attend services, Lizzy felt a bit silly just sitting there looking around, waiting for the service to begin. Though she had attended the church for a while, she still did not know many people. Tapping the screen back on, she stared at the words but did not read them. *He's kind of cute. I wonder if he has a wedding ring.* She wanted to steal another glance but didn't dare. She found she had a hard time returning to the book and concentrating on the service. When church was over, Lizzy glanced up after gathering her belongings and immediately made eye contact with the man. "Have a good week," she said with a friendly smile.

"You, too."

No ring. Lizzy smiled. *He has such friendly eyes.* Lizzy made her way out the door and into the parking lot. *Interesting ...*

~ * ~

"Guess what?" Lizzy looked at Denae with a twinkle in her eye. She opened her lunch bag and put her sandwich on the break room table. "I met someone interesting at church."

"Do tell." Denae looked up from her Caesar salad. "C'mon. Details, girl. I need details."

"He looks like he's at least 5'10 or 5'11, and he has blonde hair." Lizzy smiled. "He has such friendly eyes."

"Have you talked to him?" Denae took a bite of salad and looked at Lizzy pointedly.

The television blared away with an early afternoon soap drama. Two other women watched with rapt attention and paid Lizzy and Denae no attention. Nevertheless, Lizzy lowered her voice a bit. "Just to say 'good-morning' and 'have a good week' after the service." Lizzy's face clouded. "I don't know, though. I've seen him now for several weeks, but he hasn't made any kind of effort to talk to me, other than the usual pleasantries. I mean, I'm sitting there alone just reading on my iPad."

"Maybe he doesn't want to disturb you." Denae looked thoughtful. "I probably wouldn't talk to someone who was reading or texting. I'd feel like I was interrupting."

"But I feel like an idiot sitting there looking around. I don't know many people there yet, and since Mom can't get out to services anymore, I don't usually have anyone to talk to. Besides, the fact remains, if he was interested, he would make an effort. He could be married and just doesn't wear a ring. Or he may have a girlfriend."

"True." Denae munched on a cracker, then continued. "I still think you should try not reading and see what happens."

Lizzy sighed. "Okay but I'm going to feel like a moron. Just sayin'."

"No, you shouldn't feel that way. Lots of people just sit and wait for the service to start." Denae smiled.

Lizzy finished her sandwich and opened her cup of black cherry Greek yogurt.

"We shall see what happens, oh wise one," she said with a smile.

~ * ~

The next Monday Lizzy and Denae sat in the break room for lunch. After several minutes of chit-chat, Denae sat upright. “Hey, what happened Sunday? How did it go?”

Lizzy looked disgusted. “Nothing happened that’s what. Get this - he didn’t even sit on the same row as me this time.” Lizzy brooded silently for a moment, and Denae got up to retrieve her Lean Cuisine from the microwave. “You know, Denae, I think I just need to forget it. I mean, I tried things your way. I didn’t even open my iPad until the service started. It’s clear he’s not interested.”

Lizzy took a bite of her pickle spear and chewed thoughtfully. Denae sat down across from her and shrugged. “I guess so, but ...”

Lizzy interrupted. “Seriously. I remember someone saying once, if a guy really wants to get to know you, he will find a way to make contact. If he doesn’t, he’s not interested. Period.”

Denae nodded slowly. “That’s true. I just have a hard time believing every single guy isn’t camped out on your doorstep.” She smiled and took a bite of chicken and rice.

Lizzy grinned. “If a guy did that, I’d be calling the law, Denae.”

The women giggled. “It’s really all right, though.” Lizzy was pragmatic. “Clearly, it’s not God’s will and that’s okay. I only want His best for me.”

“You’re right of course. But I still say Mr. What’s-his-name at church is missing out big time.”

“Thank you, Denae. You’re so sweet.”

The ladies finished their lunches amid much laughter and fun as the conversation turned to lighter subjects.

~ * ~

February flew by, and Lizzy couldn’t remember when the office had been so busy. The man at church was all but forgotten. Lizzy put in more late nights during long trials than she had during her whole career in circuit records. The paperwork load in the office seemed to have increased ten-fold, and everyone felt the pressure. Lizzy started attending the evening church service on Sundays, just to allow time to catch up on her rest.

The first Saturday in March, Lizzy stretched lazily and looked at the clock. *I love Saturdays. Nothing so fine as sleeping 'til I wake up on my own.* She crawled from underneath the comforter and put on her robe. Nugget and Downton rushed down the bedside pet steps, eager to go outside.

"Okay, okay. Give me a second, kids." Lizzy yawned widely. Sherlock and Watson eyed her from the bed, but showed no signs of budging from their cozy abode.

Lizzy grabbed a light jacket and attached leashes to the dog's collars. After exploring the yard and taking care of business, they all returned to the house. Rose, who was reading in her bedroom, called a good morning and both dogs rushed in to greet her.

"Morning, Mom," Lizzy replied. "I think I'll make pancakes. Do you want some?"

"Sure, honey. Sounds great."

After a leisurely breakfast together, Lizzy showered and dressed. She spent the day cleaning, giving the dogs a bath, and enjoying a day off from the hectic pace of the office. Thankfully, the workload had finally begun to slow a bit, and she planned to attend her favorite early church service again.

While Lizzy prepared her hair and makeup the next morning, she smiled with contentment. *Life is good. Thank You, Lord. I would be perfectly happy if nothing ever changed. Thank You for safety and contentment.* She bade Rose good-bye and headed for Ripon Falls Community Church, her heart full of thankfulness and praise. She entered the sanctuary and sat in her usual spot near the back. *Now what was I reading last week?* She opened her iPad and tapped the *Kindle* app. *Oh right. So long Insecurity by Beth Moore.* Lizzy settled in to read until the service began.

She glanced up a few moments later when someone entered the other end of the row. *It's him.* Lizzy smiled briefly and said, "Good morning".

"Good morning. I'm Cooper." The man looked at her with a friendly expression.

"I'm Elizabeth. Nice to meet you." Lizzy extended her hand to shake his. They proceeded to chat until the lights dimmed, signaling the service was about to begin.

Hmmm. This is an interesting turn of events. Lizzy smiled to herself as she joined in with the singing. *Lord, are You just letting me know I certainly don't have everything all figured out?*

While she exited the sanctuary after the service concluded, Cooper came up beside her. "I'd love to hear more about you," he said hesitantly. "Would you like to get together for coffee or something sometime?"

Lizzy smiled. "Sure. That would be great." She walked to her car feeling amazed. *Wow! Just, wow!*

She pulled out of the parking lot and laughed out loud. *I never gave him any contact information. Good grief, I'm no good at this.* She shrugged. *Guess it'll just have to wait until next week.* She drove home with a grin on her face, feeling uplifted and hopeful.

~ * ~

The next Sunday dawned cloudy and cold, proving the unpredictability of March in the south. Knowing the church would be cool, Lizzy decided to wear her leather jacket, mock turtleneck, corduroys, and boots. She sat in her usual spot and opened her iPad, but within minutes, Cooper came in and sat one chair away from her. She greeted him with a smile.

After the usual pleasantries, Cooper said, "Hey, I'd still like to get together, but I don't even know your last name."

"I know, Cooper. I was thinking the same thing. My last name is Godfrey. And what's yours?"

"Lindsey. Do you have email?"

"Sure." Lizzy grabbed her purse and took out a pen. "Here, I'll write the info on your bulletin."

He handed her the pamphlet, and she scribbled out her email address. He then did the same for her. "So where do you work, Cooper?"

"I'm the manager of a privately owned office-supply store. Oh, and by the way, my friends call me Coop." He grinned. "And no cracks about chicken coops either."

Lizzy laughed out loud. "Okay, Coop, no jokes."

"How about you, Elizabeth, where do you work?"

"I'm an Administrative Assistant in the circuit court records office. We're the keeper of the high court criminal records." She briefly thought of telling him her friends called her Lizzy, but something held her back.

He nodded. "I'll bet that's interesting work."

"Oh for sure. I'm in court a lot, so I never know what I'll see from one day to the next."

The conversation continued, and Lizzy asked more questions. She learned he had never been married and was originally from Vermont. He seemed content to share about himself, and Lizzy had the passing thought that she was acting more the interviewer than usual. The service began, interrupting their talk. Lizzy easily fixed her concentration on the message of the morning and was still deep in thought while she rose to leave. Coop followed her to the lobby.

"I guess probably weekends would be the best time to get together?" he asked.

Lizzy brought herself back to the present. "Yes. I'm usually exhausted after a day at work. Saturday afternoon would work best for me. I like to sleep in Saturday mornings. The dogs and cats and I all pile in together." She grinned.

A flicker of something Lizzy couldn't quite identify flashed in his eyes at the mention of the animals, but just as quickly the look disappeared. He walked her to her car and opened the door for her. Coop gave her a warm smile. "I'll email you."

"Okay. Thanks, Coop. See you later."

Lizzy pulled out and drove away feeling quite surprised. *After all this time, someone is actually interested in me*. She smiled slightly and reached to turn up the heat. The car was still chilly. *Weird, though. I don't really feel as excited as I thought I would. He seems nice, though.* Then she frowned. *I don't think he likes animals, and that would be a definite deal breaker.* She pulled to a stop at an intersection and watched the traffic thoughtfully. *I'll check his record on-line before I agree to meet him anywhere. But I'm sure everything will turn out fine. Maybe I'm wrong about his feelings on animals.*

Lizzy changed into her comfortable jeans and a sweatshirt when she got home, then curled up in the recliner and pulled out her iPad. *Now, let's check out Mr. Lindsey.* She taped *Safari* and entered the site address for the county's public criminal records search. She then entered his name and tapped the *search* key. A slight smile touched her lips while she waited. *So cool to actually have a potential guy friend. This could be a lot of fun.*

When the search results came up, she scrolled down and stopped. The site listed six charges under his name, all of which were heard in the higher court. A sick feeling entered her stomach, and her hands began to shake. She tapped the first charge. *Aggravated Sexual Assault* was revealed on the *Charges* screen.

Lizzy swallowed slowly, disappointment and revulsion flooding her mind. *Oh no.* She proceeded to examine the other five charges and was horrified to discover all were for sexual assaults. The disposition screens indicated he pled guilty to each charge. Each had been adjudicated within the last three years. The final charge placed him on the Sex Offender Registry.

While she examined the last charge, her iPad whistled indicating an incoming email. There was a message from Cooper Lindsey.

Hi, Elizabeth - great service today wasn't it?
That message was one of Pastor Williams' best.
I'm looking forward to seeing you.
Please respond so I know I have the right address.
Fondly, Coop.

Lizzy deleted the email without a second thought and felt as though she might be sick. *This is disgusting. Oh dear Lord, thank You for protecting me. Thank You, Father.* She sat for many moments, staring at the wall and contemplating the horrors of what might have happened had she not been warned. She went to the kitchen to tell Rose. Both praised the Lord for His protection. "I mean, I hope he's attending church because he has repented and is trying travel the right path," Lizzy said sadly. "But how could I know for sure?"

"You can't, honey. He could also be a predator looking for his next victim. You just can't be too careful." Rose hugged her daughter tightly. "I'm so proud of you. You are a woman who allows the Lord to lead and guide her."

Lizzy returned her mother's hug, then pulled away. "But Mom, why me? Why would a pervert like that think I would want him? Why on earth me? What's wrong with me? I'm horrified, because he apparently thought I'd be interested."

"Sweetheart, you have a beautiful loving and accepting manner. There's nothing wrong with you." Rose took a pancake turner and deftly flipped over the two pieces of hamburger cooking in the skillet on the stove.

"Good grief, Mom. I told him I work in the circuit court records office. I told him I work with <u>criminal</u> records, and he didn't even flinch. In fact, he even commented about the interesting work." Lizzy took a bag of fries from the freezer.

"Oh my." Rose thought for a moment. "That is scary. Thank the Lord for His protection."

"You know what was really strange? I didn't talk much about myself during our conversations. A little, but you know me, I'm usually an open book. I truly believe God held my tongue. I'm so glad I didn't share much about myself."

"Me, too. Did you answer the email?"

"No. I deleted it. But I'm going to respond to him from my work email. I'll tell him I did a background check and am not comfortable with what I found. I'll let him know I don't want any further contact." Lizzy put the fries in the toaster oven to brown.

"That's smart. Otherwise, he might just think he got the wrong email address."

"My thoughts exactly." Lizzy hugged her mother again. "Thanks, Mom. I love you."

"I love you, too, honey."

~ * ~

The next Sunday, Lizzy walked to her car after the mid-morning service feeling full of confusion. She drove home thoughtfully, trying to sort out her mixed feelings. *On the one hand, I know God protected me from Coop. But on the opposite side of the spectrum, what if he was truly repentant? Should I have befriended him? Did I fail to show the love of Christ because his past concerned me? Haven't I felt that people would hold my past against me and wish they wouldn't? What if he was hurting and broken, and my rejection drives him away from God?*

Throughout the next two weeks, the issues continued to perplex her and came to mind often. She and Rose were relaxing Saturday afternoon after a thorough housecleaning, when the doorbell rang. Lizzy rose, answered the door, and squealed. "Marshall, Deb, and the girls are here, Mom," Lizzy shouted. "What an awesome surprise." The family shared hugs all around. The girls immediately went for the basket of games Rose kept on hand for just such occasions, while the adults gathered in the living room to talk.

When Marshall asked Lizzy what was new, she shared the story of her encounter with Coop. She also shared the concerns that plagued her ever since. Marshall looked at her thoughtfully. "The thing is, broken men should go to other men for guidance. That's just wisdom. When you have a man/woman relationship, the waters can quickly get muddied. You definitely did the right thing."

How simple, but how profound Marshall's thoughts were. Lizzy felt as if she was set free. "Oh, Marshall, that is just what I've been trying to figure out. Thank you. I was so afraid I might have driven the guy away from the Lord."

"No, Lizzy, you couldn't take a chance on his being a predator looking for his next victim." Deborah's tone was firm. "You did the right thing. You are a kind person, which is so sweet, but you have to be wise and smart about these things. Marshall is right. If he is truly broken, hurting, and seeking comfort and guidance, he needs to go to another Christian man."

Lizzy's heart soared, and she smiled. *Now I can put the period at the end of this episode. It's done and I can stop worrying about it.* She spent the rest of the evening enjoying her family's company and catching up on their news.

~Twenty~

The huge convention space was buzzing with multiple conversations. Round tables filled most of the room, each set with eight place settings. A goblet of ice water, a salad, and a bread plate awaited each guest. A large projector screen stood behind a podium at the front of the room. Lizzy smiled while she headed to table 45. She never missed the annual United Charities *Wear One, Bring One* luncheon. She sat at the table and greeted the woman seated to her right. "Hi, I'm Lizzy Godfrey," she said with a smile.

"Hello, Lizzy. My name is Caroline Hughes." The silver-haired sixty-something lady wore an elegant tweed skirt suit and had a lavender scarf around her neck. She looked at Lizzy intently. "This is a wonderful concept, isn't it? Providing undergarments for these women in need."

"Oh, yes. They say a lot of victims have to flee to safety with only the clothes on their backs. They don't even have time to grab a change of underwear. Thank goodness for me, it was ...." Lizzy's voice trailed off. She did not want to burden the other woman with her own story when they were there to support others.

"Go on, Lizzy." Caroline looked at her encouragingly. "I would love to hear your story."

"In a nutshell, the man I married turned abusive soon after our wedding." Lizzy played with the cloth napkin in her lap. "Oh the warning signs were there, of course," she said with chagrin. "Hindsight is twenty-twenty. But I was too naive about abuse to know what to look for. All I knew is that he was handsome, he said he loved me, I thought I loved him, and I was finally going to be married like all my friends."

"So many have been there, dear." Caroline gently placed a hand on Lizzy's arm. "You certainly aren't alone."

"True." Lizzy took a deep breath. "The abuse escalated and one evening when I was a couple of minutes late coming home from work, he tied me to a tree and ...." Her voice trailed off again as the horror of that experience flooded through her mind.

Caroline quickly jumped in. "Oh, Lizzy, if this is too painful, you don't need to share. You seemed to be so confident and at peace when you walked up. I don't want to ruin your day."

"No, I'm okay." Lizzy took a firm hold of her emotions, reminding herself that she'd *nol prossed* her case against Carl. "I think telling my story is a good thing. I keep hoping God will use it to warn others." She continued to relate the story. She paused and looked at Caroline. "I was fortunate, though, because I escaped Carl. He murdered his second wife. I watched the trial and heard portions of a journal she had been secretly keeping on a cloud storage site. She was so scared of him. In the end, all her worst fears came true."

"Oh, Lizzy, no." Caroline looked at her in horror, then retrieved a tissue from her small clutch and dabbed her eyes. "How absolutely horrible. That poor woman. These abusers are so frightening."

Lizzy nodded in agreement, then looked earnestly at Caroline. "But you know what? That's not the end of the story. I realized some important things while I watched the trial unfold. Even though I forgave Carl for what he did to me, I didn't realize how I let the experience put walls around my heart. I finally began to understand, if I was ever going to be able to trust again, I had to forgive him every time the memories surfaced. I thought forgiveness was a one-time thing, but now I know better. God has shown me so much in the past couple of years. I feel like I've grown by leaps and bounds, and I'm incredibly thankful. I would hate to have come through all the pain without growing spiritually."

"That explains the peace." Caroline gave her a warm smile. "I had a feeling you were a sister-in-Christ. God has given you some wonderful insights, Lizzy." She glanced at the vintage-style silver watch on her wrist. "They'll begin the program soon, but may I say a quick prayer for you?"

"Oh how wonderful. Yes, please." Lizzy and Caroline joined hands.

"Father God, bless this dear young woman. Continue to bring her peace and joy, and heal her from the past. Please use her in ways she has not yet even imagined. Guard her heart and be her best friend, dear Jesus. And keep her safe." Caroline gently squeezed Lizzy's hand. Lizzy returned the gesture just as the master of ceremonies approached the microphone to bring the luncheon to order.

While the ladies began to dine, the head of a local shelter for abused women was introduced and began to share statistics for Riponville. The numbers were staggering. Lizzy felt tears prick her eyes when she realized just how many suffered at the hands of abusers right in her own home town. *Even though I work in circuit records, I didn't realize the magnitude of these crimes. Domestic violence has become an epidemic. Thank You, Lord, for rescuing me. Please be with Mr. and Mrs. Carson as they have to go through life without Marcie. And Father, please touch Carl's heart and bring him to repentance.*

When the luncheon concluded, Caroline and Lizzy exchanged business cards. "Your story is so poignant, Lizzy." The women began to make their way out of the maze of tables. "I can't help but think the Lord will use you somehow. In fact," she paused thoughtfully. "Would you be willing to speak at my church? I know the ladies there would be touched by what you went through, and I'm sure they would like their daughters to be warned. What do you think?"

Lizzy froze momentarily. Speaking in front of people in court was one thing. Her part was solely to put information on the record, and few people were really paying much attention. Speaking in front of an audience that was there to hear her alone, made butterflies begin to dance in her stomach. "Oh, I don't know," she said weakly. "I've never spoken in front of a group before. I don't know if I could."

"Sweetheart, you'd do fine. Just tell your story like you told me. But I don't want to push you into something you're not comfortable with. Why don't you think about it and give me a call?"

"Okay, sounds good." Lizzy smiled. "I'll pray and let you know."

Caroline and Lizzy parted ways in the parking lot. The March day was warm and sunny with fluffy white clouds floating lazily across the sky. Flowerbeds full of daffodils and pansies decorated the end of each row of spaces. Lizzy took a deep breath of fresh, spring air and smiled happily. *What a beautiful day.* Just as she approached her car, Lizzy heard someone calling her name. She stopped and looked around, shading her eyes from the bright sunshine. Her heart quickened.

"Senator Bates, hello. It's been a long time." Her hands felt suddenly shaky, and she mentally scolded herself. *Stop it. You know he's not interested. Just treat him like you would treat any other attorney at work.* She removed her sunglasses.

"Lizzy, it's so great to see you again." Tucker smiled widely, his eyes warm and sincere. The attraction he'd felt for Lizzy had not dimmed with time, and his heart began to beat faster.

"What are you doing here?" Lizzy looked puzzled, knowing the event she'd just attended was for women.

"I was hosting a kind of 'lunch town hall' meeting over on the other side of the complex." Tucker looked a bit chagrined. "I got caught in traffic and almost didn't find a place to park. That's why I'm way over here. Were you at the United Charities event?"

"I was." Lizzy smiled. "I met the most interesting woman there. She gave me a lot to think about."

Tucker gazed at her for a moment. He wanted to get to know Lizzy better, but felt he must be sure of God's leading in the matter. He said a quick prayer for wisdom and felt complete peace to proceed.

The moment began to be awkward. Lizzy put her sunglasses back on and fumbled with her key fob. "I'd better get going, Tucker." She clicked the lock open. "I've got to get back to work so the others can go to lunch."

"Of course. I understand." He reached to open the car door for her and paused a moment before closing her in. "Lizzy, may I take you out for dinner one evening next week? I'd really love to see you again." His brown eyes were earnest. Lizzy looked at him for a long moment, surprised at the peace she felt. His presence made her feel safe somehow, and her nervousness vanished.

"I'd like that, Tucker. Let me write down my contact information for you."

"Oh that's okay." He grabbed his wallet, removed a small slip of paper, and showed it to her. "Unless something has changed, that is."

Lizzy was shocked. He'd kept the bit of paper from that day in the courtroom. A warm feeling of contentment started in her heart and swelled to cover her whole being. "Everything is the same," she said with a smile.

"Wonderful. I'll give you a call tonight. Have a wonderful afternoon." He shut the door gently, and Lizzy began to back out. He waved to her while she drove away, and she did the same. With a smile he thought might stretch off his face, Tucker made his way to his Honda.

Lizzy drove back to the courthouse, still a bit stunned but pleased at the interchange. *Lord, what are you up to now? There he was after all this time. And he asked me out. Wow*! She grinned, feeling a bit like a silly school girl. Then she thought back to her conversation with Caroline. As happy as she was to have seen Tucker again, she could not get the idea of presenting her story out of her head. Thoughts tumbled around like dancing butterflies. *Lord, is this you at work again? Do you want me to do this? I don't know about speaking in public. I'd be so nervous.* But the growing feeling of peace pervaded her thoughts. Peace about Tucker and peace about God using her story to help others. *After all, I've heard that part of the healing process for survivors is to tell their story.* Ideas began to flow. She could present not only her story, but statistics and real-life examples. *I could use some of the exhibits from Carl's trial. Those are all public record. And I could start out like I'm telling someone else's story, kind of a 'once upon a time' thing. Then gradually let them know the woman in the story is me.* Lizzy quickly jotted her ideas down on her scratch pad before settling in at her desk to enter a stack of motions.

~Twenty-One~

Tucker pushed the button and stood calmly on Lizzy's doorstep. Inside, the noise of the doorbell set off Lizzy's nerves. "Oh, Mom, I don't know about this. I'm no good at dating. Now I wish I'd never agreed." Lizzy smoothed her hands over her dark wash jeans and straightened her purple blouse. "It's been over a decade since I went out on a date. I'm a nervous wreck."

"Honey, you look beautiful. You do like Tucker, don't you?" Rose sat in her recliner and smiled. "I really think everything will be okay, but you have your phone with you, right? If there's any problem, you just call, and I'll have help on the way."

"Oh, you're right. I'm being silly." Lizzy let her breath out a huff and shook her head. "I was never much good at all this, and it hasn't gotten better with time."

"You'd better answer the door though, dear, or he's going to wonder what's going on."

"Oh, right! I'm going." Lizzy slung her bag over her shoulder. "I love you, Mom."

"Have a good time, honey." Rose smiled and went back to watching *The Waltons*.

Tucker's heart skipped a beat when Lizzy opened the door. He took in her beautiful features and admired her stylish outfit. Her dark hair gleamed in the rays the late-afternoon sun cast upon the doorway, and for a moment, he wished he could touch the shiny locks. *Woah, there, bud. Calm down.* Something warned him to keep things casual, so he kept his admiration of her to himself. He greeted her with a friendly, unassuming smile "Hi. Are you ready?"

"Ready." Lizzy swallowed hard. His gentle but manly good looks did nothing to calm her nerves. She wished she could wring the shaking from her hands like water from a wet towel. Determined not to act like a silly school-girl, she forced herself to smile brightly at him. "Where are we headed?"

"I thought we'd go to the new Italian place out on Shire Ridge Road and then a movie. Does that work?"

"Sure." They walked to Tucker's car, and he opened the passenger-side door for her. Once on their way, Lizzy asked, "What movies are playing tonight?"

"When I checked Fandango, I noticed several good ones. One is a drama. There's a comedy, too." He slowed to a stop at an intersection. A large pick-up truck pulled up beside them, windows open, with "I Heard It Through the Grapevine" pounding at ear-splitting decibels out of the speakers.

I like that song, but this really is not helping my nerves. Lizzy turned her head to get a look at the driver and was struck funny at how the teenager was totally into the song. She began to giggle at his body moves and arm gestures.

Tucker looked over and watched. "That guy's got an entire dance routine going right there in the driver's seat."

Lizzy and Tucker both burst out laughing when the red-haired youngster looked right at them and gave them a thumbs up. They responded in kind and moved on when the light turned green. The boy honked his horn, then shot ahead of them.

"That reminds me of one time when I saw a guy dancing in the median." Lizzy reached to tuck a strand of hair behind one ear. "He had what appeared to be a stick from a broom. He had his ear buds in and was dancing away with the stick, right there for all to see."

"Are you serious?"

"Oh, yes. Looked a little strange, but he was clearly having a good time." Lizzy laughed, and some of the nervous tension began to abate.

After a few moments of silence, Tucker said, "I forgot to mention, the theater is also having a special showing of *The Hobbit an Unexpected Journey Extended Edition* tonight." He kept his voice carefully neutral. "So what movie sounds good to you?"

"*The Hobbit*? Shut the front door!" Lizzy looked over at him. "I would love to see that movie in the theater again."

"You're a Tolkien fan too?" He grinned.

"Big time." Lizzy relaxed a bit more, pleased to discover this common ground. "*The Lord of the Rings* and *The Hobbit* movies are my favorites of all time."

"That settles it, then. I admit, I was hoping you'd choose that one. I have all the extended editions, but it's so fun to see them on the big screen."

"I have them all, too. I have Tolkien marathons every so often." They both laughed and began to compare notes on their favorite scenes. They also discovered each loved the movie soundtracks as well. "I'm so pleased to know someone with such excellent taste." Lizzy grinned while Tucker opened the door of Rizzoli's.

"Likewise." Tucker laughed with delight. His instincts had been spot-on. He could already envision himself spending lots of time with Lizzy as the future progressed.

~ * ~

"So then the guy says, 'No your honor, my aunt was a canibess.' Everybody was sitting there looking at him like, 'a what?' So he proceeded to tell the judge his mother's sister was a female cannibal and had eaten his siblings and left their remains somewhere in Manhattan." Tucker put his fork down and looked at her in amazement. Lizzy took a sip of water and heard Tucker's phone buzz. She put her glass down abruptly. "Do you need to get that?"

"No, its fine. I'll check it when I get home. Please go on. What on earth did the judge say to that?"

She stumbled a bit, trying to get back into her story. Carl had taken every call or text when they came in, no matter what she had to say. He informed her that his phone was vitally important and could never be ignored. Already, Tucker proved himself different. Throughout the evening, no matter how many times the phone buzzed, Tucker completely ignored the device. Their meaningful conversation included everything from books and music, to church and beliefs. He was polite and kind to the waitress, but she did not distract him for a moment. Carl had always flirted with the server, then spent half the dinner berating female diners who wore attire he thought was too tight or immodest. *So far, so good.* Lizzy enjoyed another bite of her meal while Tucker shared the story of how he got his dog, Porter, from a Jack Russell rescue organization.

After dinner, they enjoyed a short walk to the movie theater. The air had cooled somewhat from the eighty-degree afternoon, and Lizzy enjoyed the breeze softly caressing her face. "That was a wonderful meal, Tucker. Thank you. I love seafood alfredo."

Tucker put his hand in the pocket of his khakis, so he would not be tempted to take her hand. "I think I'll try that next time. It looked really good." They approached the ticket window, and Tucker ordered two for *The Hobbit*. "I think I'm going to be too full for popcorn, but Lizzy, what can I get for you? I definitely need some water."

"Water for me, too, please. And I couldn't eat another bite if you forced me."

"Water it is." He purchased their drinks, and they walked down the row of doors to their theater. "But if you change your mind during the movie and want something else to eat or drink, please tell me, okay?" Tucker looked at her with a serious expression. Lizzy was touched. He truly seemed to feel responsible for her comfort and well-being. His brown eyes radiated his desire to take care of her. "Don't worry, I'll let you know. Promise." She smiled warmly. Satisfied, he opened the door to theater five, and they made their way up to their seats.

They were watching previews when the thought hit Lizzy. *He's treating me like I'm the most important person on earth.* When she and Carl first started going out, he would look at her dreamily and abruptly interrupt her conversation with, "You're so beautiful." He would gaze at her with hunger in his eyes, as though he wanted to devour her. At the time, his fervor seemed sweet and flattering, but now she knew it was all an act meant to manipulate her. *This is amazing. I actually feel valued by Tucker. He's so polite and interested, but he doesn't have that sick lustful look in his eyes.* She basked in the feeling for a moment, then her acquired cynicism jumped in. *Let's see if this lasts. This is just the first date, after all.*

~ * ~

"Honey, you and Tucker seem to be getting along quite well. Are you feeling more comfortable with dating?" Rose pulled back the sleeves of her robe and reached for the syrup.

"I'm starting to relax." Lizzy watched a goldfinch pulling thistle from the feeder outside, and a smile touched her lips. "We've been dating for about three months now, and I'm really having fun."

"I'm so thankful, Lizzy. You need some friends outside of work. I like Tucker so far. He seems to be an easy-going and gentle man. Do you think so? You've spent a lot more time with him than I have."

Lizzy looked thoughtfully at her mother. "So far. I guess those are the operative words. He does appear to be a wonderful man. He doesn't get angry easily. He handles everyday aggravations well, like getting cut off on the road."

She picked up her mug of tea and took a sip. "He didn't even blow up over that incident when we went to see the last extended edition of *The Hobbit* movies. Somebody was trying to crawl over us during the show and knocked our popcorn tub over. He was so kind to that lady and refused to let her buy us another one."

"That is a very good sign, I think." Rose enjoyed her last bite of pancake with a strawberry on top. "Kindness is so important."

"Time will tell, I guess. But I know I would miss him if he were to drop out of my life now."

Rose gave her daughter a gentle smile. "I'm so happy for you, honey. God is in this, I can tell." Mother and daughter enjoyed the remainder of their leisurely Saturday breakfast while watching the chickadees and cardinals filling up outside.

~ * ~

"Ethan, it's good to see you." Tucker greeted his friend with a handshake, and they headed into Chick-fil-A for lunch.

Ethan looked at Tucker with a glint in his eye after they sat down. "So how is life as a Senator treating you, my friend?"

Tucker's face clouded a bit. "Hmm...how do I answer that?" He shook his head. "How's life treating you as an assistant district attorney?"

"Typical lawyer, answering a question with a question." Ethan laughed. "The DA's Office is treating me fine." He looked at Tucker intently. "What's up, my friend?"

Tucker sighed deeply. "Being in the Senate is not what I thought it would be. When I was appointed, I had all these grand ideas about making a difference. You know, standing firm and helping to make good things happen for my community and my state." He took a bite of his grilled chicken club sandwich and chewed thoughtfully. "I'm beginning to wonder if I was really cut out for politics. I think I'm a pretty easygoing guy, but I just don't know how much longer I can do this. I've been praying a lot, and I'm feeling like God may be leading me in a different direction."

"Tucker, you should come be a prosecutor. There's nothing like the feeling of knowing the guilty have been convicted for their crimes, and that you helped in the service of justice."

Ethan took a sip of his sweet iced tea. "Plus, our department has a lot of diversion type programs. We're not only about putting the criminals away. We're also trying to help them to become productive citizens. I heard they're looking for someone to head up a new program which is still in development. The idea is to allow certain first-time defendants to be admitted to the program, where they will have a list of requirements they must meet, and if they do, their charge can be dismissed."

Tucker looked at him, doubt evident in his eyes. "That sounds interesting, but remember, I've been working as a real estate attorney since I passed the bar. I haven't really focused on criminal law."

"Never too late to learn. I mean, I know you probably like the freedom of having your own practice, but seriously, you should come by the office and fill out an application. You could start out as an assistant DA. The program won't be ready to go live for a couple of years yet. With some prosecuting experience under your belt, you'd be a shoo-in to be the program director."

Tucker began to catch Ethan's excitement. He dipped a waffle fry in catsup, chewed thoughtfully, then grinned and took a sip of tea. "That does sound fascinating. And for the record, having one's own practice has its own issues and problems. Nothing major, but hassles nonetheless. I'm going to pray and see how God leads."

"I'll be praying for you, too. God may want you to stay where you are and if so, we'll pray you will know His will." Ethan flashed a jaunty grin. "But I'm personally hoping it's His will for you to come work with us. I think you'd find our office would be a great fit."

~ * ~

"Tucker, I have something important to say."

Tucker put down his coffee cup and eyed Lizzy intently. They were enjoying Saturday morning brunch at a local café. "Go on."

Lizzy fiddled with her watch. "I've met Porter, and you've met Nugget and Downton." She looked at him. "I think it's time our dogs met each other. I mean, wouldn't we have fun going to the dog park together or taking them to the mountains?"

Tucker couldn't have said what he expected her to say, but he laughed with relief. "I love it, Lizzy. That would be awesome." Then he grew thoughtful. "How should we go about arranging the meeting? Porter is an only dog, and I honestly don't know how social he'll be. I haven't exactly made an effort to get him out around other dogs, and he's really territorial about his yard."

"Nugget and Downton are, too." Lizzy thought hard, trying to remember dog training and behavior tips she'd read. "How about if we meet out by Lake Connemara? Then we can see how they react on neutral ground."

Tucker thought for a moment, then nodded. "Sounds like a good plan. How about this afternoon, or are you busy?"

"I have some things around the house I need to get done today. Would next Saturday work?"

Tucker pulled out his iPhone to check his calendar. "I have a meeting in the morning, but my afternoon is free. Shall we meet around two?"

"Perfect." Lizzy's eyes sparkled. "I'll be sure to give them a lecture beforehand on being friendly."

Tucker laughed with delight. "I'll do the same with Porter. Although, sometimes it's hard to get through to us thick-headed guys."

"Ahem." Lizzy cleared her throat and pulled a comical expression. "No comment." She then winked at him and burst out laughing.

~ * ~

Lizzy pulled on her denim Bermuda shorts, thankful the day was pleasantly warm but not humid as summer so often could be. She shrugged her way into her Salty Dog Café t-shirt and put on her Vionic™ sandals. She pulled her hair back into a pony tail and snapped the dog's leases on their collars.

"I'll be back after a while, Mom."

"All right, honey." Rose's voice drifted up from her basement study. "Have a good time."

Lizzy arrived at Lake Connemara and parked. The dogs started to leap from the car, but Lizzy put her hand out and stopped them with a firm, "Wait." She got their leashes situated, then told them, "Okay, come on."

The excited canines jumped from the car seat to the sidewalk, their ears pricked up, noses sniffing madly. Lizzy locked the car, adjusted her sunglasses, and put the keys in her pocket. She shortened the leashes, and both dogs fell obediently into place one on each side. She set off on the asphalt path which meandered its way around the lake.

When Tucker and Porter rounded a small bend, he saw Lizzy. His breath caught for a moment. *She is so beautiful.* Her dark hair gleamed in the sun, and she smiled, obviously enjoying the beautiful day. *How did I ever get so lucky?* he thought, but then internally shook his head. *No luck about it. You brought her, Lord. I know You did. Please guide us as we continue getting to know each other.*

He waved, and Lizzy caught sight of him. Her heart quickened. She looked at his t-shirt, khaki shorts, and flip-flip-flops. *Even dressed casually, he really is so handsome, in a masculine but boy-next-door sort of way. We get along so well, and I genuinely enjoy his company. I feel so blessed. Thank You, Lord. Thank You for my friend.* They both continued toward each other slowly. When they were close, Lizzy put on her best southern belle accent. “Why, Tucker Bates, I do declare. How lovely to see you and your fine dog, Porter.”

He responded in kind. “Miss Lizzy, it’s a real pleasure for Porter and me to see you again and make the acquaintance of the Misses Nugget and Downton.”

They burst out laughing and the dogs looked at them in confusion. Nugget immediately recognized Tucker and pushed forward to be petted. Tucker crouched down and caressed her soft red sable coat.

Downton pressed herself close to Lizzy, determined to protect her in this unfamiliar situation. The Sheltie soon relaxed when she recognized Tucker as the friend she’d met at home and began squirming for his attention also.

After a few moments, Lizzy wondered about Tucker’s dog. She looked around and giggled. “Not such a hot-shot now, eh, Porter?”

The Jack Russell was cowering behind Tucker, shaking from stem to stern. “Now, Porter.” Tucker tried not to laugh. “These ladies are friends. I promise.” But the dog would not be persuaded and looked at Tucker, pleading in his large brown eyes.

"Let's just walk for a bit, Tuck. Might help him to relax and then everything won't feel so intense."

Tucker fell into stride beside Lizzy with Porter on his outer side. They chit-chatted amiably, enjoying the day and catching up on all that happened since they last saw each other. When they reached a wooded area with picnic tables, they decided to sit for a while and see how the dogs reacted. After much sniffing of each other in the manner of all dogs, Nugget, Downton, and Porter apparently agreed to be friends. They sat together, listening and sniffing the air intently.

"Looks like a win, Lizzy." Tucker winked at her.

She removed her sunglasses and grinned at him. "This is great. I'm so relieved they're friends now." They sat for a while enjoying each other's company before continuing their walk around the lake. The conversation eventually waned a bit, but the silence was comfortable. Lizzy had the fleeting thought that her life was much richer as a result of Tucker's friendship. *I'm so glad the Lord brought him into my life.* She watched a female mallard make her way across the water, her ducklings swimming close behind. *I'm getting to where I can't imagine life without him. I'm not sure how I feel about that.* Determined not to allow introspection to ruin a perfectly nice moment, she put her serious thoughts aside and focused on the beauty of the summer day with her best friends.

~Twenty-Two~

"What kind of work are you in, Lizzy?" The sixty-something woman asked the question while looking through glasses perched midway down her nose. Lizzy took in her perfectly styled silver hair, her Armani™ jacket dress, and her chic croc-embossed Coach™ bag, which sat conspicuously on the table beside her. Diamond studs set in gold twinkled from her earlobes, and a diamond tennis bracelet lay on her wrist next to a gold watch. *Old money, prestige, and power, no doubt.* Lizzy reminded herself not to judge.

Tucker had been invited to speak at the July meeting of a local women's club which supported his political party, and he asked Lizzy to accompany him to the luncheon and speech. From the moment they entered the posh Gardenia Club meeting room, Lizzy felt out of place and ill at ease. The elegant surroundings were as stately as the women at the tables, who sat dropping names, gossiping, and generally trying to be impressive. Lizzy was sure her hair and makeup had wilted in the hot humid weather while they walked from the parking lot to the building. She wished she was invisible but saw nothing for it but to answer the woman's question. She swallowed her bite of chicken and cleared her throat. "I'm an Administrative Assistant with the circuit court records office."

The conversation around the small table abruptly grew quiet. Lizzy felt the disapproving looks pierce through her, attempting to gouge away any self-confidence she had left. Tucker quickly jumped in. "Lizzy's work is really fascinating. She's in the courtroom, so she sees a lot of interesting things." He looked around the table with a serious expression. "Some of the cases are sad, though. The number of people trapped by addiction is staggering."

The haughty looks around the table dissipated while Tucker spoke. "There must be something we can do," one middle-aged woman stated while she fiddled with her jeweled necklace. “I do give a nice check to my charity every month.” She smiled ingratiatingly at Tucker.

Lizzy determined she would try again. “That is so kind.” She smiled at the woman. “There are a lot of people who need to get into treatment programs, and the facilities never seem to have enough bed space available.”

The warm expression slid from the woman’s face like butter off a hot knife. She turned her head slowly to stare at Lizzy. The expression of harsh disdain in her eyes efficiently put Lizzy in her place. The woman returned her gaze to Tucker, and the smile of admiration returned. “Whatever happened to that wonderful girl you were seeing a couple of years ago?”

Tucker looked puzzled. Before Lizzy, he hadn’t dated anyone seriously in years, so he was at a complete loss. “I’m sorry, ma’am. I'm not sure what you mean.”

The woman laughed merrily. “Oh, Senator, you’re so funny. You know, Shelly Marquis. Her father is the owner of Marquis Investments in Clifton. Surely you can’t have forgotten dear Shelly. I always thought the two of you made an adorable couple. She’s such a beautiful girl. You couldn’t have forgotten her. She was Miss Riponville last year.”

Even in her best professional skirt suit and heels, Lizzy felt old and dowdy. She awkwardly continued to eat lunch, but felt as though she would choke on the food. Tucker reached under the table and gave her free hand a squeeze. She stole a glance at him, and he slyly winked at her. For the moment, his gesture reassured her heart.

Tucker looked back to the woman who asked about Shelly and smiled. “Ma’am, I’ve never dated a Shelly Marquis. I may have met her at some point on the campaign trail. I do meet a lot of people, but I’ve never spent time with anyone of that name.” The woman momentarily looked miffed but then began to gush about Tucker’s work in the Senate. Soon the luncheon was over, and Tucker was introduced. He strode to the podium with confidence and began his speech.

~ * ~

“Have a wonderful afternoon, Lizzy.” Tucker reached for the door handle of the courthouse employee entrance when Lizzy buzzed the security band with her key card. “Thanks for coming with me today.”

Lizzy smiled, thanked him for lunch, and said good-bye. Tucker returned to his Accord deep in thought. The troubled look in Lizzy’s eyes concerned him. Something was wrong. Though she still acted like her usual cheerful self, her demeanor seemed a bit forced. He left the courthouse and turned onto the interstate. Senate business demanded he spend the next few days in the capital, though he would rather have stayed at home. He prayed during his drive to Clifton. *Father, lead me and guide me. Something is wrong. Lizzy is upset, and I don’t know why. Give me wisdom, Lord. Watch over my girl.*

Lizzy’s thoughts during the afternoon went from feeling badly about herself, to questioning her relationship with Tucker. *I know I care for him, Lord, but I don’t think I could live the lifestyle of a politician’s wife, if our relationship should go in that direction. I’m just not cut out for it.* She sighed and looked at the stack of True Billed indictments, which had just come back from the Grand Jury. *Lord, please guide me. I don’t know what to do. I feel like a frumpy old bat.*

That night, Tucker called her via Skype after supper. “Lizzy, I feel like something upset you today. Can you talk about it? Did I do anything?” Brown eyes filled with concern looked into hers from the computer screen.

Lizzy sighed deeply. “Oh, no, Tucker. You didn’t do anything. I just feel so out of place in groups like the women’s club today. I felt like the crud they have their help scrape off the shoes.”

“I’m sorry, Lizzy. They were pretty snooty, weren’t they?”

“They were fawning all over you, but they clearly did not approve of me.” Lizzy felt aggravated when tears began to form. She grabbed a tissue. “I think I’m a pretty friendly person but those kinds of situations make me feel like a complete nobody. And then I get frustrated for allowing myself to feel that way."

"You do know I meant what I told that lady. About the woman she thought I'd dated? I don't know where in the world she came up with that story, but to my knowledge, I've never even met anyone by that name."

"I know, Tuck. I could tell she was just trying to get in a dig at me. Young, rich beauty queen compared to the middle-aged, average county clerk." Lizzy sighed.

"Lizzy Godfrey, you are definitely not average." Tucker's voice was warm but firm. "You are, however, a county clerk. I cannot argue with you on that particular point. Yes, you are. You are the most beautiful, talented, and interesting county clerk I've ever met."

A smile tugged at the corner of Lizzy's lips, trying with all its might to spread across her whole mouth. Finally, she gave in. "And just how many county clerks have you met, sir?"

Tucker laughed, relieved his uplifting teasing made her smile. "Okay, so only a few, but still." His look turned intense but kind. "Lizzy, you are an awesome person. Don't you ever let anyone make you feel less than the amazing woman you are."

Lizzy smiled and this time happy tears began to form. "Thank you, Tuck. That truly means a lot to me."

They talked for a few moments longer, then wished each other a good night. Tucker checked the locks on his condo door with a smile still on his face. *God is doing something wonderful in our lives. Father, I can't wait to see where You lead us.*

Lizzy felt better about the day, but still knelt before her bed with growing concerns furrowing her brow. "Help me, Lord," she prayed. "Guide and direct me. If this relationship is not of you, please show me and show Tucker. But one way or another, please use me for your glory." She wiped a tear from her eye, then snuggled down into bed. Nugget and Downton nestled close, and Sherlock and Watson sprawled at the end of the bed. *Thank you for my babies, Lord,* she thought while she drifted off. *If I end up alone, at least I'll have them.*

~ * ~

The morning of September 30th dawned, and Lizzy sat on the porch nervously awaiting Tucker's arrival. Today she would meet his parents, and she felt like a swarm of butterflies was fluttering madly in her stomach. Tucker pulled into the driveway and jumped out to open the passenger-side door for Lizzy. He sized up the situation immediately.

"Would it do any good to tell you not to be nervous?" he asked. "I promise; they can't wait to meet you. And they don't bite."

Lizzy sighed, then grinned and shook her head at how easily he'd read her. "No, Tucker, it won't do any good at all. I really want to meet them, but I'm kind of a nervous wreck."

Tucker reached over and squeezed her hand. "I understand. I felt the same way before I met your family. Try to relax, though. You're going to love Thirskton Lake."

Lizzy smiled and squeezed his hand in return. "Thanks, Tuck. I am excited about the boat trip. I love going out on the water but don't have the opportunity to do so very often."

They chatted amiably during the hour drive to Thirskton Lake. Tucker parked and gathered their things from the trunk, then they headed toward the marina. An excited call attracted Lizzy's attention.

"Tucker, honey, over here." Emilie Bates shaded her eyes with one hand and waved eagerly with the other.

"Hi, Mom." Tucker waved back and grinned. While they approached the slip, he said, "Mom, this is Lizzy Godfrey."

Emilie removed her sunglasses, and Lizzy did the same. Tucker's mother grasped her free hand warmly. "Oh, honey, I'm so happy to meet you. Come and meet my husband."

Lizzy smiled in return and followed her onto the Regal cabin cruiser. Emilie called, "Gil, here's Lizzy."

The man who turned from a coil of rope looked like an older version of Tucker. "Lizzy! Finally, we get to meet you." The handsome gentleman took Lizzy's offered hand. "We've been looking forward to this for weeks."

"I am so happy to meet you both." Lizzy smiled, and the butterflies in her stomach began to cease their frantic fluttering. "Thank you so much for inviting me out on your boat. I love the water." She looked out at the scenic lake with admiration.

"Wait 'til you see the view around the bend out there." Gilbert Bates pointed to where the view of the lake disappeared behind a line of trees. "You can see Whitby Mountain in the distance."

"We have a cabin on the mountain, Lizzy." Tucker placed the cooler in the refreshment center. "There's great skiing up there in the winter and all kinds of hiking trails and scenic views, too. Whitby Mountain is one of my favorite places."

Lizzy smiled. "Sounds amazing." She looked around. "Can I help with anything?"

Emilie took her arm. "Yes. You can come sit with me in the bow and wait for takeoff." She grinned, a sparkle lighting up her eyes. "I just love the feeling of the wind in my face while the boat rushes along."

"Me, too." Lizzy nodded happily. "There's nothing like the invigorating feeling of rushing along with my hair blowing in the breeze." She and Emilie made their way to the front of the boat and sat down. They chatted amiably while Tucker and his dad finished getting everything ready.

Soon the boat was skimming along the water. Lizzy breathed the refreshing air deeply and enjoyed the wind in her face while she watched the shoreline pass by. A few lake houses were dotted here and there, but for the most part, the scenery was the unspoiled beauty of God's magnificent creation. Lizzy completely relaxed and found she enjoyed Tucker's parents more with every passing minute. She was thrilled to share her testimony with them and to hear how they came to Jesus. Her heart rejoiced at having made the acquaintance of another brother and sister in Christ.

Emilie and Gilbert embraced Lizzy like family and found they had much in common with Tucker's friend. They immediately understood what their son saw in her and in a private moment, grinned at each other, knowing exactly what the other was thinking. This was the woman who would someday become their daughter-in-law.

Lizzy arrived home that night nearly asleep on her feet but still looked in on her mother before heading to bed. "Mom, they're such wonderful people. I can't wait for you to meet them. You're going to love them. I felt right at home." Lizzy felt happy to the core of her being.

Rose hugged her daughter tightly and smiled. "Oh, honey, I'm so thankful. I was praying all day. I hoped everything would go well and that they'd see how precious my girl is."

"Oh, Mom, I love you." Lizzy hugged her back. "Can we pray for a minute before we go to bed? I'm too tired to do much, but I just want to thank the Lord for this amazing day."

The women enjoyed a brief but heartfelt prayer time before each turned in to rest. Lizzy fell asleep thinking the wind in her face out on the lake was like the breath of God enveloping her in peace and light and blowing away the cobwebs of the past.

~Twenty-Three~

"What are you doing for Tucker's birthday?" Rose asked when Lizzy came into the kitchen to prepare breakfast. "Isn't it coming up soon?"

"Yep, his birthday is November 20th, so I still have a couple of weeks. I do have a plan, though. I'm taking him to his favorite restaurant, of course." Lizzy smiled. "But I have another surprise for him. Remember the picture Joy took, of the field of flags?" She took some eggs from the refrigerator and began cracking them into a bowl.

"Oh yes. You sent Tucker a card with the picture once, didn't you, honey?" Rose began laying strips of bacon in a pan on the stove.

"That's the one." Lizzy whipped up the eggs, then poured them into another pan. "He mentioned the other day that he loved the shot but somehow lost the card. He said he'd wanted to order a print, but also lost the artist's web site. Since his birthday is soon, my ears perked up at once." She raised her eyebrows in a comical expression, and Rose laughed while she turned the bacon slices over. "I asked Joy to make me an 11"x14" enlargement, and I took the picture to the frame shop."

Lizzy sighed with satisfaction and put two pieces of bread into the toaster while the eggs cooked. "I can't wait to see how the piece turned out. Mr. Larson is such a gifted artist with framing. I know he'll mat and frame the picture into a masterpiece."

She scooped scrambled eggs onto plates and grated some cheddar cheese on top. When the bread was toasted to perfection, she removed the slices, spread each with a layer of butter, and then topped off her piece with cherry preserves. Rose opted for blueberry. Both enjoyed their lazy Saturday mornings, and Lizzy loved having time to cook.

The women sat at the kitchen table. After saying the blessing, Rose looked at Lizzy. "So are you ready for the presentation at church this evening? Are you nervous?"

"In a word, yes." Lizzy laughed. "I've never done anything like this before." She took a bite of eggs and chewed thoughtfully. "But you know, my passion for this subject is so strong, I think it'll be okay. I want these girls to know what to watch for and how to spot red flags that can identify abusers. If my experience could save just one girl from an abusive relationship, it would be worth it."

Rose ate a bite of toast and nodded. "Honey, I think you'll do fine. You have a powerful story that will grab their attention. I'll be praying they listen and heed the warning."

~ * ~

The afternoon flew by and before she knew it, Lizzy stood off stage waiting to be introduced for the first speaking engagement of her life. She hoped she'd chosen the right outfit. Since she was speaking to teenagers, she opted for the casual look and donned her dark wash jeans, a collared long-sleeved shirt, and Birkenstock clogs. A simple gold rope necklace hung down against the red background of her shirt, and small gold earrings dangled from her lobes. Nervously, she checked her watch again, then noticed a woman walking onto the stage. "Girls, we have a special person here tonight to share with us. I hope you'll give her your complete attention. Please welcome Ms. Elizabeth Godfrey."

The small group of teens clapped while Lizzy walked to the podium and put down her satchel. "Hi, girls. Thank you for such a wonderful welcome." She looked out at the group and smiled, trying to make eye contact with each girl. "I have a story to tell you today." The girls looked interested and attentive.

Lizzy tried to relax and briefly reminded herself why she was here. "Once upon a time, there was a girl who dreamed of finding her Prince Charming one day. She longed to be a wife and mother in a home where she and her husband followed God with all their hearts. She even started a hope chest when she was about your age." Lizzy paused and looked around. "How many of you know what a hope chest is?" Only a few girls raised their hands. "A hope chest is something girls used to start back in the old days when I was your age." Lizzy gave them a jaunty grin, and the young women tittered. "Girls would collect items they hoped to use in their own homes someday. The objects in the hope chest could be anything, from her grandmother's doilies, to dishes, to children's books. The girl in our story especially loved collecting Christmas ornaments. She could just imagine the scene: she, her husband, and their children, going to get a fresh live Christmas tree that filled the room with the scent of Balsam. She could see them decorating the tree with the ornaments she'd collected. She could even picture her husband lifting their youngest up to put the angel in the place of honor on top of the tree.

"This girl finished high school without ever having a boyfriend. Her one date had ended in embarrassment and shame when she got sick in the middle of the movie. She attended college and went out on a few dates, but never found her special someone. She majored in Home Economics in college, and when she graduated with no boyfriend, she also had no prospects for a career. She felt adrift. Her plan had not come to pass. She asked God why, but He did not provide an answer. She finally found a job working in a local pet store. Though she did not understand why her dreams had not come true, she trusted that God knew best. By and by, she settled into her life but she was not content.

"When her 30th birthday loomed on the horizon, her discontent grew. Though no one ever said the words aloud, she knew people felt sorry for her because she was alone. *Nobody is single at my age*, she thought. *I feel like such a moron. I wanted to be like other people - part of a couple, with a family of my own. When, oh when, will my real life finally begin?*" Lizzy paused and looked around. The girls were looking at her intently, and she knew she had their attention.

"The woman loved Jesus. When she was a young child, she realized she was a sinner, repented of her sins, and accepted Him as her Savior. But in spite of her love for God, feelings of unhappiness continued to occupy her mind. All she could think about was her need for a husband. Though she put on a happy face to the outside world, inwardly she was discouraged. She felt she was a failure, and her life was going nowhere. With shame she imagined class reunions, where she would have nothing to show for her life.

"On Sunday, May 25th, everything changed. A man she'd never seen before attended her Sunday School class. He immediately noticed her and asked if he could sit beside her. He was kind and interested in the woman's life. He asked if he could sit with her during the church service that followed, and she agreed. After that, he asked if he could buy her lunch. Hardly believing this was actually happening to her, she agreed. During the meal, Carl gazed into her eyes and told her he had been looking for someone like her his whole life. He breathlessly quoted Proverbs 18:22 'Whoso findeth a wife findeth a good thing and obtaineth favor from the Lord.'(KJV). He took her hand and looked at her longingly. The woman was a bit taken aback, but still felt immensely flattered.

During the weeks which followed, Carl spent every spare moment with the woman. He always brought her flowers or chocolate. He declared he was in love with her and told her she was meant to be his. The woman was sure Carl was 'the one'. He must be because no one else ever felt this way about her. She soaked up his praise and flattery like a thirsty sponge.

"A few times, things happened that bothered her. Once, when he picked her up to go out for ice cream cones, he insisted she go back inside to change her jeans. They were 'body hugging' he said, and his eyes were serious and a bit angry.

"Shocked and confused, the woman dutifully went back inside. They were the same jeans she'd worn on other occasions when they'd gone out. Assuming she must have put on weight, she found a pair of khakis she kept in the back of her closet. They were from the days when she was about ten pounds heavier and were so loose she feared they might fall down. Carl looked her over sternly, then a small smile spread across his lips. He hugged her and told her she looked beautiful. He thanked her for changing and looked satisfied. While they drove to the ice-cream shop, he talked about how women everywhere wanted to wear body-hugging clothing and cared nothing for modesty. Carl told the woman he expected her to be different. She deferred to him and promised she would never wear the jeans again. But inside she was puzzled. Her parents had raised her to be a modest young lady, and she was always careful about her appearance. She did not really understand, but resolved to do whatever she needed to do to please this Godly, spiritual man."

Lizzy paused her narrative to take a sip from the bottle of water provided for her. "The woman did everything he asked," she continued. "He wanted to know what every phone conversation was about, and she always told him, feeling this was a sign he really loved her and cared about her life.

"The woman's parents were concerned. They'd met Carl and felt uneasy about him. They shared their concerns with the woman, but she waved them aside and said they did not know him like she did. When she told Carl, he looked deeply saddened. 'They don't like me because of my background. I was from a poor family growing up. They want somebody with old family money for you, not some self-made man.' The woman knew this was not so, but she didn't want to make him feel badly. He worked so hard, and she really did not understand why her parents objected. Soon he began to insist she stop spending time with them. 'They're poisoning you against me, my darling. I couldn't bear to lose you. I know we were made to be together, and I know God brought you to me to be my wife. I love you. But you'll have to decide. Do you want your parents or do you want me?'

Lizzy paused for a moment to make sure the girls were still with her. Their serious faces indicated their interest in her tale. "By and by, the woman and Carl were married. Her parents finally gave their support, realizing the wedding would go forward with or without them. Her mother knew someday, the woman would need her, and she did not want the family ties to be cut irrevocably. For the first two months, their marriage was a dream come true. The woman unpacked her hope chest and spread the treasured items around her new home. She lovingly put the Christmas ornaments in the attic, anticipating with joy their first Christmas together.

She cut her work at the pet shop back to part-time hours and thoroughly enjoyed the extra time being a homemaker. She felt she was finally where she belonged and was who she was meant to be.

"But during the third month, everything began to change. Carl announced she was no longer to call herself by the name she'd used for years. He said it sounded like a stripper name. He declared she had perverted a good Bible name and from this day forward, he would call by the name he deemed appropriate. He said he did not want to hear someone call her by her former name ever again, or she would regret it. Carl interrogated her daily about what she did all day, where she went, and who she talked to. If she visited her parents, he demanded to know what was said. He constantly fussed about her clothes, saying she'd gained weight and could no longer use the clothes she wore previously. Eventually, she began to realize, when he said 'body hugging', he actually meant any clothes that fit correctly. In an effort to win his approval once more, she went to thrift stores and tried to find oversized garments.

"The woman tried hard to be creative with their meals and cooked delicious dishes. Carl would thank her, but would then list all the things that displeased him about her preparation of the food. He was not happy with her housekeeping and would always sweep off the front porch, even when she told him she just finished the task. He took out the vacuum each evening, saying he could not live in such a pig sty, even though the woman dutifully vacuumed every day. Though she loved animals, Carl refused to allow pets inside the house. He was pleased when the woman's little terrier was hit by a car and killed. He told her she was better off without the dog, because it took too much of her time. He forbade her from getting another animal and told her to truly be a godly woman and wife, she must concentrate on her home and her husband.

"Gradually while the months passed, the woman began to feel she could do nothing right. Her life became a fog of misery. One minute, Carl would say he loved her. The next, he would berate her for the smallest perceived wrong. Nothing she did would please him. When she arrived home a few minutes late one evening, Carl yanked the driver's side door opened, grabbed her by the hair, and dragged her from the car. He accused her of hanging out with her work buddies instead of coming home where she belonged. He told her she would hand in her resignation the next day. He slapped her savagely and said he was through with her selfishness.

"He dragged her to a nearby tree, tied her to the trunk with clothesline, and went inside. The woman was terrified and humiliated. What happened? Why could she no longer do anything right? Was she so worthless she deserved to be slapped? She heard the door open and saw Carl come out and get into his red pick-up truck. To her horror, he began driving the vehicle straight at her. He barely missed hitting her, but continued to lunge his truck at her over and over from every angle. Gravel from the driveway flew from the tires and hit her in the face several times. She tried in vain to free herself, but Carl's knots were too tight. Finally, she stopped struggling and her head hung low. Carl eventually parked the truck and went back inside. He left her there all night long and in the morning, lovingly untied her bonds. He asked her why she would not submit and why she forced him to correct her constantly. After a hurried and secret phone call to her parents when Carl left for work, the woman made her escape, knowing deep within her heart, the next time, Carl would kill her."

Lizzy stopped and pulled a photograph from her folder. "Girls, the woman I've been telling you about is me. I was Carl's first wife." She paused for a moment to let that information sink in, then placed the photo on the overhead, and the image of Marcie in her wedding gown filled the screen. "This was his second wife, Marcie." The girls looked at her, expressions of confusion filling their faces. Lizzy paused and replaced the happy photograph with one from Marcie's autopsy, her face a bluish gray, the bruises obvious around her neck. "Carl murdered Marcie." Her voice caught, and she looked at the girls imploringly. "I didn't know Marcie, but her parents graciously permitted me to use her wedding portrait. This autopsy photo was admitted as evidence during Carl's trial. He is now serving a life sentence without the possibility of parole."

Lizzy turned off the overhead and leaned forward earnestly. "Over the last five years, there have been nearly three thousand domestic violence cases filed in Riponville County, and the number continues to rise every year. Nationwide, one in three female homicides is committed by a domestic partner." She looked around the group, seeking to make eye contact with each girl. "If I had been content where God placed me before I met Carl, I would never have fallen for his flattery and his lies. I truly believe I would have seen the red flags warning me something was wrong, and I would not have continued in the relationship. Even though I made a nearly fatal mistake, I believe God has now called me to warn other women about these predators."

She looked around the group again and smiled. "You are precious young ladies, valuable beyond price. The good news is, you don't have to end up in an abusive relationship like I did. There are many warning signs that will help you identify an abuser right away." Lizzy placed another sheet on the overhead. "Here are some things to look for. An abusive man will, at first, make you feel amazing. He will shower you with gifts even when he barely knows you. You'll most likely think he's the most romantic man ever. He may even quote a lot of scripture and seem to be a very spiritual man. He will want you to commit right away, rather than being friends and slowly getting to know you. Abusive men want to isolate you from your friends and family and will often become violently angry if you spend time with anyone else.

"They want to control everything about you. They will also often act like they are the victim and will say you are the one who makes them do what they do. The thing is, abuse usually starts small, like someone lighting a match." Lizzy put a picture of a burning match onto the overhead. "But the small flame will grow and grow until you have a forest fire on your hands, and you won't know how to escape. Abuse is a burning fire that will end in your destruction." The next picture illustrated acres of burning timber. "Another thing to remember is, no matter what an abuser says to you, they never change. Like I mentioned before, after an abusive event, some men will blame you and say you drove them to it. But some men will cry and plead with you to forgive them. They swear they will never do it again. They say they love you and didn't mean to hurt you." Lizzy looked out over her audience, her expression pleading with them to understand. "Do not be fooled. That line is only good until the next time he hits you. And the next time. And the next time."

The girls looked at her with serious, thoughtful expressions. Lizzy became brisk. "Now, ladies, can someone tell me how Carl showed these signs?" Several girls raised their hands. Lizzy was pleased they saw the correlations with Carl's behavior and the warning signs she'd just listed. After allowing each girl to speak, she opened a question and answer session, during which there was much good discussion on the topic.

When the questions began to wane, Lizzy wrapped up her talk. "Girls, I've told you what to look out for in an abusive man. But the most important thing you can do in your entire life is look to God. He is the only one who can truly love you unconditionally. When you're dating, ask yourself, 'Does this boy want to be more like Christ? Does he exhibit character traits of a Godly man, like faithfulness, truthfulness, kindness, and caring? Does he think about good things?' Lizzy put another card on the overhead and read the verse aloud. "Philippians 4:8 says, 'And now, dear brothers and sisters, one final thing. Fix your thoughts on what is true, and honorable, and right, and pure, and lovely, and admirable. Think about things that are excellent and worthy of praise.'" She smiled at her audience. "Obviously, no guy is going to be perfect. I'm sure you all know that." The girls laughed and nodded, and Lizzy laughed with them. She reached to tuck a strand of hair behind one ear, and looked at them knowingly. "And we girls aren't perfect either, huh? But we want to look for guys who exemplify that verse. And we need to be women who do the same. The thing is, we can't expect a guy to be what God should be to us. No guy or girl can hold up under that kind of pressure, because we're all human. Remember, only God can fulfill the deepest needs of your heart, so look to Him, not to a guy, for the relationship that will truly fulfill your life."

Lizzy gathered her papers and looked at the precious young girls before her. "Thank you, ladies, for allowing me to come talk with you. I'm going to hang out for a bit." She lowered her voice to a whisper. "Somebody said there would be brownies when I finished. I sincerely hope that's true." She winked at them and the girls giggled, then burst into applause.

Lizzy stayed for a while to enjoy refreshments and talk with the girls one on one. When she left the building and got into her car, she was tired but happy. *Thank You, Lord,* she prayed as she drove home. *Thank You for using me tonight. Protect and guide each one of those girls, Father. Keep them safe and bring just the right man into each of their lives, a man who will truly love and cherish them as You love and cherish the church.*

~ * ~

"Hi, Denae, is Lizzy here?" Tucker stood at the counter of the circuit court records office on Friday, November 19th .

Denae grinned. "She surely is." She looked toward Lizzy's workstation. "Lizzy, you have a visitor."

Lizzy glanced up. She felt the familiar rush of delight at the sight of Tucker's face. His eyes seemed to envelop her in light and made her feel safe, protected, and adored. She rose, straightened her merino wool sweater, and briskly made her way to the front.

"How may I help, sir?" Then she looked at him sternly and put a hand on her hip. "Do you need a background check?"

"No, ma'am, I do not." Tucker's eyes glinted with mischief. "Actually, I need a copy of this *True Bill*." He handed Lizzy a piece of paper on which was written the indictment number.

Lizzy was puzzled. "What? Why on earth would you need a copy of an indictment, Tuck? I mean, of course, I'll get it for you, but ..." She moved to the counter computer and rested her hand on the mouse, but then halted in confusion.

Tucker smiled, but this time his eyes turned serious. "I'm going to be down here asking for copies often. You're looking at the soon-to-be newest addition to the Riponville County District Attorney's Office."

Lizzy was shocked. "Tucker. Seriously? You're giving up real-estate law?"

He reached across the counter and gently covered her hand with his. "Yes, but I'm also giving up the Senate."

Lizzy looked at him, shocked again, and sure she misunderstood. "Did I just hear you say you're giving up the Senate? Tucker ..."

"I'll finish out my term, of course. But after that, you're going to have to put up with me nagging you to file documents for me."

Lizzy was so surprised she almost felt lightheaded. Sandra approached and put a hand gently on her shoulder. "Why don't you go take a break? You can get Mr. Bates' copy when you get back."

"Thank you, Sandra." Lizzy sniffed as sudden tears welled up in her eyes. She made her way out the secured door to stand at Tucker's side. They walked downstairs and out the front entrance of the courthouse. The air was cool, but they did not need their coats. Benches were placed here and there on the lawn, so Tucker steered Lizzy to one, and they sat down.

"Tucker, what's this all about?" Lizzy's voice was now laced with concern. *He can't give this up just for me,* she thought. *He can't. He'd be unhappy eventually and hate me for ruining his life.* She brushed invisible lint from her black slacks.

Tucker gently took her hand. "God has been working in my heart for quite a long time now. I've felt the political role was no longer for me. Ethan encouraged me to seek out a position with the DA's office. I prayed about it for months and felt God leading in that direction. I interviewed and got the job." He looked a bit chagrined. "There'll be a bit of a learning curve, of course, since I've not been involved in criminal law, but I'm excited. Cora has been hinting for months that she wants to retire, so I'll close my practice. Everything is falling into place."

Lizzy's eyes began to fill with tears. "So, Tucker, you're not doing this for me, right? That would never work. Just because I don't feel like I could ever be comfortable being part of the political scene, doesn't mean you should just give it up." She began to feel desperate. "Tucker that would not work. You'd grow to resent me for keeping you from your calling." She shook her head and pulled her hand away. "I knew this day would come. I've been praying about this for a long time. I cannot allow you to sacrifice your Senate position for me."

Tucker paused for a moment to take in her words. Here he'd been concerned she would somehow feel he was giving up or not finishing the job. *Wow, Lord,* he thought. *All this time, You've been working in both of our hearts.* He realized Lizzy was dabbing at her eyes and trying to hold back tears. His heart melted, and he knew in that moment, he could never live without her.

"Lizzy, I had no idea you felt that way." His voice was warm but firm. "Do you understand? I know you felt uncomfortable at the luncheon this summer, but I didn't realize the thought of a political life was weighing on you so heavily."

She thought for a moment and realized he was right. Though her concerns were forefront in her own mind after the luncheon, she'd kept them from Tucker. He took her hand once more. "Lizzy, look at me." She looked up, and her pain-filled eyes met his. A breeze gently mussed her shiny, dark hair. He wanted desperately to tell her he loved her but sensed the timing was still not right.

"Elizabeth Godfrey, you are so dear to me. I would have been willing to give up the Senate for you, but I assure you, this is a God thing, pure and simple. Like I said earlier, I'll finish out my term. I can do no less for the folks who voted for me, but afterwards, I'll start my new job with the DA's Office." He looked at her with an impish grin and whispered, "I have to admit, I'm quite pleased to be finished with campaigning. Being on the road so much was never my thing."

Lizzy grimaced and nodded. "It wouldn't have been mine either." She looked at him thoughtfully. "I never realized until just now but I haven't actually said anything to you about my feelings regarding politics. I've prayed about the issue so often, I just felt like I'd talked to you about it, as well." She squeezed his hand gently. "I'm so happy for you, Tucker. And I'm happy for me, too. It's going to be so nice having you around the office." They gazed into each other's eyes for a few moments. Had they not been in a public place, Tucker would have been tempted to kiss her.

Lizzy broke the moment with a regretful sigh after checking her watch. "I need to get back, Tuck."

"I understand. We'll talk later. Are we still on for dinner tomorrow night?"

They rose and began to walk to the entrance of the courthouse. "Absolutely." Lizzy went through the door he held open for her. "And remember, it's my treat for your birthday."

"All righty then. It's a deal." They both greeted the bailiff at the front desk, then walked to the stairwell. "Have a wonderful rest of your day, Lizzy." Tucker's voice was soft, his eyes full of the love he could no longer hide. "I'll talk to you tonight."

Lizzy's heart warmed while she returned to her office. The look in Tucker's eyes made her wonder if he loved her. She felt her own heart tugging toward his in response. Abruptly, the familiar feeling of fear washed away her joy. Why did this happen every time she considered a more serious relationship with Tucker? She refused to consider her conflicting feelings, telling herself she needed to get back to work.

~ * ~

"Can I meet you there, Tuck? I have some errands to run beforehand." Lizzy paced back and forth, still in her long-sleeved t-shirt and pajama pants, praying he would not object. The picture would not be ready at the frame shop until five-thirty, and she still needed time to wrap the gift.

"Sure, that's fine. Will six o'clock give you enough time or should we say six-thirty?"

Lizzy gave a silent sigh of relief. "Six-thirty will be perfect." Her voice was warm with affection. "See you tonight, Tuck."

Lizzy tapped her phone off and grinned. Everything was falling into place and apparently, he did not suspect a thing. Lizzy walked to the living room and sat on the couch. "Okay, Mom, everything is settled." She laughed delightedly. "Planning surprises is so much fun."

Rose grinned from her recliner. "How many people are coming?"

"Just five. I wanted to keep things small and cozy." Lizzy looked at her mother in awe. "Would you ever have thought I'd be doing this? I mean, I never dreamed a decent guy would come along." Her voice broke a bit. "I really care for him, Mom. Honestly, when we first started dating, I wasn't sure I could ever feel again. I thought that part of me was damaged beyond repair."

"I know, honey." Rose adjusted the blanket she'd draped over herself. "I've wondered if you'd ever be able to trust him after what you went through with Carl." She looked at Lizzy thoughtfully. "I believe Tucker is a good man, but I don't want to influence you in any way. Just know I'm praying God's plan will be accomplished and for protection for you if all is not as it seems."

"Thank you, Mom. I'm so grateful for your prayers. Tucker and I have been dating for a year now, and I've seen him in all kinds of situations. He's not perfect, of course, but he's nothing like Carl." Lizzy tucked her feet under her. "Deb, Marshall, and the girls love him. That speaks well for him. And the ladies at work all approve." She stared at the muted television. "It's weird, though, Mom. I still feel scared if I think of anything long-term. I don't understand that."

"I do, honey. You went through an incredibly horrible ordeal. You just need to take your time and follow God's leading. He will reveal His will for you and Tucker in His time."

Lizzy looked at her mother and grinned, a twinkle creeping into her eyes. "Thankfully, he's passed all the background checks with flying colors. Only one speeding ticket when he was twenty-one." The women laughed contentedly and chatted for several minutes. Lizzy finally rose. "I guess I'd better jump in the shower and get my day started."

~ * ~

Tucker greeted constituents with a smile and a handshake, but kept looking toward the door of Rizzoli's, eager to see her familiar face. When Lizzy came through the door, his eyes lit up. Her tweed jacket, pencil skirt, and heels set off her beauty to perfection. He greeted her with a warm hug, and his heart fluttered a bit at her nearness.

Lizzy smiled when she pulled back. "Hungry?" she asked a bit breathlessly. He was so handsome in his sweater, jeans, and loafers.

"Starved. Let's go." Tucker offered her his arm, and she tucked her hand in the crook of his elbow. The hostess checked the name, then escorted them to the back room.

As soon as Tucker and Lizzy entered, they heard multiple voices saying, "Surprise!"

Tucker burst into laughter and looked at Lizzy with a grin. "This is your doing I presume?"

"Guilty as charged." She grinned shamelessly. "Did we really surprise you?"

He nodded. "Completely. I didn't have a clue." He greeted his friends, then helped Lizzy with her chair. He leaned in close to her ear and whispered, "Thank you, Lizzy. This was an awesome surprise."

She turned her head, her face close to his, and whispered back, "You're welcome." For a moment, they felt like they were the only people in the restaurant. Tucker gave her a warm smile, squeezed her shoulder, and took his seat.

After a sumptuous meal and a wonderful time of conversation and fellowship, Lizzy tapped on her glass with her fork. "Ladies and gentlemen, I need to run out to the car for a moment. I'll be right back. No, Tucker," she said quickly when he began to rise to come with her. "You cannot escort me to the car." She winked at him slyly, and the group at the table laughed. "You guys keep him here. There will be no peeking." In moments, she returned, carrying a large, bulky package. The conversation quieted once again, and Lizzy spoke. "Tucker, I have a special gift for you. I hope you'll enjoy it." She smiled at him gently and handed him the package.

"Lizzy, what on earth? You didn't have to do anything. I thought this dinner was my gift."

Lizzy looked at Ethan. "You seriously need to teach him not to underestimate people. He's going to need that skill as a prosecutor." The group burst into laughter and Tucker grinned again while he began to tear away the wrapping paper. His grin faded when the beautifully framed picture came into view. He gazed at the piece for several minutes, drawn into the scene by some inexplicable force.

Finally, he spoke in a hushed voice. "Lizzy, this is ... over the top. Wow. How did you find it?"

"My friend Joy is the photographer. When you mentioned the card I sent you, and how much you loved it, I asked her to make an enlargement."

He gazed at the picture, then carefully placed it in his chair and came around to hug Lizzy tightly. "Thank you, Lizzy. Thank you. I will treasure this."

"That will look awesome in your new office, Tuck." Ethan reached for a leftover bread stick. "Gorgeous piece, Lizzy."

Tucker released her and nodded. "It will indeed." He looked at his gift again. "This picture will have a wall all to itself."

The group finished their dessert, and everyone wished Tucker a happy birthday before leaving the restaurant. Lizzy paid the bill, and she and Tucker made their way to his car. Tucker was strangely silent, and Lizzy began to worry. Had she done too much? Was the gift too extravagant? Her heart began to clench with fear.

Tucker stowed the picture carefully in the back seat. While they walked over to Lizzy's Honda, he suddenly gasped. "That's it. That's it." He looked at Lizzy in triumph. "You're the one."

"Tucker Bates, what on earth are you talking about? I don't know what was in the tiramisu, but ..." She looked at him quizzically.

"No, I just realized something amazing." His eyes were bright with excitement. They reached her car, and he took her hand. "After my accident, right before I woke up, I was dreaming. I saw a field of flags, and a woman was in the middle of them, beckoning me to join her. She said it was so amazing to walk among the flags. It was you, Lizzy. The woman was you." He shook his head, trying to understand. "I don't know how, but it's true. I have no memory of meeting you before that, but the woman in my dream was most definitely you."

Lizzy inhaled slowly. "Wow, Tucker. That is ... wow. Amazing. I know God doesn't work through dreams now like He once did, but maybe sometimes He still does."

Tucker pulled her into a warm hug and held her for a minute before reluctantly releasing her. "It's getting late. You'd better get back."

She gazed into his eyes for what seemed like hours. "Yes, I guess I should."

Just as she began to fumble in her purse for her keys, Tucker gently cupped his hand under her chin, turned her face to his, and gave her a gentle kiss. He pulled back and smiled, his heart in his eyes. "Be safe driving home."

He opened the car door and made sure she was safely inside, then watched her drive away. *I've found the one. Lord, thank You for bringing her to me. She is the most amazing woman I've ever met. Help me not to rush her and ruin this.*

Lizzy drove home in a daze. Rose met her at the door, eager to hear how the evening went. Lizzy put her purse on the dining room table, kicked off her heels, and plopped down on the couch, her face a study in confusion.

"In many ways, this was a wonderful evening, Mom." She looked off into space. "Tucker loved his picture. He was totally blown away." She sat up straight all of a sudden. "Mom, he kissed me and I actually enjoyed it. When Carl kissed me, it just felt weird. I felt creepy-crawly about his saliva getting on me. From the beginning I didn't enjoy kissing him, and after the abuse started, it was just plain gross. I hated it. But when Tucker kissed me tonight, everything was different. His kiss was what I always dreamed a kiss should be. It felt so natural. But then on the way home, I got so scared." Her voice broke into a sob, and her face reflected her genuine angst. "What's wrong with me, Mom? Tucker is a wonderful man but we've made no commitment to each other. What if he drops me now that he's kissed me?"

Seeing her child in so much emotional pain was comparable to a serrated-edged knife being driven through Rose's heart. "Oh, honey, I wish I could take the fear from your heart. I don't think he'd have invested all this time if he didn't really care about you. I feel sure Tucker is nothing like Carl. Your friends all love and approve of him." Her voice broke, and she was silent.

"Mom, are you okay? I didn't mean to upset you." Lizzy went to kneel beside by her mother in the recliner. "I'm sorry."

"Oh, honey, I'm so happy for you, but I hurt for you at the same time." She gave Lizzy a watery smile. "I've wanted my baby girl to have someone for so long, but I honestly thought it wasn't meant to be. When you met Tucker, I truly felt things were different with him."

Tears spilled from Lizzy's eyes and ran down her cheeks. "Tucker is different in every conceivable way from Carl. I feel safe and cared for when I look into his eyes. I don't know what the future holds but sometimes when I think about something serious, I get scared. And at the same time, I really do trust him and would be devastated if he left me."

She laughed then, and Rose looked at her questioningly. "I think I'm going crazy, Mom. I was in such a daze, I'm pretty sure my guardian angel drove me part of the way home. All the way, actually, because after the glow of the kiss, the fear hit and I still wasn't any good."

The women giggled, enjoying the comic relief. After a few moments, Rose said, "Honey, I'd like to pray for you. Can we talk to the Lord together?"

Lizzy took her mother's hands, and Rose prayed. "Dear Father, thank You for my Lizzy. Thank You for helping her to escape from Carl. Thank You for everything You've taught her over the past few years. Father, thank You for bringing Tucker into our lives. Thank You for this good man, and thank You that my Lizzy can have this wonderful relationship with him. Please cover them with Your love and grace, and lead them. Above all, keep their eyes always focused on You. Father, I pray You will lead Lizzy along and help her with her fears. I can't help but believe You have a purpose to be accomplished while she works through them. Help her to learn what You have for her to learn. In the precious name of Jesus, amen.

~Twenty-Four~

Each month flew by faster than the last. Tucker and Lizzy spent most of their free time together. They enjoyed shared meals, took walks in the park, enjoyed game nights with Rose, and trips to see Marshall, Deborah, and the girls. Text messages between the two flew back and forth throughout each day. Tucker began attending Ripon Falls Community Church, and they also went to small-group meetings. The fears which still tried to plague Lizzy's heart on occasion gradually abated while she continued to observe Tucker's steady, reliable behavior. Never did he push her for anything in their relationship. Though far from perfect, he exhibited an unquenchable desire to be more like Christ, and Lizzy felt her trust in him increase with every passing day. Time was proving his character to be strong and dependable. Lizzy spent time with Tucker and his parents, and Tucker spent time with Rose, Marshall, Deborah, and the girls. Emilie and Gilbert Bates adored the woman who captured their son's heart and prayed daily for God's direction. Tucker bided his time, patiently waiting on God's leading. Though they held hands and enjoyed occasional hugs and kisses, he was careful not to let their physical affection cloud their thinking. He knew when the time was right, God would move in his heart, and he would be free to share his feelings.

In early January, Tucker sat on the sofa in his parent's living room. "So Mom and Dad, what do you think? Lizzy and I have been dating for almost two years now. I thought I'd see if she and her family would like to go up to the cabin with me this year. I've tried to be careful not to move too fast. We've gotten to know each other quite well but this would be a great way for us to spend a week in close proximity. I've prayed about the idea and feel peace but I want your thoughts."

Emilie looked at her husband questioningly. Gilbert met her gaze, then turned to Tucker. "Son, I think God has given you wisdom and good sense. I can't see any problem with your idea. You have most certainly given her space and time to see you won't hurt her like her ex-husband. I think a trip away would be fun for everyone."

"Her family will be there," Emilie added. "That should put her even more at ease. Just be sure she knows you're not going to be upset with her if she doesn't feel comfortable with the idea."

Tucker nodded thoughtfully. Gilbert Bates leaned forward. "Let's pray about this." They joined hands. "Father we come to You today on behalf of Tucker and Lizzy. We know Tucker has fallen in love with her and feels she is the woman with whom he wants to spend the rest of his life. Father, I pray You would grant our son wisdom whether or not to proceed with his idea for this trip. We know Lizzy went through a terrible ordeal, and Tucker needs to be sensitive to her needs. I pray Your will be done. Please help him to know Your leading. Amen."

"Amen. Thanks, Mom and Dad." Tucker squeezed their hands tightly.

~ * ~

"So, I was thinking I would love for you and your family to join me." Tucker and Lizzy sat eating lunch at their favorite deli across from the courthouse. "The cabin has five bedrooms, so there's plenty of space."

"Wow, Tucker. The last time I went skiing was in high school, and I wasn't good at it. At all." Lizzy shook her head, but smiled. "Still, the trip does sound amazing."

"You'd love Whitby Mountain." He took a sip of coffee and continued. "Oh and there's a nice sized ice rink right near the ski lift if skating is more your thing."

"I enjoy skating." Lizzy took a bite of her sandwich and chewed thoughtfully. She looked at Tucker, her eyes taking on a glint of steel. "But by George if I'm going on a ski trip, I'm going to ski. Maybe this time I can learn to stop." She giggled a bit at his expression. "Seriously, I could go down the mountain just fine. I even enjoyed the moguls on the intermediate slope. However, stopping was a bit of a mystery. I tried just like they showed me, but it never quite worked out. If I wanted to stop, I just had to fall down." Lizzy grinned, and the determined gleam filled her eyes once more. "I'm going to study up on it, Tucker. There must be some training videos on YouTube."

Tucker's face looked like a kid's at Christmas. "So do I take that as a yes?".

"Absolutely. As long as I can get the time off." While she looked at him, her expression sobered. "I doubt Mom will feel she can go. Please don't feel badly. She loves you to pieces, but she just doesn't enjoy traveling anymore. But I know Deb, Marshall, and the girls will be over the moon excited. Marshall used to live in New Hampshire. He went skiing every winter back in the day."

"How about Millie and Kate? Have they ever skied?"

"I don't think so. But if for some reason they don't take to it, I'll go with them to the ice rink. They both love to skate."

They finished their lunch, talking excitedly about the trip. While Tucker walked Lizzy back to work, she suddenly wondered, *How am I going to pay for all this? Skiing is an expensive pastime. I don't know if Marshall and Deb can afford this. I'll have to raid my sav...*

"By the way, be sure to tell Marshall and Deb this trip is my treat." Tucker opened the door for Lizzy after she swiped her key card.

"But Tucker ..."

"No, ma'am," he said firmly, an engaging twinkle in his eyes. "If I invite you all to visit my cabin to have some winter fun, I will be picking up the tab. End of discussion."

Lizzy smiled at him warmly. "Thank you, Tucker. We're going to have a blast."

~ * ~

"How long will it take to get there, Mommy? Millie pressed her small face against the glass, watching the unfamiliar scenery with rapt attention.

"Just a few hours, honey." Deborah grinned at Marshall, who gave her a sly wink.

"Daddy, will we be able to build a snowman?" Kate asked.

"And make snow angels?" Millie looked at her sister. "We make the best double snow angels, don't we Katie?" Her sister giggled and nodded eagerly. The girls' excitement was contagious.

"From the look of the sky, I think there will definitely be snowmen and snow angels in our very near future." Marshall eyed the gray clouds rolling in. "Maybe we'll even have a snowball fight."

The girls giggled with delight and began planning all the fun they'd have. Deborah looked at Tucker's Accord ahead of them. "It was so nice of him to invite us, wasn't it, Marsh?"

"Surely was." Marshall looked at the mountain vista spreading out before them. "I really like Tucker. He's a good man. Any idea how Lizzy feels?"

Deborah's expression turned thoughtful. "She really likes him. I'd even go so far as to say I think she's in love with him, but I'm not sure she feels completely safe to admit that to herself yet. Even though he's nothing like Carl, she's still scared of making another mistake." She squeezed Marshall's knee gently. "We just have to keep praying. Thank the Lord Tucker seems to realize he has to take things slowly. Lizzy did tell me the other day, though, that she trusts him. That's huge."

"Tucker seems to be a patient man and willing to wait on God's timing. I have a good feeling about them." Marshall squeezed his wife's hand gently and gave her a smile, then returned his gaze to the road ahead.

~ * ~

After what felt like miles of gravel road winding its way through the forest, Lizzy and Tucker finally rounded a bend and before them, just beyond a wide parking area, sat the cabin. "Honey, we're home." Tucker smiled and turned to look at her.

"Oh, Tucker." Lizzy's mouth hung open. "This is beautiful. When you said cabin, I thought you meant ..." Her words trailed off while she gazed at the large log home. Evergreens surrounded the house on each side, and shrubs set off the entrance. A cobblestone walkway led to the front door, and rocking chairs sat here and there on the wrap-around porch. Snow, which had begun to fall during their trip, now accented the beautiful scene with a light blanket of white.

Tucker was opening Lizzy's door when Marshall drove up. He jumped out of the Ex-Terra and went to open the passenger door for his wife. "Tucker, when you said cabin, I thought we'd be roughing it, man." He laughed. "Guess we won't be needing those sleeping bags."

Tucker grinned, popped the trunk, and began removing luggage. "It really did start out as a cabin. When Grandpa Bates left the place to me, there was just one main room, a bedroom, and a bath. I decided to invest in remodeling and expanding so I could turn what we had into a nice vacation rental house. So far, it's worked out well, although Grandpa wouldn't recognize it anymore." He laughed remembering his grandfather. "He loved stark simplicity, but I prefer a few more modern conveniences."

"I'm with you, Tuck." Lizzy grabbed her overnight bag and pillow. She looked over at Deborah. "I'm all about the creature comforts." Her sister began to giggle, and Lizzy joined in. They were both remembering their camping trip at the beach the summer after Lizzy graduated from high school. Lizzy left the family on their own and paid for a hotel room. "You laugh, Deborah, but that tent was still like an oven by nine p.m." Lizzy looked at her sister pointedly. "I'm not into being baked to well-done after spending all day in the sun. I don't think that horrid tent ever did cool down."

Deborah giggled. "And remember the lobster episode?

Lizzy burst into gales of laughter. "Oh my word, that poor creature."

"These sound like stories I need to hear." Tucker looked at them with interest.

"Me, too." Marshall opened the back of the SUV. "I don't remember hearing any stories about a beach trip or lobsters."

"Maybe." Lizzy looked at them with a smirk on her face. "If you're both really good and behave yourselves."

Deborah shook her head and laughed again at the memories. She looked around before helping Millie and Kate with their suitcases. "Tucker, it really was a great idea to turn this into a vacation property. I'll bet you have renters every week."

"I do. I have to make sure I get my own reservations and those for Mom and Dad in early, or we miss out." Tucker led the way, and everyone headed toward the front door. He opened the lock and stepped aside so they could enter the house. Lizzy's eyes filled with admiration while she took in the great room that featured a cathedral ceiling. The open concept design encompassed the kitchen and a large dining table made of wood with finished log stumps as supports. Comfortable leather sofas played court to a massive river rock fireplace, the obvious focal point of the space. The log walls lent an air of cozy warmth to the entire room.

"Let's get settled and then I'll give you the nickel tour." Tucker gave them all an engaging smile. "I really hope you enjoy yourselves this week. I usually come up here alone, so this is a treat to have company."

"Tucker, I think I speak for everyone when I say we will most definitely have an amazing week." Marshall looked at his family, and everyone nodded enthusiastically.

Millie eyed the huge fireplace. "Can we build a fire, Daddy?"

"And roast marshmallows?" Kate's eyes danced with anticipation.

"I'm sure we'll do both, girls. But first, we need to get unpacked."

Marshall led the way back outside where they gathered up the rest of the suitcases. Tucker showed them all to their rooms and told them to take their time getting unpacked, then proceeded to his own room with a smile of contentment on his face.

Lizzy looked around the tastefully decorated guest room and felt like she'd ended up at a posh resort lodge. She laid her suitcase down on the queen-sized bed which was made of logs with an artfully carved headboard. The burgundy and green bedspread quilt and pillows added pops of color to the room. Lizzy noted several doors and went to investigate. She found a bathroom when she opened the first door. She grinned with delight. The walk-in shower encompassed one entire wall and was tiled completely with gray river stones. A lovely print of a white-tailed buck standing in the snow with craggy mountains in the background graced the wall opposite the shower. Above a rustic wood vanity, hung an oval mirror. Lizzy opened another door along the wall and discovered the commode and a small linen cupboard.

She returned to the main room and collected her overnight bag, which contained her makeup, a bottle of *Wen®* cleansing conditioner, and her other hair and skin care supplies. She unpacked everything and got her products situated on the vanity. Delighted, Lizzy looked around the bathroom again. *This is so cool. I am going to enjoy getting ready in here.* She tossed the empty overnight bag onto the bed and went to see what was behind door number two. A small walk-in closet met her eyes, which contained a good supply of cedar hangars and had plenty of room for all her things. She also noticed a small recliner next to the log dresser, so after unpacking, she plopped into its soft depths and switched on the floor lamp standing nearby.

"Lord, thank You for this wonderful opportunity," Lizzy whispered aloud. "I can't believe how beautiful this place is. Thank You for this chance to rest and relax. Help me to get to know Tucker even better this week, and please, Lord, have Your will accomplished in our relationship. You know I want Your will more than anything else in this world."

~ * ~

Lizzy and Deborah volunteered to cook supper. After a hilarious time spent laughing more than cooking, the sisters presented a delicious meal of hamburgers, fries, fruit, and chocolate-chip cookies for dessert.

"Deb, I haven't had so much fun cooking in years." Lizzy laughed while Tucker pulled out her chair and seated her at the table. "I forgot how much fun we used to have."

Deborah laughed. "I get to have fun cooking every day with two little girls I know." She winked at her daughters who giggled. "We've come up with some amazing creations."

"And Mommy says some of them were even ebdible," Kate said with a giggle. The adults laughed at the joke. "Honey, that's 'edible', not 'ebdible'," Deborah corrected lovingly. "Try it."

"Ed-i-ble," Kate said carefully.

The adults and Millie applauded her. "Good job, Kate." Tucker grinned and gave her shoulder a little squeeze. "I hope you and Millie will make us something amazing while you're here this week."

"Can we, Mommy?" both girls asked simultaneously.

"We'll see."

Tucker said grace, then looked at Lizzy across the table. "I want to hear that lobster tale, Lizzy."

Everyone burst out laughing. Tucker looked puzzled, then grinned. "Ha, ha." He shook his head. "You guys are hopeless. Oh, fair Elizabeth, please do regale us with the exciting *story* of said lobster."

Lizzy grinned and put down her burger. "Okay, so one summer, Deb and I decided to rent a house on the coast. We felt that for the week to truly be an authentic beach vacation, we should cook our own seafood."

"We don't do fishing," Deborah put in dryly. "The catching them part is all right, but no way am I putting my hands on that slimy scaly thing to get it off the hook."

The group tittered at the look on Deborah's face, and Lizzy continued. "So we go to a seafood market and pick out a lobster. They put it in a cooler for us, and back we went.

We had no idea how to cook the thing, but we figured we'd just Google for instructions. After we got back to the house, we started wondering if the lobster needed to be in water like fish do. So we fill the kitchen sink with water, shake a bunch of table salt in it, and plopped him in."

Deborah laughed. "That poor thing. I'm sure that was different salt from what's in ocean water. We probably did the critter in long before he hit the pot."

Lizzy looked thoughtful. "Yeah, I don't recall him moving at all after he went in the sink."

Deborah continued the story. "I booted up my laptop, clicked on Google, and to my horror, read an article that said the lobster would scream when we put him in the boiling water."

"We were about to be sick." Lizzy looked at Deborah, remembering the moment. "We'd had doubts about picking something alive to cook, and the screaming thing about did us in. So we hatched a plan. We put the pot on the stove and started the water heating. Deb went into the other room and turned the TV up really loud. She came back in and picked up the lid. Once the water was boiling, I grabbed the lobster, threw him in the pot, Deb clapped on the lid, and we ran to the TV room and put our hands over our ears."

Everyone snickered, picturing the scene. "So, did you hear any screaming?" Tucker asked with a grin.

"That's the crazy thing. We did! The TV was tuned to a horror movie channel, and right at the moment we entered the room, this woman lets out a blood-curdling scream." The group at the table, including Lizzy and Deborah roared with laughter. When the hilarity calmed down, Lizzy shook her head. "I'll tell you, after all that, we didn't even enjoy that lobster. Too much trauma associated with it, I guess."

"I can't stand the idea of throwing something alive into a pot of boiling water." Deborah shuddered. "After that experience, I couldn't eat lobster again if you made me."

"Me, either." Lizzy nodded emphatically and picked up a French fry. "That was the end of lobster for me."

The group thoroughly enjoyed the rest of their dinner and more entertaining reminiscing. Afterwards, Marshall and Tucker went to the mud room, returned with kindling and a couple of logs, and got a fire started. Lizzy, Millie, and Kate set up a game of Monopoly™ on the coffee table. After a relaxing evening before the blazing fire, the family headed for bed, eager for the next day to arrive when fun in the snow would be the order of the day.

~ * ~

Lizzy awoke early, showered, dressed, and got herself fixed up for the day. She put on her slippers and padded to the kitchen to start breakfast. She was standing at the sink filling the kettle, when she glanced up and looked out the window. *Oh wow*! She stopped and stared. The ground was covered with a beautiful blanket of white.

She jumped when she felt a hand on her shoulder. "Oh, I'm sorry, Lizzy. I didn't mean to scare you," Tucker apologized.

A familiar warmth came over her, and delightful waves shimmered through her at his touch. She turned off the water, trying once again to process her feelings. "No worries." She put the kettle on the stove and returned to the window where Tucker stood gazing outside. "I was just mesmerized by the view and didn't hear you come in."

They stood for a moment, and then Tucker casually took her hand. *I love the feeling when he holds my hand,* Lizzy thought. *It feels so natural, and I feel safe somehow.*

Tucker interrupted her train of thought. "Want to go out and take a walk?" His eyes were bright with delight, like a little boy with his first fire engine. "I love snow."

"Me, too." Lizzy grinned at him. "Let's do it. We can leave a note for the others."

Tucker turned off the kettle, and they both headed for the coat closet beside the front door. After they donned in coats, gloves, hats, and boots, they burst out of the door and inhaled deep breaths of the crisp clean air.

Tucker offered Lizzy his arm, and she linked her hand in the crook of his elbow, her heart nearly bursting in the joy of the moment. With delight, they began to trek their way through the snow, looking all around at the scenery which had been transformed overnight into a winter wonderland. They tromped around for almost an hour, when Lizzy reluctantly said, “Tucker, I’m starving.”

“Me, too.” He grinned at her and gently touched his gloved hand under her chin. “But first ...” He allowed the love in his heart to flow into his eyes, then drew her face to his in a gentle kiss. “Lizzy, I’m going to tell you something, but I don’t want you to be afraid. I don’t want you to feel pressured, and I don’t want you to feel rushed.”

He drew her as close as their bulky jackets would allow and put his arms around her waist. “I love you, Lizzy. I’ve never thought I would meet anyone like you. I am still amazed God brought you into my life. You have been worth the wait.” He gently kissed her again, then looked deep into her blue eyes, which contained a mixture of happiness and confusion.

“Tucker, you are so sweet, and hearing you say those words means the world to me. But ...”

Tucker put a finger to her lips. “You don’t need to say anything. Like I said, no pressure. No rush, sweetheart. I adore you, and my love is not going to waver. I’m not going anywhere. I understand you may still have issues you need to work through, and I have all the time in the world. I don’t want you to say anything until you’re ready.” He smiled and pulled her into a gentle hug.

“Thank you for understanding, Tucker.” Lizzy melted into his embrace, genuinely pleased at his declaration of love, but still feeling uncomfortable with returning the sentiment.

After giving her another squeeze and a quick kiss, Tucker released her and tucked her hand in the crook of his elbow once more. “Let’s get back. We’re going to need a good breakfast to sustain us on the slopes this morning.”

Lizzy was thankful he didn't belabor the point. Varying emotions tumbled over and over in her mind. On the one hand, she felt she did love Tucker. But fear of making another mistake still hovered in the background, an ever-present, menacing presence. She determined to put all serious thoughts from her mind for the moment, and just enjoy the day.

~ * ~

Lizzy stood at the top of the Bunny slope with Tucker and adjusted her sunglasses. "Okay, I've watched several YouTube videos about stopping, so I expect to be able to do this." She focused her mind on the task at hand, trying to put aside her turbulent emotions.

Tucker gave her shoulder a squeeze of encouragement. "Just take things slow and practice. I know you can do it."

"Here goes." She pushed off and glided down the gentle hill. She almost managed to stop, but glided to the left a bit instead of actually stopping when she intended.

Up the hill she went again, her face set with determination to figure out the process. "That was great. You've almost got it," Tucker said proudly.

Lizzy nodded absently, then gave the hill another try. This time she stopped like a pro. "All right!" Tucker put a fist in the air and cheered from the top of the hill. He skied down to join her.

"Tucker, you go on and enjoy yourself. I'm going to hang with Millie and Kate for a while." She glanced over to where an instructor was helping the girls with the basics. "I told Deb I'd ski with them today."

Tucker agreed and smiled to hide his disappointment. Enjoying himself pretty much meant spending every moment with Lizzy, but he recognized immediately he must give her some space. "Okay, then. I'm off. I've got my phone in my pocket, so just call or text if you need me."

"Will do." Lizzy waved him away. She didn't really understand why she suddenly felt smothered. An amazing, handsome, kind, Godly man, a man she truly cared for, had declared his love for her just this morning, and now she wanted to get away. *Why am I like this, Lord? Why?* She shook her head while she skied over to join the girls. *What's wrong with me?* Visions of Carl flipped through her mind like a slide show montage. His handsome face when he first told her he loved her. His cruel expression when he insisted she vacuum the whole house again because she'd missed one spot in the living room. His jaw clenched in rage while he rammed his truck toward her time after time that horrible night. His voice declaring her stupidity and worthlessness. The way he forced her to bury her little dog herself, and then informed her he would tolerate no more weeping over a stinking animal.

Tears pricked Lizzy's eyes, and she headed for the lodge, intent on escaping into the restroom for a few moments of privacy. Once safely in a stall, she prayed silently while tears streamed down her cheeks. *Lord, help me, please. I thought I was over this. Why now? I know Tucker is nothing like Carl. Father, please help me. I have forgiven Carl, and I truly don't feel bitter toward him anymore. You have allowed me to use my experiences to help others. So why can't I just let go and fall in love with Tucker?* She grabbed a tissue and dabbed her eyes. *I don't want to be afraid anymore. I hate this. I want to be normal, Lord. I just want to fall in love and have the wonderful relationship You have ordained.*

Lizzy cried and prayed for nearly ten minutes before her tears were spent. She sighed deeply, then opened the door and went to wash her hands and repair her face. *Thank goodness I thought to put a few things in my pocket*. She cleaned the streaked mascara away and dabbed a bit of concealer under her eyes.

Lizzy left the restroom feeling drained and strangely devoid of emotion. *I've got to get a grip. I do not want to ruin this trip for my family. Help me, Lord. Help me to move beyond this. I can't do this on my own*. A sudden calm came over her, and peace flooded her soul. A new resolve filled her. *With God's help, I will not let this mess with my mind anymore. I'm going to have a good day, and Carl Greene is not going to ruin things for me.* She headed back to where Millie and Kate were having their lesson. She still wanted some space from Tucker and managed to be elsewhere when he came by to check on them later. She didn't understand her feelings, so with a shrug of her shoulders and a deep sigh, she left them to the Lord. Tucker took everything in stride and remained his usual steady, easy-going self, even though he had to do some praying of his own. He did not understand Lizzy's sudden coolness toward him and prayed for wisdom. He also prayed God would meet Lizzy at her point of need.

~ * ~

The group opted to stop for supper at a nearby restaurant. After a long day in the snow, no one felt like cooking. When they returned to the cabin, everyone went their separate ways, ready for a good night's rest.

The house was dark and silent when Tucker awoke. He looked at the clock on his bedside table and rubbed his eyes. *Just after midnight,* he sat up slowly, wondering what awakened him. He felt pressed to check on Lizzy, but immediately shook his head. *No, I don't want to disturb her. She clearly needed some space today. I don't want to scare her.* But the feeling only grew stronger, so he finally crawled from beneath the covers and slipped a robe over his long-sleeved t-shirt and sweats. He put on his slippers and silently tip-toed to Lizzy's room. Carefully he opened the door, trying not to make a sound.

He heard wheezing and immediately flipped on the light. Lizzy was sitting up in bed gasping for breath. She looked at him helplessly and croaked out, "I can hardly breathe, Tucker. Help me. Please get Deb."

Tucker nodded and hurried to wake her sister. Deborah drew on her robe quickly and rushed to her sister's room. "Oh, Tucker." Deborah put her hand to her mouth in horror. "She developed asthma during her years with Carl, and it still flares up now and then. But I've never seen her this bad. She needs her inhaler." She rushed to her sister's side.

"Lizzy, where's your inhaler. Did you bring it with you?" Lizzy shook her head.

"We've got to get her to the emergency room." Tucker immediately sized up the situation and took charge. "Let me grab my wallet and keys, and I'll take her. There's a town a couple of miles away with a hospital."

"I'll go with you, Tuck. Let me go change, and I'll help get her to the car." She returned to let Marshall know what was going on. He wanted them all to go but Deborah shook her head. "I need you to stay with the girls, Marsh. They need their rest. And besides, I think Tucker needs to handle this. Just a feeling I have, but I think he needs to do this."

Marshall nodded slowly and helped her gather a few things. "Deb, you guys take the Ex Terra. I'll feel better knowing you all are in a vehicle more suited for the winter roads."

Deborah nodded and kissed him before leaving the room. "Pray for her, Marsh. She's in a really bad way."

In moments, Tucker, Deborah, and Lizzy were in the SUV and headed down the mountain. Tucker drove as fast as he dared on the snowy road and got them to the hospital in record time.

Minutes after arrival, Lizzy was admitted, given oxygen, and seen by a doctor. Soon after she received a nebulized bronchodilator treatment and IV Corticosteroids. Lizzy finally began to breathe more comfortably. "What happened to make this flare up?" she asked the doctor. "I haven't had trouble with my asthma in ages. I usually only notice it when I have a cold."

"Were you out on the slopes all day?" the doctor asked, his tone professional but kind.

"Yes."

"Most likely your flare up was due to the temperature. Cold air is a common asthma trigger."

Lizzy nodded and leaned back against her pillow. She felt weak as a kitten.

"I'm prescribing a rescue inhaler and oral corticosteroids. And no skiing tomorrow, young lady. You'll need to rest inside for the day."

"Can I get out later, though, doctor? I hate to have come all this way and not get to ski again."

"If you're feeling better after tomorrow, I don't see why not. But keep the inhaler with you." He smiled. "I'd like to have you stay with us a bit longer to be sure you don't have another attack. Then you all can take her home."

Tucker and Deborah were hanging on every word. "We'll take good care of her, doc," Tucker said firmly. "No worries there."

~ * ~

Lizzy awoke the next morning and stretched luxuriously. She lay staring at the ceiling for a moment, enjoying the warm sun streaming through the window beside the dresser. Gradually, she remembered the events of the night before and sat up slowly. She had no memory of them leaving the hospital and returning to the cabin. She crawled from the bed, took a deep breath, and smiled. There was no pain or tightness in her chest. *Looks like the meds did the job.* She frowned. *I can't believe this happened. I disturbed everybody's night.* She frowned. *I hope they're not angry. I never even thought about the cold making my asthma flare up. How could I have forgotten my inhaler?* She put on her robe and slippers and glanced at the clock. *Wow, I slept until eleven. I should be able to handle anything now. Maybe I can make up for inconveniencing everybody last night.* She went downstairs, determined to cook up a feast for supper. When she entered the kitchen, she spotted Deborah on the sofa with a book.

Her sister looked up when Lizzy came in. "Hi, sleepyhead," she said affectionately. She put her book aside and joined Lizzy in the kitchen. "Hungry?"

"Starved." Lizzy opened the refrigerator. "I'm going to make some breakfast, and then I'm going to cook up something amazing for supper tonight."

Deborah gently moved her hand and closed the refrigerator door. “You go sit down and tell me what you want to eat. I’m cooking this morning. I am also under strict orders not to allow you to lift a finger.”

Her tone brooked no disobedience, so Lizzy did as she was told though she was not happy. “Orders, huh?” Lizzy plopped down on the sofa, a bit put out with being bossed about in such a fashion. “You know you’ve always been like a mother hen where I was concerned. Which I never understood since I am the big sister.”

“I have no idea what you’re talking about.” Deborah looked at Lizzy with mock confusion.

The sisters laughed together then, and Lizzy’s mood lightened. She thought about her choices for a moment. “I think I’d like an omelet with cheese and bacon. But seriously, Deb, I feel great. I can make my own breakfast.”

“No, ma’am. You cannot.” Deborah got out a frying pan, then went to the refrigerator to get ingredients for the omelet.

Lizzy rested her head against the back of the sofa. “Where is everybody? I hope they went to the slopes. I’m so embarrassed my little episode caused you and Tucker not to get your rest. I really do want to cook a nice big supper tonight to make it up to you.”

Deborah set a carton of eggs on the counter, slammed the refrigerator door, and came to sit next to Lizzy. “You’ve got to stop that.”

“Stop what?”

“Feeling like you have to repay us for taking care of you. You didn’t ruin anybody’s night. We were really frightened, Lizzy. You could hardly breathe.”

Deborah took her sister’s hand. “I know you like to be independent but sweetie, please just let us take care of you.” She looked at Lizzy intently. “Tucker didn’t plan to leave this morning. I had to practically push him out of the door. I finally told him Marshall would think he was a bad host if he didn’t go skiing with them today.”

"Deb, you didn't." Lizzy looked aghast. "He would feel so horrible if he thought he'd neglected someone."

"Don't worry. He knew I was just teasing." Deborah lowered her voice to a whisper. "But I have it on good authority that no guy could possibly take care of you as well as your sister. And after the night you had, I didn't think two rambunctious little girls would be the best recipe for rest either."

"I'm telling you, I feel fine," Lizzy insisted. "In fact, I feel quite refreshed. I think the extra rest this morning was all I needed."

"Nevertheless, I have promised I wouldn't let you lift a finger, and lift a finger you shall not." Deborah returned to the kitchen and within fifteen minutes, a steaming omelet was placed before Lizzy for inspection.

"This smells heavenly, Deb. Thank you." Lizzy thanked the Lord for the food and dug in. "Mm. This tastes every bit as good as it smells. Good job." She gave her sister a thumbs up.

"Thank you." Deborah smiled, then looked at her sister quizzically. "So Lizzy, what's up with Tucker? I don't mean to pry if you don't want to talk about it, but he seems like a really wonderful guy."

Lizzy chewed slowly, swallowed, and took a drink of orange juice. She set the glass on the coaster. "I really care about him, Deb. I never thought I'd be able to feel this way after what happened with Carl. There are times when I think I'm really coming to love Tucker, but then I have these panic attacks. I had one yesterday on the slopes."

"Oh, honey, I'm so sorry. What scared you so? Did Tucker do something?"

"No. That's the crazy thing. He was just his normal self. I mean, he did tell me he loved me yesterday morning."

"What?" Deborah looked at her in shock. "Why was I not informed about this yesterday?" The teasing in her eyes gave her away.

"Oh, stop," Lizzy said dryly. "Believe it or not, I don't tell you everything."

Deborah sat back with a grin. "Okay, okay. Tell me what you want."

"We went for a walk in the snow early yesterday morning. While we were out in the woods, he told me he loved me. He even gave me a kiss, which I enjoyed immensely. He was so sweet, though. He said he didn't want to rush me and didn't want to scare me. At the moment, I was confused because I wanted so much to tell him I love him, too, but at the same time I was scared all to pieces. Then out on the slopes, all of a sudden I started feeling smothered and trapped. I had to go into the bathroom and pray my way through it."

Deborah looked at her soberly. "I'm so sorry. I wish there was something I could do to make the way clear for you but only God can do that." She looked thoughtful for a moment, then continued. "I'm going to tell you something, Lizzy, not to pressure you or to sway you one way or the other, but I think you should know. Tucker insisted on taking you to the ER last night, and he stayed by your side the whole night, even after you came home. We left your bedroom door open, of course, but he sat in your recliner all night. He said he wanted to make sure he was there if you woke up and needed something. When I came in this morning to check on you, he was still awake." Deborah leaned back and put her hands behind her neck, staring at the beams overhead. "Marshall and I love him, Lizzy. And I know Mom and the girls do, too. So you know you have our blessing while you think and pray about your relationship with Tucker. Again, I'm not telling you this to pressure you. I just want you to know where we are."

Lizzy continued to eat her omelet in silence. When she finished, she drank the rest of her juice and looked at Deborah. "You guys never had a good feeling about Carl, did you?"

"No, we did not. There was something about him that was just too slick. He didn't come across as sincere to us, and we were frightened for you."

"I wish I'd listened. God put all kinds of red flags up for me before I married Carl. Some I didn't know were warning signs but some I saw and didn't heed." Lizzy sighed and put her plate on the coffee table. "At least I can truly thank the Lord for having gone through that time. I can even thank him for the way I was forced to revisit a lot of feelings when Carl was on trial for Marcie's murder. I've learned so much. Sometimes we just have to go through our own difficult times in order to grow and in order to truly be able to empathize with others. God will turn evil into good if we let him."

"You are so right." Deborah smiled and rose. She grabbed Lizzy's plate and glass and took them to the kitchen.

"I'm going to go get a shower, Deb. I feel all grungy." Lizzy rose and went upstairs to her room. She took her time and enjoyed the warm water enveloping her body. The scent of Wen's Winter Cranberry Mint ™ in her hair made her inhale with pleasure. After about fifteen minutes, she reluctantly finished her shower, dried off, and dressed in jeans and a warm Irish merino wool sweater.

Deborah knocked on her door. "Come down to the den when you're done, and we'll watch a movie. I'll be down there waiting."

Lizzy put on a pair of wool socks, slid on her slippers, and hurried to join Deb in the den. "Wow, nice setup." She looked around the room. A large-screen television was mounted on one wall, and recliners were placed side by side to make eight viewing stations. One corner in the back of the room featured floor to ceiling shelves containing books, DVDs and Blu-ray discs. A conveniently placed recliner and floor lamp sat nearby. "This is more a home theater than a den." Lizzy chose a chair and put her feet up and leaned back with a grin. "Nice."

Deborah put *White Christmas* into the Blu-ray player and sat beside Lizzy to watch. The movie was one of Lizzy's favorites but she felt like she had ants in her pants. After the guys did the *Sisters* number, she turned to Deborah in desperation. "Deb, I feel like I'm going to fly all to pieces sitting here. I need a project. I promise I won't overdo but I'm going to go make a dessert for tonight." Sensing the task would be good for her sister, Deborah agreed but said she wanted to finish the movie.

Lizzy went to the kitchen and decided to make her specialty, baklava. She found the supplies she'd packed and set about making the delectable pastry. She put the pan filled with layers of dough, nuts, cinnamon, and butter on the kitchen island and was cutting the mixture into diamonds, when Tucker walked through the front door.

When he saw her in the kitchen, his eyes immediately reflected concern. He removed his jacket and tossed the garment on the couch. "Lizzy, should you be doing that? You're supposed to be resting today." The air between them took on a decidedly cooler turn. He came into the kitchen but kept a short distance from her, sensing he'd said the wrong thing. He leaned casually against the cupboards and eyed the creation in the pan. "Wait. Lizzy, are you making baklava?"

"I am."

"Baklava is one of my favorites. I didn't know you knew how to make it. Never mind what I said before. Clearly, you are feeling just fine, and who am I to interrupt an artist at work?" He grinned at her, his eyes begging her to understand.

She stopped cutting for a moment and looked at him. *Those eyes. I cannot resist those eyes. He's like a little puppy who just got scolded.*

"I appreciate that, Tucker. I will disregard your previous statement because clearly you are a patron of the culinary arts." She looked at him sternly for a moment before breaking into a smile.

Tucker laughed with relief, thankful he was forgiven.

"Actually, I've been feeling great up until a couple of minutes ago," Lizzy admitted. "All of a sudden, the wind went out of my sails, and I feel weak as a kitten."

Tucker straightened. "Let me finish. Just tell me what to do." He grabbed a bar stool from the other side of the island. "Sit right here and talk me through it."

Lizzy sat down on the stool, thankful to get off her feet. "Wash your hands first, young man." She chuckled to herself when he immediately went to comply. He returned, and Lizzy handed him the knife. "Just continue cutting the whole thing into diamonds. You'll want to get some melted butter on your fingers, and try to hold down the edges of the pastry. The Phyllo tends to stick to the knife."

He followed her instructions to the letter and expertly finished the job. "What's next?"

"Pan goes in the oven. Then we have to make the sauce."

He placed the pan in the oven and noticed the honey and sugar sitting next to the stove. "All right. How much, what temperature, and how long?"

"One cup of sugar and one cup of water, high until the sugar water starts to boil. Add one cup of honey and one teaspoon of lemon juice, then turn the heat down to low, and it'll just simmer until the pastry is done."

"Easy peasy ...

"Lemon squeezy," they both finished together. They burst out laughing, and Tucker began to prepare the sauce. When he finished, the syrupy mixture was left to simmer, and the two of them went to the den to relax and watch a movie. Deborah was just finishing *White Christmas*. Lizzy asked Tucker what selections were available, and he began reading off titles.

"I'm in the mood for something light." Lizzy thought about the choices he'd listed. "Let's go with *Last Holiday*."

"Perfect." Deborah stood up and stretched. "I love that movie."

"*Last Holiday* it is." Tucker removed the disc from its case with a flourish.

"Hey, Tucker, where are Marshall and the girls?" Lizzy realized she'd not seen them come back with Tucker.

"They decided to stay on the slopes. Millie and Kate are doing so well. They didn't want to leave."

Lizzy looked at him with concern. "Weren't you having fun, Tucker?"

He looked sheepishly at the floor for a moment, then raised his gaze to meet hers. "Not really. I missed you, and I wanted to be sure you were okay." His eyes begged for her understanding. "Besides, I wasn't feeling at the top of my game."

Lizzy remembered what Deborah said about his staying up all night watching over her. She said nothing but just nodded with a smile. Tucker started the movie and settled in the recliner behind Lizzy. About twenty minutes into the movie, Deborah decided to get a cup of tea and check on the baklava.

"Lizzy, look," she whispered after she rose. She pointed to the chair behind them.

Lizzy got up and looked around. Tucker was fast asleep. She smiled at her sister and gave her a thumbs up. Deborah walked out, but Lizzy's gaze remained on Tucker's face. Her heart lurched within her, and a lump came into her throat. In that quiet moment, with Georgia Byrd lamenting her diagnosis on the screen behind her, she knew. All fears and doubts melted away like snow in the warm sunshine. A complete peace she thought impossible flooded her entire being, and she knew. She loved this man with all her heart.

Tears welled up, and she fumbled in her pocket for a tissue. Deborah returned, whispering so she would not awaken Tucker. "I finished up the baklava. It's cooling on the counter." She noticed her sister's tears. "Lizzy, what's wrong?"

"Nothing, Deb. Everything is wonderful." Lizzy sniffed and continued to whisper. "I just realized, Deb. I am in love with Tucker. I truly didn't think I could ever feel this way, but it just kind of hit me all at once. I trust him. I really do trust him. And I love him so much it hurts."

"Oh, honey." Deborah began to weep softly and came over to hug her sister close. "I'm so happy for you. He is a wonderful man and will take the best care of you. I really believe you can trust him with your life and with your heart."

The sisters held each other while Tucker snoozed away, oblivious to the momentous change that just happened right in front of him. They eventually returned their attention to the movie, but Lizzy could not concentrate. Her mind was full of her newly realized love for the man behind her. *How do I tell him? I want the timing to be just right. Lord, help me to know what to say and when.*

~ * ~

Marshall and the girls returned around suppertime, full about tales of their exciting day. The girls were proving to be naturals at skiing but decided they wanted to go skating the next day. Over supper, they excitedly filled Lizzy in on everything she'd missed on the slopes. She promised to go skating with them, assuring everyone she would be good as new with another night of rest.

While she prepared for bed, Lizzy continued to pray for just the right way to let Tucker know she loved him. The next two days flew by, and no opportunity presented itself. The family was together most of the time, and there was no moment alone with him. She tried to show him by staying close and letting her eyes show her feelings, but Tucker remained his easy-going self and gave no evidence of catching on to her silent messages. Lizzy knew he was trying not to scare her or make her feel smothered, but she began to be exasperated.

The night before their last day, she sat in bed trying to read her scripture for the day. Realizing she'd been staring at the same page on her iPad for five minutes, she stopped and began to pray. "Father God, help me. I don't know how to tell him. I know now my love is real. You have conquered my fears and brought a love to my heart I thought would never exist for me. Help me to know what to do."

She stared at the photo print on the wall which captured a beautiful buck poised beside a mountain lake. Snow covered the ground, and moonlight covered the scene with a ghostly light. Fascinated, she got up to take a closer look. The picture's plate read: *Moonlight Stag, by Christopher Gordon.* She stopped and thought for a moment. *Christopher Gordon? That's got to be Mickey's Christopher. I wonder if Tucker knows him.* She was distracted by the picture for a moment but soon began to pace the floor, determined she needed to solve the problem of how to tell Tucker she loved him. Finally, she gave it up when the need for sleep overwhelmed her. *Lord, I have to rest. Please help me to know what to do.*

At three o'clock in the morning, she awoke with a start. *I'll just write him a note and put it under his door.* She smiled and felt peace that the idea was from God. *How beautifully simple.* She rose and went to grab her purse off the dresser. *Surely I have something to write on in here.* Finding nothing but a pen, she began to check out the drawers in the bedside tables. *Bingo! This is perfect.* She found a blank notecard from a local gift shop, obviously left behind by a former guest. She carefully wrote her simple message. "Tucker, I love you. Lizzy." With a smile, she sealed the envelope, opened her door, tiptoed to Tucker's bedroom, and slipped the note under the door. With a grin, she crept back to her room and tried to rest though she felt positively giddy. She was sure she couldn't wait until morning, but sleep eventually claimed her once more.

She awoke around seven-thirty with a jolt. *The note. Did he find it yet? Is he awake yet? How should I act? What if he's changed his mind? What if a mouse got in and toted the note away?* With that thought, she laughed at her paranoia. *Get into the shower and get a grip, woman,* she told herself firmly. She followed her own advice, though she was sure she'd never gotten ready so fast in her life. Heart pounding, she opened her door slowly. Tucker's door stood open. She walked carefully over and peeked inside. Clearly, he was already up and had started his day. His bed was made, and the room was silent. Feeling a bit deflated, Lizzy headed downstairs to make breakfast for the group. She grabbed a whisk and began mixing up a bowl of eggs, when she heard the front door open. She looked over, and Tucker's eyes met hers. He walked to her side without even removing his coat, gently put his arms around her and hugged her close. She returned his hug unreservedly, feeling safe and secure in his arms. He pulled back after a few moments, put his hand under her chin, and kissed her soundly. She returned his kiss with all the love overflowing from her heart, and neither had any further doubt as to the other's feelings. Deborah and Marshall walked in and began to applaud. Embarrassed, Tucker and Lizzy parted, but he still grasped her hand.

"Looks like we got here just in time." Marshall winked at his wife.

"Marshall, for goodness sake." Lizzy looked at him with an exasperated expression.

"We're so happy for you two." Tears welled up in Deborah's eyes. She and Marshall came close to give Tucker and Lizzy a hug.

The remainder of the day was a wonderful dreamy time of togetherness for Tucker and Lizzy. They skied during the morning hours, then spent the afternoon ice skating with Millie and Kate to allow Marshall and Deborah some alone time together. *It feels so incredibly right to be with him.* Lizzy watched Tucker skate around the rink with a niece on either side. *How could I have ever questioned? Thank you, Lord, for bringing me to this place. I don't know for sure what our future holds, but I pray if it is your will, Tucker and I will go through the rest of this life together.*

~Twenty-five~

"Lizzy, honey, what's on your mind? You've been brooding all day. Can I help?" Rose stood in the doorway of Lizzy's bathroom.

Lizzy rinsed and dabbed her face dry with a towel. "Oh, Mom, I don't know that you can. There are some things I've got to talk over with Tucker. I'm just not sure about my future with him."

"What happened, honey?" Rose's voice was laced with concern. She would be devastated if Tucker had hurt her precious girl in any way. "What did he do?"

"He didn't do anything, Mom. It's just something he said the other day about children." She pressed the towel to her eyes while tears began to form. "I realized the other day, I've never told him I can't have kids. That part of my life has been over for so long, I just didn't think about it. He's so precious to watch with Millie and Kate. It's just not fair of me to tie him down when I know he must want children of his own. I'm sure he expects me to be able to fulfill that dream for him." Lizzy's sobs came in earnest now. "His parents want grandchildren, and they deserve to have them, Mom. I have to tell him."

Rose reached to hold her daughter and rubbed her hand gently on Lizzy's back. "Oh, my sweet girl." She could not give false hope, for she did not know how important the issue of children was for Tucker. "I'll be praying that God's will be accomplished."

~ * ~

A cool March breeze caressed Lizzy's cheeks, and the trees in Riponville Park swayed slowly in the wind as if showing off their budding new leaves. "Tucker, there's something I need to tell you, and I think it will mean we can no longer see each other. But please know that I will understand." Her voice was matter-of-fact though her heart was breaking. She gripped her bottle of water as if the liquid was trying escape. She determined she would not cry.

Tucker stopped and turned to study her face. Her eyes held painful resolve, as though she knew their relationship was over. He noticed a bench beside a clump of yellow daffodils and steered them slowly over. He sat, determined not to overreact but Lizzy chose to stay standing. They were enjoying their usual Saturday morning walk in Riponville Park, during which he thought they would be planning a horseback riding outing with Lizzy's nieces. He had no clue what was going on but decided to ask simple questions and stay calm. He looked up at her. "Why, Lizzy? What's wrong? What have I done?"

Lizzy paced back and forth and tucked a strand of dark hair behind her ear. "You didn't do anything, Tucker." She sighed while sorrow overtook her. Despite her having informed the tears they were not welcome, the rebellious moisture welled up anyway. "It's me, Tuck. It's all me. I can't hold you back from your dreams. It would be selfish and unfair of me. We've got to stop this before it goes any further."

Tucker grabbed her hand and gently caressed it with his fingers. "Lizzy, sweetheart, I told you before, the Senate was not my dream. God led me not to run again. You didn't keep me from anything."

"No, Tucker, you don't understand." Lizzy pulled her hand away. She dug into her jeans pocket for a tissue. The wretched tears were determined to flow. "This is not about the Senate. It's about kids. I know you love children."

Tucker looked completely adrift. "Yes, that's true," he said carefully.

Seeing he did not understand, Lizzy took a deep breath. "This is kind of personal but here goes. About four years ago, I started having some health problems. I could feel a large growth in my abdomen. I was having issues every mon..." Lizzy paused, a bit embarrassed to be sharing such information with him. "I was having issues. I went to my gynecologist, and she found that I had several large fibroid tumors. The choices were to keep having problems, which could very likely become more severe, or have a hysterectomy." Lizzy looked past Tucker's ear and focused on the mass of purple crocuses growing on the bank behind him. "I was always so thankful I never had children with Carl. He hated kids, and his abuse would have scarred a child's life irrevocably. Plus, children would have tied me to him forever. I truly thought I would be on my own for the rest of my life. I most likely could never have become pregnant anyway because of my condition, so I had no qualms about the surgery. My mom nearly bled to death from the same type of tumors, so I felt the wise course of action was to proceed." She looked down at him with eyes full of anguish.

Tucker took her hand once more, but still looked puzzled. "Okay, so you had the surgery. Did everything go all right?"

"Yes. Honestly, it wasn't bad at all. Just took several weeks to recover, but the pain wasn't too bad. I actually enjoyed the rest."

Tucker was silent for a moment, thinking hard. "So, I still don't understand why we can't continue to see each other. What have I missed?" He looked up at her intently.

"Tucker, you know you want to have children of your own." Lizzy tried to keep her voice down even though they were alone in the quiet alcove. Sadness and frustration surged through her. *How can he not get this?*

Her voice went up an octave, and her entire face was a study in strain and angst. "I can't have children, Tucker." She pulled her hand away and pressed the tissue to her eyes once more. "I cannot have kids. Do you understand?" Sobs tried to overtake her, but she valiantly pushed them down and hiccupped miserably. "What good am I to you, Tucker? I can't have children like a normal woman." She turned away from him and walked a few paces down the path. Tucker stared after her, and all at once her words sank in and understanding dawned.

He leapt off the bench and was at her side in seconds. He gently turned her around to face him. “Elizabeth Godfrey, I love you. Not for what you can do for me or what you can give me. I love you for you.” He put a finger under her chin and raised her eyes to meet his. “Don’t you ever doubt that for a minute. Yes, I love children and I know you do, too. So maybe someday we’ll adopt. But I love you, Lizzy. For you, do you understand? If it’s just you and me forever, I will be perfectly content.”

“Oh, Tucker.” Lizzy’s tears fell in earnest and began to leave spots on her short-sleeved shirt. Tucker gathered her into his arms, and she clung to him, as though she would never let go. “Thank you,” she whispered into his ear. “Thank you, Tucker. I love you, too.” They stood wrapped in each other’s arms for many moments until they heard the sound of approaching voices.

They pulled apart and returned, hand in hand, to the main path. Though Tucker had not yet officially proposed, he clearly loved her and wanted her just for her. That thought began to wind its way deep into her soul, and Lizzy felt like singing. But all of a sudden, she had another thought that effectively squelched the music. “You’re not looking for a maid and a cook are you? Okay, cooking isn’t that bad, but cleaning is not my thing, and your house is always spotless and ...”

Tucker interrupted. “Lizzy, I have a confession to make.”

Lizzy’s heart thumped in her chest. Her face clouded, and tendrils of fear started to claw at her mind. “What?”

Tucker looked chagrined. “I hire a professional housekeeper to clean for me.”

“Are you serious?” Lizzy looked shocked.

Tucker looked like a little boy caught with his hand in the cookie jar. “I am. I hate cleaning.” He looked at her with a serious expression. “I really, really hate it.”

Lizzy laughed, and relief spread over her like the warmth of her bathrobe just out of the drier. She enjoyed the feeling for a moment, then an impish look filled her eyes. "You know, there are reasons why people choose different career paths. I'm so thankful for those who have the skill to clean professionally. Especially since I'm so bad at it."

"Exactly." Tucker nodded emphatically. "Besides, we need to support local small business endeavors, don't you think?"

Lizzy took his arm and looked at him with a grin. "Absolutely. I think that's the only right thing to do."

They laughed together in delight and continued down the path, content with the knowledge that issues had been settled to the complete satisfaction of them both.

~ * ~

Lizzy awoke with a start the morning of April fifth and looked at the clock in horror. *Oh, no. 7:15. I must have turned the alarm off instead of hitting the snooze button.* She leapt from her bed, causing looks of alarm from Downton and Nugget and irritation from Sherlock and Watson. She rushed through her morning routine and absently grabbed her old stand-by outfit: grey dress slacks, a sleeveless white blouse, and a light-weight burgundy and black cardigan. *I have got to get into the habit of choosing my clothes the night before*, she thought while she stepped into her black pumps and hurried to the kitchen. She inhaled her breakfast with a gulp, returned to the bathroom to brush her teeth, snatched up her purse and iPad, and hurried to the car.

"Drive safely, honey." Rose looked concerned. "I know you're in a rush."

"I will, Mom. Bye. I love you." Lizzy backed out and left the subdivision as quickly as she dared.

~ * ~

The courtroom was buzzing as usual, and Lizzy soon felt the day would prove to be an extension of her hurried morning. By 8:45, she was nearly overwhelmed with paperwork. She quickly worked up the sentencing sheets, pulled the corresponding indictments from the indictment cart, paper-clipped the documents together, and passed each set to the court reporter. Lizzy was so busy she did not notice when Tucker quietly slipped into the back row of the gallery.

"All rise. Court will come to order." The bailiff nearly had to shout to be heard over the noise but the hubbub began to die down. "The Honorable Judge Nathan Mills presiding."

"Please have a seat everyone." Judge Mills took the bench. The crowd was seated, and the first group was called to the front.

Still inundated with cases to be worked up, Lizzy published the indictments for the defendants before her and turned to face them. "Please raise your right hands." The defendants complied, looking at her with a variety of expressions. Lizzy continued. "Do you swear to tell the truth, the whole truth, and nothing but the truth, so help you God?" The defendants all answered in the affirmative, and the plea proceedings began. Lizzy resumed her seat and began writing furiously, trying to catch up.

So intent was she on her work that she did not notice the judge wave the defendants to the side. "Madam Clerk," he said.

Lizzy immediately rose and snapped to attention. "Yes, your honor?"

"Would you please step down to the podium?"

Lizzy's heart began to pound. *What on earth is going on?* she thought frantically. *This has never happened before. What did I do?* She did as she was bidden and took her place at the podium where the defendants had been standing to face the judge. His face was stern, but she noticed a slight twinkle in his eye. Judge Mills was always jovial and friendly toward her, and she couldn't imagine she'd done anything to anger or inconvenience him.

"Sir ... yes, you in the back." Judge Mills pointed. "Would you please come forward? I understand you wish to have a word with the clerk."

Lizzy's brow rose, and she looked around. Her expression went from one of confusion, to one of delight when she saw Tucker proceeding down the aisle. Her heart did a little skip. He looked so handsome in his charcoal grey suit, gray and white pinstripe shirt, and burgundy tie. She looked at him questioningly, but he kept his eyes on the judge. He approached and stood beside her at the podium.

"Thank you, your honor. I appreciate your allowing me this time to address the clerk. May I have your permission to proceed?"

"Absolutely." Judge Mills grinned and nodded.

Tucker turned and took Lizzy by the hand. His expressive eyes bespoke the intensity of his feelings. His love for this woman was evident to all who saw him. He took a deep breath. "Lizzy, you mean the world to me," he said softly. "I thought I would never find you. I've been looking for you all my life." His voice caught, and he paused for a moment to compose himself before he continued. "I love you more than I ever thought humanly possible." He knelt down on one knee, then took a small ring box out of his pocket. "Elizabeth Lauren Godfrey," he continued, his voice low and intimate. "Will you marry me and allow me the honor of being your husband?"

Lizzy gazed at him while tears began to fill her eyes. How far she had come. Never in her wildest dreams did she think she would ever find a man like this. No doubts or fears assailed her, and her heart was at peace, knowing God alone brought them together. The last few months of dating as a couple in love solidified everything. Tucker was her best friend. He loved her for her. He wanted only the best for her. He loved her as Christ loved the church.

She grasped his hand tightly and tried not to cry while she nodded. "I will, Tucker. Yes, I'll marry you. I love you so much."

He rose to kiss her while the crowd of surprised spectators in the gallery erupted into applause. Lizzy was aware of a camera clicking away near them. "This will probably be on the news," Tucker murmured in her ear. "I don't know how my plan got out but there's a news camera in the back."

"Oh, I don't care." Lizzy smiled happily. "I hope they captured everything because I want a copy of the DVD. Besides, all that matters to me is you."

Tucker hugged her close and kissed her again before turning to the judge. "Thank you, your honor." He had a huge smile on his face. "Is there any chance I could steal your clerk away for the afternoon?"

Judge Mills laughed and looked to the side door where Mandy stood waiting to take Lizzy's place. "Looks like Mandy is here to take over. Lizzy, you're excused for the rest of the day. But I expect to see you back here tomorrow." The twinkle in his eye belied his stern tone. "And Mr. Bates." He looked at Tucker. "I expect a wedding invitation."

"Absolutely, your honor," Tucker replied with a grin and a nod.

Lizzy gathered her belongings and amid much well-wishing and applause, the couple exited the courtroom. They spent the afternoon in Riponville Park, enjoying the beautiful spring day and making wedding plans.

~ * ~

Sunset was near, and Tucker and Lizzy were sitting on a park bench. Tucker's phone bleeped and to Lizzy's surprise, he took it from his pocket. He turned the screen toward her. "Look, sweetheart." There was a beautiful picture of the two of them in the courtroom at the exact moment Tucker proposed.

Lizzy was stunned. "What? How on earth?" Another picture came through showing them kissing. "Tucker, this is awesome. But how?"

Tucker smiled with satisfaction. "I called your friend Joy and asked her to be there. She'll give us all the pictures on a flash drive later."

Lizzy put her hand on Tucker's cheek and kissed him tenderly. "You are so amazing, my love." A mischievous glint entered her eyes. "But there is one thing you cannot take credit for."

"And what would that be?" He pretended to be deeply offended.

She gave him a grin. "How like God to see that we wore coordinating outfits on our engagement day."

Tucker laughed and looked into Lizzy's eyes with delight. He had her hold out her left hand and took a picture of the ring for Facebook. His title was 'She said yes!'. Lizzy took her phone out and updated her status to 'engaged' and he did the same. "My dear, it is now Facebook official". Tucker kissed her gently. "Do you want to head over to the restaurant for dinner now, or wait a bit?"

"Oh, Tucker, let's enjoy this beautiful sunset." Lizzy smiled at him. "I want to squeeze every bit of joy out of this day as possible." Tucker put his arm around the woman he loved, and she put her head on his shoulder. They watched the sun cast its rays across the sky, the clouds reflecting God's glory in a magnificent display of yellow, pink, orange, and red.

Lizzy was shocked when the entire restaurant full of patrons and servers at Rizzoli's applauded when they arrived. The hostess seated them, and they enjoyed a delicious meal. When they were about to make their exit, the owner came out with a beautifully decorated cake that said 'Congratulations Tucker & Lizzy'.

"Mr. Rizzoli, this is so kind of you." Lizzy smiled at him with pleasure. "I can't believe you went to so much trouble."

Mr. Rizzoli smiled, and Tucker asked if he would take a picture of them with the cake. "Of course, I take-ah your picture," he replied in his delightful Italian accent. "You two get close-uh together and put-ah the cake in between." Lizzy and Tucker obliged, and Mr. Rizzoli took several shots to make sure he got a good one. He handed Tucker the phone and wished them both the best. After taking several pictures of the cake, they both enjoyed a slice before calling it a night.

When Lizzy arrived home, she filled Rose in on the events of the day. Her mother, of course, already knew, since Tucker had asked her permission to marry Lizzy and filled her in on his proposal plan. She hugged Lizzy tightly and wept with happiness. Rose also laid to rest one final issue. Tucker had asked her if she would live with them as soon as he could buy a house with a mother-in-law suite.

"Oh, Mom." Lizzy began to cry again. "He's thought of everything."

While Lizzy prepared for bed, her heart was so full she felt she could barely breathe. After all the pain and heartache, after all the years of learning the hard lessons, God brought her to this amazing happy place. He brought her the man He'd planned for her all along, and her heart was at peace. She remembered part of a Bible verse she'd read recently. *The Lord says, 'I will give you back what you lost to the swarming locusts, the hopping locusts, the stripping locusts, and the cutting locusts'. Joel 2:25a*

Truly, You have given me more than I ever dreamed, she prayed while happy tears welled up and dripped onto Downton's coat. *Thank You, Lord. Thank You for Your mercy and grace. Thank You for bringing Tucker and me together. Help us to serve You and to follow You first and always. Bless our relationship and help us to be a blessing to others. Thank You, Father. Thank You for your amazing grace.*

She crawled into bed and fell asleep with a smile, thinking of Tucker's face and knowing they would belong to each for as long as God saw fit to leave them on the earth.

Made in the USA
Columbia, SC
26 November 2023

26703101R00150